MW00422992

PRAISE FOR TIME TRAP

~ What young adult and adult readers are saying about this epic series ~

"*Time Trap* is amazingly original and unexpected...I loved every second of reading it!"
~~ Alexandra Fedor, 15, who has read *The Book Thief, The Hunger Games,* and *Anna Karenina.*

"Time Trap is a deliciously entrapping read you won't want to put down and leaves you thirsting for more when you finish."
~~Angela Catucci, young adult

"I really liked Time Trap and loved how Micah Caida created an entire world in the first pages. I liked reading from the different characters and hearing from each of them. I would definitely read more books of this series and really want to know what happens next. I've already recommended it to a friend."
~~Duncan Calem, 14, Georgetown, TX who reads the Inheritance Series, Dark Life and Percy Jackson

"*Time Trap* will be a delight to every reader! All the ingredients you would hope to expect: a strong-willed heroine, a dangerously sexy man, an intriguing setting, and lots of unexpected turns make *Time Trap* a real page turner."

~~ Lynn Fedor, adult/mom and has read *The Hangman's Daughter, The Curse: The Belador Series,* and *The BAD Agency Series*

"I thought Time Trap's unique world was very fresh and very interesting. The history behind the characters gave them good depth and they all had nicely different personalities. Cool characters, cool plot, cool conflict. Nicely paced too, I was never bored."

~~Emily Gifford, 16, Newark NY read the *Inheritance Cycle, Harry Potter, Green Rider* series

"Reading this book is like riding on a roller coaster, getting to the top and not knowing when the next drop is."

~~ Alex Bernier, 12 years old and has also read all of *Rick Riordan's* books, the *Hunger Games,* the *Chronicles of Nick,* and the *Rangers Apprentice* series.

"Wonderfully written futuristic time travel story that keeps you begging for more. A combo of *Lord of the Flies* meets *Neverland* on steroids. I've never read anything like it. Excellent!" ~~Adam, age 28

"Creative and exciting, Time Trap was entertaining to the end! I couldn't wait to see what happened on the next page, and it's a book I would totally recommend to my friends "

~~ Emily Skeel, age 14, also read *The Hunger Games* trilogy, *Maze Runner* and *Delirium.*

TIME TRAP

USA TODAY BESTSELLER
MICAH CAIDA

Amanda –
Thanks for reading!

Copyright © 2014 Dianna Love Snell and Mary Arsenault Buckham

All rights reserved under International and Pan-American Copyright Conventions

By payment of required fees, you have been granted the *non*-exclusive, *non*-transferable right to access and read the text of this book. No part of this text may be reproduced, transmitted, downloaded, decompiled, reverse engineered, or stored in or introduced into any information storage and retrieval system, in any form or by any means, whether electronic or mechanical, now known or hereinafter invented without the express written permission of copyright owner.

Please Note

The reverse engineering, uploading, and/or distributing of this book via the internet or via any other means without the permission of the copyright owner is illegal and punishable by law. Please purchase only authorized electronic editions, and do not participate in or encourage electronic piracy of copyrighted materials. Your support of the author's rights is appreciated

No part of this book may be reproduced or transmitted in any form or by any electronic or mechanical means, including photocopying, recording or by any information storage and retrieval system, without the written permission of the publisher, except where permitted by law.

Thank you.

Cover Design and Interior format by The Killion Group
http://thekilliongroupinc.com

DEDICATION

To every teen who has faced what seems like an
insurmountable challenge.

RED MOON TRILOGY

GLOSSARY

ANASKO (uh – NAS – ko)
Be'tallia (Beh – TAHL – ya)
K'ryan (KRY – ahn)
C'raydonians (krah – DOE – nee – ahns)
croggle (KROG – ul)
dugurat (DO – gah – rat)
furkken (FUR – kin)
G'ortians (GORE – shuns)
Hy'bridt (HY – brit)
Komaen Sphere (KOE – main)
Micah Caida (MY – kah – KAY – dah)
MystiK (MISS – tick)
Neelah (NEE – lah)
Phen (FEN)
prantheer (pran – THEE – er)
Rayen (RAY – un)
Rustaad (ROO – stad)
TecKnati (tek – NAH – tee)
V'ru (VROO)
Zilya (ZEEL – ya)

CHAPTER 1

Painful starbursts exploded behind my eyes.

I clawed awake, tumbling forward, bouncing against a rough surface. Heat scorched my arms and legs. I tucked my head and shoulders. Sharp stones gouged my back and sand coated my sweaty body.

Slammed to a stop, I was flat on my face. Ears ringing. My next breath wheezed out, mouth dry as the hot dust singeing my body.

What was happening?

No answer. Brain scrambled.

"Get up, girl, *if* you value your life," someone demanded in a deep male voice that sounded old.

Don't push me right now if you value yours. I opened my gritty eyes to blinding light and a cockeyed view of an endless desert. Not a person in sight.

"Get. Up."

If he yelled one more time, he wouldn't be happy when I did make it to my feet. I bit back the snarl curling to my lips. Who was he anyway? My head still spun and my stomach wasn't much happier. Gravel bit the palms of my hands as I pushed up on shaky knees.

Every muscle screamed misery, my body battered as a kickball. I twisted around one way then the other, searching in a full circle. Still no one. Now I was dizzy.

Had I imagined that voice?

Where am I?

Blinking against the harsh sun, I struggled to my feet, weaving where I stood. Confused thoughts banged my aching skull. I rubbed my eyes, then focused and looked down at myself. Feet tucked inside short boots made of tanned skins. Familiar, but not. Buckskin material covered me from shoulders to skinned knees and I had a leather thong tied around my waist.

I swallowed, waiting for some memory to rise up from the empty gap in my mind and offer help. The longer I waited, the more nauseous I got.

Nerves had me brushing hair off my face and breathing fast, then I paused, clutching a handful of hair. I pulled the strands into view. Black. Long, thick and black.

Why didn't I know that? My heart thumped hard and picked up speed. I took a quick glance at the barren landscape.

Was this home?

I didn't know. *Why can't I remember?*

Trembling started in my knees and traveled up through my chest. I forced a deep breath through my lungs, anything to stop the rising panic. *Panic kills.*

Someone had told me that once. Who?

Still no answers. Squinting, I looked for something familiar.

Mountains. Red mountains. Wait. I *knew* those. *Think.* I begged my mind to give me something. To remember.

Nothing. Closing my eyes, I tried harder.

Bright colors flashed behind my eyes and a sharp ache stabbed my skull. Grabbing my head did little to ease the throbbing, but the pain did clear some of my brain fog.

Sandia.

The name of those mountains. Sandia. Relief flooded through me so quickly my skin tingled. *I'm just disoriented.*

"You waste time, Rayen."

I froze as I opened my eyes. *I better see him when I turn around this time.* And who was Rayen? I made a quarter turn to find the owner of that gravelly voice.

An old man. No, the shimmering *image* of an old man, an elder. This whole thing just shot up a level on the weird scale. With white stringy hair, light gray eyes and gnarled limbs, he flickered before me, the red and tan cliff rocks visible through his translucent body. Beyond that, an unbroken sky stretched overhead, wide and empty and *so* intensely blue it hurt my eyes.

The ghost man *floated* above the desert floor, legs crossed.

I was feeling a whole lot better until I saw that. "Who are–"

The ground beneath me vibrated and shifted, cutting off my words. I stumbled sideways.

"Listen," he ordered, his voice tense and urgent. "Three things you *must* know." The ghost spoke louder with each word, competing with a heavy, shuddering sound not that far away.

I chugged in a deep breath, as if that would keep my rising fear at bay, and smelled a rotted stench. Cloying decay and smoke. A warning smell I couldn't place, but something I sensed deep in my bones. Danger. I moved my head to look around, but the old man shouted, "You listening?"

Like I have a choice?

The spooky elder was determined to get his message said.

Nodding at him, I swallowed, not a spit of saliva in my mouth. The pounding of the ground seemed to come from a distance, reverberating through me. Adrenaline stirred my blood, urging me to be ready. But for what?

"First thing," he enunciated as if I was slow. "You die if you eat peanuts and you are seventeen."

Peanuts? Who cares about nuts, and isn't that technically two things? I sniffed at the air. The burning stink thickened. I reached for a knife that wasn't at my hip, but something told me it should be.

"Second. Your name Rayen."

Rayen? I'm Rayen?

If I could believe a crazy hallucination. Fear snaked through me with icy fingers, paralyzing me. *I don't know my name...or what I'm doing here...or where here is, other than recognizing those mountains.*

The ground shook harder, dust and pebbles scattering everywhere. I widened my stance to keep my balance.

That's when I caught the distinct sound of hooves pounding. Hard. Behind me...and gaining speed.

I looked over my shoulder. A beast. My muscles clenched at the sheer size of the thing. A hairy, rhino-hide gray creature blotting out the desert landscape behind it. Barreling forward, rocking back and forth on three legs, wide head low to the ground. Scary fast, churning geysers of sand and dirt, eating up distance quicker than anything its size should.

Air backed up in my lungs. "What the – "

"Third thing, Rayen," the elder shouted, his voice nearly drowned by the rumble. *"Run!"*

CHAPTER 2

Ghost Man vanished as I took off running.

Something clicked in my head, some instinct. I ran, arms pumping, and rocketed away from the beast. A quick leap over thorny bushes. My heels slammed hard rock, feet racing as if hell itself chased me.

Quick check over my shoulder.

The beast was gaining, yellow eyes burning for blood.

What *was* that thing? Shouldn't I know?

Didn't matter. Right now I had no place to hide and no idea how to escape. No trees large enough to dash behind. Nothing.

Except the mountains. They were my safe haven. I knew that, somehow. *But how do I know?* Was there a place to hide in those rocks up ahead? Maybe that beast couldn't follow me up a sharp incline.

Keep moving.

Ragged breaths chugged past my dry lips. Hot air scoarched my chest. I gagged on the creature's nauseating smell. I could hear it gaining on me. Shaking the earth beneath my panicked feet.

I'm running too hard. Won't last at this pace. My lungs were going to burst. *Have to find cover.*

Where?

Stinging sweat poured into my eyes when I lifted my gaze, searching boulders that had tumbled into a monolithic pile along the nearest ridge, as if stacked by a giant's hand.

Tell me that beast can't climb.

If I could just get far enough ahead. Reach the peak on the other side of those boulders.

I veered slightly left, pistoning my arms and breathing as hard as a small prey run to ground.

Fifty feet. *Run faster.*

Thirty feet. *Not going to make it.*

Ten feet. *Come on.* Almost there. Almost.

A roar screamed through the air.

I leaped from ground to rock. Slammed a knee. Slapped raw palms against jagged surfaces baked by the sun. Heat seared my skin. *Ignore the pain.*

Climb, climb, climb!

Scrambling like a lizard, I reached for crevices, grinding my knees and thighs.

Another scream, higher pitched this time but farther away. The thing pawed the ground. Dust erupted, choking the air.

I stretched for the next handhold and risked a quick glance back. What *did* that thing want?

At the base of the rocks, it started morphing from a huge, low-to-the-ground Rhino beast to a tall, thin whippet shape with a short, sleek coat of sand-colored hair.

And talons.

No way. No way in blue blazes. *I'm so dead.*

I bit my lip, tasting blood. *Can't quit now.* I sucked in a blast of baked air and clawed my way up the next rock. Sunlight poked through crevices. Maybe on the other side there'd be someplace to hide. Or people.

Like me? Where were my people? Friends? Family?

Did I have any?

Worry later. Right now, I'd take help from anyone I could find.

The sun roasted my exposed skin and beat down on my back. Muscles burned the harder I climbed. Blood pounded in my ears. I jammed the toes of my boots into whatever crack I could find and shoved my body higher, faster. My fingers clutched sandstone and slipped. I dug in deeper and scrambled hand-over-hand.

Hot breath licked the air around my legs.

The beast was almost on me.

A space between rocks gaped to my left. Crunching my shoulders as thin as possible, I plunged into the narrow V opening, raking my back raw.

A shaft of blue sky yawned on the other side.

Deadly panting echoed right behind me. Closing in.

Fighting panic, I scrambled forward and lunged for the far side...and too late saw nothing below.

Just air.

My feet flipped over my head. I tumbled. An ocean of sky and rusty-brown rocks blurred through my vision.

I hit hard, face planted on dirt.

Knocked the breath out of me. My head spun and every bone reverberated. I took a wheezing gasp that hurt.

"Son of a bitch!" a strange young male voice called. "Hey, dude, we got a skydiver."

Did I know the name Dude?

I opened my mouth and groaned. The only sound I could make.

"Hey, babe, where's your chute?" the same voice asked, closer.

Babe?

"Idiot, she fell from the rocks." Another voice that sounded just as young and male joined the first. "She's a mess. Leave her."

"No way she fell. From those rocks?" First male's voice. He whistled low. "Should be dead." Then he whispered, "Hey. Maybe she is. We better go."

We'll all be dead if that beast follows me. I twisted my head just enough to look up at the cliff face I'd just dove from.

There. In the crevice of dusty-red boulders loomed a shadow. Long and thin. Waiting.

Even from this distance, I felt the danger. Predator eyeing prey. But what kept it from attacking? The other people? The distance? Could that thing not shift from land animal to a winged creature and swoop down?

Beware the beast whispered through my mind.

As if I hadn't figured that out. That voice stirred a memory, almost. A female voice filled with worry. *Who is she? Why can't I remember?*

The flicker of knowing slid away faster than dust through my fingers.

Fear coiled in my chest. *I'm so confused.* The blank spots in my mind threatened me on a gut-deep level, far more than the beast did.

But I'd gotten my wish. I'd found people.

I rolled onto my back, sucking air at the pain that movement caused. My entire body complained. Body slammed twice and feeling as if I'd been squeezed from the inside out.

The second voice called from a little further away. "Come on, Taylor, move it. We gotta get out of here before—"

A high-pitched screeching noise blasted over the top of the stranger's words, followed by the echo of an older male voice. Not the ghost's voice, a different one. His words boomed through a mechanical amplifier, shouting, *"Stay where you are. Hands in the air. Stop!"*

But instead of stopping, bodies swung into action. I angled my head to figure out who was doing what. I'd thought there were only one or two people nearby, but a dozen plus young ones erupted around me. Running in all directions. Dust devils with legs.

The booming voice barked more commands. *"Stop where you are. Down on the ground. This is the APD."*

I had no problem complying. Flat on my back, I stared up at an empty, vast sky. Breathing was about all I could do.

Wonder what an APD is?

As if in answer, gravel crunched under approaching steps. A weathered face with skin as dark as mine hovered into view, indigo blue pants with a knife-sharp crease and dust-covered boots. One boot kicked my hip.

I gritted my teeth to hold back a groan of pain. *A warrior never lets a threat see you flinch.*

Had that been a random thought? Or did I know this as a truth?

"Stay right where you are, kid. No funny stuff and you won't get hurt."

Too late. Everything ached right down to the roots of my hair. And why had he called me kid? Was that anything like a dude? I dug around in my mind and came up with kid as a baby goat. Maybe I'm not the only one with scrambled brains.

The boot nudged me again. "Get up. Slow and easy."

I eyed that boot, considering what would happen if I spun his foot to face the wrong way. But he had a black metal object on his hip that could be a weapon, and I still didn't know where I was or what was going on.

Breaking his ankle didn't seem too smart.

Rolling to my side, I shuddered to my knees. That settled it. I was in no shape to fight anyone right now. I'd made the right decision not to antagonize this person. Bracing myself, I lurched up to stand and anchored my feet shoulder width apart. Wiping at my arms was a mistake. Sand and grit clung to my skin so all I did was grind it into the raw places.

The man I faced stood barely taller than me. An elder I estimated to be three times my age if that old ghost had been right about me being seventeen. Age seamed this man's face and voice. Eyes like coarse stone. "What kind of damn outfit you wearing, girl?"

He said *girl* as if I reminded him of a maggot. As for my clothes, what about *his*?

Couldn't place what he wore, but I sensed the meaning behind his words and attitude–authority.

All the elders milling around wore the same covering–blue pants, light blue shirts, everything regulated and unyielding except for the sweat stains at their armpits and lower backs.

I cast another glance at myself. No one was dressed like me. Not even the others my age. They wore a different type of uniform–unusual words and designs across their chest coverings-PMS, Mad Cow Disease, Rangers. Loose pants that sagged at their hips, colorful footwear too short to be boots. The more I looked, the less I understood. I searched my memory for what was normal or how I'd ended up here.

And found only a cold emptiness filled with dark shadows.

Nothing. How could that be?

Fear turned into a rabid animal in my chest, fighting to get out.

With no idea who I was or where I belonged, what would these people...

"You going native?" the man asked me, guffawing. He shouted over his shoulder, "Hey Burt, we got one thinks she's Pocahontas. Looks Navajo, like that other kid you got cuffed."

Pocahontas? Could that be my name, too? Judging by the way he'd treated me so far he didn't know me and didn't care. The crazy old ghost had shown more concern.

The other elder this guy called Burt had clasped metal rings on the wrists of a scrawny boy younger than me–a kid?–who looked more malnourished than dangerous. What had he meant by saying we looked Navajo? What was a Navajo? I fingered my hair again. Straight and black like the skinny kid. Was my face as sharp as his? Were my eyes brown, too?

Nausea boiled up my throat.

I didn't even know what I looked like.

Panic darted across the other young faces, but not like mine. They didn't appear confused over who they were or why they were being captured.

And no one here recognized me.

Blue lights flashed on top of a dirty white box with wheels. Was that how the elders had arrived? That form of travel seemed wrong, but I couldn't pinpoint why.

Who were these people? What did they want?

I scanned the cliff face again. The beast appeared gone. Or merged so deep into the shadow of the rocks as to be invisible. Unless?

Turning around, I eyed the male and female elders rounding up the struggling captives. Could the beast thing morph into a human? And if so, what were my chances of escaping?

"You got a name?" the man at my side barked.

I whispered through cracked, dry lips. "Rayen."

"That a first name or a last?"

I shook my head. Big mistake. Pain shot through my battered skull. The elder waited for me to answer, but the ghost hadn't given me more. "Don't know."

"Can't hear you."

"I *don't* know." Talk about the scary truth. An icy ball of terror jackknifed around inside me, but I kept my face passive, trying to figure out what to tell him. My eyes watered, but I blinked against tears. I was not one who cried. Strange, but I *knew* this.

Never expose a vulnerability rolled through my thoughts.

I might not know who I was, but some deep-seated instinct

told me to trust myself to know how to survive.

"Where you from, kid?"

Just keep asking me questions I can't answer, chewing up my insides. I shook my head.

"Don't have a last name? Don't have a home? Wrong answers, kid." The elder reached for something in his belt. "Turn around. Hands behind your back."

What choice did I have? There were too many of the blue uniforms with the black metal devices on their hips. I knew something discharged from a unit shaped like that. And even if I did try to run, that beast was out there, somewhere. I could feel its presence bone deep.

So I turned, willing to wait for my chance to escape. A narrow strip of rigid material looped against my bruised wrists. Tightened with a sharp tug.

"That'll keep you." The man sounded pleased. "Where's transport, Davis?" he shouted to someone.

"On the way," came a female answer.

"Captain's going to be glad to know we got this gang corralled before they disappeared into the Sandias," the man next to me bragged. "You were right about these kids holing up this side of the Del Agua Trail."

Del Agua. I knew the name of that trail.

Another positive sign, right?

"Folks out at Piedra Lisa Park will be happier," another laughed.

Piedra Lisa Park? I didn't know that name or what they were talking about.

A sudden jerk on my arm sent me stumbling. I couldn't swallow the groan that slid out this time.

"Keep up, kid. No lagging. We got room for one more in this van." The man spoke out of the side of his mouth as he half dragged, half-shoved me toward one of the dusty boxes with wheels and iron mesh windows. This one already jammed full of snarling, angry prisoners. All who looked my age or younger.

Wary glares taut with anger and fear sized me up, judging me.

I stiffened at the thought of being caged and helpless. And

no telling when that beast would attack again. Could it get inside these boxes? My instincts warned me this wasn't a good idea, but those same instincts didn't offer help on how to get out of this situation.

Stalling, I asked, "Where're we going?"

"Why we're taking you to the Hilton Albuquerque." The man snickered.

A Hilton Albuquerque? Could the beast get to me there? I shoved a quick look up and over my shoulder again, searching. A shadow moved down the rocks, closer. "Where?"

"Don't be a fool, girl." The man thrust a meaty hand on the top of my head and shoved me inside toward the only remaining single seat. The taint of fear and sweat filled my nose. Heads hung down, shoulders hunched. I had the sense that the others knew where we were going and that knowledge had them trembling.

I tried once more. "Where *are* you taking me?"

"Where do ya think we take juvenile delinquents who steal twelve-thousand dollars worth of valuables and destroy a business just for fun?"

Stealing? Destruction? I wrenched at the tight bond around my wrists.

I wasn't a criminal.

Was I?

CHAPTER 3

What had I done to end up *here*?

I held myself erect in the stiff seating. Must show a strong front. Hide the terror vibrating inside me.

But the weird thing? Everything I'd seen since waking up in the desert hit me as both strange and familiar. I knew what materials like glass, metal and wood were, but I couldn't recall any memory of being inside a building like this one with glass windows, some sort of metallic vents and wooden doors.

Artificially cooled air washed across my skin, a welcome break from the heat outside. But the air in this room smelled stale and claustrophobic.

Why did those people in blue uniforms, officers, bring me here when they'd left the other kids at that first place they took us? A jail. For delinquents. I understood the language and terms, but couldn't grasp the clear meaning. The words sounded strange, as if filtered through multiple layers. Just like what they called this place. School.

Sure, I knew the definition of a school, or to be schooled on a topic. But the mental path I ran along chasing down those thoughts disappeared before I could find the end.

I rubbed my wrists, glad to be uncuffed.

One of the two doors to the room opened and three people entered. Elders. Two men and a woman. The woman and one of the men appeared to be around thirty years old. The other man had aged maybe twenty more years based on the gray in his hair and deep grooves on his face.

Correction. They weren't *elders*.

I'd heard them called adults. Sounded so out of place.

"I'm Dr. Maxwell," the oldest man said as he folded his flabby body into a seat behind a large table.

I sat opposite him in a rigid chair, perfectly still and silent.

His age made him look the least threatening, but not his eyes. Stone-cold eyes that assessed and weighed everything. Dr. Maxwell pointed at the other two. "This is Mr. and Mrs. Brown, the benefactors of The Byzantine Institute of Excellence."

Institute, another word for school, but just as odd sounding as the term *adults*. I kept tucking away every little piece of new information, sick of feeling so out of place.

I looked from one face to the next. The two men had much lighter skin color, especially the doctor, with thinning hair and skin so pale and dotted with age spots. But the woman's skin looked familiar...like my own.

I considered not speaking until I had to, but I was tired of being pushed here and there. Tired of being confused. "Why am I here?"

Dr. Maxwell sat back, eyeing me with a flat gaze. "The Albuquerque PD said your fingerprints didn't match those found at the Piedra Lisa Park breakin, but neither did your prints pop up right away in their initial run through the database. Since you were captured with the gang suspected of these crimes, you'd normally be held in detention while they decide what to do with you."

I'd heard the other kids whispering about detention and something called juvie. Scared them. I held my silence and let this Dr. Maxwell finish explaining.

"The police deal with a number of Native American kids every year, most are no older than you, some are criminals and some have been turned out of their homes to survive on their own. The Browns–" He nodded at the other two adults as if I'd forgotten their names already. "Sponsor a handful of Native teens every year. The police know to contact them about potential candidates. While we wait to hear back from the detectives about your background check, you've been given the opportunity to remain here...as long as you behave and don't cause any trouble."

I wanted to ask what a Native American was, but something

told me to keep some questions to myself.

At the jail, someone had called me a savage and shoved a handful of clothes at me. They'd sent me to a small room where I'd washed off most of the dirt. I now wore a thin maroon-colored chest cover called a T-shirt that was soft against my cuts and bruises, and blue pants — no, these were called jeans. I didn't mind changing.

At least now I felt clean and people had stopped staring at me.

"Rayen?" The woman speaking to me had smooth skin, and warm hazel eyes above sharp cheeks. Like mine. But my eyes were blue. Sort of a green-blue. The eyes and cheeks I'd seen — but hadn't recognized — in a mirror when I'd changed clothes. Who doesn't know their own face?

Mrs. Brown smiled, the first welcoming expression I'd seen since opening my eyes in the desert. Her sun-colored yellow dress flattered her skin. The compassion on her face reminded me of another woman, one with straight black hair like hers and...I wanted to growl when the image never completely formed.

I realized she'd gotten quiet, waiting for me to say something. I went with the simplest reply. "Yes?"

"We're here to help you, Rayen." She sent her smile over to Mr. Brown, a tall man dressed in charcoal gray...Pants. Jacket. Shirt.

A uniform? No, something else. A *suit*?

Could that be right?

I wanted to ask if I was correct, but not now when three sets of eyes judged every breath I took.

Mr. Brown stood with his back against a wall of books...

Colors flashed in my mind again, prodding me to think harder. At least the pain wasn't as sharp this time. Those were *real* books printed on paper. My heart thumped faster at the thought that paper was precious...then I hit a blank spot again. I curled my fingers, frustrated at failing to piece together yet another shattered memory.

Mr. Brown missed nothing, arms crossed, observing me with the intensity of a wise elder, dark eyes expectant. Not an easy man to read.

When he flicked a look at Mrs. Brown, she moved closer to me, taking the chair on my right. "We've been told you have no identification."

"Yes." I wasn't sure what she expected for identification other than my face. Eye scan? That triggered another half-memory that came and went. I wanted to pound the chair arm.

"And that you are reluctant to share information. Is that correct?" she continued.

"No." I hesitated, battling over how much information to reveal. But what did I have to lose? "I just don't *have* information to share."

"Oh." She paused and seemed perplexed, but her lips turned up in a reassuring way before she spoke again. "I'd like to tell you about our Institute."

"Why?"

"Perhaps you'd fit in here."

I had no interest in joining her school, but from the minute my hands had been tied this morning, I'd lost all control of my life. For now. What could be the harm in hearing her out? I nodded just to appear agreeable.

"Our program is for teens of high school age and is different from other schools in this part of the country in that we have two unique areas of study. We use a selection process based upon the skills of each student. Our diverse program was created to offer students with unusual abilities a chance to excel in areas not often taught in other venues. Or perhaps not taught in as specific a way as how we guide students here."

What was she saying? At a loss, I gave her another nod as a prod to continue, and she kept talking.

"We pride ourselves on not only accepting students with brilliant minds who are headed for places such as MIT and Harvard, but also those who strive to develop their other senses, like their sixth sense."

I understood the words being spoken, but their culture and terms were strange. MIT? Harvard? *Sixth sense* ignited a thought. Six senses. Touch, smell, hearing, taste, sight...and intuition, power or energy. Was that right?

"Do you understand what I'm saying, Rayen?" she asked, alerting me that she could tell my mind had wandered. Again.

"Yes." That word worked a whole lot better than constantly saying no, like I'd been doing up until now.

Dr. Maxwell leaned forward, resting his arms on his desk, but his eyes hadn't warmed at all. Snake eyes. "What Mrs. Brown is trying to tell you is that she and Mr. Brown award a small number of positions to select students from less fortunate homes, depending on how the student tests. We understand that some teens run away from bad situations. We can't guarantee that you'll get a placement here without gaining permission from your family, or if you don't qualify after testing, but if you tell us the truth about who you are and where you're from, we'll assign you an academic advisor and see what we can do."

They wanted me to stay? Here? *Why?* I couldn't swallow past the knot of tension in my throat. I didn't belong here.

But I had no idea where I *did* belong.

Mrs. Brown tapped a finger on my arm. "Who's your family?"

A question I couldn't answer with yes or no. "I don't know." I was tired of being viewed as a bug with no more sense than to run under the nearest boot heel. I opened my mouth to say, *I woke up in the desert, disoriented and with a beast chasing me*, but that survival instinct kicked in again, warning me that less was more right now.

"Don't know?" Mr. Maxwell's calm face slipped, showing his true feelings. Irritation. Disgust. He glanced at Mr. Brown, his tone dismissing me from this conversation. "*We'll* know who she is by the end of the day once we get the police results on her fingerprints. I think we're done here...right?"

Mr. Brown's angular face still showed no emotion until he looked at his wife and his blue-gray eyes softened. "What do you think, sweetheart?"

Mrs. Brown swung around with a look of pleading on her face. "We haven't gotten the results of the blood test to review yet, Charles." She turned to Dr. Maxwell. "Would you check again?"

I'd known what they were doing with fingerprinting at the first place, though the ink pad they'd pressed my fingers on had seemed like a messy way to transfer prints. But I'd been puzzled over the small white bandage on my arm from where they'd jabbed me with a sharp needle. They'd drawn blood.

Everybody wanted my blood today. The beast I could almost understand, but what did these people want with it?

Dr. Maxell flipped open the top of a thin metal case with an apple-shaped emblem on the lid and started tapping at it with his fingers. "The blood results just came through and–" He leaned closer, reading something, then his forehead creased sharply before he turned to Mr. Brown. "Uh, we do need to review this report."

Mr. Brown's eyes lit with interest.

Mrs. Brown slid forward in her chair, anxious, but before she could say anything her husband shot a pointed look at me and said, "You may wait in the next room."

When I didn't move, Dr. Maxwell stood and took a step toward me.

Tired of getting dragged, shoved and jerked around by strangers, particularly the el...the adults, I jumped to my feet, arms loose, hands ready to defend myself.

Mr. Brown unfolded his arms and reached over as if to restrain the doctor, but he spoke to me. "*Please* go to the next room. Wait for us there."

Mrs. Brown stood just as quickly, putting herself between me and the doctor, gently cupping my arm. If either of the men had touched me, I couldn't say what would have happened, but her touch reached past the need to fight—to defend myself.

She looked up at me, smiling reassurance, and indicated a door with her free hand. "There's a waiting room right in there. We'll send someone for you in a moment, okay?"

I let out a breath that had backed up in my chest and nodded before turning for a second door that exited the room. As I passed through and pulled the door almost closed behind me, Dr. Maxwell spoke in a low, excited voice, but too quiet for me to understand.

I paused with the door ajar at my back and focused my full attention on his words. Heat bloomed in my chest, surprising me, then it radiated out through my body as I concentrated.

The more I focused, the clearer the voices sounded.

Dr. Maxwell was saying, "...I'm telling you there are markers in her blood like nothing we've had before."

Mrs. Brown asked, "What specific markers?"

"With just one pass through the new software program, her DNA spiked alerts in four of our profile areas with the strongest being algorithmic–"

I didn't understand the next part, a string of strange letters and numbers. I'd heard of "software" and "DNA" at some point. Software versus hardware. DNA determined ancestry. I could almost hear the words coming from something inanimate as it instructed me.

Mrs. Brown spoke up. "I say we put her in the computer science program and see what she does."

What happened to 'we can't guarantee you placement without getting your family's permission'?

And what of my family? Did they exist? Did they know what had happened to me? Were they looking for me? A dark ache stabbed at me. A hole so large it threatened to swallow me.

The door suddenly snapped shut at my back and I opened my eyes, quickly taking in my surroundings.

I stood inside a larger room that had chairs placed around the walls. There were three doors and several small tables that weren't as tall as my knees.

And someone watched me–a young male. I corrected myself, mentally searching for words I'd heard in the last few hours. This young one would be a teen or kid, but the young ones captured with me had not called each other teens. Maybe because the adults often said it in a negative way.

A couple of the boys close to my age had called other males *guys*. That had seemed acceptable to all of them.

Trying to talk like everyone else here could only help me.

This...*guy* lounged in one of the chairs that appeared more padded and comfortable than the one I'd had in the doctor's room. This new stranger had skin a deeper brown color than mine, closer in shade to that of the drink he held in a bottle with writing half hidden by his fingers. His short black hair curled in tight circles, matching the color of his pants and shirt, but his shirt had...*buttons*. Yes, buttons was the right word.

Brown eyes watched me with an edge of intelligence that demanded others notice him.

Not sure of any order to the seating, I strolled over to the first open chair. One of the small wooden tables separated us. I sank into the soft material, sighing over how good it felt against my abused body.

"New recruit?" the guy asked.

Would there be an end to the questions I couldn't answer any time soon? I flipped through my knowledge and came up with the word recruit. It meant being called to a task. I weighed what had been said before and after I'd left the meeting, deciding on another simple answer. "Possibly."

"I'm Nicholas. You certainly appear to be new recruit material, since you're adorned with that leg iron."

I glanced down at my leg that still throbbed with pain.

Punishment for not listening to my instincts earlier when I'd first arrived here at this school. Those instincts had warned me not to jump at an opportunity that had "too easy" stamped all over it.

But my gut had badgered me to escape at my first chance.

The adults in blue clothes who'd delivered me to this place had turned their backs for a few seconds outside, long enough for me to try to vanish. But the minute I'd stepped through what looked like an exit gateway, a bolt of energy screamed through my left leg, the one with the wicked-looking metal ankle bracelet those adults had attached. I'd fallen to my knees, writhing in pain, then dragged myself away from the invisible field of current just as one of them walked up.

The man had chuckled and pointed to the metal contraption. "Guess I don't have to warn you what'll happen if you try to run with that latched to you. These fine people take in low-life scum and you half-breeds. You best show your appreciation and don't give 'em no trouble. Or you won't like where we take you next."

That might register on my barometer of concern if I had any idea where I was to begin with.

"Hey, just kiddin' with you, sweetheart," Nicholas said in a lighthearted tone, bringing me back to the present with a snap. "Don't feel singled out. Recruits who arrive via government channels rather than being enrolled by family wear a security device until the front office receives all the records. The

Institute is responsible for you. No big deal. They can't risk being sued if you wander off the property. Not as though you're in prison or something."

That made sense, except for being sued, whatever that was. So this school had a place that gathered records. I hoped they would find information on me, something that would fill me in on my history. Who my people were.

Unless they found out I was a criminal. I didn't feel like one, but would a criminal think of herself as such?

Nicholas leaned forward in his chair. "Where do you hail from?"

This guy didn't sound like any of the kids I'd met earlier. He had a stiff way of talking and sounded more like one of the adults. I asked, "Hail from?"

"Your point of origin. Home."

I couldn't say 'I don't know' one more time without losing my temper, so I summed it up all at once. "I know my name's Rayen, but not where I'm from. I have no idea what I'm doing here or if I'll stay. I hit my head in the desert and can't remember anything." I'd heard the kids I'd been captured with talking in the van–about me. One had made a comment that I could have lost my memory from the fall.

Sounded like an explanation for the empty spots in my mind.

"Word to the wise, sweetheart." Nicholas glanced at me sideways. "Don't tell anyone you've suffered a head injury."

I didn't see how that could complicate my life any more than it already was since I had to work through everything minute by minute at this point. Besides, what other reason would I have for not knowing answers? But he was the first person since Ghost Man to offer advice without a sneer. I asked, "Why not?"

He scratched his ear and took his time, as if thinking very hard or hesitant to share. At last he said, "If Dr. Maxwell thinks you're damaged goods you'll be withdrawn from here so fast you'll get whiplash. Then you'll end up in the detention center hospital. Those who go there experience *mutatio*."

Hospital? I thought I might have heard that term before but not enough to track.

I felt like I was being tested, but still asked, "What's *mutatio?*"

Smiling with regal superiority, Nicholas explained, "It's Latin. Means change."

Before I could ask what exactly he meant, one of the doors not connected to Dr. Maxwell's room opened and a female entered...no, I should call her a *girl* or *teenager*. That's what the uniforms had called me and another female close to my age when I was at the police station.

This one looked a year or so younger than me. She came bouncing into the room. White wires ran from her ears to a tiny pink metal square on her hip. She wore an orange, green and purple dress with wide side pockets. The dress was draped over striped purple-and-white tights that disappeared into scuffed black boots with three-inch-thick heels. She'd twisted her yellow-and-lavender hair into eight or ten ponytails that stuck out in all directions.

Every ponytail was tied with a different color ribbon that moved with the rhythmic shake of her hips.

Nothing matched on her, including her eyes...one brown and one green.

Two different color eyes?

She paused, took one look at me with those unusual eyes, then her lips curled in a quirky half-moon curve full of curiosity. She removed a wire from one ear. Her gaze slid over to Nicholas who said, "Where's your broom, Gabby? Wouldn't want you caught with no transportation."

I couldn't understand the connection, but read insult in her face just fine before she covered it with a wicked smile.

"Nick, you're such a flirt. Careful or I might turn you into a horny toad," she replied in a singsong voice, then snapped her fingers. "Oh, wait, someone already did." She laughed, a fluttery sound that danced through the room.

Nick gave her an indulgent smile that didn't quite reach his eyes, seeming more amused than insulted. "What would we do without eye candy in this place? I salute whomever scours the country to decorate our halls with sweet things to entertain the male student body."

I kept my face neutral, glad not to be the center of attention.

Derision in his voice keyed a memory I couldn't pin down beyond the distinct feeling of anger over being ridiculed for my differences at one time. I felt a fleeting camaraderie with this girl who smiled at him in spite of the demeaning insinuation beneath his words.

Gabby continued swinging her hips back and forth as if to some secret musical beat. "What you doing up here, Nick? Waiting for an optimum snitch opportunity?"

I tried to follow their conversation, but little made any sense. Nicholas enjoyed taunting this Gabby in a way that *sounded* harmless. I had my doubts. On the other hand, Gabby acted as if this was all just funny when I had the strangest sense that she kept her guard up the whole time.

But what did I know? Nothing.

Nicholas chuckled. "What brings *you* here, Gabby? You lose your crystal ball and get stuck having to navigate your way around humans?"

Her laughter tinkled with a sly undertone. "Oh, to be a mere mortal." She pranced past Nicholas and out the last door that opened into a hallway.

"She's schizo," Nicholas muttered. "Stay clear of that one."

"What do you mean by schizo?"

"Crazy. Rumor is she hears voices." He spun a finger around his ear.

I talk to ghosts. No way I was going to admit that, but I did catch the warning note about Gabby in what Nicholas said.

Just then the door from Dr. Maxwell's office opened again and another girl came into the room, as different from Gabby as the sun from the moon. This one wore her auburn hair straight and chin length, vibrant pink on her lips, and had a round face with such perfect features I peered close to see if she was real. Where Gabby had been a lightning display this girl was regal with her ice-blue eyes and russet-red dress that stopped at the middle of her thighs and a white jacket with the sleeves shoved up.

She held a fistful of papers and a thick, dull-green book against her chest, and cast a surprised glance at me. "I'm Hannah. You must be Rayen."

When I gave my usual nod, she said, "I've been asked to

show you around the school and take you to class."

"Class?"

Her eyes rolled with impatience before she said, "You've been assigned to Mr. Suarez's computer science class in room 217."

"Oh." A learning program. But with a *person* instructing?

"Follow me." She issued that directive as though ordering people around came naturally to her.

Nicholas spoke up and this time his voice had a smooth texture. "How's it going, Hannah banana?"

I studied Nicholas to figure out what had caused him to change from speaking in a somewhat superior way to one of light-hearted teasing.

Hannah even sounded different when she addressed him in a soft tone. "Fi-ine. And you, Nick?"

"Never better."

There were undercurrents here, but it was one more thing I couldn't figure out.

I stood. *Why am I being sent to a class? I just want to find out who I am. Where I came from. My family.* The last being the most important.

As I started to move, Nicholas whispered behind me, "Remember, sweetheart. Tell no one."

Lifting my hand to acknowledge I'd remembered his warning about my head injury, I murmured, "Thanks." And I *was* thankful that he'd cautioned me before I made the mistake of adding to my problems.

The hospital sounded like a place to avoid no matter what.

Nicholas raised his voice just above a whisper, but I knew he spoke to me. "Any time. You need anything, you let me know."

The only thing I needed was to fill the gaping hole in my memory and I doubted he could do that. I followed Hannah out into a hallway, but something Gabby had said nudged me to ask Hannah, "Do you know what *snitch* means?"

She gave me a strange look as though I'd asked her how many noses I had on my face. When she realized I was serious, she huffed out a noisy breath, answering as if she recited a definition. "A snitch is someone who takes you into their confidence and acts like a close friend, then shares that information with an adversary or enemy, quite often in trade for something they want. Got it?"

"Yeah." Another name for a traitor. I had one more question. "What do you know about Nicholas?"

Her smile tilted with a sly angle. "He's at the top of his class in computer science. He's very popular with all the girls. And..." She swept a long look at me. "And he's off limits to you, but you should be polite to him."

"Why?" I ignored why he had limits and focused on her last words. "Are people mean to him?"

"Are you serious? No. He's their only child."

"Whose only child?"

"The Browns. They adopted him."

My stomach dropped. I'd just spoken openly with Nicholas *Brown*, someone who could easily tell his parents that I was damaged goods.

Mrs. Brown had been my only advocate so far, but what would happen when she found out I was not suitable for this place?

I might not have wanted to be here to begin with, but I certainly didn't want to go to that hospital and end up *mutatio*.

CHAPTER 4

I had Hannah to thank for my full stomach, even if she had seemed put out to sit with me in the dining hall, as if my presence detracted from her. While I ate something with no flavor, she'd scanned her nails, the ceiling, the other kids. Did everything to ignore me. Which was fine with me. Food helped revive me some, but now I had a new challenge to face.

More people to meet. Me, the strange one. I felt like I stood out even wearing their clothes.

We'd run into students during lunch, but Hannah had spared me more questions by keeping the conversations turned to her, as though she knew I didn't want to answer questions.

Didn't being a better option than *couldn't*. But I doubted it was actually in Hannah's nature to do anything kind for someone she deemed unworthy. And she'd clearly passed that judgment on me.

I matched her pace as she moved down the sterile walkways in the building. Everything smelled well-scrubbed, but confining. She still carried the papers and the book with the hard green cover. It had to be two inches thick. I wanted to hold that book and touch the papers, but I wouldn't ask.

Every time I said more than yes or no, people looked at me as though I lacked brains. Same as Hannah's perpetual expression when she addressed me.

My internal defenses continued to bellow for me to escape.

Not going to happen this time until I knew how to leave without getting zapped by an electric charge.

Or knew *where* I was going.

She walked me up to a sliding metal door she opened by

pushing a button as she explained, "Computer Science is on level two. This is the closest elevator to the administrative offices. You'll find another one at the south end of the building."

When she stepped inside the small room that would hold maybe ten people pressed together, I took my place next to her, holding my breath. The elevator, as she called it, moved slowly upwards.

Another new sensation. Not dangerous, but uncomfortable.

Exiting the elevator, Hannah pointed out areas of the school, explaining things in a bored voice.

A tone dinged three times overhead from some hidden source.

She waved a hand at rooms we passed that were full of kids. "That's the final bell to be in class on time, but it takes a moment for the instructor to get things rolling so we're fine."

She pointed out plaques on the wall touting someone's accomplishments and droned on about what had inspired the creation of the school, but my mind drifted.

I cut my gaze left, then right, taking in each classroom as we passed open doors. Heads turned my way, curious expressions, but not a flicker of recognition on my part or theirs. I'd never been here before or surely someone would have recognized me by now.

What would my fingerprints reveal? And couldn't those be altered? Why not search their records for my face or retina scan, which couldn't be altered so easily?

I stopped midstride. How did I know fingerprints could be changed...or about retina identity scans? No one had mentioned that. Should I?

Only if I wanted to be treated like a moron again.

Hannah had been in the middle of describing something about the school. Her monotonous voice faded as she kept walking then paused, looked around and spoke in a snippy tone. "Rayen."

"Sorry." I caught up to her.

She drew a deep breath, expelling the air slowly with a brief shake of her head then continued on whatever she'd been talking about. "As I was saying, the Browns are richer than

God. They bought this place four years ago for the Institute. *If you make it through here, you're pretty much guaranteed a spot in a top college. You're fortunate the Browns aren't just loaded, but nice people to be so generous.*"

I zeroed in on the one word that didn't track for me. "Nice? Then why'd they give me this leg bracelet?"

She glanced at my ankle where the metal cuff barely showed below the bottom of my jeans, then met my gaze with her dismissive one. "It's a security measure that Dr. Maxwell requires...for *some* students. Just until the staff is sure the student is ready to stay here."

Meaning, Dr. Maxwell expected a certain number of students to try to escape. If this place was so good, and the Browns were such nice people, why would anyone want to run away? More questions without answers. I didn't ask Hannah since I hadn't heard one note of understanding in her voice.

Not for someone like me who didn't fit in with her kind.

Stopping in front of the last open door in the hallway, Hannah rapped on the doorframe with her knuckles. She broke out a bright smile for someone inside and said, "I have the new student the office sent you the text about."

Text? I didn't ask.

Hannah backed up, clearing the way for a thin man to step out into the hallway. He wore a white shirt with half sleeves and pants the color of the desert. Strange clothes to me, but from the way everyone had reacted to my simple buckskin sack dress, as one person called what I'd been wearing in the desert, *I* was the strange one here. I wished they'd given me back my boots, which were more comfortable than the shoes I now wore. Sneakers.

Did that mean they made it easy to sneak around? If so, that might be useful.

Altering her voice to a superior one that reminded me of Nicholas, Hannah addressed the skinny man. "This is Rayen. No last name." She turned to me, stabbing me with a serious gaze. "This is Mr. Suarez, your beginning computer science instructor. The Institute will give you additional classes once they know your academic level and *if* you'll be staying." Her look said that wasn't likely and she didn't care anyway. She handed several sheets of paper to Mr. Suarez then edged a step closer to me and thrust the book she'd been carrying at me.

I held it carefully, my fingers moving with respect and awe over the texture of the cover.

She tapped the hard cover. "You probably won't get time to read much by the end of the day, if you *can* read, but this book will help you familiarize yourself with the school guidelines and programs offered. *If* you stay around, finish it this week. Oh, I almost forgot. You're to be at Dr. Maxwell's office at five o'clock today to meet with them again."

The way she kept emphasizing *if* was starting to wear on me.

She tossed her head and turned away, prancing toward the classroom.

I asked, "Why?"

Hannah jerked around as though spooked, then recovered to snap, "Why *what*?"

"Why do I meet them at five o'clock?"

"To speak with the. . ." She glanced at Mr. Suarez and said, "Need a minute." When he nodded, she closed the distance between us and spoke in a low, tight voice. "Look, I agreed to bring you, but I didn't take you on as an understudy. Did you forget you got picked up by the cops this morning?"

"No." Cops must be another term for police, but how did *she* know they'd captured me?

"Then I'll make this simple. From what I heard, the detectives investigating the Piedra Lisa Park robberies are coming by to speak with Dr. Maxwell. You wouldn't know anything about that now would you?"

I ignored her sarcastic tone. "No." At least, I hoped not.

"Better hope not, because if they find anything tying you to the crime spree that's been going on, they'll take you with them." A smug glow lit her eyes. "Just be sure to be in Dr. Maxwell's office at five sharp or losing permanent placement here will be the least of your worries. You'll be sent...somewhere else."

She gave me another dismissive glare then walked calmly into the classroom.

Permanent placement? I didn't want to stay here. But

neither did I want to be shunted off to someplace worse.

Why had I left my home?

Did I *have* a home? My gut said yes.

"Let's go, Rayen," Mr. Suarez said with a cool politeness, lifting his chin toward the classroom. His voice was less hostile than Dr. Maxwell's and not nearly as superior sounding as Nicholas's had been.

I mentally marked Mr. Suarez as not a threat. Besides, like everything else today, I had no choice but to comply.

I hated having no say over my life.

A low murmur clouded the room until I walked in and everyone stopped talking to look. At me. I'd faced a sentient beast out in the desert. This shouldn't be worse, but my stomach kinked at moving deeper into the room. Fifteen pairs of eyes took stock and judged me on the spot.

Not a friendly face among them.

Actually there were sixteen counting Hannah, but she ignored me. She'd taken her seat on the right side of the room and had her chin down, focused on setting up a slim rectangular unit on her desk. It was similar to the one with the apple-shaped emblem that Dr. Maxwell had used.

Based on the wide eyes and snorts of barely suppressed laughter, especially from the girls in the room, the general consensus was that I didn't belong.

I couldn't agree more.

"This is Rayen," Mr. Suarez informed the room, then he told me, "Take one of the two seats in the back on the left, but don't turn on the monitor."

I passed small metal tables with light colored wood surfaces that each held two keyboards and two flat panels...I dug around in my mind and the word "screen" floated up then "monitor." Each table had room for two students.

Monitors and keyboards.

Finally, something clicked. I knew what a monitor was, and a keyboard.

Maybe coming in here would rattle my memory.

Most of the kids seemed to be my age. As I walked toward the last desk on the left, one of the guys I passed studied me with blatant interest, then softly said, "Hel-looo, baby."

I might not grasp every meaning, but I did understand that wolfish look, especially when the girl next to him hissed something angry under her breath. He just kept smiling at me. I might not belong here and had no idea who I was, but I knew when a boy was interested, and recognized female jealousy.

Some things were universal. But she wasted her energy. I had no interest in him or his leer.

I kept my eyes on the back corner. All I had to do was stay out of trouble and make it to the meeting in Dr. Maxwell's office at five o'clock.

Mr. Suarez stepped behind his desk. He muttered something about finishing rollcall as he glanced up and down, eyes searching out each student after saying a name.

I settled into my chair, glad not to be in the front on display any longer.

The teacher scanned the room again. "Where's Tony?"

When no one answered, Mr. Suarez scribbled on a paper pad, then turned and wrote words on a white wall behind him that read:

Deadline for the Top Ten Competition: May 15, 2013

Wait, I understood that. The words at least, but not what they meant.

The instructor set down his pad. "Deadline for this year's competition. That's two weeks from today, folks."

I toyed with the date in my mind, but 2013 triggered no concrete memories. Surely something significant had happened this year in my life.

The more I studied the date it did feel familiar, and pressing. Significant. *Why?*

I was starting to hate that three-letter word.

Every time I tried to concentrate hard on anything, an ache bit into my forehead with sharp teeth. I rubbed my temple then dropped my hand. My fingers touched the green book.

As Mr. Suarez started talking about the project, I propped the book on my desktop and opened it, reading the first page of introduction. Hannah was right about how long it'd take to get through this thing, but I couldn't get past how special holding a book felt.

Mr. Suarez paused.

The silence drew my attention.

He looked right at me when he spoke. "For those of you who are new, the Top Ten Computer Project's a special event the Browns created where our best ten students in computer science will have a chance to compete for a full scholarship to any of the top ten universities in this country. You'll each be assigned a partner for the first phase."

Excitement flittered through the room, but I couldn't have been less interested. I was locked on my book, blocking out Mr. Suarez's voice so I could read as much as possible in what time I had. I started scanning the pages fast, really fast. Then I felt heat, or energy, swirl in my chest. The same type of feeling I'd had earlier when I listened to the Browns and Dr. Maxwell talk behind the partially closed door.

I clutched the book tighter and the energy rolled down my arms until my fingers tingled.

Pages fluttered past as if I fanned the pages, but I only held the book.

I caught every word, comprehended every sentence.

In less than a minute, I'd finished the book. And slammed it shut, earning a hard stare from a girl at the next table over. Her gaze ended with a frown that said, "freak."

Pushing the book away, I looked at my trembling hands.

Was that normal?

Was *I* normal?

"Miss Landers and Miss Pearson make up the next team," Mr. Suarez said, calling out names to match up partners for the project.

I took a couple of breaths to settle myself and did a quick head count again, relieved at the uneven number of students. *No one to match me up with?*

That suited me just fine. I'd only end up proving how clueless I was about everything in this room and in this school, except for the monitor and keyboard in front of me. I might not know how these units worked, but I was sure I'd seen something like them before.

"Whoa, I know you're not startin' my favorite class widdout

me, Mr. S," someone announced as he entered the room. A husky-built guy with chopped-off black hair and an olive tint to his skin.

He looked about my age but had an attitude years older. His dark-brown, calculating eyes searched out each of the other five girls in the classroom, and gifted them with a wink and a cocky grin.

I noted that all the girls returned his attention with varying degrees of smiles.

Even Hannah, whose lips quirked when she tossed a brief glance his way.

Mr. Suarez paused to frown. "You're late, Tony. I told you the first day of school I don't tolerate tardiness from anyone."

"My apologies, Mr. S. A young lady needed my personal assistance." His hands moved constantly, as expressive as his I'm-the-man tone. Here, there, touching a silver medallion at his neck, punctuating his words in the air. "Being a gentleman and all yourself, I know you wouldn'ta wanted me leavin' the young lady on her own."

"What kind of assistance?" the instructor asked, wary-eyed.

This Tony guy beamed a sneaky-cat grin I didn't buy any more than I bought the grandiose performance.

And what was this guy's strange accent?

Tony opened his hands in a what-else gesture. "New kid from Jersey and Italian, like me. Got lost her first day. I delivered her safe and sound to the front office. But I didn't waste no time humpin' it here. Like I said, sorry I was late, Mr. S, but I'm ready for the Top Ten Project. Seein's how my last name starts with an S, I'm thinkin' I'm paired up with the delicious Miss Georgiana Sanderson, right?"

A look came over Mr. Suarez's face that knocked the foundation out from under Tony's grin. "Miss Sanderson has been paired up. In fact, everyone has a partner. In light of your charitable nature to help new students–"

No. No way. Don't do it. I sat up straighter.

"–you'll be teamed up with our newest student. Rayen." Mr. Suarez pointed in my direction. "Take your seat, Tony."

Tony's eyes finally lit on me. All his smug attitude slid away leaving disbelief. He stepped over to the teacher and lowered his voice, but my sharp hearing caught every word he said.

"You kiddin', Mr. S, right? You know how bitchin' I am on computers. I need someone who can hang with me, not..." Tony cut a harsh glance at me then his face smoothed, all charm by the time he faced Mr. Suarez again. "Not somebody just off the reservation."

One of Mr. Suarez's eyebrows arched at a sharp angle. "If this was so important you should've been punctual and I'm going to pretend I didn't hear that last comment. Rayen is your Top Ten partner until I say differently. Take your seat."

"But—"

"Now, or you're out of the competition altogether."

That had Tony snapping to attention.

I'd grabbed the seat closest to the corner from which I now watched as Tony swaggered down the center of the room, scowling. As he drew closer, I could see part of an image in black ink that crawled up his neck, peeking out from beneath the collar of his shirt. The design was a creature with sharp pinchers.

Some memory niggled at me. Neck markings meant something, but what?

When Tony reached my table, he dropped into the chair and crossed his arms.

The minute Mr. Suarez turned to the white board again, Tony leaned over, a nasty smile on his face when he whispered, "Find a way to disappear or I'll do it for you, sweet cheeks."

CHAPTER 5

"Unfreakinbelievable!"

I ignored Tony's latest outburst since we'd left Mr. Suarez's classroom and concentrated on searching the equipment room for a computer we'd been instructed to rebuild.

I couldn't stop thinking about how I'd read that green book in seconds, yet I now stood here staring in confusion at tables filled with equipment that had monitors.

Wish I could get through this assignment as easily as I fanned through that book.

Much of the terminology in the classroom hadn't clicked for me. When Suarez had explained the principles of what he expected to see built from outdated equipment in storage, I'd rolled my eyes. The jumbled words still spun through my mind, some pinging a trickle of memory but others sliding past.

I hadn't minded that Tony dragged his feet to leave the classroom since it meant everyone else had already been here, chosen the parts they wanted, and left. Now it was only the two of us. Not ideal, but easier to escape one than a roomful.

This Top Ten Project had something to do with taking an old computer and rebuilding it into an AI or Artificial Intelligence unit. I did understand those terms, had heard of a computer and an AI somewhere, but I knew as much about turning a computer into an AI as I did about flying to Mars.

At least, I didn't think I could build an AI unit or fly to any of the other planets in the solar system. Though I did know the planets, and knowledge of space travel tapped at the edge of my mind.

Not that I expected anyone to keep me in this program, but

until I met with Dr. Maxwell at five o'clock I might as well pick my way through this clutter to see if I could find something to use. The green book had made multiple references to accessing information on the computer, so apparently computers were used to store a lot of documentation and records.

If one of these worked, I wanted to see if I could use it to find out something about myself.

Tony shoved a monitor dusty with age out of his way, grumbling, "I should be with four-point-oh Sanderson, not some mute who doesn't even understand English."

I swallowed my smile. Tony *would* think I was unable to speak since I'd refused to answer any of his obnoxious questions like what tribe had I come from. How many scalps I'd traded to get into this place? Did I have a clue how lucky I was that they let the terminally clueless into the Institute?

Did I even know where Jersey was?

No.

I'd shrugged in answer that time, amused when Tony went off on a rant over how he wished he were back in Jersey if this was as good as it got here.

He pitched a thing he'd called a mouse into a box of miscellaneous parts and turned on me. "You're not screwing up my chance at MIT."

That term again. MIT what?

Crossing my arms, I faced him, more curious than anything to see what this blowhard would do next. He might have two inches on me since I was maybe five and a half feet tall, but he was the one terminally clueless if he thought his loud mouth intimidated me.

Just then the door over in the corner opened and a girl backed into the room, humming a strange, but interesting, tune as she dragged a cart with cleaning products, a broom and dust mop.

But there was no mistaking all that bizarre color. Gabby.

Still humming, she turned around and jerked back when she saw us, dropping her can of drink that rolled across the room, sloshing brown liquid everywhere.

Tony jumped sideways. "What the 'ell? Watch whatcha

doin'."

I gave him a dark look of warning. The poor girl had been startled. Just an accident.

"My bad," she said, sounding amused until she let out a weary sigh and grabbed a towel from her cart. She dropped to all fours to wipe up the mess.

"What're you doin' here anyhow, sweet cheeks?" Tony asked in his Mr. Nice Guy voice–*Were all girls "sweet cheeks" to this guy?*–but he looked around warily as if keeping an eye out for Mr. Suarez.

Gabby drew an exaggerated breath, eyes staring up in serious thought when she answered, "Getting ready for the prom, but I'm still waiting for my white mice and glass slippers to arrive. Until they do, I'm relegated to two hours of cleaning up. An unfair penalty for telling the truth."

Mice and glass slippers?

Tony rolled his eyes, dismissing her with a shake of his head, muttering, "Good practice. World needs more hamburger flippers."

"Your ridiculous opinion has been duly noted." She smiled sweetly at him with eyes twinkling as if she knew her reaction bothered him.

He turned his back on her and mumbled, "First Sacagawea. Now Cindereller."

Sacaga-who?

Shrugging at his back, Gabby bumped her shoulder into the mop hooked on her cart, knocking the stick loose. She had quick reflexes, grabbing the mop handle before it whacked Tony in the head. But when she slapped her other hand down for balance, it landed on my foot and her finger grazed the skin of my bare ankle just as I thought, *If I'm Sacagawea and she's Cindereller, that must make Tony the Jersey Jerk.*

"Jersey Jerk. That's too funn–" Gabby sucked in a breath and shoved up on her knees, snatching her hand off my foot. For a few seconds she sat there, staring ahead, frozen. Silent.

Tony kept muttering to himself, so apparently he hadn't heard her, but I'd caught what she'd said.

Had she heard my thoughts?

I'd had weirder things than *that* happen today already, so I kept my face blank and acted as if I hadn't heard her. I returned to moving computer parts around on the table.

That must have worked to convince her I'd heard nothing, because her shoulders slumped, as if in relief. She continued cleaning up the spilled liquid.

The door still stood propped open with her cart half in and half out.

Temptation hit me square in the chest. All at once, I wanted to leave, even just far enough to find a place to sit and think. Anything would be better than being stuck as Tony's shadow for the rest of the day, as Mr. Suarez had instructed me to do. I didn't want to build a computer or go to another class. I wanted to go home, wherever that was.

With Tony distracted removing the cover off one computer, I slipped out the door. Two steps into the hallway I smelled something rank, and familiar.

The beast. I swung around, looking everywhere until I spied a black bird, a raven maybe, perched on the top edge of an open door at the end of the hallway.

So it *could* morph into a winged creature. But why hadn't the thing done that out in the desert?

Instead of questioning my good fortune that I'd escaped it once, I backed up, slowly. I stepped into the room again, tugging Gabby's cart all the way inside and closing the door. Sweat dampened my palms.

Tony turned around, scowling at me, but an undercurrent of worry he hadn't managed to hide tinged his words. Something was bothering him. "Suarez finds you here doin' nothin' he's hangin' it on me. You gonna help or not?"

With that beast outside, waiting, I needed to figure out a plan. A way to escape. One that wouldn't get these two hurt. The thing might look like a simple bird right now, but no telling what it could become in the next minute.

I stepped over to the last worktable where...*what were those*? Laptops. That's what Tony had called the thin units that opened like a book. A mix of styles and colors sat open in rows, facing forward like good little soldiers. I started fumbling with the closest one.

Appeased, Tony returned to tinkering with a computer on

his side of the room.

Nothing happened to the one I'd chosen, no flickering lights when I hit a couple of buttons, so I stared at the worktable as if one of the devices would choose me. I had a hard time believing what had been left here would work at all if the cracked faces and beat up exteriors were any indication of functionality. But if I managed to get one of these turned on, maybe I could send a message for help.

I paused. How'd I know these things could do that? Searching my thoughts ended in a blank again. I felt eyes on me and glanced over at Gabby who still sat on the floor with a curious squint in her gaze, though she said nothing.

She shot Tony a weighted look then made some decision and stood up next to me. "The universe can be a strange and wonderful place..." She paused, glancing over at Tony for a moment before adding, "If not for those who should have remained a glint in their parents' eyes. Don't you agree?"

Nicholas's warning about Gabby came back to me, but this girl didn't seem dangerous. Just unusual, different from the others, but so was I in their eyes.

And other than Nicholas, she'd been the only friendly one around my age so far. But Nicholas might be *snitching* on me at this very minute.

Gabby didn't wait on my answer, moving ahead to say, "We didn't get a chance to meet earlier. I'm Gabby."

I started to offer my hand to her–some strange reflex that felt like what I should do to greet someone–but I left my arms hanging at my side, wary of touching anyone.

On the other hand, she didn't reach out either.

Where had I gotten that stupid idea anyhow?

Tony turned halfway, took one look at the taunting smile Gabby sent him and shook his head in disgust before giving us his back.

I got it. She wanted to poke at Tony by being friendly with me.

"I'm Rayen." I was glad to offer her something in return, even if it was only my name. All I had for now.

Tony paused when I mentioned my name, shook his head and muttered something about low placement standards.

Gabby studied me with her odd, mismatched eyes. "I presume you're one of the chosen few offered a spot on the Top Ten Project."

How could I answer that? I was none of those things, but I *was* here for the stupid project. Had it not been offered to others, like Gabby? I lifted my shoulders and let them drop.

"Ah, the rare humble academic. Found a suitable computer yet?"

I shook my head.

Tony kept his back to us when he said, "Fat chance of Sacagawea pickin' a decent computer." He sent a pompous smile over his shoulder and told Gabby, "Why don't you call up your fairy godmother, sweet cheeks? See if a magic wand can help her."

When he returned to whatever held his attention, Gabby's lips curved up. She touched her finger to her lips, looking as though a devious idea fueled her thoughts before she whispered to me, "Put your hand out and see which computer calls to you."

I lifted an eyebrow. Was that really how it was done?

She released one of her bubbling laughs that bordered on scary then lifted her shoulders in a what-can-it-hurt motion.

I sighed and turned back to the table. I had no reason to treat her with caution or condescension the way Nicholas had, because she seemed nice and harmless. I put my hand out and waved it over the top of each laptop.

"Ah, for love of Einstein, are you two for real?" Tony complained, crossing the room, a scowl on his face. "What *are* you doin'?"

Gabby rounded on him with an expression of excitement. "Perhaps she'll prove that you techno-ites are not all full of dull stuffing," she taunted. "Rayen is using her sensory skills to select the perfect computer, which requires the unique ability of energy touch. Please don't try it or you might hurt yourself and I wouldn't be able to help you. My magic wand only works if you possess a heart."

I smiled, playing along with her teasing while I searched for a computer that showed some promise, anything to get Tony off my back. I mean, what could it hurt to go along with her? It wasn't like I knew what I was doing anyhow.

Tony smacked a hand on his forehead. "Oh, no, don't tell me you're one of those woo-woo students from the east wing."

Gabby struck a pose with one shoulder cocked up and her chin held high. "Careful or I'll call my flying monkeys."

"For the love of..." Tony mumbled, pulling out a small handheld device he started thumbing. "Say your name's Gabby, huh?"

I'd seen those handheld units used earlier. Communication devices. *A phone.* Tony could call someone and–

I moved to reach for him, but my extended hand yanked toward a laptop, jerking me forward with the motion.

My fingers gripped a scuffed-up machine in the second row that had a scratched black case. *Weird.* I caught Gabby's startled look, but she said nothing so I wasn't going to acknowledge it. I lifted the computer and made room for it on the front of the worktable.

Oblivious to us, Tony waved his phone, chuckling. "Oh, yeah, this explains everything. Gabrielle Lin." He glanced up, his flinty gaze more calculating than friendly this time. "You don't look Chinese."

"Oh, dear, really? Because you certainly appear to be the spitting image of an A-hole."

"Ah...major screw up." Tony focused again on his phone screen. "Says here you're sixteen." He eyed her up and down as if doubting her age then went back to reading. "Psychological profile...delusions, antisocial personality syndrome, alien...they got that right. What planet you from, babe?"

Right then and there I decided that if I ended up staying here I'd figure out how to build a computer from scratch on my own before I asked Tony for anything.

Prancing around happily, Gabby ignored Tony and snagged the wire attached to the laptop that had responded to my hand. Had pulled me to it. I hadn't even felt heat inside me this time. Did that happen with others...or just me?

She stuck the metal prongs at the end of the wire into the wall. Must be the power source.

I tried to concentrate on what was happening with the

laptop, but my mind still worked on what to do with that threat outside our room. What was that bird-beast doing?

I once again considered using Tony's phone to call in help, but who would we call? Teachers? Dr. Maxwell? I'd been warned not to cause any trouble. Besides, I knew better than to try convincing the Jersey Jerk that a rabid, shape-shifting, predatory threat was loose in the hallway. Tony wanted a reason to get rid of me and that beast might morph into something else by the time someone got here.

Best case, I'd end up looking like a bigger idiot or a troublemaker.

Worst case, the bird could kill whoever showed up *and* us. But the bird-thing had seemed interested only in me so I just needed to keep my head down until five o'clock when I hopefully got some answers.

I realized Gabby was waiting for me to do something. When I didn't, she finally pressed the button near the top of the keyboard.

The computer whirred to life.

Still tapping keys on his phone, Tony paid no attention to us. "Ah, now we gettin' to the good stuff. Kicked outta the last two schools for disciplinary reasons, but...this can't be right. No way Cindereller tested that high." Tony frowned. More thumb typing.

The laptop in front of me buzzed with energy. I punched a couple of keys, surprised to find that my fingers knew how to form words as quickly as I thought them.

Standing at my right shoulder, Gabby hummed something quietly to herself until an image of circles appeared on the screen. She brightened at that and said, "Ah, you've found the entrance, but do you know the password?"

I shook my head.

She cocked her head, ponytails flopping to one side, laughing silently. "I like to keep my finger on life's Escape key. Try hitting that, Jedi."

I knew that key, but couldn't very well say so after I hadn't hit it. I pressed ESC.

Nothing happened. The three circles of banded colors that mixed with copper, gold and silver, kept spinning and turning, passing over and around each other.

Gabby gave the computer a confused look and leaned closer, mumbling, "Wonder what's wrong?"

Tony appeared on the other side of me. "Nothin' other than two morons do not a computer tech make."

Ignoring the loudmouth, I kept manipulating keys in hopes of clearing the screen, but nothing would let me past those circles.

Gabby angled herself forward, talking across me to address Tony on the other side. "Perhaps there's a better way for a computer savvy one such as yourself to garner the attention of the Browns. Such as letting Mr. Suarez know how gifted you are in hacking confidential records."

Tony dropped his voice low. "You threatenin' me, sweet cheeks?"

"Threat is such an unattractive word. Think of it as inspired relationship building," Gabby said, not the least bit intimidated by Tony.

"Who they gonna believe?" He scoffed. "Me or some psycho babe with zero computer ability?"

"And here I thought you found *all* my records, placing you in the caliber of a true mastermind as opposed to petty thief."

"Yeah, I found them, but records can be doctored. Not that you didn't show an impressive level of skill pluggin' in that power cord. Now you two are pickin' out a computer like itsa Ouija board. Can't wait to see what's next."

I lifted my hands to hold up between those two, or I tried to, but something tugged my fingers back to the computer.

Then I caught a swooshing noise outside in the hallway.

So intent on arguing, Tony and Gabby missed the flying dark shadow flashing past the glass window.

I glanced over in time to see black wings flapping. What would that thing morph into next? And would it stay outside this room? Even if it only wanted me, would it harm Gabby or Tony if they got in the way?

I had to get out of here and draw the beast-bird away, then figure out how to not get caught again. Something told me I'd only been lucky last time, but I couldn't stay here and be the reason these two got hurt.

Gabby waved a hand, dismissing Tony, and sounding bored with their verbal game. "Some people have the gift of touch, an unfortunate shortcoming in those who don't."

Tony waggled his fingers and eyebrows, smiling. "I got plenty of touch, babe. My fingers can make that laptop sing."

Gabby glanced at my hands with a knowing look and murmured, "Don't think you've got her touch."

"Ya think? She can't even get the screen to open."

I tried to lift my hands again, but my fingers were heavy as weighted metal and drawn to the keys as if they were pure magnets. This wasn't helping my immediate goal of escaping this room. More than that, I didn't think this was normal.

Gabby looked up at me, her face calm and sincere. "Just ignore Tony and open your senses to–"

Tony hooted as if he hadn't heard anything so ridiculous in years.

In a surprising change from her earlier teasing, Gabby growled and grabbed my right wrist as if forgetting her wariness about touching. She snatched my hand off the keyboard and shoved it palm out toward the monitor, speaking past me at Tony the whole time as if *he* was the clueless one. "Everything has energy. You just have to–"

My arm sucked into the screen.

Gabby shrieked and gripped my wrist tighter, trying to hold me back.

I tried to back away, too, but whatever had latched onto me wasn't turning loose.

The raven slammed against the glass window, beating its wings to get into the room. Tony and Gabby were both shouting so loudly, I doubted anyone heard the thing but me.

Tony repeated, "What the f–" He clamped his hand on my left arm, yanking to pull me back.

He was strong. I hoped he'd win the tug o' war, but my hand kept sinking further into the monitor...then my arm started shimmering.

In the next instant, I was sucked all the way inside, my body twisting into a kaleidoscope of colors. Heat ripped through me from my arms to my chest then through my legs.

Gabby blurred into a colorful stretched shape beside me.

Tony's grip tightened on my arm as we all spun into a bright orange-red vortex.

CHAPTER 6

I slammed up and down, over and around, freefalling in a vacuum of cold air. Someone screamed. Gabby? Her foot kicked my arm, grazing me then gone.

Another shout. Tony?

No time to think.

Slam.

For the third time in less than a day, I crashed into a hard, unyielding surface. This time a knee jammed my spine. An elbow gouged my stomach.

"Get your effin' foot off my ribs," Tony growled from somewhere nearby.

Everything was black. I couldn't see.

I squeezed my eyes tight then cracked them open. I sucked air. My eyes adjusted slowly. Feeble light and barely visible shapes came into focus.

Another room. This one metal. Round walls. Blinking red-orange light.

Where was I now?

Not any more familiar to me than the desert or school had been. I pulled into a sitting position. No bones broken but bruises on top of bruises. How much could a body take? When my vision adjusted further, I realized I could make out details. An eerie red glow washed across everything. I licked my lips, mouth dry as a dust bowl.

Gabby groaned.

"You two okay?" My words echoed in the cramped space.

I could see enough to notice Gabby cocked her head one way then the other, sending ribbons and hair flying. "I'll live."

Twisting, I found Tony, head in his hands. He drew his knees to his chest then lifted his head and grasped the metal disk hanging from a chain around his neck. A talisman?

I nudged him with my elbow. "You alive?"

His head popped up. "Yeah, I'm alive." In a quiet voice, he added, "What the freak just happened?"

"Don't know." My standard answer for the day and doing nothing to ease my sense of dread. I rolled to my feet, biting back a groan. Complaining wouldn't help anything.

I fisted my hands to stop the trembling. Were these things really happening or was this some bizarre dream? Nightmare more like it. Tony and Gabby were real though, so this must be. At least I wasn't the only one confused this time.

But that didn't offer any comfort.

This space reminded me of a large, round version of the elevator but three times the size. Wouldn't this thing have a door or hatch? Maybe a reverse button to take us back? One I'd jab in a heartbeat.

I stumbled toward an arch of smooth metal with purple light seeping around the edges. Possible entry and exit point? With my hands splayed open, I connected with the cool surface and felt for a button, control, anything, but stopped when the wall hummed under my fingers.

Buzzing metal, a vibration. I wish that was a good sign, but the noise and vibration climbed up my spine like claws.

Gabby asked, "Smell that?"

I hadn't until now and caught a whiff of a scent that immediately put me on alert for the sentient beast.

But this was a different smell. Sulfuric.

Even so, some deep, primitive sense of survival warned me that we had to get out of here. Now.

"Rayen?" Gabby's earlier happy voice was gone, replaced by a low guarded tone that transmitted equal concern. "I can't explain it, but I feel this is a bad place to be."

"Agreed. But how do we get out of this thing?" I ran my hands over the arched door again, searching for a release mechanism.

Tony called over, "Wait a minute. Why try to get out of here when we might need to *be* here to go back?"

I glanced over my shoulder, keeping an eye on both of them while I kept touching the metal, hoping to find some release mechanism. Tony pulled himself quickly to his feet then braced his hands on his knees. "Think I'm gonna puke."

Gabby shuddered. "Eew. Just kill me now if you do."

Tony put his hand on the wall and groaned.

I might have chuckled at seeing the loudmouth brought low if I weren't so concerned about where we were and how in the world we'd ended up here. The last thing I remembered was Gabby sticking my hand on that laptop monitor...no, *in* the monitor.

Gabby unfolded her arms and shifted from the floor to her knees to a standing position, her face pale in the pulsing red haze. But she shook herself, as if preparing for whatever she had to face, and straightened her spine. She stepped up next to me. "Got any idea where we are?"

"No." There had to be a lever or button somewhere to open a door or hatch.

"Either of you ever see anything like this before?" Gabby asked louder but calmly, even though I caught the way she clenched her fingers.

Tony grumbled, "No."

I admitted, "I don't know."

"What kinda answer is that?" Tony's bravado returned in full force. "Either you've seen somethin' like this before or not. It's a yes or no question."

"I *said* I didn't know." I turned back to patting the wall, urgency driving me. Not sure why. The smell? The buzz?

"Look, Sacagawea, now's not the time to be cryptic." Tony stood and stepped toward me, his chin up, his whole attitude set for a fight.

"*Now's* a good time to give it a rest," Gabby interceded in an even tone, but sounding much more serious than she had before. She angled her head, staring at me as if she tried to reach inside me to get an answer her own way.

If she could dig something out of my mind that'd help, I was all for it. But she just shrugged.

Tony argued, "No, I won't give it a rest. We're here because of her."

"Not really," Gabby corrected. "*I* put her hand on the monitor and I saw *you* grab her arm, so that would seem to implicate all of us equally, don't you think?"

Tony wouldn't relent, studying me as if he couldn't decide what to think. "Whatcha mean when you say you can't remember, Sacagawea?"

Why play with words or avoid the obvious at this point? Besides, Nicholas had probably already told the Browns about my head injury so how could it matter if these two knew?

"I'm saying my mind's a black hole." My voice burned dark with frustration crowding my throat. I slammed one hand against the metal. For all the good that did. But we couldn't just keep on standing here. Waiting for whatever had caused that smell to return.

My skin chilled at the idea of being trapped in here. I knew on some primal level that we had to escape. Now.

"Like *amnesia*?" Gabby asked, her tone too bright in the face of Tony's incredulity. "How fabulous. That means you get to start over, clean slate. Make your life whatever you want."

Just when I thought I had an ally I could depend upon...

I faced her. "Yeah. Just like amnesia, but I'd rather have my original life back than a new one."

"Oh, in that case I'll help you hunt for it," she offered as if we were looking for a lost shoe. The red flashing light looked different in her green eye than it did in her brown eye.

"You can't have amnesia," Tony scoffed, getting his teeth behind his words. "We just got here. No way could you—"

"I'm saying I had amnesia back at the other place. The school. Nothing's changed here." Except for my sense that staying trapped in this space could be dangerous. "Look, we'll talk about that more when we have time. For now we've got to get moving."

"Why?" Tony asked, oblivious to the red pulsing light that kept increasing in intensity. He held up his hand and huffed out a hard breath as if trying to be reasonable. "Let's use logic. If this thing we're in brought us here, wherever here is, then it should take us back, right?"

He had a point, but the metallic hum chose that moment to grow into a low whine that picked up in volume. What was happening?

Tony covered his ears. "That's frickin' awful."

"Still want to stay in here, Jersey?" Gabby called to him.

I had to yell even louder over the screech. "Help me find a way out. Gabby, you search this side of the room and I'll search the other."

"What're we looking for?" she called back, surprising me when she jumped into action.

"A handle. A button. I don't know–something. There's got to be a lever to open a hatch on this thing."

Tony dropped his hands and shouted, "Oh, come on, you two. Maybe whatever sent us here is *sending* us back. Ever think of that?"

Gabby yelled back, "If you're not going to help us, I'd say it's been nice knowing you, but I'd hate to die with a lie like that on my conscience." She swiped her hands back and forth frantically over the metal faster and faster. "That smell's getting worse and it feels...hostile."

The hairs were already standing up on my arms from the same thought.

"What smell?" Tony demanded, but his voice sounded shaky. "Hostile? You tryin' to pull more woo-woo crap? Tryin' to scare me? Won't work."

I don't know who he was trying to convince, but I heard the truth beneath his words. Jersey Jerk *was* scared.

Deep down scared.

Gabby coughed, but she'd started pounding the metal wall on her side of the container, working her way back closer to me.

I whirled around to Tony. "That." I pointed to the pulsing blood-red light, now beating like a heart on overdrive. "Is going to kill us if we don't get out of here. Now."

"A light's gonna kill us? You on crack? Tell ya what. You two do the woo-woo thing and I'll use the computer in my phone."

Giving up, I turned back to the wall. Missing something. But what? *Think.*

I came up blank. Too many holes in my memory. All I could do was pound palm then fist against the wall. A flat, smooth wall that was heating up. Not good. Not good at all.

"I got it," Gabby said, excited, stopping to push flyaway hairs from her face. "Maybe we have to do what we did with the computer."

"Meaning?"

"The two of us," she nodded at Tony, who was busy punching his smart phone and cursing when nothing happened. "We need to touch you. Maybe that will make the door open?"

Tony paused. "Forget about that. I hold hands with girls I date, not two loonies tryin' to get me killed." He jammed the phone back in his pocket.

This wasn't getting us anywhere.

The whine of machinery reached crescendo pitch. Nothing to lose.

"Let's try it," I shouted over the screeching metal.

Gabby moved past Tony where he stood close to the arched panel and stopped next to me. I latched my hand onto Gabby's wrist, feeling static vibration beneath her skin even through her sleeve.

I picked up terror, but determination, too.

She actually growled a sound of frustration and lurched for Tony's arm. The look on his face said he couldn't decide whether to pull away or not, but he didn't.

Nothing happened.

"Great," Tony snapped in my direction. "What now?"

I was fresh out of ideas. And time.

A whirring scream split the room, tearing my brain apart, making all of us double over.

"*Don't let go!*" I shouted, even as I wanted to jam both hands over my ears. "Think!"

Tony shouted, "*Think?* That's all you've got? Think."

If we did get out of this room, I was going to shut him up even if it meant using my foot to plug that yapping hole.

But right now I had nothing more than what Gabby suggested. I yelled, "Think getting out. Open. Something!"

The room started rocking, gyrating with the three of us.

Gabby tightened her grip. "Open up. Open sesame," she shouted. "Time to go. Beam me up, Scotty."

Tony grumbled something unintelligible.

I lowered my head, blocking out as much as I could of Gabby's terror and Tony's lack of faith, the stench, the vibrations. *Out. Gotta get out.*

I leaned my entire body against the closed doorway, tugging Gabby and Tony toward it at the same time. Lights flashed wildly and the noise hit ear-bleeding level.

We were going to die.

All at once, energy burst inside my chest.

The walls shimmered around us.

Then an opening appeared as all three of us tumbled face forward into the purple light.

CHAPTER 7

I lay sprawled on my back on shin-deep grass in a wide-open space...if this was really grass. At least it was softer than desert dirt. My fingers found a blade and tugged. It stretched. The rubbery stuff was an odd mix of brown and aqua with bumpy yellow specks. I inhaled a big lungful of warm, moist air, waiting for my racing heart to quiet.

That might not happen any time soon with me staring up into a purple sky with green streaks through it. Where was I now?

Green streaks and a big red ball that didn't glow like a sun. It pulsed instead.

A chillingly eerie sight I had no reference for.

"I think we've just gone where no man has gone before," Gabby crooned. "That looks like a moon. It's got shadows...craters. . .or maybe it's a face?"

"Okay, Sigourney Weaver and Princess Leia," Tony groused, his voice coming from somewhere off to my left. "Where the freak have you two got us to now?"

Good question. Better question was why hadn't we left Tony trapped in that metal room? A tempting idea. "Who's Sigourney Weaver and Princess Leia?"

I got a look from both Tony and Gabby at that. Tony laughed. "You're serious. Ever watch *Alien* or *Star Wars*?"

I shook my head.

Gabby sat up and smiled, unbothered by my answer.

Tony's mouth dropped open, speechless.

Gabby swiveled her shoulders, a dazed look of wonder on her face as she took in her surroundings. "Check out the sick colors in this place."

"Sick, as in unhealthy?" I asked.

"Ah, no, that means they're gorgeous and amazing." She smiled, framing a picture with her index fingers and thumbs, clearly someone who lived in the moment. Wildflowers of neon-pink and intense black, with sharp spikes and even square shapes sprouted here and there.

Tony speared Gabby with a hard look. "You happy 'bout this?"

She muttered something to herself then said, "I'm not entirely sure I'm even conscious and will admit to feeling a bit out of my element right now–"

"A bit?" Tony chuckled sarcastically.

"–but you shouldn't take life so seriously. It's not permanent after all. And to be honest, I was looking for a change of scenery."

I might not always understand the things she said, but Gabby had held up pretty well through this and wasn't bawling her eyes out. As she was the one person not giving me a hard time for being here, I could better handle her strange ways than Tony's abrasive attitude.

He was already reaching for his phone–did he sleep with that thing?–so that should keep him content for a moment.

Or so I thought.

He squinted at my leg. "What're you wearin'? A cuff?"

Out of reflex, I looked down. I'd forgotten about my ankle bracelet. Had it stopped working? The thing was still locked on, but I hadn't felt any electric shock, not even a tingle. Or maybe it just hadn't activated yet.

When I didn't answer, Tony muttered, "Suarez stuck me with a freakin' criminal. This day just gets better."

I rolled to my knees. Every muscle groaned in protest. Was being beaten and bruised my normal state?

And landing in strange places?

Scanning the terrain, all I found beyond the dry grassy area surrounding us and the metal contraption at my back was an encroaching jungle that loomed on all sides.

A deadly quiet jungle.

No sounds. No breath of a breeze. Nothing.

Tony stood and trudged over to the metal thing that had spit us out and sealed itself back to a solid cylinder again. He started smacking one palm against the structure over and over, his other hand still clutching his phone that he waved around.

"What the freak are *you* doing?" Gabby asked, mimicking Tony's voice as she slid to her knees before standing. "Think your cell provider has coverage here?"

"Look. I'm just tryin' to get back inside. I put more faith in technology than this–" he waved his hand to indicate the unreal world around them.

"But we just got out–"

"You two wanted out of this thing. Me?" Tony jerked his thumb toward himself. "Got dragged along. We came here in this pod thing. Logic dictates it's the only way back. So you can hang aroun' and sightsee, but I'm findin' my way home."

Just then the metal pod started spinning counterclockwise, causing Tony to stagger backwards. "What the--"

His last words were swallowed in a bang and puff of red clay dust. When the air cleared, the pod had disappeared.

"Nooo!" Tony screamed, his hands thrown wide, his eyes wider. "It can't . . ."

But it could, and had.

I felt as sick to my stomach as Tony looked. Staying inside that thing had worried me, but that *was* the way we got here.

Gabby stared at the open spot for a moment, stunned silent.

I didn't say a word. I'd heard something new beneath Tony's cocky arrogance. Panic. The kind of panic when your whole world has spiraled out of control and you can't stop it.

For the second time today, I knew how that felt, otherwise I might not be taking this so calmly myself.

Calm on the outside anyhow. If they could look deep inside me they'd see chaos swirling into a tornado, threatening to destroy me.

Tony gave his phone a longing look then dropped his arm and started circling where the pod had been, his movements getting more and more frantic. He ground out an oath and yelled, "Okay, fine. No 9-1-1 here. No 4-1-1. No cell tower. So what now? And what *is* this place?" He spat the last words at me.

As if I've got all the answers? I bit back my temper, determined to leave my senses tuned to our surroundings. "How should I know? I don't know what happened back in that equipment room or where we are or how we'll get out of here, but I do know our best chance at surviving is if we work together."

Tony's face said he supported no one's plan but his own. Especially someone who didn't know the Princess or Sigourney people. I saw his reaction as simple denial about what was going on and I even understood it to some degree.

I didn't expect a complete change in Tony's personality, but we couldn't survive by fighting each other.

Strength in numbers.

Even if we were only three.

My instincts told me that, and I knew, somehow, that I should trust them, especially in this place.

Gabby stood to one side staring at the jungle then swung around looking from me to Tony. "She's right, you know. We have no idea what kind of place we've just been dumped into. Unless you can teleport us with that smart phone we have no way out until we figure out how we got here. Can you counter that logic or is bitching and moaning your only plan?"

I took a long look at her. Was this the same girl we'd traveled here with? The one who hadn't seemed to take much of anything seriously back at the school? She'd laid out Tony's options in simple terms and managed to point out his abrasive attitude without sounding as if she'd attacked him.

After a moment of digesting that, Tony held up a hand. "Enough. I got your point. I'm just sayin' logic dictates that the way back is the way we came. Until that pod returns, I agree. We find out as much as we can about this place and if there's anyone else here. 'Specially if they can help us."

I'd been wondering the same thing. Were we alone, or not? If we found others here, would they be friend or enemy? And I had no idea why, but I was sure I'd encountered enemies before — enemies other than the beast-bird. Bad ones.

Tony added, "While I'm stuck here, I want no more touchin' any electronics without clearin' it through me first since neither one of you babes has a clue what you're playin' with. Agreed?"

Hard not to agree with that since computers seemed to be his passion. I didn't care for his "babes" comment, but nodded anyhow.

Gabby grinned. "As long as you agree to be open to using our other senses here."

"Sure, sweet cakes. Whatever you say." Tony shook his head and made a snorting sound that indicated how little he thought of her suggestion.

She added, "If you want to return the way we came here, keep in mind that the computer screen reacted to *Rayen's* touch and sucked in *her* hand."

Let's not keep pointing that out, okay?

Tony said nothing, but distrust stirred in his gaze.

I played the whole event back through my mind and had no more answers about what had happened than they did. I'd felt a surge of energy wick up my arm and into my body the minute my palm disappeared into the screen.

Pulling my hair away from my face and wiping perspiration off my neck, I rolled my shoulders, ready to talk about something else when I noticed Gabby cocking her head. Her yellow-and-lavender ponytails bobbed when she looked up, intent on something in the distant sky.

"What is it?" I asked, following the direction of her gaze across two hundred feet of open space that ended in a slashing dark line of massive trees. The beginning of the dense jungle vegetation.

"Can you hear that?" she asked, her voice soft, but no humor this time. Something had her entire focus.

I shook my head.

"Don't know, but . . . "

I didn't have to ask her more as I started hearing what she did, a heavy *whap, whap, whap* sound. I glanced around but didn't see anything.

Until Gabby inhaled a quick breath and pointed up.

"What the heck's that?" Tony demanded, his gaze following her finger. "Sounds like—"

I shushed him with a raised hand then moved to stand next to Gabby, both of us facing the direction of the racket. My shoulder bumped hers and I got a jolt of an image. Not a clear image but a clear sense of danger.

She tensed the way she had back in the equipment room when she'd repeated my thought about Tony, but when I said nothing to expose her she continued quietly staring in the direction of the noise.

"Any idea what it looks like?" I'd realized that Gabby had gifts she kept hidden. Based on *my* reception since waking up in the desert, and Tony's taunting just because I was different, I didn't blame her for protecting her secrets.

She murmured, "I'm trying to see it in my mind...but it's not like anything I can explain."

Tony made a disgusted growl. "If you savants are done doin' a mind meld thing, would someone please tell me what the heck is goin' on?"

Gabby's fingers twisted the skirt of her dress. "If you'd shut up long enough to hear and look up, you'd know."

The warning in her tone must have worked. Tony froze then glanced in the direction where we stared. "I don't–oh, crap."

That summed up my feelings as the moving object started taking shape.

Not object but objects. A good dozen or so of the largest maroon-and-black bat-like creatures I'd ever seen.

I didn't know where I'd seen bats before but bits and pieces of my thoughts were functioning at times, at least whenever my brain seemed pressed to figure a way out of trouble.

Like now. We had to get away from these big dark flying creatures.

First, I had to determine which direction they were headed.

They easily had wingspans of four to five feet across, blackening the sky as they swarmed nearer.

"Are those...bats?" Tony said to no one in particular as the swooping wings grew louder the nearer they came. "Aren't bats nocturnal and only eat insects?"

Tony's last words had been more hopeful than reassuring.

Gabby's voice sounded squeezed from her lungs, getting higher by the second. "This could be nighttime in this place with that red moon, and we may *look* like insects to them."

"Let's not hang around to find out," I shouted. "*Run!*"

I didn't have to say it twice as all three of us took off toward the closest trees, which were across the field.

Tony yelled, "We'll never make the trees in time!"

I checked to the left of us. The bats were still gaining altitude so they might not actually dive toward us, but we were going to intersect their path and end up running beneath them before we reached the tree line. I kept moving rather than risk a bad guess that they weren't going to fold their wings and plummet toward us.

We'd almost made cover when tiny acidic pellets hit my face and arms, stinging my skin.

"Ouch!" Gabby swatted the air around her face.

Tony slapped his head. "They're *spittin'* at us."

I thought it was obvious, but still shouted, "Keep your face turned away."

After a hundred feet of running flat out, the grass gave way to thick, vine-strangled vegetation. Plate-sized leaves whacked my face. Gnarled roots, some knee-high, snagged my shins, and thorns raked the skin on my arms. Another hundred feet and we'd reached the tree canopy.

Panting and slowing once we'd plowed fifteen feet into the thick growth of trees, I stopped and squatted until I could peer through a break in the twisted limbs back toward the grassy field.

"Gone," I whispered, catching my breath as I scanned the sky, or what I could see of it by moving back and forth until I found a sizeable opening in the towering trees. Deep purple ribbons appeared through gaps, but no green streaks that had been there when we'd first arrived. That throbbing red moon still mocked us though. Inside this forest, we'd entered a world of shiny copper and brown colors, red vines, dripping hollow sounds and shadows that shimmied.

Creepy, but safer than where we'd been. Away from oversized bats.

At least, I hoped we were safer.

That sprint had been no real effort for me, but Tony had his hands on his knees, dragging in deep breaths of the thick, damp air. He whistled. "What's this place? Jurassic Park goes techno? That was close."

Jurassic Park? I gave up trying to figure out the things Tony said.

"At least the bats didn't come after us," Gabby pointed out, just as winded as Tony, with hair falling loose from her ponytails.

Tony ignored Gabby, turning to me. "Now what, Touchy Feely?"

"How should I know?" I was getting tired of him expecting me to have answers, because he blamed me for this problem, then complaining about the answers he got. "What's *your* great idea?"

Tony's face screwed up in pure disgust. "Drop me in a city and I'll find my way, but out here? Not my thing. *My* idea would've been not comin' here in the first place. What *did* you do to that computer to make this happen?"

"I didn't do anything," I muttered, but not with any conviction.

"You musta hit a combination of keys."

"You think we're here because of a typo, genius?" Gabby chided. "Oh, yeah, that's scientific."

Tony started pacing a wide oval path between me and Gabby. Couldn't he be still for a minute? He slapped orange-and-blue-striped palm fronds out of his way. "Everything in science has an explanation. We just have to figure out how we ended up here."

Lifting her hands to her colorful ponytails, Gabby started fixing the loose ones. She passed me one of her stretchy loops. "You need this."

"Thanks." It took a few twists to pull my thick length of hair back. At least now it wasn't swinging around, swatting me in the face any more.

Gabby started in on Tony again. "That's the thing about you science types. So locked into a narrow way of thinking. You just can't wrap your mind around the possibility that all things do not have a tidy scientific answer."

I couldn't accept everything that had happened today too easily myself, but we had bigger problems to worry about. My mind had been stingy with memories, but now wanted to make it up to me by raising one survival concern after another.

"Since we have no idea how long we'll be stuck here, we need a plan to find water and food. And to figure out what's poisonous or not."

Gabby's eyes lit up. "Since Tony clearly doesn't trust our judgment, he can taste everything first."

"Very funny," Tony grumbled, still beating a circular path.

One look at where we'd just come tearing through the weeds and bushes introduced a new problem. The vegetation had already started growing back as I watched, which meant moving around would only get us lost when the path covered over, even if I left markers.

When Tony passed a bush with yellow and orange flowers, he flipped his hand at one, scattering petals everywhere.

Gabby shoved a disgusted look at him. "I don't know what your problem is but I bet I can't pronounce it."

The squinty glare he shot back at her said he hadn't found that funny, but he did avoid touching the next vine he passed that supported a bright pink flower the size of his face.

I leaned my head back, searching above us for fruit in the trees, but saw nothing obvious. If we didn't recognize something edible soon, what were we going to eat?

When I brought my chin back down, Tony had paused, standing with his arms crossed next to another huge pink blossom. This one had brilliant green spots.

And petals that moved in and out as if...breathing?

I rubbed my eyes. That couldn't be. Right?

Had to be the wind causing the movement, but I didn't feel a breeze stirring the thick air.

I would have dismissed the flower, but I noticed Gabby studying one just like it next to Tony's left knee.

"We need a plan," Tony said, unfolding his arms and slapping the phone against his thigh in a rhythmic tap.

Hadn't I just said that?

That brought Gabby's attention back up with a sharp chin lift. "How are we supposed to come up with a plan when we have no information to go on?"

Tony swung his arms out. "I don't know. Maybe we start with finding something we can use for weapons."

Strange as this seemed, I was about to say he had a valid

point. Tony swung his hand that held his phone out and back toward his thigh at the moment I realized that flower really *was* drawing a breath.

I yelled, "look out," but the pink petals lunged up, sucking tight around Tony's hand and arm before he had a chance to react.

Everything happened in a burst of seconds.

Fast as a coiled snake, a tendril of the vine lashed out from beneath the flower and raced around the wrist that Tony frantically tried to jerk free.

Tony shouted, *"What the—"*

I dove for him, but landed in an empty space as the vine snatched him off his feet and slithered away, dragging Tony deeper into the jungle. He made garbled noises.

"Grab him," I shouted at Gabby, who had the best shot at getting to Tony before he passed her and disappeared.

She hadn't looked overly athletic until she lunged for him and managed to barely snag his ankles.

I jumped up and raced after both of them.

"Raaayen!" Gabby yelled, flopping behind Tony as his body cut through vegetation slapping right and left like a shark ripping through water.

Picking up speed, I caught glimpses of Gabby's hair flying behind her and her face plowing up silvery dirt. Her body acted as dead weight to slow the momentum of the slithering vine, but not by much.

I pushed harder to get ahead of both of them, leaping over fallen trees and dodging wide bushes as I passed Gabby. Humidity soaked my clothes and sweat ran down my back.

Whipping around a tree, the vine seemed to slow for a second.

I saw my opening and threw myself toward Tony and grabbed at his free arm. Got it. Now Gabby and I could both be anchors. Maybe the vine would hit a spot it couldn't pull all three of us through.

Sounded good. Wasn't. We were getting beat to pieces and, even with my ankle restraint gouging a deep furrow through feather-fine soil and decomposing leaves, nothing slowed us down.

If anything, the vine started moving faster.

"Don't let go!" I yelled.

My last words hadn't been necessary.

Fuzzy brown tendrils snaked up from the main vine and circled down Tony's body to snag Gabby around her wrist. They were lashed together as if one elongated body.

A second tendril whipped around Tony's arm until it reached my wrist.

Let go and risk being able to catch up again? Or–?

There wasn't enough time to think it through as the sticky brown length wrapped and triple lashed my wrist to Tony's arm.

Terror rode through Gabby and Tony's faces.

I couldn't be distracted when I had to find a way to free us.

Like fragile tails tied to a windborne kite, we swept across the jungle floor, bouncing up and down, banging back and forth, being thwacked against plants, small trees and leaves with prickly thorns.

At last, the vine started to slow.

I raised my head, gritting my teeth against the burning pain of being dragged over uneven ground. I spied a wide-girthed tree ahead, larger than any others nearby. One so big that little grew anywhere in the immediate area except for a huge bush with jagged leaves at the tree's base.

Dark, oozing, orange spots and bumpy shapes dotted the weathered tree bark, some looking uncannily like faces. Small faces.

But the tree wasn't the biggest threat. The bush surrounding its base sported another pink blossom, like the one that had attacked Tony. Only this flower was massive. The petals were wider than my shoulders. They sucked in and fanned out in a breathing motion. The center area had what looked like a pile of black sticks...that started spreading.

The sticks moved until they lined the opening like teeth, sharp and clicking when the mouth of the plant snapped closed then opened again.

"Tony, watch–" The words choked in my throat when a vine branch curled around my neck, tightening.

"*Hellllpppp!*" Tony's frantic plea came out muffled as

another vine wrapped his head, covering his mouth and nose.

I'd hit my limit of being knocked around and attacked.

Anger shot through me and sent strength to my tight muscles.

Energy started building in my chest, wicking its way up through my arms and down through my legs. Everything slowed. Sounds dulled. I could feel each beat of my heart thrum in my ears.

Then that energy exploded inside me, boiling my blood, hotter and hotter, until my mind and body moved with the speed of a lightning strike.

Purely on instinct, I swung my only free hand in a slashing chop toward the vine branch that was shutting off my air supply. My one thought, *cut, cut, cut.*

And I did. I lanced the tendrils as though my fingers were small knives, and air once again flowed into my lungs.

I had no idea why that worked, but the vine dragging the three of us stopped moving forward. Instead, it began wrapping layer after layer around Gabby, Tony and me. Like a spider cocooning its prey.

I wrenched aching muscles, forcing myself to wiggle forward, past Tony and Gabby, struggling until I could yank each of my legs free to stand between them and the host bush. With everything I had in me, I stomped the vine with my foot, focusing on the word *crush* as I did.

Nothing.

Brown tendrils wrapped Tony's forehead, mummy like, leaving only his eyes void of any arrogance, just pleading silently for me to save him.

Gabby gasped and wheezed.

The vine was strangling her to death.

I focused harder. I thought *break* as I shoved my heel down with a vicious blast on the vine.

Again, nothing.

One last effort. Squeezing my eyes until flashes of light burst in my head, I called up all the energy into one last thought.

Kill.

Then I heard it. The shuddering of live wood ripped asunder

and an unearthly howl of pain. The bush screamed.

CHAPTER 8

My heart slammed my chest with every ear-splitting wail from the massive pink flower at the base of the tree.

Had I killed Gabby and Tony by attacking the vine?

The tension wrapping their bodies snapped.

All at once, thick vines connecting them to the tree splintered as strips of the plant shriveled.

I drew a breath and staggered over to reach down and grab them each by one hand, then I pulled, dragging them from the bindings still wrapped around their bodies. Uprooting one of these trees would be easier. Where had that wild energy gone? I still had adrenalin pulsing through me, but not that hot power. I yanked harder.

Their bindings splintered this time, allowing me to drag them clear of the bush.

Tony clawed his hands over his head until every last clinging stem remnant had disappeared, leaving cuts. His skin was flush, his breathing heavy. He reached into his shirt, yanked out the metal disk and kissed it hard.

"What's that?" I asked.

"Saint C." Tony eyed me. At my blank expression, he added, "You know. St. Christopher. Patron saint of travelers."

I didn't have a clue what he was talking about.

Gabby fell over on the ground, hissing, cradling her wrists, which flushed bright red.

Feeling lightheaded myself, I knelt beside her. "You okay?"

She released her wrists, sat up and shoved hair off of her face, visibly shaken, but she took a breath and muttered, "I will be after I kill Tony."

"That thing attacked me," Tony mumbled, the fight having gone out of him.

"After you attacked another flower. Maybe it wanted to eat your phone."

"My phone?" Tony lifted his hand, realized he still had his phone and said, "Hallefreakinlujah." Relief spread across his face until he frowned at Gabby. "What the heck are you talkin' 'bout the flower bein' mad? It's a plant."

"*Everything* in any world is alive," Gabby said. "Just because you can't make something fit into memory chips, processors and motherboards doesn't mean it lacks value or survival instincts of its own. We have to be careful in this place."

"It was a *freakin' flower*, for cryin' out loud. Who woulda thought it'd try to eat me?"

"You've got a point. I'd expect a plant to be more discriminating." She rubbed the raw skin around her wrists.

A leaf fell out of Gabby's hair. She picked it up and shrugged to herself then gave up a half-hearted smile. She did look a year younger physically than I was, but she had the tough core of someone who'd fought her own battles for a long time. Whatever life she'd led had taught her how to adapt, because she'd been taking everything in stride better than Tony had so far.

More than anything, this plant attack proved how much we needed each other. I hoped Tony realized that now. "Let's call this progress on the learning curve and move on. No harm, no..." I almost had the word, but it vanished.

"No foul?" Gabby smiled.

"Yeah." That sounded right, though I didn't have a clue where the saying had come from. Another crumb from my brain.

Tony muttered something in my direction that sounded like, "I'm gonna have to start callin' you Xena after that."

Another name that meant nothing to me.

Once Gabby reached her feet, she dusted off her ripped dress and asked me in the quiet voice of a conspirator, "What *did* you do to that vine?"

Not a question I wanted to answer. Or *could* answer with any confidence.

"Don't know," I admitted, and decided a lie would be better for now until I could figure a few things out for myself. Besides, that battle had drained me to the point it was hard to dredge up thoughts, much less words. Muscle fatigue from the inside out. "It all happened so fast. Everything's a blur."

Though I *had* figured out something just now. Where I'd been out of *my* element in that school, there was something primitive here that called to my blood. Did my family live in a place similar to this? I didn't think I'd ever seen anything like the vegetation or bats in this place, but I had a strong sense of having survived off the land at some point in my life.

That I'd been expected to fight and protect. Or die.

Gabby stared at me again with that deep look, as if trying to read everything I hadn't said about getting away from the vine, but the sound of Tony thrashing away from us drew our attention.

"Where you going?" she called to him then shot a questioning look at me as if I had a clue what that crazy Jersey Jerk was up to now.

"Home," Tony flung over his shoulder, steadily stomping deeper into the jungle, evidently trying to retrace the route the vine had dragged us.

"There's nothing back there," I called out.

Tony stopped as if pulled taut by an invisible wire. He turned partially to say, "Back in this direction is where the pod was. Might come again. Who knows? Gotta be better than dyin' in this hole."

Now he sounded worse than terrified.

He sounded defeated.

I glanced at the quivering bush, the one that had nearly devoured the three of us. My gaze traveled up the towering trunk where I caught sight of the small faces I'd noticed before. One looking more and more like a sad child in the shadows of the dim forest light.

Gabby's gaze bounced between Tony and me, searching for an answer in a place that held none. "You think we should go with him?"

"No." I meant it. My gut told me the pod was dangerous. But then, standing around or going deeper into the jungle could be, too. I shook my head and admitted, "But splitting up isn't an option either."

In the few seconds that I hesitated, leaves and branches started weaving across the path behind Tony. Once we left this place the chances of finding our way back here, or anywhere else, were dismal.

We were stronger as a unit of three. We could survive this if we kept our heads. I believed that at a level deep enough that it drove me to compromise.

I headed for what I could see of the path he left. "Let's go, before we lose him."

"We don't have that kind of luck," Gabby grumbled close behind. "But I'm not jumping in again if he gets attacked because of stupidity."

"How long do you think that'll be?" I asked, afraid we'd find out sooner rather than later.

CHAPTER 9

Someone's got to admit we're lost. Might as well be me.

I paused to lean against a broad tree trunk and dropped my head back, feeling the wood squish around my head. But when I shoved the heel of my hand at it, I hit a rock-hard surface. Had the bark anticipated the strike? I wiped sweat out of my eyes and rubbed at my ankle cuff that caused a drag on each step. I might be in better shape than either of those two, but I was exhausted and thirsty. "This isn't working. I don't think we're getting any closer to where we started out."

I'd hiked over mounds of gnarled roots, hacking bushes with unyielding branches using nothing more than my hands–minus the super power I'd fought the vine with–and was hungry enough to start gnawing on my own arm.

Gabby slipped into a crouch. The chafed, reddened skin around her wrists hadn't gotten any worse, but no better either. She chugged a harsh breath, her hair now wearing as many twigs as ribbons. "Maybe Rayen's right." She exhaled heavily, looking at Tony. "Not sure we're making any progress going this way."

"What is it about girls? You always side with her. Ever think *I* might be the one who's right?" Tony crowed. Or it would have been a crow if he hadn't been as winded as the rest of us. He stood with his legs braced in a wide V, hands on his hips, his chest heaving.

Gabby cocked her head, tapping a finger to her cheek. "Hasn't got anything to do with gender, but let me think about it. You right? No. *You* called her Xena. Change your mind about her being a warrior princess?"

"A crazy one," he mumbled.

If we didn't find water soon, being right or wrong wouldn't matter. Besides, Tony had lost some of his edge after that scrape with death. And to be honest, I couldn't in good faith say that returning to the pod area was a bad idea.

But we needed to hydrate.

Could we find anything in this place that would be safe to drink?

I'd worry about that when we found some liquid. With as much as we were sweating, dehydration was a given. I'd gotten more light-headed with each step and I was sure a small furry rodent had slept in my mouth for a week.

"I'm not taking sides," Gabby added. "Nor am I arguing with the logic of going back to the pod area, but I don't think you know where you're going and rushing forward isn't safe."

Tony's gaze turned hard as tempered steel for a few seconds, then remorse washed all that away. Something was driving him even beyond the basic desire we all had to return home. Some fear that hid inside his anxiety and shook beneath his words. "I haven't figured out what the freak happened to get us here or where the freak here is, but I can't be late checkin' back in with Suarez this afternoon. I've got a lot on the line for this Top Ten Project. A *lot*."

"Like what?" Gabby asked, her voice holding no bite.

Tony looked as though he would tell her the truth, but his gaze shifted from worried to arrogant, quickly shielding whatever vulnerability he wanted to keep hidden. He cracked his knuckles, burning off energy even when he was exhausted. "Unlike you two, I *am* going to MIT."

Between dealing with the beast-turned-bird back at the school and getting sucked into this alternate dimension, I'd forgotten about my own time pressure. I had to be in Dr. Maxwell's office by five o'clock.

I *had* to find out who I was.

Of everywhere I'd been since opening my eyes today, the school offered me the best place to learn who I was and somewhere safe while I figured that out.

Except for the beast that was still there. But I'd take my chances with it to get Gabby and Tony back to safety. I didn't fit into their world, but I believed they were in *this* world because of me.

And right now, worrying about anything except escaping here and getting back to the school was laughable.

Gabby huffed an exasperated breath at Tony. "You're not the only one with time issues."

"Oh, yeah?" Tony said. "What's pushin' on you, sweet cakes?"

"You, right now." She dismissed him with a wave of one hand, and started stretching as if she had a routine that relaxed her.

Tony ignored her and pinned me with a "what now?" glare.

I hadn't asked to be in charge and if Tony thought he had all the answers he could start sharing. "Okay, genius, if you want to keep going, we need water. Got ideas on where to find it?"

Tony looked surprised to be put on the spot, but all he offered was a tired shake of his head. "Told you. I'm out of my element here."

Great.

"Gabby?" I asked, not expecting much, but with her gifts she might be able to find water. When she gave me a confused look, I said gently, "You have some abilities. I'm not asking you to share what they are, but I dug my fingers into the ground during the last stop and didn't reach moisture."

She nodded, took a deep breath and closed her eyes. "I'm not a diviner," she murmured, though I didn't have a clue what that meant. "But I'll give this a try."

I shot a look at Tony to warn him not to ridicule her, but he actually watched her intently as if he hoped she could do something.

Gabby dropped her head back and held her arms out to each side in a motion of opening up to the world. Her lips moved silently then she frowned and lowered her arms. When she opened her eyes, she cocked her head, listening for something. "Hear that?"

"What?" Tony looked around. "You hear water, maybe moving like a stream or river?"

She twisted her head one direction, then another, getting a fix on what I couldn't hear. But she'd heard those bats before, way sooner than I had, so I turned my head in the direction she faced...and caught a faint sound.

A high whine that sounded like a cry.

"Is that a child?" Gabby stood straighter, pointing in the direction we'd been heading. "That way."

"A kid?" Tony looked confused. "I thought you were divining for water?"

Gabby turned on him and snapped, "I'm not a magic wand! I hear what I hear and right now it's the sound of a child crying. Some things are more important than you."

Tony jerked back. I didn't blame him. Our rainbow butterfly had fangs. What had triggered that reaction in Gabby? The child's cry?

"I hear it, too," I confirmed.

Tony slapped his forehead. "That could be *anything* in this place." He dropped his hand and said in a calm, logical voice, "Computers aren't computers, flowers aren't flowers so why should a cryin' kid be a cryin' kid?"

He had a point.

Gabby paid no attention to him, her voice turning to steel. "I don't have an answer for you and that still sounds like a child. It could be hurt. Who's to say someone else isn't here if we are and I'd think you'd be interested in checking it out if that child arrived here in a pod as well."

The gears started turning in Tony's head. "You're absolutely right, sweet cakes. We can't risk that bein' a child left alone in this place. Let's get humpin'."

Surprise at his quick shift in attitude showed in Gabby's face. "Uh, okay."

I almost wished she hadn't handed him such a convincing argument for checking out the noise. Tony perked up the minute he realized the arrival of another person might open the path to go home, which meant he'd go charging forward without thinking about the dangers.

Tony looked right and left, anxious to move out. "Which way, sweet cakes? That kid's our GPS to the pod area."

Gabby turned toward the sound of the child's voice. "This way."

"Wait." I grabbed her arm, feeling sudden determination

rigid in her muscles. "It could be a trap."

In the moment that I touched her, I caught a buzz under her skin and saw a visual of Gabby as a young child, alone, crying. Who'd left her to fend for herself?

And how had I seen that?

"Or it could be just a child," she said emphatically, shaking off my hand. "We haven't found water or a way back. If there's a child here then there may be other people here. Regardless, are you willing to gamble a child's life and leave a vulnerable kid exposed to this place?"

Something inside me shouted, "No," that I'd defended younger ones before, but I had no idea when or where. Nothing felt right in this place, but if I was perfectly honest with myself, nothing had felt right since opening my eyes this morning.

"What's it going to be, Rayen?" Gabby asked, fidgeting to get going.

Tony added, "Like you said, we can't split up."

More than that, Tony had just admitted that he trusted my judgment. Something not to be taken lightly. Not if we were going to make it out of this alive.

Were they right to trust me?

I didn't have a reason to stop them from going to the child other than sensing that sounds had been used as bait for traps at some point in my life. On the other hand, I couldn't honestly live with the thought of ignoring a child in need. "We'll go, but if it *is* a child let's not race straight to it without a plan."

"Agreed," Gabby said and Tony nodded.

I didn't like the thought of walking back toward the clearing where the sound was coming from, not with my gut still screaming the metal pod area wasn't a safe place to be, even if it was our only connection to the school. But I raised a hand, indicating to Gabby to lead the way with Tony following and me taking up the rear.

Not an ideal setup for defense, but I felt better suited for this terrain than those two and could keep an eye on both of them this way.

The hike back to the clearing seemed to take a lot less time as the cry grew louder, though decreasing in intensity as if the child, or whatever, was winding down from full pitch bawling to a pathetic whimper.

I noted purple light again through a break in the trees. But this time, the green stripes were back. The way the sky had looked when we'd fallen out of the pod. Call me superstitious, but I had an uncomfortable feeling about that sky.

I jogged past Tony, calling to Gabby. "Wait up."

"What now?" she asked in a snappish tone. I looked at her more closely. Maybe I'd heard exhaustion.

"We agreed to scope this out before walking up to the noise," I pointed out.

A child in distress clearly bothered Gabby on some internal level, but she nodded a reluctant agreement. "As long as...if it's a child we're going to help it and not just make a dash for the pod, right? If there is a pod."

I nodded. "If it is a child, and alone, we'll take care of it."

"We doin' this today?" Tony stood with his thumbs hooked in the pockets of his jeans, waiting. Sweat beaded down the side of his face, streaking through patches of dirt. He might have been a self-centered jerk at the school, but he'd been working with us better since the flower attack and I could tell he moved like someone capable of defending himself.

I turned and eased cautiously toward the whimpering sound. When I reached the tree line, I crouched low, waving the other two down, making sure they hugged the multi-colored foliage enough to avoid being blatantly visible to anything in the grass clearing.

And there she was in a patch of packed-down earth. A small girl. Maybe five or six years old, curled on her side into a fetal position, hiccupping air like someone who'd cried out every last ounce of emotion.

She looked so tiny and alone out there.

But the flower that attacked Tony had been the vulnerable-looking bait of a carnivorous plant and this place was riddled with danger.

The child was dead center in the clearing of the odd-colored grasses mixed with patches of bare ground. She wore a silvery dress, gold jewelry, sparkly shoes and her hair was braided and curled as if she'd been dressed for a party. Why didn't she look like us–ragged from running for our lives?

Had a pod dropped her here, too, or was she just lost?

Tony whispered in my ear as he squatted up against me. "There's no pod. We in the same spot where we arrived earlier?"

I shared the disappointment in his voice, since I couldn't deny hoping the appearance of a child meant adults would be nearby and show us the way home. But Tony was being calm so I answered him by pointing to where we'd clearly beaten down the grass while running from the bats earlier. The trail started from a flat area of grass, roughly conical in shape where the pod had been recently.

So the grass did not grow back out there the way the jungle had?

Gabby flanked me on the other side. "So what's the plan?"

A battle raged inside me, a tug-of-war between my drive to protect an innocent and the strong sense that I was right to be wary. "I'll go get the girl. You two sit tight."

"What if the pod comes back while you're there?" Tony asked. "We should all go so we can be together if that happens."

Gabby wasn't agreeing or arguing, but I knew from her response to the child's cry that she'd go along with anything that would allow her to help with the...*kid*.

I shook my head. "Based on how that metal thing brought us here and left, we'll have plenty of time for you to reach it if it shows up. I need you to watch my back. I can't explain why, but I have a feeling this is some kind of a snare. If something happens to me, I don't want you caught out there, too."

A sudden thrumming started. The vibration came from below ground. The pod? Or something else?

I fought to keep my balance. *What the–?*

Gabby floundered where she knelt beside me, her arms flapping to keep her balance. Tony cursed and growled.

The earth movement shifted from a tremor through the ground to an eruption of rocks and dirt out in the open space. Something alive emerged from beneath the surface on the other side of the child, near the dark jungle where it bordered the far side of the grassy clearing.

Like a giant crocodile on steroids, the creature's head with a long snout burst out of the ground. Huge eyes stuck off each side of its head. The body kept coming. It used multiple arms to drag itself up. Had to be twelve, maybe fifteen, feet tall when it stood upright on two feet the size of giant palm leaves, but with talons. Thick hide covered in scales and a wide mouth full of pointed teeth. It let out a wild screech. A metal-tearing-against-metal roar.

Tony sat up on his knees, eyes bulging. *"What the freak is that?"*

Color drained from Gabby's face. She stared open-mouthed at the beast emerging from beneath the ground then squeezed out a whisper. "The child."

A trap. I hated being right.

Just as much as I hated what I had to do next.

CHAPTER 10

I wanted no argument and made that clear with my tone. "I'll go. You two stay here." When Tony stood, I shook my head. "If I don't reach the little girl, you won't either, so don't follow me."

When Tony opened his mouth to argue, I gave a pointed look at Gabby whose attention remained locked on the kid.

He caught my meaning to watch out for her, but clearly struggled to make the right choice. At the blowhard's core, he was male and had probably been raised to protect females, but based on what had happened with that deadly vine, we both knew I had the best shot at saving that child. Even Tony had to admit that I was far faster than either of them.

With a reluctant nod, he finally said, "Don't hit a pothole, Xena."

The whole exchange took seconds I couldn't afford to waste so I had no time to ask what a pothole was.

Gabby had been paralyzed by the deadly scene unfolding until I gave her shoulder a quick squeeze of encouragement, ignored her terror and shoved to my feet. I took off running toward the child.

"*Rayen!*" Gabby shouted behind me, delayed reaction kicking in.

I couldn't turn around. Had to trust Tony to do his part to hold Gabby back and keep her safe. This was now a foot race against the roaring creature that had emerged all the way out of the ground. Dull orange scales with bright blue swirling lines covered its body in dizzying patterns.

It shook off dirt like a wet dog and swung its enormous head toward where Tony and Gabby hovered at the tree line.

I risked a glance over my shoulder, relieved to see that Tony restrained Gabby. They were in the open, but not far from the jungle's edge.

Booming steps rocked the ground.

I whipped my head back into the race.

The strange croco-monster had dropped down on four of its limbs and ran with a side-to-side movement at a thundering speed. Bulging black eyes streaked with yellow veins flared wildly at me then dismissed me as too insignificant to get in the way of reaching its initial, and easier prey–the little girl. Two thick arms dangled from the monster's upper body. Hands large enough to rip a human body in half or swat a grown man into next week had three thick-boned fingers each, with curled claws.

This was not the Beast that had chased me in the desert. This was worse.

The child let out a hair-splitting cry.

With the ground shifting the closer the monster came, I did a quick double-step to stay on my feet.

Forcing my legs to spin faster, I matched pace with the monster and angled my body into a headon collision course. I waved my arms and shouted wildly for the child to get up and escape.

She didn't move.

"Get away. Move. Run!" I bellowed. Using all I had left, I sprinted the last few yards toward her.

The little girl crawled to her knees, twisting about, staring at the monster. Wide-eyed, her panicked cry was drowned out by the *thud, thud, thud* of the predator bearing down on her.

With an extra surge, I threw myself toward her, scooping her with my arms and hitting the ground hard, rolling to the right. But I had her safely cocooned.

The ground rumbled and vibrated as the croco-monster catapulted past. So close I could smell its strange sour odor, feel the blast of its hide scrape my upper arms.

Safe?

Not hardly. Maybe Tony had been right to focus on the pod to get out of this place.

Pushing back to my feet and hugging the child to me, I made a quick sprint to the jungle edge on the other side from Gabby and Tony. I careened around, facing the back of the monster. It skidded to a stop, snorting and stomping the ground.

The little girl in my arms quivered. Too scared to make a noise. I felt her heart beating like bird wings as I stepped deeper into the jungle edge. I moved us behind the biggest, baddest palm-like frond, hoping to soothe her by being hidden.

Where was the monster?

Had it given up chasing me and the child. Why?

I heard shouting. Inhaling air into my starved lungs, I shifted the child against my chest and eased back out into the open space until I could see Gabby and Tony. They waved their hands and shouted taunts at the croco-monster.

They were the reason the monster had lost interest in us, but that appeared to be the extent of Tony and Gabby's planning.

How was I going to keep those two from being eaten?

I couldn't leave the little girl alone. Neither could I risk her life by rushing back into the monster's path.

Before I came up with a plan, the creature lunged forward and barreled toward Tony and Gabby who stopped yelling and turned to run back toward the jungle.

Chugging air as if I'd never get enough, I set the girl on the ground.

She crumpled to her knees, clinging to my leg as a lifeline.

"Stay here. You'll be okay," I gasped, trying to untangle my legs without harming her and hoping she understood my words. I patted her feather-light hair to keep her calm. Would she stay put?

No time to think as a cry of wild noises went up from deep in the jungle on Gabby and Tony's side of the clearing.

But Gabby and Tony had stopped shouting. They were looking around then all of a sudden stood transfixed at the edge of the clearing.

Who, or what, was making all that noise?

"Keep going!" I leaned forward to punctuate my words with my body. I waved at Gabby and Tony, yelling, "Don't stop. *Run!"*

Neither one moved, two bodies as rigid as trees.

What was wrong with them?

In a blink, twenty children varying in ages, sizes and looks exploded from the jungle on both sides of Gabby and Tony. The newcomers raced toward the monster, rather than away.

There *were* others in this place. And they were crazy.

None appeared younger than ten or older than me. All of them followed a tall male I'd call a boy, who appeared to be seventeen or eighteen. Hard muscle wrapped his body and he carried a rough-looking spear as a warrior would.

Not a boy. And dangerous.

He took two long strides on powerful legs and used his forward movement to throw his spear, stabbing the croco-monster between plating in its chest.

The monster bounced back as if it had hit an invisible wall, then fell over on its side, writhing in pain. A couple of the kids levitated, hovering in the air over the beast, shouting taunts and waving sticks and fists.

How'd they do that?

Even from here, I could see the terror in Tony and Gabby's faces.

I pulled my leg free of the child's grip and took a step toward them.

Something sharp stuck me in the back, and felt like it broke the skin.

Swinging around, I almost tripped on the little girl as I prepared to fight whatever had hit me...two boys maybe twelve or thirteen at the most. Both pointed lethal looking, if primitive, spears at my chest. Where had these boys come from? The jungle?

Finding more people here would be good news if not for these two trying to skewer me.

The boys wore ragged, mud-splattered tunics to their knees. One youngster had flame-red hair spiraling out from his head and his face was mottled in leaf-colored hues on one side of his forehead. Skin colors that shifted and changed to pale yellows. The other boy had brown hair to his shoulders and glowing purple eyes.

Was everything in this place weird? And deadly? Even little

boys?

That redhaired one was the shorter of the two and had a threatening look for someone that young. He ordered, "Get down on your knees. Hands on your head."

Good news? I understood their words. But I ignored his order, demanding, "Who are you?"

They pointed the razor-sharp tips closer to my chest. "Move, and you die."

And I'd thought the school had been a trial.

My back stung where one of them had already stabbed me. Nothing worse than a cut...as long as that stick had no poison on the tip.

So I know what poison is?

This was not the time to add a check mark to my ongoing list of what I did and didn't know. What I knew for certain right now was that this little warrior meant what he said.

But I didn't care. "That thing." I hitched my shoulder toward the still-roaring croco-monster. "Is going to kill...my friends."

"They're safe...from the croggle."

"A croggle?" I glanced over my shoulder. Ah, the monster. "If this is just my scrambled brain having a nightmare, I hope I wake up soon," I muttered and gently untangled my foot again from the child at my ankles. When I did, both boys looked down.

Not trained very well to lower their guard so easily.

I twirled around, catching both spears at once and pitching them aside then spun back to check on Gabby and Tony. Same spot.

What was that monster, the croggle, doing?

Nothing, because that band of shrieking children were beating it for all they were worth. They used a net of woven vines, crude three-pronged weapons, clubs and spears like the two boys had held on me. Their mighty leader called out orders and took the lead in beating on the croggle.

Why didn't he just grab another spear and kill the thing?

Did he want to kill it or was he only training his little warriors? The kids I'd seen floating before were no longer in the air, but had joined the others. Maybe their ability to remain airborne was limited.

I took a step and heard from behind me, "Last warning. You move, you die, tek-nah-tee."

What was a tek-nah-tee?

When I turned around, both kids had their weapons again. How'd they manage that without my seeing them? I'd pitched the long sticks a good distance to my right, far enough I should have heard or seen them going for the spears.

Didn't matter. I had to get to Gabby and Tony. But if I ran toward my friends, one of these two–or both–might gut me with a spear.

Maybe I could move us in that direction. "Why aren't you helping your friends with that monster?" Neither one answered. "What are all of you doing here?" I made sure they heard the lack of patience in my voice. "What *is* this place?"

Still no answer.

The little girl huddled in the same spot near my legs, eyes glazed over in shock, probably over how she got here since she wasn't dressed like this bunch.

I had a hunch that she'd gotten spit out of a pod, too.

I could appreciate that scared, shaky feeling.

More annoyed this time, Red Hair raised his voice. "Down on your knees. Now!"

"No." I waited to see if either one would make a move. When all they did was exchange a look of confusion with each other, I angled my head around to see how the battle was going.

Their tall leader had a club in one hand and something that could be a sword in the other, not giving the monster–croggle–an inch. Stab. Thwack. Stab. He had golden-brown hair and strange light purplish skin with aqua and dark-blue markings. Broad shoulders and muscled arms that swung a club the size of my leg with no more effort than if he held a thin stick.

But spearing the thick-hided creature with sharp points and clubbing it just enraged the thing rather than scaring it off or killing the monster.

In spite of now being stretched out on the ground, the croggle howled all of a sudden and lashed out with its giant tail, knocking two children out cold.

Then it rolled onto its belly, trying to right itself.

I could hear the boys behind me suck in their breaths.

Things were not looking good for the humans–assuming anyone present was human–and here I stood being useless, pinned in place by two half-sized guards.

No way.

I twisted toward the boys once more, surprising them for the second time when I yanked away both spears. "I need these."

Mouths open, they stared at their empty hands.

Nodding at the little girl at my feet, I shouted, "Take care of her."

And I was off.

To commit suicide? Possibly, but I'd bet there were kids with spears standing behind Gabby and Tony, too. I couldn't just hang around and wait for that croggle thing to kill the attackers then go after Gabby and Tony the minute it got tired of being beaten.

And to be perfectly honest, charging toward a threat felt bone-deep right, as odd as that sounded. As natural as breathing, I knew I'd done this before...somewhere.

I was almost upon the monster before the other kids noticed me. The guy in charge whipped around with shock riding his face then a fierce mask slipped into place. The younger ones seemed confused, as if trying to figure out if I was friend or foe.

No time to explain.

The leader kept his gaze on me, all the while roaring orders at the children, drawing them away from the croggle, and me.

Tossing down one spear to free up a hand, I flipped the other spear over in my right hand into a natural position for attack. Energy swirled in my chest, like before, but faster and stronger. Power shot through my arms and legs until I thought it would consume me.

Using my speed to run up the blunt scaly tail of the croggle, I pushed off and landed on its back. When my momentum slowed at the thing's neck, I clenched a curved horn sticking out the back of its head to hold myself steady as it moved underneath me. My muscles expanded and thickened with every blasting beat of my heart.

The spear began to smolder under my fingers as if burning. That was new.

I ignored everything except focusing on killing this threat, and trusting instincts I sensed were as much a part of me as the strange energy building inside me. I didn't think I could reach the monster's side eyes, or break through the skull to its brain. But I had to try.

When I drew back with the spear, a row of scales around the neck flapped out and back, out and back. Breathing?

Just as had happened in the jungle when I battled the vine, more energy rushed through me, but this time it was like molten lava.

I held the spear poised above the neck flaps.

The monster exhaled. Its scales flipped open.

A shout of *"Tenadori"* burst from my throat. I thrust the spear downward between scales in the neck.

The sharpened stick struck membrane that resisted.

My muscles bunched. Heat exploded through my body and rocketed through my arms. I powered another shove deeper into the monster until something inside gave with a spurt of stinking gray-blue ooze that spewed out.

The croggle thrashed hard, tossing me like a leaf, high and far, in an arc through the air.

I slammed on my back, knocking the breath out of me. My lungs begged for oxygen. After a few seconds I sucked in air, head ringing and the rest of me feeling like a flattened bug. My body complained from head to toe, but I pushed up on my elbows in time to see the monster spasm again, glow bright then explode into blue flames.

The high-pitched squeal of an animal in agony rolled on and on until the thing shuddered once more and collapsed on the ground with so much force I felt the blast in my chest.

Scales curled back in the intense heat that blew away from the monster and rushed across the flattened grasses, scorching my skin just like the desert had earlier.

That seemed years ago.

Young voices started shouting in anger then a deep male voice boomed orders to back away and said something else I couldn't hear.

Probably the leader.

But the monster was dead. A croggle, whatever that was. Within seconds, the thing turned into a bubbling mass of scorched skin and scales.

I'd never get that acrid smell out of my nose. My head spun from the effort of pushing myself up. I let my aching head thud back to the ground, unable to force my body to move another inch.

Gabby started yelling and chaos erupted.

I should move. Get to Gabby and Tony.

Can't breathe yet. Wheeze, pain, wheeze.

Who were these people, all kids, and that older boy? *A guy,* I corrected myself. Anyone that powerfully built was no boy.

But why did everyone sound so angry? The threat was dead.

Thoughts skittered through my head. I coughed and pulled in air, breathing in short gasps, staring up during brief snatches of lucidity.

Purple sky. Single red moon.

No green streaks now.

I closed my eyes, hearing a groan. Mine. I hoped Gabby and Tony were safe now that the croggle was dead.

Quiet. Then footsteps marching toward me. That same deep voice I'd been hearing ordered, "Stand up."

I opened my eyes. The violet-skinned leader's face suddenly shifted into view. Hair, more gold than brown now, fell to his shoulders. Were my eyes playing games with me? His hair changed to multi-colored browns, grays, and burnt orange, all muted colors. Interesting.

Different, but interesting.

Brown and black straps that looked like leather crisscrossed his chest, if such a thing as leather existed here. Loops on the straps held dagger-type knives and flat metallic discs with jagged hooks. Throwing blades. He wore woven links of the leathery material around his waist like a belt that drooped over a short groin covering created out of a plum-colored tanned hide. A longer blade hung at his hip. Bold aqua and deep-blue designs slashed along legs of roped muscle that stopped at short, dark-gray boots with orange and green fur.

Strange didn't end there.

His eyes were unusual, too. Almost too light to be human and they were first aqua then hazel...now reddish-brown and glowing with fury. I noted several of the kids with similar skin, but theirs changed as if shifting from camouflage colors to one shade of violet.

Maybe I'd hit my head too hard. Again.

The dark markings, graphics actually, on the leader's skin remained fixed in place. I had a feeling that meant something significant about him.

He repeated, "Stand. Up." But with more force.

Hopefully, I could reason with him since I'd helped slay their monster. I forced myself to roll over onto my stomach and pushed to my knees then my feet. When I stood I had to bend my neck to look up at him.

He studied me from the ground up, much like someone would observe a new species. Had he not seen a girl before?

An idea came to me.

Back when I first met Gabby, I'd thought shaking hands was a form of friendship. I dug through my brain for any help. I believed it *was* a sign of not being hostile so I took the risk of extending my hand.

He ignored me, his eyes burning like hot coals when his nostrils flared in anger.

I'd been sure that shaking was some universal sign of non-enemy, but maybe not.

"Two hands," the leader demanded, voice as grim as his face.

I didn't think I was familiar with this greeting. *Then again, I don't know what I do and don't know.* It wasn't as though I could remember ever being taught protocols any more than I knew where I'd learned how to fight. And I definitely didn't remember ever being chased by a morphing beast or fighting a croggle, but I'd survived both, so I saw no problem in going along with the request, even as terse as it sounded.

I stuck out my other hand, both palms up to show I was no threat.

The leader raised his spear to my throat. "Don't move."

I figured that out on my own.

A skinny kid around fourteen I hadn't noticed before came

out of nowhere and lashed red vines around both of my wrists before I could blink.

I glared at the leader. Purple just topped the list of my least favorite colors. "A little unappreciative after I helped you kill that thing."

"You destroyed it."

"Agreed." I enjoyed a moment of pride over having the skill–and strange internal power–to defeat a monster that huge. Something flickered in my memory.

A ceremonial moment after I'd completed a similar kill.

But the look on the leader's face didn't say thank you.

Instead he snarled, "You destroyed *all* the croggle, leaving not an inch of skin or bones to be used. You *ruined* meat that could have fed our village for two weeks. And now that we have to deal with your arrival our hunting trip is curtailed."

Just. My. Luck. "Only trying to help you keep these children safe."

A female, maybe sixteen, stepped up to the leader. So there *were* girls here. She wore a muted burgundy tunic with a braided gold edge that stopped short of her knees and ankle-high skin boots like the rest of them. The boots were made of material that reminded me of animal skin, supple and breathable. Her hair fell in dark ringlets woven of blond and black, surrounding a stunning face...until her dull gray eyes slapped me with icy hatred.

Ignoring my claim about trying to help, the leader spoke to the girl. "Is the child safe, Etoi?"

"Yes, Callan."

"Did you contain the other two?"

"Yes. The second team has them bound and waiting for your signal to return to the village."

Just as I'd figured, this group had caught Gabby and Tony.

What little good will I had toward anyone at this point was quickly sliding away, but I had to stay calm until I could figure out how to free Gabby and Tony. And after that, a way for the three of us to escape.

I'd draw on that strange energy inside me when the time came. I just had to be careful around these small children.

This Callan guy wheeled around to address the glum-faced pack of children circling him. They ranged in ages from ten to fifteen with mixed eye, hair and skin colors as if none were related, but dressed in three basic colors–mostly browns, a smattering of deep-reds and one golden color.

Their leader might be older than me, maybe even eighteen or nineteen now that I'd studied him more. Hard to tell when someone had the honed edge of a warrior. He told his band, "We'll find another food source we can defeat, or we'll find something better for food. But now we must return to the village." I heard a couple of rumbling grumbles, quickly suppressed. The leader obviously had the unhappy group under control.

Someone poked me with the tip of a spear to get me moving. "Ouch." I called out to Callan, "Would you tell them to stop stabbing me?"

He again ignored me, striding ahead to lead the way.

Just let me get my hands on another spear and I'd put a couple of holes in him. As I had no choice but to follow, I asked him, "Why are you taking us prisoner?"

He didn't slow his stride or turn around. Instead he ordered, "Silence, tek-nah-tee."

That word again. *What* did it mean?

Hopefully someone at this village we were going to was more open-minded than this guy.

The two boys behind me spoke between themselves. One mumbled, "What do you think *he'll* do with *three* tek-nah-tees?"

When the second boy answered, his voice was flush with respect...or fear. "What would you do if a tek-nah-tee killed your brother the way his died? You saw what–"

"Don't talk about that. I couldn't eat for two days after seeing the vid of what happened to him."

Who was this "he" they were talking about? Their leader?

Should I be more concerned about being thought of as a tek-nah-tee, whatever that was, or finding out what this Callan had in mind for us?

Both sounded deadly and unavoidable.

CHAPTER 11

There had to be a way to escape without harming a child, but I hadn't come up with it yet and only young ones surrounded me. And even if I did figure that out, I wasn't sure I could get Gabby and Tony free fast enough before one of these miniature terrors speared them. And the sticks they used were lethal.

I followed the blond-haired girl called Etoi who plodded along behind the leader. Callan. Nice name that didn't reflect his personality.

I raised my voice. "Where're we going, Callan?"

Not a word or motion of acknowledgment. Again. He just kept marching at a brutalizing pace through the thick and muggy forest. If he followed a path, I was having a hard time detecting it, especially with the way the jungle grew back so quickly. Something niggled in my memory that I should be able to read a trail. But why?

I spoke louder this time. "Who are you people?"

Etoi made a disparaging sound in her throat, "You teks really think we're so easily fooled?"

I was tired of being called names I didn't recognize, but doubted Etoi would believe me if I argued that I did not know what a tek was. Would she answer if I made it sound as though I talked to her this time instead of Callan? "Is the village far?"

Silence.

"Is the village your home?" I pecked away at her, going for tiny bits of information in hopes she'd slip and give me something.

Etoi shook her head until her ringlets danced. She chuckled

sarcastically, but finally spoke, emphasizing her words that had a funny accent beneath them. "Don't be a dugurat."

"A dugurat?"

"As if you don't know," Etoi muttered. "You put them here."

Walking third captive in line behind me, Tony spoke up. "Think she just called you a moron in another language, Xena."

I cast him a droll glare over my shoulder.

Gabby, who was right behind me cut in. "Astute observation from someone who has probably been called that in *every* language."

When I faced forward, Etoi turned around, walking backwards. "Make fun all you want because you will–"

"*Enough*, Etoi." Callan cut her off.

Her eyes transmitted a promise of retaliation for getting her yelled at, as if I'd caused her to be in trouble. She spun around and stomped away.

"Never thought I'd miss being at school," Gabby murmured as she moved closer behind me.

I gave a quick check over my shoulder at Gabby. She now wore a wary, distant look I started to think might be the first honest face she'd shown since I'd met her.

She trudged along looking like some exotic flower left out in the heat too long. Her ponytails and ribbons drooped, as did her shoulders.

Next to the droopy flower, I probably looked like a wilted weed. But I had a sense of this being my normal state.

Trudging along two steps behind Gabby, Tony had a grim set to his mouth and squared shoulders. As if he'd felt me watching him for a moment, he lifted his eyes and gave a half-smile with as much humor as a man going to his death. "The teachers will never believe us *if* we make it back to the Institute."

What could matter so much for him to worry more about a school project than the trouble we faced? I tried to encourage him. "We'll get out of this."

A sharp poke in my ribs took my breath.

I swung back around to face forward and found Etoi walking backwards again with one of the sword-type weapons.

Some kind of grayish-brown hardwood with the tight grain of
dense wood that had been honed to a lethal edge and deadly
tip. Her lips thinned with menace. That's when I noticed Callan
had moved several long strides ahead of her, providing Etoi a
chance to speak freely again.

Fueling my own expression with plenty of foul mood from a
long day chocked with pain, I lifted my vine-wrapped hands in
a quick move and shoved the tip of her sword away from my
chest.

She flipped the blade back in place just as quickly. "I'm not
one of the children to easily disarm." Her smile promised pain
if I gave her reason to justify slashing my stomach open. In
fact, her expression dared me to fight back so she'd have an
excuse. "You have no value here and would be wise to
remember that."

She seemed to like hearing herself talk. I changed my tactic
to a more friendly approach. "At least tell me where *here* is."

"Don't act as stupid as you look, tek-nah-tee."

I turned that on her. "If you're as intelligent as *you* look,
you'd realize I'm telling the truth and have no idea what a tek-
nah-tee is or where I am." *A pretty consistent state of mind for
me today.*

Tight lines across her face eased in thought. She clearly
considered whether I spoke the truth, but in the end she scoffed
at me. "Don't think to play tricks with me. They won't work.
You know very well where you are since there is no way for
you to be here without a tek knowing. And what's that on your
leg? We don't wear anything like that." She pointed to the
restraint banding my ankle.

I hesitated to answer. I didn't want to say I'd been cuffed as
a security measure since that would give this bunch even more
reason to think of me as a threat.

Etoi's smug smile deepened. "Obviously another tek device
you plan to use against us."

"You're wrong."

Quick as a thought, Callan was once again marching only
one step ahead of Etoi, his back an imposing figure that
dwarfed her. She didn't realize he'd returned. He swung his
head around, dark eyes scanning over his shoulder. His gaze

settled first on me, pausing long enough for me to cock an accusatorial eyebrow at him that turned his face even harder, then his eyes landed impatiently on Etoi.

He spoke in a quiet voice ripe with iron authority. "Take a flank position, Etoi."

She tensed at having been caught disobeying his earlier order to be silent and clenched her lips in a rigid line before nodding. Moving six feet to my right, she took point over a string of children walking parallel with our line.

I slowed briefly, thinking. How'd I know the word *point* meant to take the lead? Another puzzle piece slipped through my fractured thoughts.

No one deviated from that arrow-straight direction until we approached a puke-green fog hovering just above the low-growing jungle vegetation. I could probably stretch my hands from one side to the other across the patch of mist.

"Is that green crap what I'm smellin' that stinks so bad?" Tony asked no one in particular. "What *is* that stuff?"

Callan lifted his hand and signaled to his line of children as he angled his direction to avoid the green mist.

Never-let-it-go Tony quipped, "You fight monster croggles, but you're afraid of a little fog?"

When Callan once again didn't respond, Etoi couldn't pass up an opportunity as her group came closer to ours with Callan's shift in direction. She clearly wouldn't be silenced for long, which made me wonder at her status in this group. Her smile lacked kindness when she said, "As if you don't know the fog will peel the skin off your bones...slowly, and painfully. However, if you wish to pretend otherwise, by all means step into it. I'd enjoy hearing you scream."

Tony scoffed at her. "Dream on, babe."

Guess she didn't rank being called sweet cheeks or sweet cakes.

In the next few steps, the fog was just ahead and to the left of Callan as he shifted the line right, giving the stench zone a wide berth.

I wrinkled my nose at the rotting sweet-sour smell. Just how dangerous could a patch of green translucent fog be?

As deadly as a pretty flower?

What gave it the rotting odor?

I tossed a warning over my shoulder to Tony and Gabby. "Let's not test it, okay?"

Tony answered, "Got no plans to touch any of this crap even if it does sound like Amazon girl's only tryin' to yank our chains."

Etoi pointed at a small, pink lizard-looking creature with a perfectly round head and eyes at the ends of two prongs that stuck off the top. "Perhaps the eegak will teach you a lesson." She aimed her wooden sword to prod the funny-looking lizard that had brown and white dots splattered across its pink body. It scurried between the broad leaves of low-growing plants, the pencil-shaped body and tail stretched as long as my forearm.

All at once, the lizard paused, head sticking up, tongue flickering. Etoi poked the sword tip again and the lizard took off at a run, bulging eyes locked ahead as it raced and lunged into the fog.

At first contact, the lizard squealed a hideous high-pitched sound as its skin literally peeled off its little body. Small legs kicked at a phantom attacker as it writhed in a grotesque ball of muscle and bone. And then *pifft*, like water hitting a hot surface, it disappeared.

That explained the disgusting smell.

Gabby gagged as if she was going to throw up. "Gross."

Tony just whistled. "Daa-yum."

Out of the corner of my eye, I watched Etoi's calm face during the whole event. I asked, "It doesn't bother you to see something innocent die that way?"

She kept marching forward as she spoke. "Most animals know to avoid the fog unless they're being chased, except for the eegak. They are almost as stupid as a dugurat who has no survival instinct." Then she added, "Nothing innocent should die, but—" Her gaze slid to me with lethal intent. "Teks aren't innocent."

Callan must have had enough of her. "Etoi, go ahead to alert Mathias of our arrival."

That must have been something she wanted to do. Lowering her head, Etoi took off, quickly passing Callan and disappearing into the jungle ahead of him at a fast trot.

Would Mathias be the *he* I'd heard those boys talking about earlier? The one we were marching toward? The possibility that he might be more dangerous than Callan had me making another attempt at communication. "Is Mathias in charge of this place?"

Callan still ignored me.

At the mention of Mathias, the mottled, colored skin on most of the kids started moving, changing shape and position, even to different colors on some.

But nothing moved on Callan's skin.

I couldn't really fault him for his silence. *A wise warrior reveals little to the enemy.*

Who'd taught me these lessons that fluttered into my mind as if sent on the wind?

Callan lifted his hand and extended one finger up.

The children who had been flanking us moved over to our main line, some filling in gaps between me, Gabby and Tony. I glanced back to catch Gabby's eye and she nodded, letting me know she was fine for now even if we were too far apart to hear each other without yelling.

Tony gave me a similar nod and mouthed, *We're with ya, Xena.*

We might be in trouble up to our armpits, but we were finally in this together. First time I really believed that since we'd landed here.

In the next few steps, Callan and our party emerged from the jungle into a wide-open area...completely shrouded in another green fog.

But this band of green mist was huge, rising three times as tall as me and spreading a half-mile wide.

Had Callan marched us here just to force me, Gabby and Tony into a mist dense enough to kill all three of us? If so, Callan had better be prepared to die, because I wouldn't go meekly to my death, or allow any of my group to step a foot into that stuff without a fight.

"We're not going in there," I warned him.

The stoic warrior finally turned to acknowledge me. "You'll not be harmed if you follow directly behind me and your other two follow you."

Could I trust anyone in this place? No. I didn't know how I'd called up the strange energy that had helped me stop the killer flower and defeat the croggle, but I believed I could call it forth again if someone pushed me to defend myself and the other two.

I slowed my pace and asked, "What if we don't follow you?"

Callan took a moment answering, a tight smile playing around his mouth as if he looked forward to a worthy opponent. "Please resist. Not that I need more proof that you are tek-nah-tee who have killed nineteen of our smallest children–so far. But it would simplify my life to gain a decision now instead of later. The question is what do you think *I* will do if you refuse to follow?"

In other words, walk forward and risk entering this fog that we might not be immune to even if Callan and his followers were, or stand firm and end up gutted.

Tough call since he thought the three of us were tek-nah-tees who'd killed children...and someone's brother. I could understand wanting to punish anyone who harmed those unable to defend themselves, but even without knowing my true identity I was sure I could never hurt an innocent. Especially a little one.

I would *not* willingly die–or let Gabby and Tony pay the price–for someone else's crimes.

CHAPTER 12

Faced with choosing between entering fog that could flay us alive and facing a pack of weapon-wielding opponents, even if they were kids, I picked what I hoped was the better of the two options.

I told Callan, "I've never harmed a child and I saved that young girl from the croggle. We're not this tek-nah-tee thing you keep accusing us of being. A warrior's word is worth his life. If you give yours that you're telling the truth, we'll follow you, but if either Gabby or Tony are harmed you'd better hope I don't live. Because I will make you pay."

Callan took my measure with a steady, clear-eyed gaze and said, "I give my word that I speak the truth. If you and your friends remain in line along with the others, the three of you will pass through the fog with no harm."

The word *friends* raised something strong within me. A sense of bond I couldn't assign to the brief relationship I had with Gabby and Tony, but at this point we were in this nightmare together and had to depend on each other. And it wasn't as though I knew if I had any friends or not.

Could I accept this unknown guy's word?

Did I have a choice at this point? No. "Thank you."

He leaned close and added, in a far more menacing tone, "I've also given my word to destroy every tek-nah-tee I meet as long as I draw a breath. I swore my life to this vow. Do not test me again."

I knew when I was butting my head against a rock wall and nodded to Mount Callan to show my acknowledgement. Angling around, I snagged Gabby and Tony's attention and called back, "They're going to make a path. Stay exactly behind the person in front of you."

Gabby paled but her eyes sharpened with determination. She swung around, speaking to Tony, then she and Tony faced forward, both giving me tense nods of understanding.

I hoped I wasn't leading them to their deaths when I told Callan, "We're ready."

The leader gave me another look of promised retribution then turned his back to me and raised his arms. A spear clutched in one hand and the other hand empty. He spoke in a strange language, murmuring until the fog parted, rolling back to the right and left, leaving a three-foot-wide tunnel. Just enough room to move through while still needing to be careful. Then he strode forward.

What had Tony just said a few moments ago? *Daa-yum.*

I followed, tensing when I felt the cool residue of the fog tingle on my skin, but no burning sensation. Fifty steps ahead the tunnel finally ended at a massive cavern-like space enclosed by the towering fog on all sides, but open overhead. Looking up, the sky reminded me of the striking blue one that had spanned from horizon to horizon back at the Institute, except this one undulated from a deep blue-purple shade to a vibrant red-purple. And that blood-red moon glared down on us.

I didn't know anything about the school I'd left, but right now I agreed with Gabby about missing that place.

At least the school had made more sense than wherever we were now. Once Gabby, Tony and all the warrior children behind me were inside the misty barrier, the path through the fog closed.

With my group safe for the moment, I turned around and took in the village. Some of the unusual trees and bushes had been cut down, leaving a few trunks high enough to be stools. But those trunks were strange shades, some mustard yellow and others blueish gray. Vines and branches crisscrossed above, stretching from tree to tree and covering an area three times the size of Mr. Suarez's classroom.

Young children who stood no taller than my waist moved around inside this area, being watched or herded by others who were closer to thirteen or fourteen years old. Some of them sat around a pile of glowing rocks as if hovered over a campfire, but there were no flames. Others pounded what appeared to be plant fibers into cloth. Two little girls stood facing each other, a small orange gourd hovering in the air between them. It was suspended in air. No strings or levers visible. Another little boy with wild cinnamon hair levitated his body a good foot off the ground. Like the two had done while fighting the croggle.

They all paused to take note of Callan's return and us three strangers among them.

Silence swept around the interior walls of the village that appeared to be made of massive feathers strung on a vine running between trees. The feathers hung vertically side-by-side. All the colors imaginable, but there were more dust-brown feathers with vibrant red or orange streaks than any other.

I didn't want to know what kind of bird had a feather as tall and wide as my body.

Callan handed his spear off to one of his half-sized soldiers, then turned to me. "You. Come with me."

"What about my–"

A spear tip nipped me in the back, hard enough to break skin. Again.

I hissed at the new wound but followed the leader through a willowy hallway composed of more feathers. I heard multiple footsteps trailing behind, and could only hope Tony and Gabby were being herded to the same place as me.

I needed them close if the chance to escape presented itself, but I resisted the urge to turn around and earn one more hole in my back. I had enough cuts and bruises for one day, and figured I'd hear something if either of them were harmed.

And for once, I didn't think Tony would stir up trouble.

But what about this Mathias that I was pretty sure I was about to meet? Would he be as hardheaded as that brute Callan ahead of me?

Hard to imagine, but based on my luck today I wouldn't be surprised.

At the end of the passageway, I followed Callan into a room about twelve feet square. The corners were rounded where the giant feathers, solid mauve and lavender ones this time, overlapped. Just like the rest of the village I'd seen, this space also had no ceiling, and was open to the sky.

A female teen stood with her back to us while she listened to Etoi who spoke in a low, agitated voice.

"...they pretend to know nothing. One has the mark on his neck and a strange smell, another has some metal device on her leg, and still Callan brings this threat back to our village. Why did he not kill them when he could? You must tell Mathias–"

"Zilya." Callan announced his presence with a voice sharp as a knife slicing air.

Still standing with her back to us, the other girl, this Zilya I guessed, said, "That will be all, Etoi."

Color splashed her cheeks, but Etoi donned a calm expression and dipped her blond head at Zilya in a respectful manner then headed out through a different opening. She spared me a terse, just-wait glance on her way out.

I smiled, showing just enough teeth to let her know she need not wait on my account.

A swish of movement drew my eyes back to finally see this Zilya.

She turned around gracefully, looking as though everything about her contained that same graceful quality, and paused. Her attention landed on Callan first, her eyes widening in question. His stern face didn't budge. Her tunic-style gown was an odd yellowish, almost golden, material, not shiny, but elegant in its simplicity. Strange half-moon designs were sewn in a deeper burnished gold down the front. She stood eye-level to me, but her regal posture gave her the illusion of being taller.

Spikey, white-blond hair haloed over her head, so pale it reflected lavender highlights from the sky, luminous against the bright gold feathers of the wall at her back. She had a smattering of little raised, jewel-like dots, some maybe a sixteenth of an inch thick, and some the size of my smallest fingernail fanning out from her left eye. The dots started as black then shifted to iridescent as they spread across her high cheekbone.

I didn't think she was beautiful so much as compelling, but I knew Tony would be drooling if he were standing here.

What about Callan? Was he as dazzled by her?

I cut my eyes at him.

His gaze bumped into mine, hung there a second studying me, then he looked away, frowning as if caught.

I turned back to the girl. Zilya took me in with one long, cool appraisal, but her voice lashed out at Callan. "I understand there are two others."

"Yes."

"Bring them. Mathias will be here in a moment."

Callan didn't move.

Zilya's face softened when she added in a coy tone, "Don't worry. I'll be safe."

That sounded so flirty-sweet it was nauseating. Either she didn't see me as dangerous or she felt capable of defending herself. I wondered which.

He let out a huff of air. "I'm sure you can take care of yourself. Mathias may want to speak to each one independently."

Zilya's mouth tightened as if intolerant of anyone countering her orders. "As *I* am council to the Governing House, I *advise* you to bring the other two here for Mathias."

Some issue played out between them. I didn't care as long as their friction didn't have a negative bearing on Gabby, Tony or me.

Callan turned and disappeared through the opening.

I might as well start arguing in the defense of our position now. "You must believe *I'm* not a threat or you wouldn't send your. . .your guard away."

She cocked her head at that, her eyes cold and calculating. "I am hardly defenseless and *he* is not my guard. I need no guard."

If she'd seen what I did to that croggle, she might rethink her statement, but pointing that out would work against my goal of convincing someone in this place not to kill us. Before I could say anything else, another guy entered, striding so quickly the gold robe he wore whipped against his legs.

He stopped the minute he saw me. "Who is this?"

Zilya answered in a surprisingly humble tone. "One of the three captives, Mathias. I sent Callan for the other two."

So this was their leader? As tall as Callan, this Mathias might not match Callan in muscle tone, but he carried himself as a king, shoulders back, eyes ahead. He had skin darker than mine. Reminded me of Nicholas from back at school, except Mathias had warm eyes that held a depth of understanding that made him approachable. Strange for me to think that when he was in charge of this group and they had captured us.

His eyes didn't fit his age. Not that he had lines or wrinkles, but he wore years of living on his face that said he'd seen far more than others with his seventeen or eighteen years. He asked me, "What are you doing here?"

No matter where I went, I was doomed to be asked questions I couldn't answer. "I don't know."

Zilya interjected, "This is yet another tek trick, no doubt."

Mathias crossed his arms, irritation boiling in his face. "What new challenge have you brought to us?"

"None." Who did these people think we were? "We're not who you think we are."

Zilya answered, "In this sphere, you are either one of us or our enemy. There is no third option. So where does that leave you?"

The enemy. Someone they claimed had killed children.

CHAPTER 13

Muffled footsteps approached the chamber. I turned as Gabby and Tony entered the feather-encased room ahead of Callan.

Mathias moved over to stand alongside Zilya where they both faced us. Callan chose a position on the side where he could observe everyone. And look foreboding.

Gabby had the same red vine wrapped around her wrist as Tony and I did, but her forearms were now a deeper pink. Had the heat or humidity caused that, was it still a reaction to the fight with the killer-flower bush, or was her skin just extra sensitive? She stepped over to my right.

Tony stopped short behind me. "Your shirt's torn and you're bleeding. They stuck those spears in your back, didn't they?"

"It's okay, Tony."

He stepped up beside me on my left, his dark eyes conveying rage at Callan. "She risks her *life* for your bunch of munchkin soldiers, or whatever those brats are out there, and you let them *stab* her?"

Callan might as well have been formed of granite, right down to his glare. Turning me into a sieve clearly didn't bother him at all.

Ignoring Tony's outburst, Zilya moved her head in tiny fractions as she considered the three of us, particularly Gabby.

That's when Tony noticed Zilya.

I leaned over and whispered, "Shut your mouth, Jersey, unless you want to catch some demon fly in this place."

His mouth snapped shut and he speared me with a glare that felt more natural than his concern about my injured body.

Mathias addressed Callan. "Is it true we have a new portal site to watch?"

"Yes, in the area where we killed the croggle two months back."

By the subtle move of Mathias's head, I had the feeling this was unwelcome news for some reason. Mathias spoke to Callan. "I understand these teks were trying to capture one of our new arrivals."

"Now wait a minute!" I snapped. "I *saved* that little girl from that croggle monster."

Callan sliced a meaningful look at Mathias. "The child *was* unharmed when I arrived, but I still don't know where they came from *and* she destroyed every piece of the croggle by torching it before we could harvest any of the parts."

The loathing Mathias swung at me this time turned his eyes a brutal shade of purple, almost black. "That meat would have fed us for several weeks. The bones and skin offered additional shelter for those who cannot create their own."

I turned to Callan. "I had no idea that you intended to *eat* that thing." It sure hadn't looked appetizing. But Callan was doing his stone-faced warrior impression. No help there so I turned back to Mathias. "I only attacked the monster because I thought it was going to hurt the children fighting it."

A silent conversation seemed to flow across Mathias and Callan's hard gazes. Mathias finally nodded and said, "We haven't explored every inch of this realm. I will allow that there *could* be...other captives."

Captives like us...or did he mean *they* were captives?

Unconvinced, Callan crossed his arms, the muscles in his biceps clenching and unclenching. "They did not arrive in the area we normally monitor when the stripes appear in the sky or we'd have seen them when they ejected." He paused, his long fingers curled into fists, then he cast a suspicious look at my ankle. "What is that ring on your leg called?"

I shrugged, trying to come up with a bland description that didn't scream criminal.

Unfortunately, Tony decided to help me out. "It's an

electronic monitoring device." At the blank looks, he added, "You know. Remote surveillance via an electronic device attached to a person or vehicle." He winked at me. "That way their whereabouts can be monitored using GPS which reports their position via a cell phone network back to a control center."

"To control a prisoner?" Zilya offered.

Thanks, Tony. Why not tell them I was suspected of theft and destruction while you're at it?

Tony swallowed and avoided looking at me. "No, it's a tracking device." He let out a dark chuckle. "But this place is kryptonite for technology."

"You think this is funny?" Zilya demanded, a frown creasing her face.

Tony raised his bound hands. "It was a joke, sister. Just a joke."

Her frown deepened. If I had dug a pit for myself, Tony threatened to turn it into a bottomless hole. But before I could kick him into silence Zilya spoke to Mathias. "They do not dress as us so they could be high-ranking tek-nah-tee. They may wear strange uniforms thinking to confuse or trick us."

Now we were being judged by what we wore? "What do our clothes have to do with anything? We're not tek-nah-tees, whatever they are. We're here by accident." I hoped to distance myself, Tony and Gabby from whatever had killed children and the brother of somebody in this room. I felt certain the person those two boys had referenced as losing a brother was part of this discussion. Mathias or Callan?

I also wanted to alert Tony and Gabby that being a tek-nah-tee was not a positive point, and even worse that Zilya inferred we might be high-ranking.

Callan's penetrating gaze cut across the room to me with the precision of a honed knife and held the warmth of an ice storm. "Does SEOH think us so stupid as to believe this ruse? To send a bunch of vid players in here to *pretend* to be what you're not? To what purpose?"

I lifted my hands, palms out, and shook my head. "I would love to know what someone in this place was talking about. I don't know what CO is. What does C and O stand for?"

Zilya's glower suggested she addressed a moron. "Is this the part in your script where I spell S-E-O-H and explain who that monster is? So sincere sounding. Save your effort for when you stand in front of a recorder again, vid player."

"I'm *not* a player or a vid whatever." Wait, had she said a *vid*? I did know what a vid was–the short version of video–and that players performed in them. At last, a reference point for things that were coming back to me in bits and pieces.

"A great loss to young tek-nah-tee males, no doubt," Zilya sneered, then paused and said louder, "Our houses do not allow vids or fictitious tales shared. *We are* immune to your training."

Gabby piped up, saying, "Sounds like a boring-ass house to grow up in, if you ask me."

Zilya scrutinized Gabby. After studying her closely, Zilya paused then her eyes flared with disbelief. "What house are you from?"

Why did she say *house* as if it was more than a dwelling?

Gabby gave a wry laugh, letting everyone know she found Zilya's question absurd. "This month? I'm stuck in a dorm room. No house, thanks to dear old dad."

Based upon Zilya's blistering scowl, that had been the wrong answer. "They think everything is funny, Mathias. Shall we see how much they laugh when they face death?"

His drawn-out sigh spoke of lost patience.

I doubted his could equal mine, but I was making no headway with the current conversation. Time for a different approach. "This is the truth. We don't know where we are or how we got here. If you can tell us how to get back, we'll be on our way."

Zilya started to speak, but fell silent when Mathias raised his hand. "We will not release you to report back to SEOH."

Gabby muttered low, but not low enough. "What exactly are you accusing us of?"

Zilya's attention returned to Gabby in a way that sent spikes of worry running along my spine, especially when Zilya demanded, "Look at me."

Gabby straightened her spine and leaned forward, only her eyes defying Zilya. "Get your fill."

"Your eyes do not match."

Irritation rushed out with Gabby's next breath. "Yeah, well. Some of us must rise above the mundane."

Reacting as if she'd been slapped, Zilya's fingers tightened on the folds of her tunic then opened slowly with a forced effort. She ordered Gabby, "Show me your ears."

Gabby raised an eyebrow at Tony then me. He said nothing and I pushed up one shoulder, letting her know that while I thought it sounded ridiculous it was not an unreasonable demand. I hoped she wouldn't antagonize Zilya further.

I checked Callan for a barometer of the room. He'd unfolded his arms and now had one hand clutching his chin in a thoughtful pose. Darker blond than his hair, his eyebrows were tucked low over his unusual, yet always intense, gaze. The unguarded moment vanished when he shifted his attention and caught me staring at him. His arms folded back over his chest and his chin cocked up with arrogance.

Lifting her constrained hands, Gabby brushed back lavender-and-yellow strands of hair that had fallen loose around her face. When she did, she exposed first her left ear that had six earrings spiked through the outer curve, each one a similar thin silver ring except for the last yin-yang shape hanging from a tiny wire at the lobe of that ear. When Gabby turned her head to show the other side, only the matching half of the yin-yang earring dangled from her right ear.

I tucked away the fact that I recognized the yin-yang design, intending to ask Gabby about it later. Whatever she could tell me about the design might trigger more memories.

I'd have found nothing notable about her earrings if not for Zilya's sharp intake of air and Mathias's double blink in surprise.

Even Callan registered a moment of shock before hiding his reaction.

What could be so significant about jewelry?

I studied Zilya closer this time, noting the delicate earring shaped as a swan inside a sliver of moon that dangled at the base of *her* right ear. She wore only one more earring inserted above that one. A small cut stone that blazed gold.

Mathias seemed to want all the information before making a

decision, which gave me hope. As the leader, he might weigh what we said and not be quick to order our deaths. When he spoke, he addressed all three of us. "Where are you from?"

Tony said, "A school in Albuquerque, New Mexico."

Mathias shook his head. "I know nothing of Albuquerque or New Mexico."

Great, talk about hitting a wall in the conversation. Actually, beyond knowing the Sandia Mountains, I'd never heard of Albuquerque or New Mexico either before today, but I wasn't admitting that. Recalling how Etoi had treated me like an idiot when I'd suggested this was her home, I asked Mathias, "How'd *you* come here?"

Zilya answered instead. "Stop the ridiculous questions. Do you really think to convince us you are not tek-nah-tee?"

"Not really."

Zilya's face brightened, Mathias looked disgusted and Callan's countenance took a deadly shift.

I explained, "If I knew what a tek-nah-tee was I could convince you we're not that, but I have no idea what those are or where we are or how we got here. That puts us at a huge disadvantage in trying to prove our innocence."

Tony interjected, "Look at us and look at you. We obviously come from somewhere different. Show us a picture of a tek-nah-tee that looks like us. What else about us reminds you of them?"

Every time Zilya's attention landed on Tony her expression turned more evil. "I would say you smell like them, but you wear a scent clearly meant to confuse us."

"You mean the cologne I'm wearing? That's Davidoff's Hot Water." Tony grinned. "It doesn't confuse women where I come from, babe. It attracts them."

"I admit that it does mask your stench."

"My what?"

Mathias had been studying Tony and angled his head, peering closer at him. "You have a mark on your neck. Explain it."

Tony gave him a frown that questioned his IQ. "My tattoo? The Blood Scorpions...from Jersey."

Mathias did that visual exchange with Callan again then ordered Tony, "Uncover the entire marking."

"No problem, dude." Tony reached for his collar and pulled the material aside, turning his head to show off the image I'd noted earlier. A twisted, deadly looking thing with a claw. I now recognized the art behind Tony's ear as a scorpion, with another claw in the fold of his neck and a swirled tail sneaking down Tony's back.

Tony grinned at Zilya with a wink. "Like it?"

"There is no family banner as yet," Mathias pointed out.

Tony rolled his eyes, insult sparking in his words. "What? The Blood Scorpions control the west side of Camden. That's all anyone needs to know about touching me or my family."

Where Mathias and Zilya had turned wary of Gabby, they were not the least cautious of Tony. In fact, Zilya's fingers quivered with a surge of anger. "Your arrogance knows no boundaries."

Gabby muttered, "She's got your number, Jersey boy."

Tony held his bound arms in front of him, hands up. "It ain't braggin' if you can do it."

"Then you admit you are one of the mighty teks?" Zilya quizzed Tony.

I opened my mouth to object and Callan warned me, "Do not interfere or this discussion ends now."

Meaning things could deteriorate further. Not good.

Callan had kept any show of his emotions locked down tight, everywhere but his eyes. Fury stoked his gaze to the fiery shade of brown. I could swear the colors on his skin shifted a tiny bit. So his markings did move. What caused that? Mathias and Zilya hated tek-nah-tees, but Callan wanted blood.

I clenched my jaw, forcing myself to remain silent when I smelled a trap being set for the Jersey Jerk.

Tony swelled with the implication that they thought he was special. He gifted Zilya with a beaming smile. "Nobody handles technology better than me back home. I *am* the man."

Smiles could say a lot of things.

Zilya's said she'd just heard the answer she wanted.

Mathias turned solemn, but pain and anger riddled his gaze. When he spoke to Tony, his words came out with quiet authority. "Enjoy your superiority for the short time you can. You shall be the first to pay for the transgressions of your people."

"What're you talkin' about?" Tony, brows furrowed, turned to me. "What's goin' on?"

I couldn't see a benefit in remaining silent at this point. "They think you're a tek-nah-tee, Tony. Something or someone they believe to be their enemy."

Tony's cockiness disappeared in a flash. "Whoa, everybody. That's not me." He swung a worried face to Mathias then Zilya. "I'm a geek guy. A babe magnet. A lover, not a fighter."

Zilya's posture stiffened. Anger spiked her breathing. "First you want us to believe you are a genius of technology. *Now* you want me to believe you are *not* tek-nah-tee?"

I had a feeling the less this girl talked to Tony, the better off the three of us would be. And if this conversation didn't improve soon we'd face a bloody resolution. Forcing a calm in my voice I hoped would hide the worry squeezing my chest, I asked Mathias, "What's it going to take to convince you we're not whatever this tek person is? A strong ruler would be sure before jumping to conclusions."

His eyebrows tightened in a brief flinch at my subtle strike to his leadership skills, but he lifted his hand and all conversation paused. "Fine. You want a fair judgment, even though your kind is not acquainted with such practice? How did you travel here?"

Tony jumped in, trying to be Mr. Helpful. "I can tell you that."

I bumped Tony's leg with my foot, but he was undeterred. "Rayen here did some woo-woo with the computer and–"

Callan broke in. "*Computer?*"

Zilya froze.

Mathias opened his mouth but said nothing.

"Yeah, a computer. Never seen one?" Tony asked, his ego expanding by the second.

Mathias cut in. "Does this computer have a name?"

Tony made a half-laughing noise deep in his throat. "They all have names. Mac, Apple, IBM, Dell and a pile of others."

Once again, Mathias shared another of those looks with Callan that hinted of communicating, but I read this one to mean the mention of a computer had been significant. But if I tried to keep Tony quiet now Callan would think I had something to hide and I sensed he was the one we should worry about most.

Addressing Tony once more, Zilya said, "You were explaining how you traveled here."

"Right. Where was I?" Tony's eyes lit up again and he nodded in my direction. "So she sticks her hand *into* the computer screen and the next thing we know, bam, we're sittin' in some pod that spits us out where that nuclear crocodile climbed out of the ground."

"Pod?" Mathias frowned.

"That thing that spins then vanishes."

"Ah, I see. You *did* travel to the sphere in a transender." Mathias's voice flattened, removing any hope of sympathy for Tony or me. "Take them to the Isolation Unit, Callan."

Callan waved his hand at us and ordered, "Follow me."

"You don't believe him?" I asked Mathias, waving a hand at Tony.

He cocked his head as though he thought my question strange. "Of course, I believe him. I'm *sure* he's tek-nah-tee."

What had Tony said that ended all speculation on their part? I demanded, "But why?"

Mathias spoke in the most matter of fact way. "Because tek-nah-tees are the only ones who can travel here voluntarily through the transenders. They are the only ones who can visit the sphere."

Tony sputtered a protest as he and Gabby were being herded toward the opening to the corridor.

Callan turned to me, no mercy in that face.

My hands were damp with a deep panic that our stay in this place had taken a disastrous turn. I made one last attempt to find out our future from Mathias. "What's the Isolation Unit?"

"Where we hold prisoners."

That might give us a chance to figure a way to escape. "How long will you keep us there?"

"For a short time."

"Then what?"

Thinking on that for a moment before answering, Mathias said, "I have not decided about you and the other girl."

Zilya finished the thought for him. "But *that* one–" She pointed at Tony. "–will be the first tek-nah-tee punished for the deaths of our children. He will pay with his life."

Tony's face washed clean of color.

Gabby's mouth dropped open.

I felt the same way, but unlike Tony or Gabby, I knew I could stop these people. I wouldn't let them kill Tony.

Mathias glared at Zilya, but didn't counter her claim.

Callan stepped toward me in a threatening move.

I searched inside myself, calling upon the energy I'd experienced earlier, the power that could break these vines around my wrists and give me a fighting chance at getting all of us out of here alive.

Nothing happened.

Not even a flicker.

CHAPTER 14

Returning from the Isolation Unit, Callan padded down the walkway to Mathias's private domain and paused at the door when he saw Etoi and Zilya.

Some days, those two were almost as much trouble as the TecKnatis and so caught up in their conversation that neither heard him approach. How many times had he drilled them in training that to be unaware is to welcome death?

Of course, a fully-grown prantheer hadn't heard him sneak up on her lair last week either, but she'd been caring for her cubs. Not gossiping.

Etoi worked on a basket of dried tullee pods for seasoning a stew and complained to Zilya, "The one who calls himself Tony is a TeK. He must die."

Zilya nodded. "Yes, I know." She sat on a separate mat spinning katoni threads into a skein the weavers used to embellish the hems of gilded tunics.

Poor use of labor. Left to Callan, he'd have everyone train to fight and build defenses when not gathering food or hunting. Decorating clothes was a foolish use of time when faced with survival. But Mathias had pointed out that the simple task of sewing allowed those too young to hunt or gather food alone to have a feeling of worth.

That's why Mathias made an excellent leader.

But then there were *those* who felt that physical training was beneath their House level.

And Etoi and Zilya were not little children who needed to be coddled to have a sense of worth.

"Why does *he* still live?" Etoi's focus stayed locked on the topic of the TeK captive with the tenacity of a dugurat latched onto a last meal.

Zilya gave a dainty shrug. "I would use that Tony for croggle bait myself, but Mathias decides the fate of the prisoners."

"He is too soft. You should–"

"But he is our leader. I can only advise, not force his hand if he chooses to ignore my counsel."

"*You* should be leader here."

Callan almost stepped inside to let Etoi know he'd heard her traitorous comment, but he wanted to hear Zilya's reply.

"I will always regret having you with me the night I was captured, but I have to admit that I am selfish enough to be glad for your company. I am fortunate to have a champion such as you, Etoi, but to challenge Mathias for his position would be foolish on my part."

Callan agreed, but didn't hear the outrage in her response that he'd expect from a Gild female who should strike down impertinence against a leader, not preen under adulation.

Zilya added, "Let's finish here soon. I have much to worry over besides the prisoners."

Nodding her head in concession, Etoi still grumbled, "I just believe all TecKnati should be punished."

"As do I."

Callan could not listen to these two carry on any longer. No one had more reason than him to feel deep hatred for the TecKnati who had killed his twin brother, but Mathias was the eldest of the Governing House and had studied MystiK law since taking his first steps. His word was final and Callan would uphold the law here just as he would at home, even if it meant laying down his life to do so.

He'd failed once. That wouldn't happen again.

Making himself heard as he stepped in, Callan asked, "Where is Mathias?"

Zilya's surprised gaze shot up to his, then she calmly returned to winding her thread. "Checking on our new child."

Callan called to Mathias, mind to mind. *This is Callan. We need to talk.*

Mathias answered, *I'm on my way to my chamber. Meet me there*.

Speaking out loud, Callan said, "For one so busy as you claim, I would think you'd have more to do than sew, Zilya."

She tensed at realizing he'd overheard her conversation.

"What would you have her do?" Etoi argued in her usual surly tone. Her lack of respect knew no bounds.

"You could *both* use more training."

Etoi leaped to her feet, hands fisted and shoulders tight. "You wish you had more warriors like me."

"If you'd train as hard as you gossip, then I'd agree."

Growling, she lunged at Callan who only lifted a hand. Etoi smacked against the invisible surface of his power and bounced back, yelping and rubbing her nose that now trickled with blood.

He grinned. "You can put a bandage on your nose, but there's no cure for stupidity. On the positive side, those who act without thinking will eventually clean up the gene pool."

"Must you?" Zilya asked Callan.

"I did nothing except defend myself in the least painful way from someone who should take care whom she attacks."

Murder raged in Etoi's eyes. "In this Sphere, you are not of Gild or Rubio level. You are not your brother, only a second son who is unfit to rule the Warrior House."

Zilya went very still, her eyes raised watching Callan.

Etoi's words sliced through him back and forth, cleaving his heart with each reminder that he'd failed to protect his twin brother's back. Jornn should have been the next Warrior House ruler, but the TecKnati had murdered him. After torturing Jornn to the point of disembowelment, they'd cut a triangle where his heart had been and that was the last vision their mother had of her son's body.

Callan's last memory of his closest friend in the world.

But the TecKnati had not broken Callan and neither would some spiteful elite-Gild-wannabe like Etoi. He forced a smile to his lips and told her, "You're right. I will not rule my House, but I never wanted to, where you will *always* lust after the life of a Gild female and the closest you will ever come is cleaning their hygiene facilities."

His strike slapped the arrogance off of her bitter face and silenced her. He pointed at the door. "Go."

Wisely, Zilya stood and pushed a bowl at Etoi as though she had made the decision for them to leave. "Meet me in my chambers."

Etoi gripped the woven bowl with fingers so tight they turned white at the knuckles, but she left without another word.

Once Etoi was clearly out of earshot, Zilya whispered, "When did you realize you had *that* ability?"

"Stopping Etoi with my hand?"

"Yes."

"It's new and not of any significant use yet." Not that he'd let *her* know when any of his G'ortian gifts reached full potential. He could use those powers with fighting croggles if not for some defense mechanism the TeKs had put around the areas where the monsters lived.

Stepping up next to Callan, Zilya said in a sultry voice, "I'm *always* willing to train. When will you be available for a private session?"

Back home, men lost their wits when Zilya walked into a building. She was stunning and rare, and they all wanted her. *Not me.* He'd been interested, once, back when he was fifteen and before she'd been promised to his brother. Then Callan had investigated her as he would anyone who might have proven a threat at some point to his brother.

Beneath the layers of Zilya's beauty lay a deadly trap of deceit and a heart of ice. Sharing his opinion of Zilya with Jornn had caused an argument Callan didn't want to remember. He told her, "I'll let you know when I'm training grunts again."

Her eyes narrowed to angry slits. "Insulting me is dangerous."

"No, dangling you in front of a croggle is dangerous. Insulting you is rude."

"You can pretend the rules are different here, but nothing has changed at home."

Not having to deal with political issues at home was the only upside he'd found to being in this pit of death. "That's there. This is here."

Her chin lifted and her eyes flared with warning. "When we return–"

Mathias walked in. "Is there a problem?"

"Of course not. I was just leaving." Zilya's face glowed with a smile for the one person she believed would push Callan to do her bidding even here.

She was wrong.

If no one else had been able to force Callan to take Jornn's place as leader, what made her think she had any more power?

Once Zilya left, Mathias faced Callan. "You should try to get along with her."

Callan held up his hand. "Please, no lectures on Zilya today."

The weary sigh that escaped Mathias spoke of long days and nights trying to keep a band of children alive. At the moment, that meant providing for over sixty MystiK children stolen from the Ten Cities of the K'ryan Renaissance. Many of whom were barely past nine years old. Callan didn't envy him.

Mathias moved on. "In that case, tell me what you couldn't share about our captives when everyone was here."

"The girl with the long black hair who leads the trio is dangerous." Pretty, too, but then Zilya proved that physical attractiveness meant very little when it came to character.

"More dangerous than the TeK male?"

"Yes. Have you decided *she's* not TecKnati?" Callan didn't think she was, but he'd reserve final judgment until he had all the information. The fact that she'd been found in the company of his enemy and defended that same TeK counted against her.

"She doesn't appear to be TeK. However, that doesn't clear up who or what she is." Mathias waved toward the far wall for them to sit in two ocean-blue chairs he'd carved from the base of chopped-down terrian trees. "I'll have to ask V'ru, which reminds me. Would you spend some time with him?"

"*Train* V'ru?" Callan didn't even try to hide his shock.

"No, just talk to him. He's adjusting, but not as quickly as I'd hoped."

Words were not Callan's strength. He didn't know how to comfort anyone. "Can't Zilya talk to him?"

"V'ru likes Zilya, but he doesn't look up to her. He idolizes you."

That made it even worse. Callan wanted no one idolizing him, but he owed a debt to V'ru who had given Callan valuable information that helped in investigating Jornn's death. As a powerful G'ortian and a prodigy of the Records House, V'ru was better than any Cyberprocessor when it came to producing immediate information. And Callan wasn't entirely sure that V'ru hadn't been following him the night they were both captured. "I hate that he's here."

"I understand, but we lost a lot of children before V'ru arrived. I was barely keeping this village alive on what little we'd figured out was edible through trial and error."

"I'm glad we have V'ru's unlimited knowledge at hand, but he shouldn't be here."

"No MystiK should. He'll settle in."

Seemed like a good time to change the subject back to why Callan had stopped by. "You need to train."

Mathias groaned. "I'm proficient with the spear. That's enough."

Not if Mathias intended to spend tonight in the woods alone, but Callan didn't want to add to his leader's worries by reminding him. "You missed the last two training sessions."

"I'll make you a deal."

Now Callan groaned, sure of what was coming. He pushed up from the chair and stepped over to where two shoulder-high spears were stabbed in the ground next to the feather wall. When Mathias stood, Callan lifted a spear and tossed it at him. "Fine. We both train."

Mathias grinned and caught the weapon with one hand then moved to the center of the room. He began stretching, using the staff for support. "If I must train to fight croggles, you must train to fight SEOH."

Here came one of Mathias's "leader" lessons.

Callan crossed his arms and spread his feet apart, ready to work Mathias to the point of distraction. "If you say so. I'm ready to meet him on the battlefield."

"That you are, but as leader of all the TecKnati, SEOH will never fight fairly, *or* on a physical battlefield."

"I have no intention of fighting fairly either. Not against someone who got away with killing three future MystiK leaders without sanction." Jornn had been one of those. "Our treaty isn't worth the spell that was cast on it."

Mathias paused from a contorted stretch and straightened. "Yes it is. The sanction worked just as the spell on the treaty was intended. At the moment each of those underaged MystiKs were murdered, SEOH and two other TeK dignitaries lost their seventeen-year-old sons. An eye for an eye. A future leader for a future leader."

"But no one *knows* that's why those TeKs died. You want to know what really chafes my hide? The whole thing got covered up."

"I'll admit that SEOH is a genius when it comes to battle strategy."

Callan scowled at Mathias. "How can you praise him?"

"Do not misunderstand me. I do not praise him, but you were the one who taught me to thoroughly evaluate an enemy. I am only doing that."

"I said to look for an enemy's weak spot, because they always have one. Never underestimate an opponent."

Mathias nodded as he began moving through exercises while Callan gave hand signals of different attack and defense positions. Shove straight out, pull back to his chest, then a half spin to the right, another shove, a half spin left. Mathias said, "SEOH is a sociopath, and a clever one. My point was that he ran a brilliant damage control campaign to camouflage the deaths of the three TeK children who *appeared* to have collapsed from asphyxiation. Easy to accomplish with the technology at his fingertips."

"*Only* because idiots believed his lies," Callan ground out, disgusted. "I couldn't believe that even MystiKs bought into SEOH's claim." Callan dropped his voice to emulate SEOH's from the black-ban vid and struck a politician's pose with a hand over his chest. "Our planet has experienced a *rare* phenomenon."

Mathias snorted at the imitation. "Maybe we need a vid player as a ruler."

"That's the problem. Our citizens are lazy sheep. They accept anything spoken through a microphone or seen on a vid screen as truth."

"I concur, but no average person will dispute SEOH's statements when his claims are backed up by scientists."

Callan never understood how people could be so easy to trick. Couldn't they use their brains? "How stupid can anyone be to believe that fine particles from a meteor had passed through the atmosphere to cause the sudden deaths of three TeK boys?"

"Naïve, not stupid," Mathias corrected.

With one quick move, Callan struck unexpectedly and had Mathias on his back, the spear at Mathias's throat. "Never allow *anything* to distract you."

When Callan stepped away, Mathias climbed to his feet and snatched back the weapon, grumbling something about payback.

"You were saying?" Callan smiled.

"Just wait until I test you on MystiK law." Mathias nodded for Callan to resume, then stabbed and moved with the intense conviction that Callan had been looking for. Mathias continued, "All I'm saying is you must study the way SEOH handled that situation. Instead of allowing rumors of three mysterious TeK deaths to surface, he offered major credits to families who, quote, 'also had children die of unexplained deaths' during that same time frame."

"I understand. With so many families coming forward whether they had an unexplained death or not, the three TeKs killed by our treaty were buried in the flood of reports."

Mathias nodded, lifting his arm to swipe sweat from his brow. "*That* is a TeK strength you must plan to confront when you return."

"I can't fight press conferences." If he could, Callan would have destroyed SEOH a long time ago.

"To be a strong leader, you must also learn how to fight political battles, Callan."

Callan ignored the comment about being a leader, determined not to argue with Mathias today of all days. He turned to find a water gourd near the chairs that he handed Mathias who upended it for a long drink then set it aside.

Mathias pressed on with his lesson. "When SEOH uses charm to sway the masses while he kills MystiKs, you must be just as creative when it comes to striking back."

"I'm the sword arm of Warrior House, not the mouth."

"And *that's* only one reason SEOH is successful."

Callan's entire body tightened at the insinuation that he was at fault for SEOH's success.

When Mathias noticed Callan's face, he stumbled in his movements and held the spear across his chest. "Save that look for a croggle or the enemy. I have enough nightmares."

Callan gained control of his anger and wiped all expression from his face.

Angling his head in a show of thanks, Mathias went on. "I meant no criticism of the Warrior House, but of the fact that none of our Houses work together. A sword arm alone will not save us. If we continue fighting the way we always have, we'll eventually lose everything."

Callan agreed about the lack of cohesion between Houses, but he *would* kill the man who took Jornn's life...if he ever got out of this Sphere. The moment Jornn's soul had left his physical body, his brother's spirit had spoken in Callan's mind saying, "I'm sorry to leave you, brother. SEOH has murdered me and, as decreed by the treaty, he's punished by the loss of his own son. But there will be more. Do *not* let him win."

SEOH may not have struck the blow with his hand, but he'd ordered the vicious killing. In one instant, Callan lost the equivalent of a limb and became the next in line to rule the Warrior House, except he wasn't ruler material.

But duty rarely took ability into account.

Callan would fulfill his brother's last command once he figured out how. "You're right. If our Houses weren't so competitive, secretive, and paranoid over protecting their powers they might communicate and know the treaty has been broken. As it is, the leaders of all seven Houses will not know that three MystiKs have been murdered by the TecKnati until our elders meet at the upcoming BIRG Con, expecting to indoctrinate new leaders and sign another worthless treaty. By that point, there may be no future generation to take the reins. What will our people do when they realize children from all Houses have gone missing? Will they figure out that the TecKnati have been capturing us? I tell you this as truth. The Warrior House will seek retribution, but will the other six make SEOH pay?"

"I don't know. SEOH has to be expecting retaliation at the BIRG Con. I have to hope our leaders would put aside their differences and unite the minute they realize genocide is under way and, at that point, turn on the TeKs." Mathias paused, lowering his spear. "This could mean war."

"It should."

"But can we fight the TecKnati?"

"United, I believe we could, but not when our leaders only meet once every five years at the BIRG Con. SEOH has had the luxury of time for planning." Callan lifted his spear and gave a silent defensive order to Mathias to keep him training. Maybe when Mathias returned to his Governing House, he'd be able to show his elders that one could govern and protect at the same time.

Mathias agreed, "We have proven the power of shared knowledge and communication to survive in this Sphere. There is no value in hoarding information if the price is our future." Mathias made a difficult maneuver that included a back flip. He landed decisively, grinning.

"Well done." Callan could see a strong MystiK society if the Houses joined resources the way he, Mathias and other young MystiKs had done to survive this Sphere. But MystiKs didn't question the status quo, content to believe they were safe as long as they stayed inside the ten secured cities, content with their own corner of power. And the TecKnati population appeared as easily misled.

Both MystiKs and TecKnatis had lived in uneasy peace since the K'ryan Syndrome when an infection had wiped out ninety percent of civilization a hundred and six years ago.

But the peace would last no longer.

Callan changed up the training. "Now without your hands."

Mathias balanced the spear on one arm and used his kinetic ability to roll the rod up his arm and dipped his head forward as it traveled across his shoulders. "Can you see the Warrior House ever being as forthcoming back home?"

"Security has always called for a certain amount of autonomy and maintaining classified information." Callan conceded the point though. "We have thick-headed seniors, too. The old ones have been in control for too long. They refuse to change the way things have always been done. Time for new blood, younger blood, but SEOH is wiping out our next generation before that can happen."

With a new hand signal from Callan, Mathias flipped the spear in the air, caught it and went into a series of attack positions. "No argument on that point. Sadly, the TecKnati's ability to communicate better than we do is why we're sitting in this Sphere."

Callan vowed, "One day I *will* prove that SEOH is a cold-blooded killer and see him sent to a cage worse than this place."

"That's probably one reason SEOH's glad to have you in here."

"I'm sure." Callan glanced up at the sky, always keeping an eye out for change. "Think this Sphere is the only world SEOH's created?"

"Quite possibly. According to V'ru, the engineering of an artificial planet such as this one takes an enormous amount of credits that even SEOH's ANASKO Corporation would hesitate to spend twice. The media vids V'ru allowed me to review showed SEOH bragging about the plants and animals gathered as a result of his space exploration program. He touted the TeKs for donating generously to create a suitable host location for the study of adaptability."

"Adapt or die, in our case."

"Yes. Most people would assume SEOH meant the ability of his alien plant and animal specimens to adapt to *our* world, not that *we* would be doing the adapting." Mathias lifted the spear and began timed maneuvers that required rapid hand-over-hand defensive and offensive moves. "I think SEOH saw this as the perfect place to put captured MystiKs while justifying the expense of building this Sphere to his board of twelve. He probably convinced them this would be a sort of training area prior to relocating people–MystiKs–to other planets."

Callan dodged forward with the speed of a striking snake and snatched the spear from Mathias, flipped it once into an attack pose, then handed the weapon back to a scowling Mathias. Callan grinned, continuing. "I've heard that rumor about relocation. You think SEOH's really going to try to wipe out MystiKs by shipping us off to another planet?"

"No." Mathias paused, thinking as he cradled the spear. "I think his primary goal is to remove those of us approaching eighteen–take us out of circulation, especially G'ortians."

Callan avoided discussing his G'ortian status since that was yet another reason his family had been disappointed when he refused to accept his role as a leader. More powerful than other MystiKs, G'ortians only came along once every seven generations. Callan had experienced some gifts since birth, such as immediate telepathic ability that usually developed several years later. But his kinetics were a recent revelation and undependable as yet. He pushed the conversation back to SEOH. "I keep trying to figure out SEOH's end game for putting us in here. What's your guess?"

"To prevent us from taking our places as the next level of leaders within our Houses."

"Sure, but SEOH's also putting TeK children in jeopardy every time a MystiK child dies here. Even TeKs will eventually raise an alarm if they lose enough children."

"I've thought on that quite a bit. I don't believe the TeKs are losing children." Mathias jabbed the spear into the ground and took a breath, wiping a sheen of sweat from above his mouth.

"Why not? The treaty decrees retribution." Not that Callan wanted to see any child die, but without a consequence SEOH would continue capturing MystiKs.

"I believe this Sphere is their answer to neutralizing us."

Callan argued, "But the treaty–"

"–stated that a TecKnati or a MystiK child would die in response to an intentional death caused by either group." Mathias drew a couple of breaths. "SEOH probably thought little of that clause at the time it was written. Rumors say he scoffed at the notion that anything supernatural would reach beyond our people to affect the TecKnati, and him in particular."

"SEOH was the fool there. Underestimating your opponent is shortsighted and dangerous." Callan had drummed that into his young warriors.

"Quite true, but when our MystiK forefathers negotiated the current treaty, the TeKs had never before experienced more than occasional interruptions in their technology caused by MystiK powers that they dismissed as coincidental. SEOH had no reason to believe our leaders could infuse any real power into that one retaliatory clause in the treaty. Not until he paid the price for ignorance and arrogance with his own son's death. Sending captured MystiKs to this Sphere is evidence that he's worried now."

Callan pondered on that, not liking the direction of his thoughts. "So you're saying SEOH has changed his tactics and there's no consequence?"

"He may not want to *believe* in our powers, but he has to know that MystiK power was behind the failure of ANASKO'S HERMES shuttle *and* the death of his son at the same moment your brother died." Mathias dropped his gaze to the ground. "My father and our House led the drive to stop that launch. As the Governing House, we should have been better prepared for the reaction. We anticipated a backlash, but no one expected SEOH to send an assassin after three of our future leaders or to orchestrate a plan for genocide."

There was little Callan could say to that admission, but Mathias did not deserve to carry the blame for those deaths. The only person responsible was SEOH. Callan walked over to lift the other spear and turned back. "Through resting?"

Once Mathias raised his weapon, Callan attacked. Strike, dodge, strike. Callan admitted, "Our elders must accept the need for change. Had all seven Houses worked together, my warriors would have been brought in to perform a covert attack on ANASKO's shuttle launch that no one could have pinned on the MystiKs. That being said, regardless of any mistakes, at least your father took an action when we had to do something. We can't allow SEOH to bring another deadly version of the K-Virus into our world again."

Mathias's father had led the charge against space exploration for years. Callan respected that. MystiKs believed the dangerous K-Virus that annihilated so much of the world's population five generations ago had originated in outer space. In his thinking, every effort SEOH took to expand space exploration placed the entire world's population at risk.

"The threat of the K-Virus won't stop SEOH from trying to ship us off planet," Mathias said, and shot forward, jabbing the spear.

Callan spun away from the sharp tip. He landed with his feet set to intercept a second attack, but Mathias was laughing too hard to follow through. Callan gave him his due and dipped his head slightly in a nod, the equivalent of high praise for getting that close to an elite warrior. "You're improving."

Shrugging, Mathias swung the spear up in front of his chest, holding it horizontally with two hands. Callan lifted his spear with two hands as if he wielded a sword, striking the wooden bar from different angles as Mathias blocked. Callan thought out loud. "With the threat of facing another K-Virus, does SEOH really think our Houses will go along with shipping MystiKs to a new planet?"

"Perhaps. There are MystiKs who believe in SEOH's relocation program as a chance for our people to rule their own world. I heard many excited about SEOH's announcement of his new HERMES shuttle plans. The ad campaign went viral within minutes. If I saw one more ad for Hermes, God of Travel, I threatened to destroy my Cyberprocessor."

"Foolish MystiKs and TeKs. Yet again, they hear only what they want to hear."

Mathias quipped, "I wonder if any of them realize Hermes was also the god of trickery and thieving."

Callan answered with a wry smile. Could Mathias be right about SEOH's reasoning behind using the Sphere as a cage for MystiK children?

After the K'ryan Syndrome wiped out billions of people, every generation of MystiKs since then had become more powerful in using their abilities. Gifts the MystiKs considered as natural as breathing, but TecKnati saw as supernatural freakishness. Now the G'ortians showed signs of unexpected levels of abilities that, if combined, threatened a power capable of impeding technological advancement the MystiKs deemed reckless.

Now that Callan thought on the specifics of the treaty–just as Mathias had intended during this training session–he realized Mathias hadn't answered his earlier question. "Why do you think no TeK children are dying at home?"

Swinging the spear tip up and down in fast arcs, Mathias blocked, breathing hard as he answered. "The treaty is written in such a way that if an underaged MystiK dies by the hand of, or order of, a TeK as a premeditated act, a TeK child of equal rank will lose his or her life immediately. The idea was that no parent would willingly sacrifice his own child, and if someone who was not a parent killed a child, that the penalty would be great enough to force the people to rise up against the person responsible."

"But, as I mentioned, the loophole in the treaty is *lack of knowledge* of this heinous act." Callan worked through the logic in his mind. "What about a *beast* that belongs to SEOH?" *If I'd studied with Jornn back when he went through government training I'd know the terms of the treaty better.*

"I assume you don't mean sentient beasts, which were outlawed long ago and would still cause a TeK death if SEOH directed the animal to kill a MystiK child. Even SEOH wouldn't risk the death penalty that possessing one of those beasts carries."

"No, I mean what about a regular *living* animal?"

"If a TeK owns a living creature who attacks a MystiK who then dies, but the TeK did *not* train the animal to kill, that would be considered an accident, leaving TeK children safe."

"You think that's true even of things in here like croggles?" Callan started understanding where Mathias was going with his train of thought and put the blunt end of his spear on the ground.

A bit winded, Mathias lowered his spear as well. "SEOH did put the croggles and other deadly elements retrieved from planetary exploration into this Sphere, but those creatures are naturally hostile. SEOH isn't directing the plants, animals or the poisoned liquids. So as long as we die here, killed by natural events, he's found a way around the treaty language."

Callan's skin chilled at the possibility of what Mathias was saying. SEOH could capture thousands of children, ship them here to die, and get away with murder.

Again.

Footsteps approached at a fast clip from down the hall, then Etoi rushed into the room without requesting entrance, as always. "There's a corruption in the fog barrier."

Mathias frowned. "That might only be the atmospheric change we experienced a couple of months ago."

Callan snatched up his spear. "Or it might be something more significant."

Any change to the fog compromised the safety of the village. He ran out with Mathias and Etoi close behind.

CHAPTER 15

I didn't like it, but I had to finally admit I had no idea how to escape this place. The Isolation Unit we were stuck in was some kind of hut made of bright green reeds that vibrated with a low-level hum. Every time I approached the sides of the chamber, the reeds increased their vibration, which didn't reassure me.

But I kept that to myself.

I had failed Gabby and Tony. Where was that power in my chest when I needed it?

"That bitch blondie, wants to kill me," Tony said as he paced ten steps across and back, for the umpteenth time.

"You mean the one with the white-blonde hair?"

"Yeah, that one." Tony flapped his hand at me. "Point is we've gotta escape."

"Keep your voice down, would you?" I'd been trying to ignore him since we'd been thrust into this stagnant room that had a minty sweet smell.

That should be a refreshing scent, but it wasn't. Or maybe I was just suspicious of everything from flowers to children.

And why shouldn't I be? I was trapped in a hut constructed of a plant that I should be able to rip to shreds given what I'd done to that killer vine earlier. But my energy had abandoned me when we needed it most. The power humming in these walls keyed my senses that any attack might have deadly consequences. No mercy anywhere in this place. When Callan marched us here, not an ounce of sympathy had flickered in his eyes. He'd lifted his hand and an opening had appeared just long enough for me, Gabby and Tony to walk through, then the doorway disappeared.

No windows, no door.

No clue how to get free, or help Gabby.

I walked over to where she sat cross-legged, huddled in the center of the floor, her teeth clenched in pain. She rocked back and forth, cupping first one wrist then the other in her lap. Sweat beaded across her forehead.

"Any better?" I asked, concerned about the deepening raw welts ringing her wrists. Red streaks had started running up her arms in jagged lines that indicated infection. Had it started earlier, when I'd noticed pink on her wrists after the killer flower had strapped her wrist to Tony? Or had the dull-red vines used for constraint done this?

"I don't think I can use 'better' to describe the pain." Gabby spoke between her chattering teeth and tried to grit out a smile. "More like somewhere between having your appendix cut out without anesthesia and being burned to death."

All of our wrists were unbound now. My wrists and Tony's showed no skin reaction like hers. We had to get her out of here, back to the school where someone could help her.

"I'm not stayin' here," Tony continued babbling and pacing. "These guys are serious whack jobs."

"We'll figure a way out of here as soon as we can," I said, hoping to shut him up.

Nope. Tony pounded over to where I knelt next to Gabby, but kept his focus only on me. "'As soon as we can' is fine for you two. *I'm* on death row."

Fighting the urge to snap at him, I asked Gabby. "Let me see your arms."

She lifted her chin, indecision playing hard through her flushed face.

I understood her hesitation. She shielded her secret gift by avoiding touch. I offered quietly, "You can trust me when I say I'll not judge you or share anything about your gift."

After the things she'd seen me do today, she must have decided I was telling her the truth, because air wheezed out of her with relief.

I braced myself to touch her skin, prepared for any image or sensation when I gently scooped her arm in my hand.

Fragmented images scattered through my mind, mixed with her burning pain and fear of dying. What I picked up came in pieces, meaning she could hide her thoughts somewhat, but not very well while her body fought an infection.

The red lines continued to crawl up her arms, raging hot as if acid etched deep into her skin.

I detected an odor of something building that my mind labeled as gangrene, but this didn't fit with the vision of rotting flesh that followed the name. I didn't have time to question what I knew or how much I knew, but I was sure these streaks could kill her if we didn't stop the strange infection.

"We'll be okay," I reassured Gabby and released her arm before she could catch the desperation in my mind.

"Of course *you two* will be fine," Tony continued ranting from where he'd paced to the other side of the room again. "Meanwhile I'll be sacrificed to the god of Loony Land. Or the goddess. But you don't care, which figures. Won't be the first time I'm thrown under the bus. The *last* time was by people I thought were friends."

I understood Tony's fear of being put to death, especially for something he hadn't done. He should realize I wouldn't let this bunch harm him or Gabby without a fight, regardless of my sporadic superpower, but I didn't have the patience to figure out what Tony meant by a bus. I buried my need to strike at something out of frustration and told him, "No one is going to die. It's probably just a scare tactic." At least, I hoped so. "Put your mouth to some use for once. See if you can get us some health aid here."

"You mean medical attention?"

I shot him a look that had him backing up.

"You don't get it. They don't care if *any* of us lives or dies." Tony stomped back over and drew in a deep breath as if ready to unleash a snarl, but stopped and whistled between his teeth on the next exhale. "Whoa, babe," he said, bending over to examine Gabby's arm more closely, really seeing her this time. "Daa-yum. That's bad."

"Not helping, Tony," I snapped. "Need medicine."

"No problem. I'm on it." Tony spun around and got within a foot of the wall and yelled, "Hey, a-holes, you hear me?"

Diplomatic, Tony was not, but loud he was.

Someone should respond. I had clearly been hearing noises on the other side of the reeds since we'd been deposited here. Mostly kid voices that sounded as though they were in a play area.

Laughable to think children played in this place.

Tony balled his fist and smacked it on the wall, only to earn a quick blast of energy zapping him. He jerked his hand back, yelping. "You sorry-sack-of-skunk-crap! Man, that stings."

"Try your feet?" I suggested. "The soles might insulate you from the shock."

"Why don't *you* try, Xena?" Tony demanded, still shaking his hand, no humor anywhere in his voice. "Instead of givin' orders. Do somethin'."

"Fine." I stood and approached the nearest wall, giving it a solid thwack with my sneaker-covered foot. That earned me a small tingle, but nothing like the static power that had surged when I'd hovered my palm near the reeds earlier. I raised my voice and shouted, "You? Out there. We need medical assistance. *Now!*"

"And *food*," Tony called from the other side of the cramped room before mumbling, "Who asks for 'medical assistance'? This isn't a five-star hotel." Then he put more force in his voice again. "More water, too."

But nothing happened.

Except the voices had quieted.

I thought back on Zilya's reaction to Gabby. The blonde who acted like a queen had expected Gabby to know what she'd been talking about with houses. Zilya and Mathias had taken issue mostly with Tony, and maybe me, but not Gabby. That gave me an idea. I raised my voice. "Tell Mathias the Gabby girl needs help. She could be dying."

I looked over at Gabby quickly and mouthed the words, *Not true.*

Gabby, being the astute person she was, offered a tight, small nod.

I wished there hadn't been some truth in my claim. That she didn't look as if she could get sicker, and die, if we didn't get help.

Tony and I kept the shouting up, sometimes one at a time, sometimes both together, until our voices sounded hoarse, our throats raw.

Nothing.

In fact, even the scurrying noises around the chamber had diminished.

So maybe we were making some progress. But not much and not soon enough if the pain lines on Gabby's face were any indication. Sweat glistened everywhere. Blotchy pink patches covered her death-white skin.

Tony opened his mouth for another blast, but I waved him off. "Save your energy. We have to find another way."

Gabby glanced at me, her voice fighting to sound strong, but coming out thin. "What about what you did to the attack-vine earlier?"

I'd hoped that wouldn't come up for discussion again.

Tony glanced at me, his expression confused. "Yeah, how'd that vine just die?"

I crossed the room to squat by Gabby again, buying myself a few minutes. Gabby and Tony wanted answers. So did I, but I didn't have any. I finally offered what I could. "Let's say I didn't do anything consciously."

"So what? You were knocked out and somethin' happened?" Tony demanded, looking for a scientific answer he could wrap his head around.

"No, more like a thought."

"A get-us-out-of-this-mess thought?" Tony's tone made it clear he labeled that answer as woo-woo.

Too bad it was the truth, or as close to the truth as I could manage.

Gabby managed a weak smile of reassurance. "Whatever you did, you saved our lives, Rayen. Thanks."

"She also managed to get us stuck here in the first place if her touch–as *you* pointed out–is doing these things." The stress of worrying about his life had brought back the abrasive Tony. He glared at me as if I'd planned the trip through the computer. "That crazy girl wants me dead and if that happens I let people down. If you don't get us out of this hell-hole, I'm so going to kick somebody's ass."

"Mine?"

Tony had a moment when I thought he'd say yes, but he shook his head. "I don't hit girls, but I wouldn't mind going a round with that Callan."

He gained a bit of respect from me for his personal code, but did Tony really think he could match up with Callan? He'd earn my appreciation if he'd just shut his broken trap. My body ached from toe to head. I had no idea who I was or how I'd ended up in this mess. And I was tired to the bone, mostly of taking grief all day. "I'd take care threatening Callan."

Tony scoffed at me. "Where I come from we'd eat a pretty boy like him for lunch."

When I didn't reply, Tony taunted, "What's the matter, Xena? No *come back*?"

Out of ideas and patience, I stood up, ready to give Tony the target he'd been wanting.

The changes in my stance should have warned him I had no tolerance for aggression right now, but he just kept on pushing me. "How'd you even end up in Suarez's class to begin with anyhow? That ain't a class for the short bus kids...or criminals."

Whatever a bus was sounded even more insulting this time.

Ready to silence that mouth, I took one step forward then stopped. I suddenly sensed another presence inside the hut.

What the . . .?

The old man I'd seen back when I'd first opened my eyes in the desert took a filmy shape beside Gabby. Sitting with legs crossed, he hovered a foot above the ground again, speaking in that gravelly voice. "A warrior fights to defend others and for honor. A child strikes out in anger. There is no place for a child on this journey."

Easy for you to say. But as long as Ghost Man was back, I could use more information.

"Who am I?" I asked before the vision could vanish again. I might not make it back to the school to learn what had been discovered about my family. But here was a chance. Maybe my only one.

Tony stopped jawing and for a blessed moment went silent.

Gabby paused in rocking to look up at me with curiosity

swimming through her mismatched eyes. She glanced next to her at the empty spot where I stared then back at me and whispered, "You okay, Rayen?"

Neither she nor Tony seemed able to see the old man.

How could I answer that when I questioned my sanity at the moment? I kept my eyes on the filmy figure. "Answer me."

The ghost with the weathered face had been staring off into the distance. His gaze shifted to meet mine. "You know what you need to know for now."

Fury boiled up my throat. "Who. Am. I? Either tell me or stay away from me you old goat."

Tony whistled behind him. "She's gone completely off the reservation, Gabby."

"Just shut up, would you," Gabby snapped, sounding weaker than before.

I glanced away from the vision long enough to check on her. When I looked back up the old one was gone. *Fine. Like I need one more animal in this zoo?*

"So now you're talking to invisible friends, Xena?"

Clenching my hands into tight knots of frustration, I stepped toward Tony, determined to shut that yapping trap.

Tony's eyes widened in surprised. His hands curled in reaction and he came up on his toes, prepared to defend himself. "You gonna use your super juice on me?"

"Cut it out," Gabby grumbled. "We need to work together, not fight amongst ourselves. Doing that plays into their hands."

I didn't want to listen. I wanted to do something to burn off the frustration churning my insides.

The old man's voice whispered in my mind. *Are you a warrior or a child?*

I stopped in the middle of the hut, but couldn't say if it was out of deference to Gabby or the old man's taunts. "She's right. If we allow them to divide us they'll win."

Gabby groaned and bent over.

I dropped down next to her. "What's happening?"

"I can't close my hands. My arms feel like...the muscles are hardening."

Tony squatted on the other side of her and carefully lifted hair from her neck then hissed and pointed to gain my attention without speaking.

Leaning closer, I saw what he was trying to keep Gabby from knowing. The red lines were climbing up and around her neck. If the muscles in her neck hardened, she wouldn't be able to breathe.

CHAPTER 16

Brushing the gauzy, moss-green wisps from his hair, Callan warned Mathias, "If Etoi sends me on another fool's errand, she won't like the punishment."

"But you said it might have been a serious breach in our security."

"If the fog had actually *corrupted*, it would have been. She knows the difference between a hollow eucalypoon mist that's floated loose and a break in the fog curtain."

Mathias swatted a swatch of green off his shoulder. "They look similar and it *was* quite a large mist cloud, taller than either of us and twice as wide. She can be annoying, but sometimes you just have to overlook it."

"And that is why you govern and I protect," Callan pointed out. "I don't have your patience. Where'd you send her?"

"To check on the prisoners."

Callan chuckled. Etoi hated guard duty. She'd probably sneak off and find Zilya to gossip with, but he didn't care as long as they were both out of his hair. "What are you going to do about the captives? We can't keep them without feeding them, and we don't have enough food to share."

"I don't know." Mathias sounded weary and not from just the trek to check on their defenses.

Callan offered, "In her usual bloodthirsty way, Zilya suggested we stake out that Tony as croggle bait."

Mathias's lips quirked at that. "She does have a homicidal streak."

"I do, too, when it comes to TecKnati," Callan admitted, though he'd never kill in cold blood. That would put him on the level with his enemy, lower than scum on the bottom of his boot.

"You would execute someone without a fair judgment?"

"No, but we're at war and many of ours have died. If you're right and there's no sanction happening back home, SEOH owes us TeK deaths in return for the children we've lost. It's the treaty. It's the *law*. Right?"

"Believe me, I'd like to personally enforce that law if we could use it specifically against SEOH," Mathias muttered.

The dire sound of his tone caused Callan to poke at him. "And here I thought only the Warrior House sought to solve issues with fighting first–as we're so often accused..." He paused until Mathias swallowed a grin and added, "Rather than negotiate a problem to death like the Governing House. It's *your* House that preaches against vengeance."

"Living here has caused me to reevaluate many things, but I digress. We're agreed that the mouthy one with the skin ink mark is a TecKnati, right?"

Callan nodded. "He's the best candidate of the three. What about the girl with bi-colored eyes, excessive earrings that only the most powerful MystiKs are allowed to wear and...did you sense anything from her?"

"Yes. She has a gift or gifts, but she clearly wasn't going to admit that to us. Not unusual for a Hy'bridt MystiK, the only explanation for those eyes. Except the colors she wore were all over the place...but so were the clothes on the TeK one." Mathias paused. "And what was a Hy'bridt doing with *him*?"

"I don't know. I've never seen TeKs dressed that way. Based on what little we know, I'd say she's as MystiK as that Tony is TecKnati."

"We'll have to talk to the Hy'bridt some more and see if we can figure out what she's doing here. Makes no sense."

Callan swallowed a growl of irritation. Why would Mathias believe anything that Hy'bridt said? "I don't trust any MystiK that hangs out with a TecKnati. I told you when I first got here that I think a MystiK traitor has to be working with the TecKnatis to help them trap us. Who's to say that person isn't a Hy'bridt?"

Mathias slowed next to the hut where several girls and a couple of young boys prepared food. He gave them a word of encouragement and snagged a bowl of buri berries, then continued on toward his chambers, not missing a beat in the conversation. "Hy'bridts are supposed to be as loyal as they are powerful."

"Maybe," Callan allowed, taking a handful of berries to refresh his dry throat. "But loyal to whom? And what about the other girl?" The taller one with midnight-black hair and skin the color of brewed tea. His mind fought to sum her up in one word, but narrowed it down to two–deadly and attractive–much like some of the plants in this Sphere. She was a prime example of whatever group she belonged to, with her keen blue eyes, slashed cheekbones and a body that filled out her strange clothes nicely.

But anyone who associated with a TeK, even an exotic female, fell clearly within Callan's definition of enemy. Especially after watching her single-handedly annihilate a croggle.

"That one with the black hair throws me," Mathias admitted. "I didn't understand her name. Xena?"

"I don't think that's her real name. I heard both the TeK and the Hy'bridt call her Rayen and she doesn't strike me as a TeK. Rayen has the skills of a Warrior. You know TeKs would rather push a button than dirty their hands fighting."

"Except for their Scouts." Mathias sounded resigned.

"They are the exception."

"But that Rayen has no TeK markings, nor does she have marks such as those of your Warrior House."

"I know," Callan admitted, trying to put the pieces together. "Plus she has that device attached to her leg."

"Do you think she meant to destroy the croggle?"

Callan hated all things related to the TecKnati, but to falsely accuse anyone would be dishonorable. Without honor, a man was nothing. "Much as it still angers me that she destroyed our food, she did so with only one of our spears and the croggle *had* neutralized two of our hunters with its tail right before she attacked. That supports her claim that she thought children were in danger."

"How did she destroy the beast?"

"That was strange. Her power burned the croggle from the inside out. Blue flame, very hot. No TeK has ever been known to have our gifts, and few of our own have that level of power."

Mathias munched quietly on a mouthful of berries for a moment. "If she's not TeK and not MystiK, what then? Could she be a different type of G'ortian?"

Callan stared off, considering that possibility. "I don't know. What I do know is that she's the most dangerous of the three."

"But in spite of the power she displayed in battle, she didn't try to harm any of you on the way to the village?"

"No." Callan could see why Mathias hesitated to pass judgment on the two girls, but the mouthy male *was* a TeK.

And no TeK deserved to walk away free.

When Mathias looked up at the sky, Callan did as well, noting the subtle shift of color overhead that had begun undulating from the deep blue-purple shade toward a vibrant red-purple. A hint of green stripes began appearing above the forest side of the village.

Mathias sighed, a sound heavy with the weight of responsibility on his shoulders. "We'll have to figure out what to do with those other two captives later, but the TeK does not spend the night in our village."

"Agreed, but wait to deal with him until I return from checking the original transender site for new arrivals." Callan didn't want anyone at risk while he was gone.

"We need our strongest four to make that run and Jaxxson can't go. He has to watch the little girl we brought back for any signs of reaction to the Sphere."

True. They couldn't wait until Jaxxson declared the child stable or they might risk losing another one dumped in the Sphere with no defenses. Callan said, "I'll have to take just Etoi and Zilya."

"No." Mathias shook his head. "Not after losing Sebi. You can't go with fewer than four capable fighters and we have no one old enough or experienced enough yet to take Jaxxson's spot. I can't risk losing any of you and definitely not all of you. I'll go."

Callan understood the worry in Mathias's voice, but he couldn't include Mathias on this run even though he was capable in battle. Mathias had been too distracted lately with problems inside the village and now he had three captives to pass judgment on...

The captives. That gave Callan an idea how to convince Mathias to stay behind. "You can't leave the village with those three in the Isolation Unit. That's a security risk."

Mathias lifted his large hand and rubbed his temple, thinking. "Are any of the younger hunters capable of joining you?"

"None are ready to face TecKnati Scouts. The captive, Rayen, easily disarmed two of my best-trained young hunters."

"That still leaves us with only three runners. We have to stick with working four in teams of two. Otherwise it's too dangerous."

Callan suggested, "Maybe Zilya's idea about the TeK deserves consideration. If he dies, it's on the heads of the TeK Scouts."

"To use Tony as croggle bait?"

"Why not?"

Mathias laughed. "I'm not sure a croggle would have that one. Even if we did want to take the TeK with us, I sense that the dark-haired girl will not allow those other two to be harmed. That's why we have to be careful how we deal with this Tony."

Callan held up his hand. "I'm not concerned with any leniency for the TeK. And as for this Rayen, she may be strong, but she has *not* proven herself to be a MystiK as yet. If she is aligned with that Tony, it means she *has* to know a TeK will turn on his own mother to save his life."

"True. What're you suggesting?"

"With the right motivation," Callan said, weighing his words. "Rayen may not fight us to take Tony and, even if she does, she can't stop *both* of us."

"You would stake him like a sacrificial–"

Etoi came running up. "Mathias!"

Callan growled under his breath, but Etoi never gave him a chance to say a word.

"The girl captive with the strange eyes is very ill. The other two are yelling for help. They say she is dying."

Callan looked to Mathias, inspiration firing his smile. "Now we'll find out which one Rayen is willing to save."

CHAPTER 17

I paced the isolation hut, cursing Mathias and Zilya. I couldn't believe Mathias was going to let Gabby die.

Zilya might. She'd made it clear that Tony's life meant nothing to her. But I'd thought for sure that Mathias had shown an unusual interest in Gabby, and in a positive way earlier. So why hadn't they come to check on her by now?

"Come on, babe, keep your eyes open," Tony told Gabby in a concerned voice that I wouldn't have thought possible at one time. Tony sat next to her, using a strip of cloth I'd torn from the bottom of my shirt to brush sweat off of Gabby's forehead.

For someone who could be so abrasive at times, Tony had picked up quickly on Gabby's aversion to being touched. He'd been careful not to stress her worse by making any contact with her skin.

I could do no more than Tony right now since I had no idea how to help Gabby either. I'd taken turns calling for help again, but hadn't heard a sound in a long while.

Gabby lifted her head. It wobbled a little as she leaned back against the arm and shoulder Tony had put behind her for a support. "Water. My throat's burning."

Tony looked at me.

I fisted my hands and turned to beat against the wall of the hut regardless of what the energy sizzling through the structure did to me. And it did hurt. Badly.

But a section the size of an opening started wavering.

I stepped back into a defensive position in front of Tony and Gabby.

When the opening finally appeared, Mathias entered first and stepped to the side. That allowed room for Callan to duck his head and walk in, a guarded expression in place. Mathias had a serene look, which I trusted as much as I trusted anything else in this strange, hostile world.

Not one bit.

Mathias started to speak, but my frustration knew no limit right then.

"What's wrong with you people? You accuse us of being some murdering tek-nah-tees but you place no higher value on life either, do you?"

I'd expected Mathias to snap right back at me, not to turn rigid as a statue at my accusation as if I'd slapped him. Or maybe insulted him. I'd feel bad for yelling at him since he seemed to be the only calm one in the bunch, but Gabby had gotten worse during each minute that Mathias had ignored our calls for help.

He drew a breath and spoke with the authority I'd heard in our earlier meeting. "We have to make the run to check for new children dropped from the transenders."

Tony piped up. "What's that got to do with Gabby bein' sick?"

Callan's only reaction to Tony's words was a tightening of his jaw. His gaze moved to me and his words came out with a hard clip. "We need four who are experienced enough to do this. The young ones lack the strength and skill to face the challenges of this transender location."

"Still waitin' on the punch line, dude," Tony groused.

Callan turned on Tony. "Shut up, tek-nah-tee."

I couldn't deal with both of them. "Tony, please."

Gabby moaned and shivered.

When Mathias's attention shifted to Gabby, his face scrunched with concern. So he finally noticed the puffy red skin on Gabby's arms? He demanded, "What's wrong with her?"

Shaking his head, Tony gave him a look of rank disgust. "What the eff do you think we've been yellin' about for so long? She's having some kind of reaction. Needs a doctor. D.O.C.T.O.R. You got one?"

Dismissing him with a curt lift of his chin and speaking once again to me, Mathias said, "We do have a healer–"

"Great." My relief flooded out in that one word.

"But as I was explaining," he continued. "He is one of only four qualified to go on the observation run."

"Be serious," Tony argued. "You gonna send him out someplace to *maybe* find someone while Gabby gets worse?"

That stoked the fire that had simmered in Callan's eyes since he'd walked into the hut. He turned all that fury on Tony. "If not for *your* kind, we wouldn't have to go looking for children dumped in this place. If not for *your* kind we wouldn't fear those children being eaten by a croggle or harmed by deadly plants. Don't lay her sickness or possible death at our feet when your SEOH is behind all this."

Tony looked at me. "Who's he talkin' about?"

"I don't know." And right now it didn't matter, because I was tired of waiting on help for Gabby and didn't want everyone to keep talking about her dying in front of her. I figured Callan wanted something and getting to that point sooner would be in Gabby's best interest, but I posed my question to both Callan and Mathias.

"What's it going to take for us to get help for Gabby?"

A vein in Callan's neck pulsed, restrained power waiting to be unleashed. I wasn't going to like what he had to say. His lips parted to speak, but before he uttered a word his gaze drifted down to where I'd torn the bottom half of my shirt off for Gabby. He stared at my exposed skin as if he hadn't expected to see that and had lost track of the conversation.

I shifted my stance, crossing my arms as I did.

He jerked his attention up. I quirked an eyebrow to let him know I'd caught him studying my body. I enjoyed the moment of catching his control slip. It had been oddly...flattering.

Not something I'd let *him* know.

When Callan didn't answer my question, Mathias jumped in, saying, "I have sent for our healer. We will see if he can do anything first."

I hadn't heard Mathias request anyone to come here, but in the next moment I heard a male voice outside the hut announce, "Jaxxson coming in."

The opening appeared again. The guy who stepped forward had blond hair, a dark honey shade, and eyes so rich a brown and ringed by thick lashes that they appeared outlined in black. Naked chest showed above his skirt-like covering that reached his ankles. He was athletic looking, but had a lithe, sinewy build as compared to Callan's muscular physique. I personally found Callan more attractive.

Not that my opinion would matter to either of them.

Callan's gaze tracked over to me and I merely lifted an eyebrow in response. That sent his attention back to Mathias.

"Take a look at the girl's arms," Mathias directed the healer, his voice less hostile but no less authoritative.

As Jaxxson stepped past me, he nodded once, either a sign of respect or just sizing up the stranger in their midst. Then he knelt on the opposite side of Gabby from Tony, keeping his movements slow, as if not to overwhelm or scare her.

Wise move. Even the most docile animal would attack when in pain.

Gabby pushed herself to sit up straight, wincing with the effort. She'd been so tough all day I'd come to understand that putting up a strong front was a matter of pride with her.

Jaxxson reached forward, then paused before touching her and asked, "May I?"

She shook her head and raised glazed eyes to me.

I gave Jaxxson's back a don't-you-dare-try-anything threatening glare. I explained, "She doesn't like to be touched."

"I'm a healer." Jaxxson spoke gently to Gabby, but hostility danced beneath his words as if coming here to care for a prisoner wasted his precious time. A possible tek-nah-tee prisoner.

"Can you open your arms just to show him," I asked Gabby, wanting her to get the help she needed.

She gritted her teeth, but she forced her arms to unbend half way, which appeared to be all she could manage with her limbs swollen.

Jaxxson looked over his shoulder at me and asked, "How'd this happen?"

I unflexed my balled hands. "We had to fight off some monster plant that was trying to suck us inside a pink flower.

Its vine wrapped her wrist." They weren't showing an appropriate amount of concern, so I glanced in Callan's direction and added, "Gabby's having a bad reaction to that...*or* those red vines *your little soldier* wrapped around her wrists."

Mathias sent Callan a pointed look filled with silent questions. Callan asked, "Pink flower? Green spots? A frazzle vine?" He used his palms to air sketch a shape. "Blossoms this big? Then one huge flower head on the host bush?"

"Sounds like it." I stepped toward Gabby. "Whatever it was, she's been the only one of us to react. I think your red restraint vines made things worse."

Mathias asked Jaxxson, "Can you do anything for her?"

"Yes, but I'll need to move her back to the healing hut."

I immediately tensed. Last thing I wanted was to allow them to take Gabby anywhere alone. Especially if it meant her being isolated and vulnerable. "Why can't you help her here?"

Callan cut me off. "Because his supplies are in the healing hut, but that will have to wait until we get back. We need Jaxxson and have to leave soon."

Not good enough. I stepped toward Callan. "She's getting sicker by the minute. She can't wait for later."

"She doesn't have a house," Mathias argued.

I snarled, "I don't care if she doesn't have a tent, she could die from this. Are you willing to let that happen after we saved that little girl?"

Guilt slid through Callan's hard expression, but he looked as though he'd come to some conclusion. "I told you we have to run the transender lines then we *also* have to hunt for food."

Not my fault, I wanted to answer but instead said, "What do you mean by running these lines?"

He drew a deep breath as if just listening to me took all his patience. "Do not play games with me. The tek–"

"*I'm not a tek-nah-tee!*" I roared. "I don't know who or what they are, but I'm starting to wonder about what kind of people *you* are if you're willing to leave her–" I pointed at Gabby. "–in pain."

"That is *your* problem," Callan charged. "Mine is saving our children." He paused as if wrestling his temper under control, then added in a calmer voice, "But we may be able to work out something favorable for everyone."

Finally. The trade I'd been expecting. "What do you want?"

"A fourth person to go with us who can...help defend against a croggle. I will allow Jaxxson to remain and tend to the girl, but in exchange we need another person. We'll take the one who can't deny he is tek with us."

I looked at Tony, easily reading the thoughts behind his ashen face. He believed once Callan and Mathias took him away he'd never return. He'd already said once that he expected to get thrown under a bus. Was this the bus?

Worse, the resigned look on his face said he thought I would agree.

I didn't want to leave Gabby alone, but neither could I let Tony walk out of here with someone who'd marked him for death. Keeping my eyes on Tony, I announced, "No. I'll go instead."

A whole swarm of demon flies could have set up camp in Tony's open mouth before he recovered to shout, "Are you crazy?" He slapped his leg. "What am I sayin'? Of course, you're crazy. First you're talkin' to an inv–"

"*Tony!*" I gave that warning in a voice that threatened serious harm if he said another word. Then I turned to Callan, "What's it going to be?"

He swung a stunned gaze on me. That had clearly not been the answer he'd been looking for, but that was the only one he was getting. I sensed a lot more not being said out loud between Callan and Mathias when they faced each other, the dilemma of what to do hanging between them.

Mathias started, "I don't know that we–"

Divide and conquer came to mind, but I didn't sense any real dissent between these two.

Cutting off Mathias, I swung to Callan, to get the terms straight. "Before I go though I want *your* word–as a warrior–that no harm will come to either of them while I'm gone."

Something shifted in Callan's eyes that made me think he rarely had to put his word on the line and, in that moment, I had a gut feeling that he took his honor to heart.

Then again, that perception might've been nothing more than the result of too many knocks to my head today.

Callan stepped in front of me, tight muscles in his face flexing as if fighting his temper again. When he spoke, each word had the bite of jagged ice. "And what if I choose not to agree to your terms?"

I crossed my arms and tilted my head up, our noses only inches apart. "Then prepare for things to get ugly. Because if you don't help Gabby, or if you try to take Tony out of here, it's going to get bloody and I promise you there will not be four of you in shape to make the rescue run when I'm done."

Mathias asked Callan, "If there's a child to save, would we be better served to take a trained warrior than a..."

Smooth approach on Mathias's part to give Callan an out by suggesting that someone who could fight would be of more benefit than a tek-nah-tee they only wanted to sacrifice.

While everyone waited in silence, Callan finally gave a single nod of agreement.

I didn't want to admit it, but I admired the fact that Callan put the needs of the children ahead of his desire to punish a tek-nah-tee.

That was until he added, "If the sick girl is with Jaxxson until we return, there is no way for this one–" he bent his head toward me.

If I told him my name, would he stop calling me *this one*?

"–to get to her if she escapes. If she runs or tries to interfere with us in any way–"

"I *won't*." I was tired of hearing threats. "I'm not going to abandon my friends or cause any problem...as long as Jaxxson heals her. Are we through negotiating?"

Mathias didn't chuckle, but his eyes creased with an odd humor, as if stifling a half-smile at Callan.

Callan's eyes still seethed, probably from my having demanded his word as a warrior again. "I have agreed but know this–if *any* of you try to escape while I'm outside the village, the other two will pay dearly."

"Understood," I said then turned and dropped down in front of Gabby. When I told Jaxxson, "I need a minute," I made it clear that was an order, not a request.

Jaxxson gave me a testy look, but stood and moved to where Mathias and Callan waited.

Gabby still fought to hold herself upright. "Don't leave, Rayen. They can't be trusted."

Tony had recovered from his surprise and leaned in. "Look, Xena...Rayen, I don't want–"

I cut in, keeping my voice low. "Both of you listen up. Gabby, we need you healthy. Soon." I gave her a meaningful look I hoped she understood – that she had to be in shape to run the minute we found a way out of here. When her infection-dulled eyes lit with understanding and she nodded, I turned to Tony. "I don't know what a bus is, short or otherwise, but I'm not throwing you under anything. Take care of Gabby while I'm gone and...be ready when I return."

As if the day hadn't been filled with enough surprises, for once Tony not only was speechless, he actually looked like he agreed with me.

I then rose and strode over to the three waiting for me. I nodded toward Callan. "You ready?"

"Rayen!" Gabby pushed up to her knees, refusing Tony's offer to help her up, which would have meant his fingers touching her exposed arm.

Seeing her in such pain twisted my gut. "Yeah, Gabby?"

"Be safe." Her eyes said a whole lot more. "And come back."

"Plan on it." My gaze slid to Jaxxson who had waited next to the opening that had once again appeared in the wall. He didn't look any happier about the arrangement than I was, but I didn't care. My words were as hard as stone when I warned the healer, "I promise you I *will* be back, and I had better find her safe and healthy."

I didn't wait for a reply as I turned, following Callan and Mathias out the door into the purple light that was becoming a noticeably darker reddish-purple.

Once outside and far enough away from the hut that neither Gabby nor Tony could easily hear them, Callan glanced over his shoulder at me. "It's unwise to offer promises you have no way of knowing for sure you can fulfill."

"What? Telling Gabby and Tony that I was coming back?" I'd already fought one croggle practically alone, so how much harder could it be this time? If he hoped to rattle my confidence, he wasted his breath. I simply pointed out, "Croggles don't seem too hard to kill."

Callan's lips curved with a knowing smile when he cast another look at me. "The croggle you fought was a clumsy adolescent. The ones living around the transender site we go to now are full-grown creatures. Three times as large. Can't be stopped with a spear and not the least bit clumsy."

Now he tells me. "So how do we kill it?"

"That is the problem of the one keeping it busy if there is a child to save."

I didn't even waste my breath asking who he intended to send out to be croggle bait.

CHAPTER 18

If I die here, how long will it take my dad to notice I'm missing if the school doesn't notify him?

Months. And Gabby considered that generous on her part.

One school hadn't noticed when she'd missed classes for two weeks.

She followed along behind Jaxxson, ignoring him since he ignored her. Outside the Isolation Unit, everything in the village was cast in intense reddish-purples from that jacked up sky. Moving around had given her a small burst of energy, or an adrenaline spike over facing a new unknown. She kept forcing one foot in front of the other, struggling to catch her breath in the humidity that wrapped around her and squeezed, reminding her of childhood summers in Saigon, Bangkok and Singapore. Mostly Singapore. Surviving that had been hard enough after her mom cashed out, but then her dad buried himself so deep in his work he'd forgotten he had a daughter.

A burden he'd pawned off on one private school after another since then.

She coughed and stumbled, catching her balance. Must not lag behind the grouchy healer from this weird world.

"Drink more of the water I gave you unless you enjoy coughing," Jaxxson said without turning around. The only words he'd spoken to her since leaving the neon-green hut this group used for a jail. "And keep up. You're not the only one who needs my attention."

She caught what his terse words hadn't said, that she imposed on his valuable time. Especially since he considered her an enemy, some freaky whatever they kept calling her,

Tony and Rayen–techno-somethings. As if.

She had the brain power to be a techno-whiz, but lacked the passion for anything mechanical or electronic. Numbers she loved, the rest? Bleh.

Jaxxson crossed into a less dense area. Not wide open like the grassy space where the metal pod had spit them out, more like trails wrapped in between trees where the underbrush had been cleared. Lots of trails, tons of big trees but no people, except for the sound of children, but she couldn't see any. The trees weren't brown or gray-skinned and the leaves weren't green. They were every color but. If not for working so hard to stay upright, she'd pause to admire the wicked colors, but not right now.

With Rayen dragged along on a hunting expedition that might involve killing croggles and Tony stuck in that prison unit, Gabby had to find out as much as she could while she was semi-free. Getting Jaxxson to talk at all would be tough, but he might if she started with a subject that interested him.

She asked in a scratchy voice, "How many kids are here in Camp Croggle?"

"Water," he ordered again.

Not a lively conversationalist.

She made a face at his back, or tried to but her face muscles weren't cooperating. Why should she be surprised at Jaxxson? He was just another self-consumed brainiac healer, like her father, right down to the bedside manners of a turnip. Only her dad *was* a physician, not some wannabe doc like Jaxxson.

A real doctor would have realized the reason she *hadn't* kept drinking was because she couldn't. Getting the lip of the water bag he'd hung around her neck up to her mouth became more impossible as her condition deteriorated.

Her swollen arms were so tight they didn't want to bend and neither did her puffed-up fingers that felt as though the skin would split any minute. But her throat ached with a dry, burning heat so she fumbled with the bag made of strange, aqua-colored leather hanging from a woven grass lanyard. She managed to lift the opening to her lips.

And pour *some* water in her mouth.

The rest ran down her chin and chest, dribbling over the

front of her dress that was dirty from being dragged through the jungle. The multi-colored cloth would hide most of the wet stains. Dropping the water sack to lay against her chest again, she swiped a fat hand at her face and missed half the water still trickling down. Sort of like getting a shot of Novocain in her arms, hands and face...but without the pain relief.

She focused on Jaxxson's back walking ahead of her and asked, "Where's this healing hut?"

"We're close."

"Where did Rayen, Mathias and Callan go?"

Not a word. The old silent treatment?

Being the new kid at a new school every six to eight months when her nanosurgeon-dad-turned-consultant accepted new contracts with different national and international medical programs meant a lot of stares and silence from her peers. You'd think after that, and being ignored by her dad for the past six years, she'd have gotten used to being treated as an inanimate object. A useless dead weight.

But she hadn't.

On the other hand, she should be glad Jaxxson hadn't looked back at her the whole time she'd followed him since she could probably beat out the *Creature Of The Deep* for a scary-looking award. Her filthy arms and face were swollen and streaked with red lines, hair stuck out unintentionally all over the place and sweat glued her clothes to her body.

Not that she should care, but grouchy up ahead looked like he'd stepped out of a television ad for sexy shaving cream with that sarong wrapped around his waist, his nicely-defined chest, smooth, olive-tone skin over an appealing masculine face and taut muscles that flexed across his back.

Wait. Back muscles?

That had nothing to do with shaving cream ads.

The infection must be frying her brain. Had to be the only reason she'd consider anyone who was even remotely related to medicine attractive. Underneath all that prime packaging lived the cold heart of an arrogant male with a God complex.

She'd met plenty over the years.

Sons of a few of her father's associates had taken an interest in her, until they clued into the fact she wasn't her mother, the classic trophy wife.

Gabby had set her sights on being anything but. The more anti-trophy-worthy she could make herself, the better.

Jaxxson came to a sudden halt in front of a massive tree that reminded her of giant California redwoods you could drive a car through. Except this one's striped bark had a tiger-skin look to it and, way up high, polka-dotted yellow leaves flickered beneath that crimson-red daytime moon. But the moon had trekked some from one side of the sky to the other since she'd first seen it, like the arc of a sun going from horizon to horizon.

She kept plodding along to close the distance between her and Jaxxson. Why had he stopped here?

He turned with his arms crossed, as if waiting on an errant child. His dark-brown eyes swept up and down her, pausing on her face before he looked away.

I look that gross, huh?

Like she cared what he thought? But to be honest, the boys usually found her attractive, so on some what-the-hell-is-wrong-with-you level his action did sting.

When she finally reached him, he said, "Ready?"

"For what?"

"To enter the healing hut."

He was joking, right?

"I hate to point out the obvious, you being a medical professional and all," she said in a perky sarcastic voice she managed to dredge up in spite of the pain. "But it's a tree and I can't climb. I know, I'm self-diagnosing, and you doctors hate that, but I'm just saving you from a possible malpractice suit." In case he needed a demonstration, she raised her sausage fingers and unbendable arms as high as she could, grimacing. The pain had increased as her heart rate picked up from walking, and worrying.

He shook his head as if she were particularly slow or clueless. "Come on." He reached for her arm.

She flinched and stepped back, her voice coming out brisk, to make sure he understood. "Don't touch me."

"Don't give me orders," he warned. "I have enough to do without having to deal with someone like you."

"What do you mean 'someone like me'?"

"Think I haven't noticed you're a Hy'bridt?"

Did he mean hybrid? Like a mixed breed? A mongrel. "A what?"

"Mismatched eyes. Sign of a Hy'bridt."

Yeah, right. Everyone saw her different eyes before they saw her and marked her a freak without a single word of getting to know her. That's why she made a point of being the first one to put some distance between herself and strangers before someone had the opportunity to snub her. "I've been slammed by better than you, buster."

He jerked at her words. "I didn't touch you and I harm no one."

This whole conversation had gotten weirder than she could deal with until she found relief from this infection.

A battle of emotions warred through his gaze until he settled on irritated, his default emotion from what she could tell. He ground out his next words. "*You* wanted my help. If you don't go into the hut soon, that infection could reach your brain and, if it does, I won't be able to stop it from killing you."

Could reach her brain?

Was he telling her the truth or just trying to scare her? Either way, he was doing a damn good job of rattling her.

In fact, swallowing was becoming more difficult, especially getting past the lump of panic jamming her throat. "What do you want me to do? If your hut is inside this tree, show me the door."

"Door?"

She lifted her eyebrows. Was she speaking another language all of a sudden? "Yes. How else do you get in and out?"

"You have two different eye colors and *claim* to not be tek-nah-tee, yet you must be one or the other."

"One or the other what?"

"You waste my time!"

And you're making me crazy! She bared her clenched teeth. "I get it. You're important, but I'm not fluent in idiot and you're not making any sense. What does any of this one-kind-or-another thing have to do with getting inside this tree?"

"Tek-nah-tees can't enter this tree." His eyes flickered with a thought, something he battled about within himself until he looked up, whispering something silently that reminded her of her father when his patience ran out. Then he glanced back at her. "You have mixed eyes yet you don't see the passage?"

One more snipe about her screwy colored eyes and he was going to end up seeing stars circling his head.

She took in the bark on the tree trunk, searching for a line or something that would indicate a doorway. Something that would prove she was *not* a tek-nah-tee. "Give me a hint."

"Put both hands up on the tree," he said, enunciating each word slowly.

She started to tell him she wasn't the moron here who thought she could walk through a tree. Giving him a we'll-play-your-little-game glare, she gritted her teeth and moved right up against the bark so she didn't have to reach far to touch it. She pushed her aching hands forward, past her hips, and then she paused, anticipating the pain of her over-sensitive palms hitting the striped bark.

But her hands touched nothing, kept moving as they disappeared into the tree that gave no more resistance than a cloud.

The unexpected lack of solidity startled her and she fell forward with no chance of getting her arms up to block her fall.

She squeezed her eyes closed and hunched her shoulders, preparing to hit face first.

And stopped in mid-air.

An arm scooped around her waist right before her face should have smashed into the ground.

She opened her eyes.

Yep, that smooth flat surface she stared at had to be the floor, because the two feet in odd sandals also in view matched the ones Jaxxson wore.

He hoisted her up to stand on her own and released her, stepping back with a strange expression. A mix of confusion and surprise.

Yeah, she was freaky, but this guy had no idea just how weird.

Want to talk freaky? Take a look at this place.

Awe stretched through her voice when she said, "This has got to be the most rockin' tree house I've ever seen." The room looked about fifteen feet across and more like an apartment than a doctor's office. Nothing cold and sterile here.

She sniffed. Eucalyptus? Sort of. And something else just as soothing. Sage? Or maybe lavender? It could be from the rough-hewn wood of the tree walls, toned down from the outside stripes. How cool was this to be inside the heart of a living, breathing tree?

Or were they? "Is this tree still alive?"

"Of course it is." He strolled away.

She scrunched up her face and silently mimicked his words *Of course it is,* but he didn't see her.

Jaxxson stopped at a wall where an odd assortment of dried plants hung from a vine line. He pulled a wooden bowl off a crude shelf and sat it on a large slab table that was covered with a soft-looking gray skin of some kind. Reaching for several dried plants, he used a polished rock to crush the leaves into the bowl.

Definitely not like any kind of hospital or clinic that she'd ever seen.

Glancing up higher, there appeared to be another room accessed by a hand-hewn ladder, like a loft. She asked, "You live here?"

Putting down the bowl, he turned to her, a furrow between his brows as if he still tried to figure out something about her. "This is my temporary quarters until we find a way home."

So he wasn't from here either.

"Where's home?" she asked, trying to figure out the emotion beneath his words. He'd gone from adversarial to quiet since she'd stepped inside this place. Maybe the scents in here had a calming effect on him, too.

He took his time answering. "Back through the transender."

"You mean that–" Just then she noticed something new about the table in front of him. No table legs. Nothing between the slab and the floor. "Is that, uh, floating on its own?"

He looked down at the space beneath the slab then back at her. "Of course it is. I need you to sit on the surface so I can treat you."

She started to tell him the thing was too high when the slab suddenly levitated down low enough for her to easily slide onto it.

But she didn't move. Had that really happened or was this guy some kind of magician, which could mean he was fooling her about everything, even being a healer.

He ordered, "Sit."

Considering all the bizarre things she'd encountered since Rayen's hand had been sucked into that computer screen, Gabby decided to just roll with this for now. She inched herself onto the slab, waiting for it to slam to the floor at any second, Jaxxson reached for his bowl of ground-up leaf mixture. He grasped a handful that he let sift through his fingers as if checking to see if the texture suited him. Then he added some liquid from another bowl.

Was he a healer...or a witchdoctor?

What if that evil-eyed tile girl had convinced Mathias to do this as a set up?

Scary second thoughts bombarded Gabby. Her heart rate increased like a sprinter going for a record and her breathing shortened until it came in pants.

What exactly was that stuff Jaxxson held? Would it do more harm than the red vines? What if he'd brought her here to interrogate then kill? She knew nothing about tek-nah-tees. Would he believe her?

He paused, cocking his head to one side. "Why are you becoming more distressed?"

Had he read her thoughts? Without touching her? To hide her surprise at his question, she asked him one. "What kind of doctor are you?"

"Heal-er," he said in an exaggerated voice of impatience. "Understand?"

She buried her worry under her temper. "Oh, I understand. Doc-tor A-hole. Got it."

If not for the dire circumstances, she'd get a laugh at the dumbfounded look on his face that said he had no idea what she'd just called him. And male ego, being what it was, meant he'd never admit to not knowing.

Instead he frowned even more and reached for a basket on the floor. He pulled two puce-looking dried flowers out, tossed those in his bowl then continued crushing that with the leaves.

He eyed her again, trying to decide something. When he finally made up his mind, he said, "I'm from the healing house. But I'm not called whatever you are calling me."

"Why not?"

He paused in thought. "There are many names for what I do, but I have not studied them all."

Odd answer. Who were these people? But no matter how much effort it took, she had to keep the conversation going, hoping to find out something useful. "I was born in China. Hong Kong, but we moved around a lot."

Digesting that for a moment, he asked, "*Your* home?"

"No." Her neck muscles ached, getting tight like her arms, but she didn't want to stop the tentative truce. That much she'd learned from her dad. The number of real discussions with him could be measured on the fingers of one hand, but if she did get him to talk, she made darn sure she kept him talking.

Jaxxson pondered a few seconds then asked, "If you're not tek-nah-tee, where *are* you from?"

Her heart did a double bounce at the word "if." Here was a chance to convince him she wasn't tek-nah-tee and open the door for his friends to consider that Tony and Rayen might not be either.

She carefully explained, "I live in Albuquerque, New Mexico for now, but my dad consults all over the world so I've lived everywhere–Berlin, Dubai, Singapore. What about you?"

The silence that met her words raised hairs along her neck. The intensity of his stillness sent her pulse skyrocketing and with each hard pump of her heart she could swear she felt the infection spread.

She started breathing in shorter, rougher gasps.

Jaxxson grabbed a handful of his mixture again, sandwiching it between his palms. He shook his head as if grappling with something he couldn't comprehend. "I live in City Four."

She shook her head. A city called by a number? "Four?"

As if reading her mind again he explained, "Yes, YEG/4."

What was he talking about? Had she heard him right? Her eyes blurred then cleared. She wheezed a breath in and out.

He squatted down in front of her, real concern showing on

his face for the first time. "I have to rub this on your wrists at the infection origin. Right now."

That meant touching her. She swallowed past her dry lips, and her fear. "No. Give me the bowl. I'll do it."

"How will you do that with fingers that refuse to work?"

She didn't have an answer for him. Her head was splitting and it was getting harder and harder to swallow.

"This will not work without my touch," he added.

"Why?"

"You're serious? Were you born of this millennium?"

Pain blazed through her. She snapped at him. "Of course not, I was born in..." Her chest wouldn't expand. She forced out, "1997."

His eyes widened as he whispered, "Not possible."

"Oh, really? When were you born...uhggg..." She flailed her arms at her neck, unable to reach her throat.

Jaxxson reached for her, his face ripped with anxiety and anger. "*You lie. Who are you? Don't close your eyes!*"

His fingers latched tight onto one of her wrists.

She tried to protest, but couldn't. Words snagged in her closing throat. Her vision blurred. Pain raged through her wrist, her whole body. She jerked her arm, but couldn't pull away and started falling back, back, back into a bottomless void.

Jaxxson's bewildered thoughts burst into her mind.

She lies.

1997 is impossible.

I was born in 2162.

CHAPTER 19

I stalked behind Zilya who followed Etoi as Callan led all of us through another tunnel in the green fog that protected the village. The air seemed to have thickened, clawing at my skin and making each breath labored, even though we were not yet in the jungle.

Zilya had traded her queenly robes for a leaner, two-piece look similar to Etoi's. The tops covered their breasts and tied at the necks. The bottom parts stopped mid-thigh. Pants...no, I'd heard them called shorts.

Where? At the school? Or somewhere else?

The material hugged their bodies like soft deerskin.

But deerskin was tan colored. Not spotted like a leopard.

Leopards have spots. If that was correct, more fragmented memories and knowledge were sifting through the black hole in my mind.

We exited on the opposite side of the village from where I'd originally entered. I set my bearings according to the red moon—as Gabby had labeled it—that had moved halfway across the sky. Hard to believe that a full day hadn't passed yet since we'd arrived here. Or had it?

Callan picked up his near-silent pace, moving us quickly over a narrow strip of open land, through dead grayish and yellow-orange vegetation to a copse of trees that looked more like forest than jungle. The minute the four of us reached the first tall trees with ghost branches, gnarled and white, Callan swung around and said, "This is good."

Etoi carried two spears and whispered something to Zilya as they both stopped.

When Zilya's gaze intercepted mine, she lost her chuckle and fumbled with the short spear Etoi handed her. Could the delicate Zilya handle that weapon and hold her own? Guess I'd find out soon.

Callan ordered, "Etoi will lead, then Zilya, me, then her."

Her? "My name's Rayen."

Etoi protested, "I won't have *her* behind Zilya or me."

So much for trying to get on a first-name basis. I felt a smidgen of sympathy for Callan who always seemed one word from losing his patience with Etoi.

Zilya didn't interfere, other than allowing Callan to see that she, too, wasn't comfortable with me following her.

Callan's skin deepened in hue when he drew a long breath as if that would wash away his frustration with outspoken Etoi. "If the three of us don't return to the village, the other two prisoners will be executed. She–" Callan nodded at me. "–knows this and won't try to escape or harm one of us. And since you *should* know the most vulnerable position is the last in line, does that mean you wish to take her place?"

Understanding brightened Zilya's eyes once she grasped Callan's logic. "Good plan. How do you want to split up?"

Etoi opened her mouth to voice her opinion and Callan glared her into silence. "You take Etoi, Zilya, and I'll take...her."

"Why?" Zilya demanded.

That snapped the latch on Callan's temper. He stepped over to her, his body swelled with restrained fury, his color one shade now–deep violet. "Etoi is too impulsive to be put with her and heeds only you. I'm the best one to deal with the captive if she creates a problem. We don't have the time to argue with a child's life potentially depending on us. You're of the Governing House, not the Warrior House. Need I remind you who is in charge out here? Force me to waste another breath explaining and you'll regret it."

"We'll discuss this further with Mathias when we return." Zilya stood firm and spoke with authority, but everything else about her seemed to shrink back from his anger. Flags of embarrassment waved in her cheeks. She didn't wilt like a flower that had been trampled, but withdrew in respect of the foot that could smash her.

Interesting dynamics. Now if only I could use that tension to my advantage to get myself, Gabby and Tony free.

Callan sent me a look of discomfort at having his group's flaws laid out in front of a stranger, but when he spoke to Etoi, his voice was that of a leader. "Are we clear?"

"Of course."

She'd answered in a respectful tone that I didn't believe for a minute, but it seemed to mollify everyone's temper. I didn't know why I wanted to do it, but I decided to help out Callan by distracting his attention from the other two.

I asked him, "How long is it going to take to get where we're going?"

"Not long. Let's get moving."

Etoi took off into the undergrowth with Zilya right behind. Zilya's white-blond spikes of hair bounced above the vegetation, keeping her visible.

Callan stepped away and tossed over his shoulder, "Keep up."

I smiled and waved my hand in a keep-moving motion. "I won't lose you."

He headed into the forest at a brisk pace, slapping chocolate-hued branches out of his way with sharp swings of his sword. I noticed which plants he tended to sidestep— orangish pink, and deep blue ones. Some were spiky and others furry like soft chick-down. So I knew what chick-down was, huh?

A loud caw overhead alerted me to a gray-yellow bird. At least I thought it was a bird, except for the long scaly tail that drooped behind it. The tail broke off into four individual lengths, like different sized whips.

"Watch that," Callan ordered, halting me in my stride.

I shoved my gaze in the direction he pointed and saw a very small bear-type animal, all fluffy and furry until the critter's neck extended once again as long as its body. Half its head opened up to expose three rows of lethal, slicing fangs that were almost as large as the animal's wide paws.

"What is that?" I didn't realize I'd spoken out loud until Callan made a snort sound.

"It's called a muttrapper."

"Is it as lethal as it looks?"

"Worse. Each of those teeth is tipped in poison."

"Nice mutt-whatever. Be a nice mutt-rapper," I murmured as I sidestepped around the critter. "Guess this means you're saving me for the croggle."

He glanced at me, puzzlement staining his expression. "If I wanted to feed you to something, I'd have told you to pet the muttrapper."

He'd sounded insulted. What'd I say wrong? "Just joking. I appreciate the warning," I said to his back as he marched ahead. This bunch didn't have much sense of humor.

Fine by me. Now, I could drop my mask of subservient prisoner and focus on the important things, like keeping track of where I was in relation to the village.

Callan followed a trail deeper into landscape thick with vines as large as my legs, leaves of yellow, red and rust.

I tried to memorize as many landmarks as possible in order to return on my own if I needed to, but the trees were so huge they blocked out any distant view. So I started noting shapes of trees like the one I'd just passed that hunched over like an ancient elder. Another towering one dead ahead split into five arms, with long, thin branches like fingers reaching toward the changing sky. Everything in this place seemed oversized, twisted and lethal.

What made this place a sphere? That's what Mathias had called it. Who *were* Callan, Mathias, Zilya and the others, and where had they come from if this was not their home?

They clearly weren't happy about being here and it wasn't by choice, so what had happened? Were they prisoners, too? Maybe I could convince them to work with us and find a way home...but where was *their* home?

And what was the possibility of Callan working with Tony–the one he'd deemed an enemy tek-nah-tee beyond any doubt–in any lifetime? Zero.

That put me back to where I'd started, which wasn't much of a place to be, considering I had no idea what the word "home" meant to me either. And if I didn't get back to the Institute, I wouldn't find out what information my fingerprints had revealed.

Even if I did, would that give me my memory?

What about that healer who was hopefully taking care of Gabby? Could he heal more than the body? Like finding my lost memories? I asked Callan, "Can your healer work on any part of the body?"

Callan snapped at me, "You feeling ill?"

"No."

"Then be quiet and keep up."

So much for a friendly conversation.

I managed to stay on pace just fine and, like Callan, I moved ghost-quiet in this setting, which made me wonder if being in the wild was familiar to me. Had I hunted at one time?

Slipping up close to him, I whispered, "Right behind you."

Smooth muscles flexed with his fluid movements. The mottled colors on his skin shifted a tiny bit. Did emotion affect the change? He'd never admit I'd surprised him.

With Etoi and Zilya moving along seven to eight steps ahead of Callan, I tried once more to engage the hard-nosed warrior in a conversation. "Why are you here?"

He wouldn't answer.

"What is this place? Did you get into trouble to be sent here?"

He sent an implacable expression over his shoulder that should unnerve me if I had that kind of temperament, but I was finding I didn't have many docile bones in my body.

I kept verbally poking at him, telling myself it was only to get information. Not because I wanted to break through that stony wall and make him interact with me as someone other than a prisoner. "How long have you been here?"

"Be quiet, tek-nah-tee," he growled.

"Thought I made it clear that I am not a tek-nah-tee."

"Anyone who walks with the enemy and protects the enemy *is* the enemy."

That told me the cost of defending Tony and stepping in to take his place. "You going to tell me what a tek-nah-tee is?"

"Vermin. You're all vermin." He spat the words.

Vermin? That sounded familiar. "You think I'm a...rodent? A rat?"

He shook his head as if to himself and muttered something that would be dark if it had color. "Calling you a rat would be unkind–"

There was hope for this conversation.

"–to rats. Tek-nah-tee are more like cockroaches. Single-minded, stupid insects with no regard for what's decent. No other creature than the cockroach has survived every devastation in our world."

His attitude annoyed me on a level I couldn't explain. More than feeling irritated. He compared me to something disgusting. That cut me when I shouldn't care what this stranger thought. I changed the direction of my next question. "So where do the tek-nah-tees stay in this place?"

He swung around so fast I almost ran into him and had to throw my hands against his chest to stop myself.

My pulse pounded at touching him.

He stood there for a second, long enough for me to feel his heart thrumming a fast beat before he backed away from my touch. I dropped my hands, fighting an awkward feeling at the way he made it clear how much he detested being touched by me. He walked backwards so I had to follow, but not as close as before.

After a silent couple of steps, he said, "You *know* tek-nah-tees only visit this world to drop off incoming mystik passengers or spy on those of us who still live. Why do you ask these questions?"

I juggled what I knew to this point. I could understand his hostility if the tek-nah-tee forced kids into this scary place and killed them, but I still didn't understand why he seemed convinced that I was one. I had no mark on my neck like the one on Tony that had created a stir with them.

"You're an intelligent person, Callan. Think this through. You have no solid proof that I'm a tek-nah-tee. If you could open your mind to the idea that I might *not* be your enemy, then maybe we could help each other."

To be fair, there was some chance I could be a tek-nah-tee since I had no memory prior to this morning, but I would not harm a child and, without any real proof, I refused to be marked as a child killer.

Callan turned around and picked his sure-footed way through an undulating area of roots–*had that root just moved?*– and uneven, hard-packed red dirt when the path leveled out.

Was he actually entertaining the possibility of what I suggested?

I thought so, until he muttered, "I will *not* be tricked again by a tek-nah-tee." He turned to me again and jabbed the spear at my chest, point first, but stopped short of breaking skin.

Furious at the mere threat of attack, I caught the shaft before the tip had any chance of doing damage. Yanking the end up and toward me, I brought us face-to-face, feeling smug when we stood so close I could see sparks of red firing through his eyes that were now a somber brown in this shadowed light. His nose flared as if he'd caught a wild scent and his gaze dropped to my mouth.

My thoughts skidded to a halt, long enough for the anger to bleed out of me. I had the craziest thought of wanting to run my finger across that sculpted mouth to force a smile, just to see what he looked like happy.

A flash of movement drew my eyes to a flutter of rainbow-colored wings the size of my two hands spread open. Four flapping wings on a furry body that had a chipmunk-looking head, beady black eyes and small legs with claws that were extended as it flew towards Callan. Large and lethal claws.

Shaking himself from whatever had happened for those few seconds, he snarled at me. "Don't think to use your powers on me without suffering repercussion."

I ignored his words, too focused on the threat. I spun away and broke a dead limb thick as my thumb from a tree and leaned back, prepared to throw my make-do spear at the attacking bird.

Callan took one look over his shoulder and dove at me, grabbing my arm. "No!"

We both lost our balance. I toppled backwards, landing hard against the ground, one shoulder scraping a tree. He came down on my chest with a thunk, knocking the breath from me. I groaned, but kept my eyes open, searching for the threatening bird thing.

The flying critter had landed on a small sapling at Callan's feet but now flew back up into the tree, squeaking in terror the whole way.

The little bird animal landed on a branch and turned to keep an eye on me as if *I* presented the real threat.

I let out a pained breath and relaxed my guard. The minute I did, I noticed every curved muscle, and other parts, draped over me. A distinct masculine scent tangled up my next breath.

The heat I felt building inside this time had nothing to do with preparing to fight a battle.

He pushed up on his arms, sharp breaths squeezing out between clenched jaws. I could swear embarrassment skittered across his face before his eyes hardened and he snapped, "Have you no brain?"

"Evidently not, because I try to save you from being attacked and end up catching the devil for it."

The surprise on his face was comical. "Save me? From a dallymoth?"

"Moth? Aren't those like butterflies? That thing's no moth. I saw teeth and claws."

He growled another dark word I didn't catch. "Teeth for eating insects with hard shells and claws for grabbing branches as it flies around spinning thread...which we use for weaving. You frightened it so badly I bet the thing doesn't make a strand of thread to harvest for another week. Do you have to kill *everything* that helps us survive?"

My face heated so fast I had to be glowing red with humiliation. I shot back at him, "I only meant to protect you. Wasted energy on my part."

My answer must have stalled his brain because he stared at me slack-jawed.

I'd have laughed at his expression if I could find one thing funny about this situation. "Get off me."

Now he looked embarrassed. Good.

He shoved up to his feet, stood there a minute debating something, then offered his hand.

I slapped it away and struggled to a standing position. "How am I to know what's dangerous or not in this place? You got a book or a list of things not to kill?"

Callan had no answer to that. He just stared at me for

several long seconds then lifted the spear and turned back to whatever trail he followed.

"Is there a problem?" Zilya called out, coming back to us, her eyes a deep purple with intensity.

I watched Callan's face for a sign of how he'd explain this. Depending on the way he answered, I could end up with my wrists bound again...or worse.

He waved off Zilya. "A dallymoth frightened her."

Etoi roared with laughter. "Our youngest children don't fear dallymoths."

I narrowed my eyes at Callan who ignored me, his don't-cross-me mask back in place. By the time I'd dusted myself off, Zilya and Etoi were waiting for us.

Etoi kept a sly eye on Callan, whose curt voice made it clear he blamed me for this delay, which improved her mood significantly. Especially when Callan stepped over to me and dropped his voice to a menacing level. "The sky is changing faster. Hold us up again and I'll leave you staked until we return."

I held up my hands. "Just a mistake."

"Don't make one when we reach the transender," he warned. "If you cause us to lose a child, I'll kill you myself and leave what's left for the croggle."

Just when I thought we might have reached a friendly understanding, but no. "I won't let anything hurt a child."

Whether Callan believed me or not was yet to be seen, but I saw something in his gaze that hinted at a change in spite of his cold voice.

That he might truly believe I'd tried to protect him.

If so, that had to fly in the face of my being a tek-nah-tee. Didn't it? But it probably also rubbed for any girl to protect a warrior such as Callan.

What had he said? That he would not be tricked by his enemy again. In that case, I might be reading more into his reactions than was there.

This time, Callan set a faster pace.

I jogged in step behind him, waiting for Etoi and Zilya to pull ahead once more as they had last time. Over roots, around trees growing thicker, beneath leaves everywhere. Easy to get lost in a matter of minutes.

When Callan gave a hand signal with two fingers, Zilya split off to the left with Etoi. Callan spoke over his shoulder to me in a whisper. "Follow me. Do *not* make noise."

"What's happening?"

"Don't make noise means to keep your mouth closed."

I mimicked him silently behind his back at his snippy tone and whispered, "I can't help you unless I understand what's going on."

He looked up at the changing sky for answers to his silent questions and hissed.

I started to ask what now, but saw the green stripes whipping across the sky like giant brush strokes.

Callan started running. "The sky's changing faster than before."

"What does that mean?" I jumped over downed trees, chasing after him. "Why'd you split up from the others?"

He answered in a low voice sharp with impatience. "The sky stripes when the transender arrives to deliver children and sometimes scouts. Our teams divide as we approach..." He must have decided I really was confused, because he kept explaining. "That way, if one team is penned in by a croggle or a different threat, the other team can help the child. We may be too late."

"What if—"

"Shhh," he snarled. "When a child is delivered, Zilya and Etoi will distract the threat. I'll hand off the child to you to protect then I'll draw the croggle away so they can escape. Each team knows their duty. No arguments."

That sounded like Callan had to be the last one to escape the croggle. Wouldn't that be harder to do alone? When the forest started to open up ahead, Callan stopped abruptly and dropped into a crouch behind paper-thin bushes that barely hid anything. I dropped into a crouch beside him.

I studied the quiet area, thinking this might be the wrong place when I heard his sudden growl of anger.

Something was up.

Searching further to my left, I spied Zilya and Etoi hunkered down, too.

I could feel the double beat of my heart racing as I inhaled the acrid scent of the blood-colored earth. Sweat ran down my face and dripped into my eyes, blinding me.

I leaned my mouth near Callan's ear, noting how he forced himself to remain still when he obviously was bothered by me being so close. Could I use that to my advantage at some point?

I asked, "What's the problem?"

"Tek-nah-tee scouts."

Lifting up, inch-by-inch, I braced myself on my arms and managed to see through a gap in the intense orange-and-black leaves. An area that looked similar to the same grassy field where I'd fought the croggle monster earlier fanned out before us. The trampled rubbery grass here had gray-blue bloodstains darkening the ground.

But there was no dead monster carcass. Was this the right field?

So what happened to the croggle? Or were those bloodstains from something else?

A sudden movement to the left snagged my attention.

No monster, but two people. The tek-nah-tee scouts? Both males in their early twenties, each holding the arm of a little boy, a toddler, no older than three or four, with bright red hair and horror etched in his tear-streaked face.

The two guys wore shiny, metallic gray one-piece clothing that covered them from neck to boots. The way they carried themselves, their demeanor reminded me of the people in uniforms who'd arrested me near the Sandia Mountains this morning. That seemed forever ago and these two scouts were far more lethal looking than the elders who'd carted me to the Institute. Dark, short-cropped hair gave these two young men an aggressive and harsh appearance. Unmerciful.

And they both had menacing designs painted–inked?–in black on their exposed forearms. Tattoos.

So those were tek-nah-tees, huh?

Now I understood why Mathias thought Tony was one since he had that same short hair with an arrogant cut to his chin, a scorpion tattoo and he strutted with attitude the way those two moved.

One scout clutched a metal instrument. A flint-gray box that fit in the hand he raised and pointed at the child.

The other scout, with a wide forehead and dull eyes, shook his head. "You know we can't kill any of them unless you want to explain a tek death back home."

The first male laughed, a cold chilling sound, eyes trained on the small boy stumbling between them. "Don't be so serious, Phen. I won't kill the package. But I can play with the furkken brat."

I wanted to ask Callan what furkken meant, but from the way a muscle jumped in his jaw I took it as a curse or derogatory term.

"Not with me here. Do it on your own time so I don't get charged with misconduct. SEOH could have vids in this area. Let's get our surveillance done and go home. This is as good a place as any to dump the incomer."

"A little further in the middle. That way the croggle has a better chance of catching dinner. Need to keep the livestock fed, and feeding him there means we won't have to walk through the blood to reach the transender to leave."

The child cried out, startling the guy with the gray box.

His hand twitched, or he must have hit a button and the child screamed in pain. A single burst of terror.

I launched myself forward.

Callan shouted something at Zilya, but I'd already exploded from cover, racing toward the little boy.

The scouts were so surprised by the toddler's sudden wailing they weren't looking up as I charged them.

The guy holding the box lifted his head a second before I reached him, and I took advantage of the shock on his face. Moving fast and hard, I hooked an arm around his neck, slamming him to the ground.

The small box dropped from his fingertips.

I punted the strange weapon further away and spun to meet the second scout who'd abandoned the child to jump in.

Then the battle really started.

The second guy attacked me. A child's terror-filled cries clawed the air.

Hurt a child? Pay the price.

I drove jabs at him over and over, not sure how I knew to

fight this way but going on instinct. Connected with soft flesh a few times, hard bone more. Callan had joined the fray with Etoi standing back, her spear pointed at all of us.

I lost my balance. The ground had shifted beneath me. One too many hits to my head maybe?

My gaze strayed to the child just as Zilya snatched him up and rushed away from the battle.

The distraction cost me a rock-hard fist in my ribs. I sucked air at the blow, the only pause I took before immediately returning the favor with a brutal right cut to the scout's face.

Cartilage shattered. Blood geysered from a broken nose.

That was worth the ache in my knuckles.

But the tek scouts were well trained. They didn't back down. Continued to rain hammering blows just as punishing and with vicious precision.

Staggering back, I stumbled, then caught my balance in time to see that the scout I'd been fighting now stared past me, toward the trees.

Where Zilya held the child.

The scout sneered at me and moved toward Zilya.

Protect the child.

A blazing haze of fury clouded my vision. Hot energy started building inside me.

I yanked the scout back around. The tek-nah-tee only laughed, fists up and moving like lightning, raining hits over me again and again, the strikes pummeling my shoulders and head.

Anger so molten it threatened to sear my insides whipped through me. Strong enough that I wouldn't back down either. Instead I fought the scout harder, forcing him away from Zilya and the boy.

Over the grunts of the attackers, I heard Callan shouting at Zilya and Etoi to run.

With one last surge, I knocked the scout backwards ten feet, rolling over and over, with me right after him.

The scout landed on his feet, spotted the gray box and scooped it up. He swung around, pointing it at Zilya.

I ignored everything except charging forward and knocking the scout's hand away just as the box buzzed.

The gray box went flying another thirty feet away from the tek-nah-tee. My next punch landed under his jaw, snapping his head back and causing him to stumble around, arms flailing to keep his balance.

But then I stumbled sideways, too, trying to keep my own feet stable again.

That's when I realized the ground really was shifting back and forth beneath me. My feet flew out from under me. I hit hard at the same time the scout went down.

Callan and the other grappling scout hit the ground as the earthquake erupted.

Not an earthquake, but a violent tremor. One I recognized. If I was right, that shaking announced a greater threat.

Croggle.

Rolling to my knees, then my feet, breathing hard, I glanced around. Callan and both of the scouts had snapped to their feet, shuffling with their arms stretched out to keep upright. Dirt and rocks exploded into the air when the croggle burst from beneath the ground.

Callan hadn't been joking about this beast being larger than the one I'd killed earlier.

This one could kill all of us with the swipe of one claw.

Struggling to keep Etoi on her feet and moving the child deeper toward the tree line, Zilya looked back first at me then at Callan who yelled, "Protect him," then turned back to face the croggle.

Zilya stared at me as if she couldn't believe I would stand next to Callan and fight the croggle.

Callan glanced at me and shouted, "*Go!*"

I shook my head. Seeing Callan's eyes warm, even for a fleeting second, sent my heartbeat thudding at a crazy speed.

The trembling stopped. Everything went deathly silent.

Callan raised his spear toward the monster, as if one weapon was going to stop that thing.

A toothpick against a mountain.

With the scouts stunned, watching the greater threat, I inched slowly over to stand within a few steps of Callan, my voice soft. "Got a plan?"

"Stay alive?"

"Good as anything I've got."

He spared me a quick glance, but in that moment I saw something I wanted to call respect in his gaze. Probably my imagination, but it gave me a warm feeling I needed right then.

If I ran now, I'd have no chance to prove I was not tek-nah-tee. If I fought alongside him and convinced him I wasn't his enemy, I had a chance to save myself and my friends.

The scout who'd zapped the little boy turned to run toward a spot where the transender pod had beaten down the grass.

The second guy held his ground. No, he stood locked in fear, his face pale beneath blood dripping from where I'd damaged skin and bone. Callan had pummeled the other guy worse.

So three against one giant beast. Not favorable odds.

Didn't matter. We'd never make the woods before the thing reached us. Facing the beast gave us a better chance than being caught from behind.

The fleeing scout stopped before he reached the transender landing spot, searching the ground for something.

The box.

He dove for it, grasping in a smooth somersault move that landed him back on his feet in position to aim the device at the monster.

Callan and the second scout both shouted, "*Nooo!*"

The tek-nah-tee with the metal box paid no heed to their warning yells. He hit the button.

Must have been a stronger charge than what he'd used on the child. Blue bolts of electricity arced all over the croggle's head, lighting up his skin where it shocked him. But whatever zap that little box had spewed out meant nothing more than spitting in the eye of a wild beast.

The croggle stood up on its two hind legs, tall as a five-level building, and roared so loud I thought my eardrums would burst. It lunged forward, pounding the ground when it hit, tossing all of us off our feet again.

Enraging the croggle with an electric charge had accomplished only one thing–to zero the monster in on the person who'd zapped him. The idiot scout had no chance to move before the croggle swung its massive jaws at him.

The first bite cut him in half at the waist, leaving two legs standing. The rest of him disappeared between churning earth, spewing blood and severed body parts.

With the croggle distracted, Callan shouted, "*Runnn!*"

Sounded good to me. I scrambled to my feet, ready to sprint toward the forest cover.

I caught sight of the other scout, paralyzed with fear.

"Get out of here," I called, but the guy either couldn't hear me, or was so petrified nothing registered. If the fool stayed where he was he'd be dead in moments. The croggle was already shifting his ungainly size around, seeking new prey.

Leave the guy? He'd die for sure.

"Let the croggle have him," Callan yelled at me as he dashed toward safety.

At that moment, the croggle's bulging black eyes streaked with yellow veins flared wildly in the direction of the tek-nah-tee and roared, ready to kill.

CHAPTER 20

Rearing up again, the croggle prepared to lunge in another attack.

I screamed again at the scout. *"Run!"*

He stayed frozen in place between me and the croggle.

As the monster arched forward then plunged down, I ran full out, smashing into the scout, my body throttling us both forward. The monster's hot breath rushed past us ahead of its jaws slamming the empty space where the scout had stood seconds ago.

The scout rolled twice with the momentum from my blow, which must have shaken him out of his stupor. Jumping up, he yelled something at me that I couldn't hear over a loud whine.

I was too busy scrambling away from the monster now that the scout could save himself. When I turned to see the beast's position, a massive claw swung toward me with hyper-speed.

I twisted to dive away, but didn't move fast enough to dodge the sharp tip of a claw the size of my forearm. It raked a burning slash across my stomach and side. Arching in pain, I forced myself to keep scrambling, barely avoiding the solid thump of a foot pummeling the ground where my head had just been.

"Ayeeee! Here! Here!" I heard Callan shouting somewhere nearby. "Croggle. This way."

Smart guy. Taunt the monster away. Then what?

Rolling my head to the side, I saw the scout sprawled on the ground with Etoi on top of him, a spear at his chest.

The tek-nah-tee yelled up at her, veins in his throat standing out.

I couldn't make out anything he said.

Etoi pushed the tip of the spear into the scout's chest and yelled right back. That shut him down.

Scary girl.

Further away, Callan kept distracting the monster as he shot back and forth so fast in front of the creature that I could barely see Callan's legs move. But a person could only do that for so long before he gave out or made a mistake and got caught.

I couldn't leave him to deal with the croggle alone, not when he could've gotten away with the others if I hadn't stayed to save the scout. Callan's enemy.

Clenching my teeth, I clamped a hand on the wound gouged deepest at my side and struggled to my feet. Where had the power within me gone? What had brought it on?

The scout heading toward the child.

If that's what it took to bring on the energy, I imagined the croggle turning on that little boy after it killed me and Callan.

At once, heat churned in my middle. I staggered toward the croggle now down on all its limbs, pounding the ground and snorting, snapping at Callan. Power swirled inside me, building. I started jogging.

Callan split his attention for a second, glancing my way, and roared, "Stop. *Nooo!*"

I couldn't look. No distractions. Moving my feet faster forced blood to gush around my fingers. I felt dizzy and shook it off, growling. The power coiled tight then expanded. I yelled at Callan. "*A spear!*"

Fury made the veins stand out on his forehead.

Two more steps and I'd reach the croggle.

I jumped on the monster's tail that was taller than me at its thickest part. And almost fell off. Grabbing a scale, I hoisted myself back to my feet. Would the monster notice something that weighed little more than one of its scales? I climbed toward the air flap that moved in and out, just as it had on the smaller croggle, only this was like climbing a mountain, not a hill.

Callan dodged right and left, keeping the monster confused as he worked his way around to the monster's side. He yelled at me. "Catch!"

I braced my feet to free one hand. If I moved my hand from the gash, I'd bleed out faster. When Callan threw the spear, I caught it and flipped the spear around, ready to stab the monster the second its breathing hole flapped open again.

The beast howled, shaking its bulk and snapping its jaws, the sound of giant teeth grinding. Massive feet stomped and the smell of raw sewage reeked in the air. Its twenty-foot tail lashed back and forth then curved, the tip swatting me off like an annoying fly.

I cartwheeled in the air and landed on my back with a dull thud when I hit the ground, my fingers still clutching the spear.

Callan had raced away, yelling and waving his hands to hold the monster's attention. Even with his speed, he was too far away to reach me in time to offer any help.

Jaws as wide as the transender pod swung around to me. Black eyes streaked with yellow rage turned on me.

Callan's voice reached me above all the noise. *"Rayen!"*

He said my name.

A small thing, but hearing that gave me a renewed surge to fight. I had to tap the red-hot energy I felt spinning inside me, but how?

Callan bellowed at the top of his lungs, running straight at the monster.

The croggle paused, head swinging over to Callan for just an instant before whipping back around to lunge at me. Razor-teethed jaws opened to cut me in half.

That was the extra second I needed.

Power detonated inside me once more. I knew it wouldn't last.

I rolled to my feet, pain lashing my middle and the world spinning around me. I yelled, *"Tenadori!"* and grasped the spear with both hands, ramming the lethal point into the croggle's massive foot.

I focused all my thoughts on *die and burn!*

An inferno of heat pulsed through me into the spear and blasted into the foot. Blue flames and smoke shot from the monster's air flap. It bellowed in anguish. Scales glowed fiery red.

I released the spear and fell backwards. Warm liquid gushed from my wound and ran across my stomach and chest. My heart thumped slower and slower.

The croggle kicked its legs then crashed over on its side, shaking and emitting a screech that rattled the trees.

Closing my eyes, I drew a gurgly breath, sick of smelling the stench of death.

What about Callan and the others?

Footsteps pounded up. I peeled my eyes open.

Callan walked up to me, chest heaving for air. He dropped down beside me, his eyes now reddish-golden. "You look worse than the croggle."

"I don't want...to hear grief...for killing him."

Shaking his head, he released a breath that almost sounded like a chuckle, but raspy as if he hadn't done it in a while. Warm hands covered my stomach. I gasped and jerked at the pain racking my body.

What humor I'd seen in Callan's face a moment ago fled quickly beneath a grim mask, the severity of my injuries written in the worry lines creasing his forehead. "Got to get you out of here before that thing bleeds out and you drown in croggle blood."

"Doubt I'll make it. Go. Save the child. But–" I drew another rattling breath. "Please...let my friends go."

Zilya's face popped into view. Confusion scrambled the color in her eyes. "You should have let that scout die."

I breathed out, "Couldn't let that beast...kill anyone."

"He's an *enemy*." She placed her hands on her hips. "Why would you help a tek? Protecting your own?"

"No." I scowled at her, gritting my teeth when Callan pressed harder. "Can I just die . . . in peace?"

Callan's gaze never left mine when he said, "Leave her alone, Zilya." Then he told me, "You will not die...yet."

Now that Zilya had pointed out how I'd, once again, protected their enemy, I wondered if Callan wanted the honor of killing me himself.

I closed my eyes, trying to separate myself from the pain snaking through every inch of my body.

The cries of a child approaching forced my eyes open to

find Etoi hovered in my line of sight. She told Zilya, "I think this little one is reacting to the Sphere. He already has a rash on his arms and legs."

Callan kept his hands in place, applying pressure that tortured me as he turned to address Zilya over his shoulder. "Where's the prisoner?"

"Tied to a tree."

"Take the child to Jaxxson."

"What about *her*?"

Now I'm her *again?* I fought to stay alert when all I wanted to do was close my eyes and withdraw from the jagged ache clawing my stomach. Had Callan been telling the truth that I wouldn't die?

Callan shook his head as if debating with himself. "Leave her with me. We'll follow once she can walk."

He expects me to get up and walk? After losing a couple of quarts of blood and with a gaping wound?

As usual, Etoi had an opinion. "This one killed a fully grown croggle. She protected a tek. Why save her?"

Hmph. I'd graduated to 'her' then back to 'this one.' At this rate, I'd be 'it' next.

Callan still pressed on the wound.

I hissed, nauseous from the streaking pain.

The struggle to figure out something warred in Callan's face. "How'd you kill these croggles? Our spears can't pierce the hide of a grown one, but you stab him in the foot and he dies."

Something I could do better than warrior-guy? *Sweet,* as Tony would say.

Throat dry and fighting dizziness, I opened my hands but couldn't lift them from where my arms had flopped down beside me. "With these. Not sure how it works." I took short breaths, which was all I could handle. "I feel an energy. . . then I think about...what I want to happen. That's how I killed the flower vine that...attacked Tony. Just worked." My eyes fluttered closed. Too much effort to keep them open.

No doubt they'd think I was insane and lock me away in that isolation hut forever...if I lived.

"Wake up," he ordered.

I didn't want to, but forced my lids halfway open, just enough to see the blurry image of Callan still kneeling next to me and arguing with Zilya. "She doesn't wear her hair like the tek-nah-tee females and no obvious marks on her body."

Zilya glared an easy message to interpret. She didn't want Callan discounting her theory that I was the enemy. "We'll discuss this later, but no matter how great a warrior you are, you risk someone like her using that power to kill you."

Looking up at Callan, I tried to speak, but it came out as a whisper.

He leaned closer to me. "What?"

Licking dry lips, I whispered, "My word...as a warrior. I will not use my power against you."

The respect that had shined in Callan's eyes earlier took on new meaning now. He believed I was not tek-nah-tee or at least he had reservations about condemning me. I could see it.

He said nothing to me, but he told Zilya, "Get moving. The child needs Jaxxson. I'll deal with this. That's final."

Did I have the beginning of an ally in Callan? An alliance that might help Gabby and Tony once I made it back to the village.

If I made it back.

"The blood still flows too fast," Etoi pointed out in a smug tone. "The decision of her fate may no longer rest in your hands. Staying here may draw another croggle."

He snarled something at Etoi I didn't get and scooped me into his arms.

Bad move. Pain ripped through my chest. Felt as though the croggle chewed on me. I'd lost too much blood. I licked my dry lips and tried to say, "Please don't hurt Gabby and Tony," but nothing came out.

Darkness closed over me.

CHAPTER 21

Cold. Her teeth chattered.

Gabby hated the cold. She wanted out of here. But where was here? She fought, clawing her way out of this frigid hole.

"Can you hear me?" a deep male voice asked.

Sure, I can hear you, which means there are two of us stuck in here. Got any idea how to get out?

No one answered her.

Too bad. He had a nice voice. She'd like to see the body and face attached to it. But like everyone else in her world, he seemed to have walked away from her.

As usual, she'd have to find her own way out of hell.

First she had to figure out what kind of place her father had dumped her into this time. Her teeth chattered more.

Something heavy covered her, taking the edge off her chill, but not by much.

Why couldn't her dad find a private school near a beach? She might actually apply herself and stick around if she had sand, water and tanned guys in board shorts.

Had she been sent to Antarctica?

I've gotten out of worse places. I think.

Drawing on all the energy she could muster, she ordered her eyes to open. Her lids weren't cooperating. Like they were glued shut.

The weight over her body increased, the new layer tucked against her. Which helped. A lot. The shivering slowed. Her arms and legs felt heavier.

Fine. She could sleep now that she was warm again.

"Come on, wake up," the male voice ordered.

She really would like to see who she had as a hell-mate. Giving it one more try, she pried open her eyes and stared up at a guy with a naked chest. A really nice naked chest and beautiful dark, sinfully delicious eyes. "Aren't you cold?"

He chuckled. Had a nice smile on his oh-so-nice face. "No, I'm not the one fighting off a fever."

Fever? She stared at him, trying to decide if she was truly awake then turned her head, taking in her surroundings. Dried weeds hung from vines. Ladder over there that went up to a loft. Odd shaped walls of wood.

A deep breath of lavender eucalyptus snapped her jumbled thoughts into order.

I get it. She was still in this freaky world with...her eyes shifted back to hot, bare-chest guy...medicine man. Jaxxson, aka the healer, and not naked, unless he'd ditched the sarong.

He must have levitated the slab table she was stretched out on because she could only see from the middle of his abs up. He didn't have a body all cut with muscle like that guy Callan, but she found she liked Jaxxson's lean physique. More her style. Her gaze kept climbing higher up his tanned skin, up to the stern chin, up to the sharp cheeks and... smack, back to the dark brown eyes observing her with wary caution.

What had she done or said to get that look? Had the mixture he'd crushed in that bowl caused her to babble something about her ability to hear other people's thoughts? "What happened to me?"

"The infection accelerated when you got upset. It spiked sharply, cutting off your air supply. You started suffocating. I treated you, then checked on the new child brought into our village."

Infection. From the vines. Right.

But he wasn't telling her something. She'd been burning up and in pain. He'd mixed a poultice of some type in a bowl then she started getting worse to the point that...

Glaring at him with unveiled accusation, she asked, "Did you touch me?"

"Yes."

"I told you not to." She dug those last moments of lucidity up from the dregs of her mind, recalled him grabbing her wrist.

She'd heard a thought just as she'd lost consciousness.

What had he been thinking?

What had they been talking about?

Irritation migrated back into Jaxxson's face. "If I *hadn't* touched you, you wouldn't be here to berate me for executing the duty I'm sworn to perform, which is saving a life if I can. Even one who lacks appreciation."

She thumped her fingers against the table slab, accepting that she owed him and was behaving like a wounded animal. "Thank you."

"You're welcome."

They stared at each other, a visual stand off until he lifted two fingers to graze his chin as he speculated on something. "About touching you."

Here it comes. *What's wrong with you? Why won't you let anyone touch you? That's not normal.* "Go ahead. Ask."

"Why do you fear touch? How have you survived to this age without allowing any physical contact?"

She hadn't expected that second question.

No one had cared that she hadn't been embraced in years, not after she'd convinced her father and the staffs at multiple schools that she had very sensitive skin and touching caused her actual pain. It hadn't taken long for word to get around that she was the weird kid to be avoided. She'd never so much as held hands with a boy much less kissed one.

If a brief touch opened the path to another person's mind, the idea of an intimate contact such as kissing terrified her.

She didn't want inside anyone else's mind again.

She never wanted to cause another death.

Jaxxson waited quietly for her answer, showing patience she hadn't thought he possessed when she'd first followed him from the Isolation Unit. People never believed the truth. So she gave him the same patent answer she handed to everyone who asked about her phobia.

"No big deal. My skin is sensitive so I don't like to be manhandled. That's it." With her reaction to the vine, that should be an easy sale this time.

"Why are you lying?"

How had he known that? "Are you a mind reader?"

He studied her with narrowed eyes. "Mind *reader*?" Then he stared straight ahead, thinking. "An outdated term, but that would make sense."

Awestruck at what he was admitting, she whispered, "You *did* hear my thoughts didn't you?"

"No. That would be inappropriate to enter your mind without an invitation." His shoulders lifted in dismissal. "It was simple to see that you lied. I used my empathic ability to read the changes in your body."

Good grief. *Someone weirder than me.*

He reminded her, "You still haven't answered my question. Why did you lie when you are clearly disturbed by being touched? I'll grant that you did have a reaction to the vine, but I don't believe that's the reason you avoid contact."

Something he'd said a moment ago struck her. "Did you say it would be inappropriate to enter a mind uninvited?"

"Yes."

"So you can enter someone else's mind if they invite you?"

"Yes, of course. Why is that surprising? It's a simple matter of training for some and bonding for others."

"So I'm not the only one," she murmured to herself.

"You try to hide this ability by not touching? Why?"

This had to be the most bizarre conversation she'd ever had. How could he act as though picking up thoughts was as natural as breathing? What would be the point in trying to lie again with someone like him? She admitted, "You're right. I hear thoughts through touch, but I hate it."

She especially hated the day she'd heard her mother's thoughts about sleeping with another man who wasn't Gabby's dad. Barely ten years old, Gabby had blurted out, "Why were you in bed with that man?"

"What man?" her mom had stammered, squeezing Gabby's hand harder.

"The yellow-haired one. At the Four Seasons where we've had tea. The hotel."

Her mother had backed up from her, demanding in a frightened voice, "How'd you know?"

Gabby told the truth. "I saw it in your mind." She raised their joined hands and looked at them, whispering, "I see things when I touch you."

That was the day her mother backed away from Gabby with a look of horror on her face. Her mom normally only drank at home, but she grabbed a bottle of liquor and jumped in her convertible Mercedes, squealing tires when she tore away from their home. Hours later, the police arrived to inform Gabby's father that her mother had died in a single car collision. She'd been ejected when she lost control and the car rolled down an embankment.

Gabby developed her skin phobia the day she killed her mother.

"Did you hear me?" Jaxxson said, snapping his fingers in front of her face.

"No. What?"

"I asked why you listen to other people's thoughts via touch if it bothers you? And to do so is wrong anyhow."

Her temper came back with a vengeance. "I hate to point out the obvious, but *if* I could prevent hearing them, don't you think I would?"

Jaxxson dropped his arms to his side, angling his head and frowning with exasperation. "Our children learn to shield their minds by the time they can write their names."

"You can do this, too?"

"Of course."

Pushing herself up, she scooted back to sit up. To get out of a vulnerable position. Lying down reminded her of too many visits with mental health professionals. She lifted her wrists to find the swelling had gone down, her hands flexed normally again. So Jaxxson was some kind of doctor after all, but he'd also been able to access her thoughts while she was out of it.

She asked point blank, "I'm having a hard time accepting that you didn't listen to my thoughts."

"Entering someone's mind when they are defenseless is no different than entering someone's home uninvited. I am not an intruder."

Where were these people from? "I've never met anyone else who can do this."

"So you were telling the truth."

"About what?" She had the feeling she was about to find

out what had caused that wariness still hanging in his gaze.

"That you were born in 1997."

"Oh, that. Well, of course, it's the truth." Her whole body relaxed. "Look at me. Don't I *look* sixteen?"

She might have gotten an early gift from the booby fairy, but she had a baby face that had never been mistaken for being older.

What was the big deal about her age?

Then out of nowhere, the thoughts she'd heard from Jaxxson's mind a second before she'd lost consciousness rushed forward.

She lies. . . impossible. . .I was born in–.

Her jaw dropped. "Now I remember. I had no way to stop myself from hearing *your* thoughts. You were thinking about being born in...2162." No way. No freakin' way. Unless . . ."What planet are you from?"

"It's known as Earth."

"That can't be possible. I'm from Earth, too, and 2162 hasn't happened yet."

But he was shaking his head. "I don't understand. How can you be here?"

"Right back at ya."

"What?"

She gave him a half grin, feeling it wobble around the edges as she grappled with what she was saying. "It means I'm asking you the same question. Really? Seriously? If you were born in 2162 then what year do *you* live in?"

"2179."

No way. "Are we in some kind of weird time travel warp?"

"No, the tek-nah-tee would never risk sending one of *us* back in time."

This conversation got stranger by the minute. If not for seeing purple and green striped skies, having traveled here through a computer, fought killer flowers and watched giant croco-monsters climb out of the ground, Gabby might actually be surprised by meeting someone from the future.

She reminded herself to roll with it. "What are these tek-nah-tees? Bad boy teckies or what? Sounds like naughty techs."

After a long moment, the suspicion and irritation that had held his face hostage disappeared. He actually smiled and folded his arms, starting off explaining by spelling MystiK and TecKnati. "Many years ago, civilization divided up between the MystiKs and the TecKnati. The TecKnati excelled in science and technology while our MystiKs developed gifted skills and supernatural powers with each generation becoming stronger."

"Why'd the TeK dudes put you in this place? And if this isn't a time warp, where am I?"

"V'ru says this Sphere is an artificial planet. A satellite."

"V'ru? Is that a guy or a girl? A MystiK or a TecKnati?"

Jaxxson looked as if he couldn't decide if she was joking. "A male MystiK. V'ru is from the Records House, a rare G'ortian no less."

"Does that mean he keeps journals for you?"

"His gift is much more sophisticated than that. Upon being captured and arriving here, he assessed the contents of this Sphere and began identifying the plants and animals that are from other planets the TecKnati have been exploring and placing in this Sphere. The TecKnati are capturing young MystiKs and sending us here, using this as a holding facility."

Was this Jaxxson for real? "Why?"

"We're in constant conflict with the TecKnati. They see our gifts and powers as impeding research and expansion plans in space that they feel will assure us natural resources and a better way of life as our world rebuilds. We see their technology as exposing us to greater risks outside of earth and threatening our ability to continue developing powers due to health risks caused by technology."

"Who'd have thought?" she murmured.

"The TecKnatis are at heart fearful of any threat against their supremacy. We now believe SEOH, their leader, plans to rid our world of powerful MystiK rulers who pose a greater threat to TecKnati than before, even though the TecKnati claim no respect for our powers."

"So the TeK guys want to get rid of you and have all of earth for themselves?"

Jaxxson nodded. "Currently they control the ten cities, but

that's not enough for them."

"Your whole world is limited to only ten cities?"

"Yes. Our records indicate that once there were many more, but now..." He shrugged and glanced away.

"What happened?"

"The K'ryan Syndrome wiped out populated areas around the world, including North America, leaving small groups of people in isolated outposts. As the survivors joined up, they made their way to ten cities that were still physically intact and capable of sustaining a sizable population."

Unfreakingbelievable. Gabby couldn't form a thought, but Jaxxson didn't seem to notice and kept talking.

"The great TecKnati minds came from those sequestered in remote research locations and labs. Powerful MystiKs developed from those who had chosen a more simplistic way of life, living in areas away from any civilization. Each of the cities in the new world is encircled by an energy field that is controlled by the TecKnatis, as is all travel between cities."

"Why do you need an energy field?"

"For protection. The virus didn't kill everyone. One particular group became rabid and, even though they were destroyed, there is fear that other infected humans might come to the cities. I admit the energy field keeps us safe, but there is a price to pay for giving TecKnati that power over us."

"So that's what's going on in the future." She didn't want to tell him his world sounded like it sucked, big time, and she had another burning question. "How did we end up here? In this Sphere place?" she wondered aloud.

"Wait a moment." Jaxxson walked away and lifted a stump that had been cut from the middle of a tree trunk and brought it over to place next to her.

Gabby enjoyed the rare opportunity of admiring a male up close while he was unaware that she checked him out. Jaxxson's lean body flexed with hidden strength. She'd never spent time with someone who looked like him.

Get real. She'd never spent time up close with any guys.

He sat down, now on eye level with her, which she appreciated. He admitted, "I don't understand how or why the three of you arrived...if you are not TecKnati."

"There's not much else I can say other than we're not. At some point, you have to decide to believe me or not." She hoped he took that in the spirit it was offered.

He nodded. "Until I see differently, I accept that you were not sent by SEOH. As for your being here, I can only think that the TecKnati made some error to bring someone into this Sphere from the past. V'ru says there is evidence of TeK time-travel research, but every confirmed report indicates that as yet they can only send a person into the past, not bring one forward."

She was so going to blow Tony's mind when she told him all this. *If* she told him. "You said the TecKnati never send someone like *you* back. What did you mean?"

"TecKnati would never send a MystiK into the past and risk MystiKs alerting the world to the strategies of TecKnati in the future, otherwise MystiKs would become even more powerful over time. A bigger threat to TeKs. TeKs send only their own kind into the past."

"Time travel," she whispered, marveling at what was going on in the future one minute and still in shock the next.

"But we have no report of this being successful so they may have killed everyone they experimented on. They don't value life as we do so we think they are only sending those they consider disposable on missions to the past."

"How would they know if they were successful?"

"I don't know for sure. Our reports confirm that the TecKnati have not found a way to communicate with someone once that person enters their time travel portal. And since the TecKnati are very good about shouting their accomplishments to all the cities, I trust we would've heard if they'd succeeded in teleporting to the past and returning. At least, that's our most recent news."

"How would you know in this place?"

"MystiK children are dropped here fairly regularly. The older ones arriving bring reports from home."

"Wow, this is over-the-top crazy," she murmured. "And people think *I'm* a freak."

"Why?"

She gave him her best duh look. "Because I hear thoughts.

Where I come from that brands you as strange, a sideshow act, to be avoided at all costs."

Jaxxson's face tightened and his eyes darkened. Why did that make him angry?

Shaking his head as though what she'd shared was irrational, he said, "Although I've not studied all ancient worlds, I knew our gifts were not once celebrated and appreciated as they are now. But I had no idea those with our abilities who lived two centuries back were persecuted."

"Persecuted is a strong word," she argued, thinking of the entire civilizations lost or abused at the hands of evil people.

"It's not strong enough if you've spent your life without basic human comfort because of being born with a gift. To treat one as that in our MystiK world is to face punishment, because the gifted are rebuilding our world and protecting our future."

Good grief. He made her sound like something special.

Valued.

She couldn't wrap her head around that.

Or that he came from the future.

If not for having Rayen and Tony on this whacked-out trip, she'd think this was all some insomnia-induced dream. Speaking of Rayen and Tony, she had to do her part and get as much information as possible on how to get out of this place. She'd been so engrossed by talk of the future–could that all be true?–she didn't know where to start. Since Jaxxson claimed to be a captive as well, she led with that.

"I've figured out that none of you want to be here," Gabby began. "Can't you escape?"

"No. Only TecKnati scouts can operate the transenders."

"That metal thing that spit us out here?" She described it further.

"Yes."

If only TecKnati could operate the pods, what did that say about going home to Albuquerque? Had that little girl Rayen rescued traveled in their same pod since she was dumped in the clearing they'd been ejected into?

What a weird place, but one where her strange ability was accepted. No, celebrated as special. And Jaxxson could teach her so much.

Staying here had huge benefits, for a short time anyway, while she learned from Jaxxson, but she had to help Tony and Rayen find a way home. This was a dangerous place where people with abilities were held as prisoners.

And too easily died.

She could see why everyone had reacted so strongly to her, Tony and Rayen.

Still, where had Jaxxson's antagonism from earlier gone when he'd seen her as a hybrid or whatever that word was? "I appreciate that you're no longer looking at me like I'm a devil spawn, but what changed your mind about 'my kind' as you called me?"

He took a moment to answer, looking chagrined. "In my world, one with your unusual eyes is called a Hy'bridt, and is revered above all other MystiKs. The majority are women, who are allowed choices other MystiKs are not."

Revered? *Fat chance that'd ever happen back home.* "What kind of choices?"

A muscle twitched in his jaw and his words came out loaded with resentment. "Such as the one in my family who *should* have been the next healer sent to YEG/4. City Four. But it would have meant traveling from ORD/1 where we both lived."

"What's city one and four?"

He thought on that a moment then lifted a finger. "I understand what you're asking. Where would these cities be in your world?" When she nodded, he explained, "Due to my need to understand medicinal resources available in each of our ten cities, I had to study the development of different lands. At one time ORD/1, or City One, was known as Chicago and YEG/4, or City Four, was called Edmonton."

"Those are definitely in North America," she acknowledged. "So what happened with this Hy'bridt girl? How old was she?"

"She'd reached eighteen, her age of maturity, and chose not to leave home. I was sent instead."

"How old were you?"

"Thirteen."

Outrage surged through her on his behalf. She'd been sent here and shuttled there since an early age with no regard to how difficult the changes had been on her. "That's so wrong. How could they do that to you? You were just a kid."

"MystiKs are considered mature at eighteen and expected to take their respective places in society at that moment. Thirteen is not a child in our world. Healers are rare and, with the exception of Hy'bridts, few are female. For that reason, we're trained from birth, prepared to go anywhere at any time."

She waved off that comment, refusing to accept that it was okay to do that to an adolescent. "Regardless. You deserve to feel ticked off about being screwed."

He smiled. "Ticked off? Screwed?"

"Ticked off means angry, po'd, really, really frustrated," she clarified. "And screwed is, well, it means that no one considered what it meant for you to be yanked out of your home and shipped across your world."

"Ah. Interesting terms, yet accurate assessments."

"Sounds like the world hasn't improved since my time." She put her hand on her forehead. "I can't believe I'm sitting here talking to someone from the future. Tony would go bat-crazy if he was here."

"Why?"

"He'd kill to find out what happens with technology and science in the future." At Jaxxson's look of horror, she said, "Wait, I don't really mean 'kill' as in bloodshed. Just another slang word that means he'd really like to know all this. That'd give him an edge in a special school project. I think Tony believes he's the next Steve Jobs."

"Who?"

Now *that* was funny. "Never mind."

Jaxxson stood. "I'd like to continue our conversation, but I must check on the little girl who arrived today."

The one Rayen saved. Pushing away the paper-thin coverings that appeared to be made of pounded leaves, Gabby swung her feet around, dangling them off the side. "Is the little girl sick?"

"I don't know yet. I'm watching for a reaction."

"To what?"

"The Sphere. MystiK gifts and powers are drawn from natural elements in their surroundings. When new MystiKs arrive here we have to observe them constantly. Some react negatively to the elements in the Sphere right away, some later on and some not at all. We've lost children early on by not recognizing the signs. I must return you to the unit before I can see the child."

She didn't want to go back to jail. "I'll go with you."

"Callan, who oversees our security, would *not* be happy with that decision."

"Because he thinks I'll try to escape. I won't." Before he could argue further, she raised a hand, palm out to stall him. "And you *know* I'm telling the truth."

Sighing, he ran his hand over his sandy-blond hair, considering what she said and clearly in a hurry to get moving.

Gabby wouldn't lose this opportunity. "I'd like to ask you questions about how to block other people's thoughts. I'm tired of constantly worrying over being touched."

The healer in him considered her request, but he shook his head. "If you did try to leave, which I'd understand, I'd be forced to contain you and would rather not harm you."

Bottom line? He had powers he had yet to reveal. She got it and let her hand fall to her side. "I promise to be your shadow and follow orders."

"I'm sorry, but I can't do this." He looked at the table and it floated down until her feet reached the floor.

He suddenly became very still. His eyes stared vacantly but concern gripped his face.

Gabby held her breath.

When his eyes focused on her again, he said, "I'm being summoned for the little girl. There's a problem."

"We helped save that child. Take me with you. I'll help."

He hesitated and then seemed to make up his mind. "Fine. But know that even though I believe you're not TecKnati, Mathias believes you are one and as the leader of the Governing House here, his word is final. If you make any unauthorized move, I *will* stop you."

Hair danced on Gabby's arms at the threat in his tone. This was not the guy who had patiently explained his world to her. She swallowed as she said, "I understand."

Following him to where she'd have to pass through the wall

of the tree again, she rationalized that she'd only agreed to not try to escape. She'd said nothing about using this opportunity to find a way out of the village and the trick for passing through the wall of fog. There had to be a plan for emergency exits with all these children in one place.

What if Jaxxson *thought* there was an emergency?

Would he and the others herd the younger children out of the village?

Gabby had activated a few alarms in her past. Could she get away with it here?

CHAPTER 22

When I opened my eyes again, I was propped up against something that sloped back.

I saw soft golden-brown hair that fell across Callan's head and touched his shoulders.

He knelt beside me, bent over, muttering more of those strange, vicious words he said as if they belonged only to him. I enjoyed a moment of studying the strong muscles in his neck and the way his shoulders flexed when he moved. He muttered some more. "...stupid to keep a furkken tek alive...they don't have powers...how could Rayen kill the...no other explanation..."

I smiled over hearing my name again and moved my hand to grasp his arm with a weak grip.

He stilled, lifting his head slowly until molten brown eyes met mine. "About time you're awake."

Sort of awake. My head floated in a fog, but I did feel alive. The pulse in his wrist raced beneath my fingers. I had the strangest impulse to put my hand over his heart and feel each beat.

But I didn't want to bring back his stony face.

I tried to speak and managed only a growl from my dry throat.

Slowly, he tugged his arm away from my hold.

He reached for a furry round shape the size of a large coconut cut in half, but I didn't think coconuts came in shades of dark pink or had furry hides. Come to think of it, was I even sure I knew what a coconut was. Too much to still grapple with. After he gave me a drink that had a tart and sweet taste, he put the nut down and touched a finger to my stomach.

I flinched at the sharp ache, but the killer pain from before had worn itself down to a constant throb. Somewhere between close to dying and now, I must have passed out. How could I still be alive?

"What'd you do to me?" I asked.

"I closed your wounds."

"Really?" I stretched my neck forward to see my abdomen below my half shirt, all that was left after ripping off a cloth for Gabby. The gash from the croggle's claw was now a red welt that ran in a wide line from my left side across my stomach. My arms had several similar welts.

Something tickled my memory about healing, but I couldn't put a finger on it. "What'd you use to close the gashes?"

Studying on his answer, he finally said, "My hands. How would you repair a wound?"

"I don't know. No wonder you thought I'd be able to walk back to the village."

"You can't yet. Not until your internal organs heal."

"Can you fix those, too?"

Confusion fed through his voice. "I can help...but I don't have Jaxxson's skills. Plus I've drained my power getting your wound closed. You have to complete your healing."

"I don't know how to heal anything." Or could I? "Can you show me?" *Since you have magic hands.*

Things had been going along so well, but that question rallied his suspicions. "Tek-nah-tees can't heal with hands either."

"Then wouldn't this be a good test if you'd show me what I need to do and let me try?" Unless I failed and gave him the proof he needed that I was a tek-nah-tee. But would he kill me after keeping me alive? Only one way to find out.

Still he hesitated to make a move.

"Afraid I'm telling the truth, Callan?"

"*Fear* a tek?"

Now I'd insulted him. "I meant, are you willing to take the risk that I might not be one? Me? I'd take that challenge, but you might not–"

He leaned forward, some decision made, and ordered,

"Spread your hands over your wound."

I moved my arms that were still heavy with weakness. Once I got my hands settled over the scar on my stomach, he spread his fingers and covered my hands with his.

A tingle of energy vibrated where he touched me, but I felt nothing changing inside my abdomen. "What else?"

"You have to see the injuries in your mind and focus on repairing the organs."

This would not be the time to admit I didn't see anything in my mind. "I've got a headache like you can't imagine. Think it's interfering with my vision." His expression became even more suspicious, if anything. I had to make this work. "I'm asking for a little help to get me started, that's all."

His sigh came out weighted with irritation then he said, "Lift your hands."

When I did, he slid his beneath mine and spread his fingers over my skin.

The minute I placed my hands over his, I felt warm energy flooding my body. The weight of his touch didn't hurt as I expected after having suffered earlier when he'd touched my wound. His touch felt right, comforting.

For the first time since coming awake in the desert, I didn't feel so alone.

Closing my eyes, I opened my mind as if I'd done this before and this time I did see something. A healing river of heat traveled from my hands down through his and inside me. I saw the shredded damage inside my belly...but how?

Was I seeing it through his eyes?

I pushed the swirling energy like a tidal wave from ravaged organs to torn veins and arteries, amazed at the way my body responded as it began to heal.

Renewed strength poured through me. Ready to be whole again, I shoved the energy hard throughout my belly and side so quickly it ricocheted back to my hands.

He grunted in surprise, having been the conduit between my hands and body.

I opened my eyes and closed my fingers around his. He had large hands, calloused fingers. I felt a pulse beating through his hands, pumping harder the longer he stayed still.

His face was so close to mine, I could see each long brown eyelash around his intense eyes. Was he breathing faster?

From the effect of healing me...or being so close?

I was breathing pretty fast myself.

As for my organs, my heart beat just fine, pumping with the speed of a cougar running across an open field. I was afraid to move and break whatever spell had wound around us.

My gaze moved to his lips, so firm and masculine.

That pushed everything out of my mind except one strumming thought. *I wish he'd kiss me.*

He leaned toward me as if drawn by my thought.

My heartbeat raced out of control. Our faces were inches apart. I could smell his warm skin, a musky scent heated from battling the croggle.

Movement drew my eyes to his chest where the strange colors on his skin shifted, a lot, morphing in hue and shape. I whispered, "Why does your skin change?"

He jerked back, withdrew his hands and stood. The shapes on his skin became fixed again. "Are you healed?"

What happened? Did his strange skin embarrass him?

I didn't think so. No, I sensed anger, but why?

"Are you healed or not?" he repeated, snapping out the words as if I was taking a long time to decide if I wanted to live or not.

I surveyed my stomach. Where I'd had a long welt before there was now a smaller scar line. Looking up at him, I said, "Looks like it. Thank you for saving my life."

It took him a few minutes to decide on a reply. "You're welcome."

Accepting my appreciation hadn't been easy for him, especially from someone he believed to be his enemy.

But joining hands with him to heal myself must have cracked his conviction. "So we're clear now that I'm not a tek-nah-tee, right?"

"I haven't decided. How'd you make the croggle burn?"

So much for *no tek-nah-tee can heal himself.* I had no better answer about the croggle now than the one I'd given him earlier. "I wish I knew."

"Let me know when *you're* ready to risk the truth."

Disgusted, he turned, searching the distance. "Time to go."

I uncurled my fingers, regretting the loss of touching him. Even without my memory, I knew on a deep level that I had never met a boy like him, and yet the word boy just didn't fit in the same sentence with Callan. Besides being ripped with muscle, he had an air of maturity that came from carrying responsibility for many lives.

Warrior, through and through.

I still wanted him to kiss me.

A sure sign that I'd taken too many hits to my head today. Twisting, I pushed up to my feet.

And caught his gaze whip to my chest. My half shirt had ridden up dangerously high but still protected my modesty, though barely. I gave a little tug on the torn edge and heat ignited in his eyes, simmering beneath a barrier of strong will.

Snapping up the spear that had been stabbed in the ground, he turned to walk. "Keep up."

I tried out a few steps and suffered no sharp pains so I hurried to catch up, striding beside him as much as I could along the narrow path. The area around us confused me.

"This looks different than where we passed through earlier on our way here."

"It is," he said, not slowing or looking at me.

I took in our surroundings that seemed more open, less thick brush and lush vegetation as before. I couldn't help but point out, "Seems like it'd be easier to have your village in this terrain. Less lethal than near the jungle."

He made a scoffing sound that ended with him saying, "Think we're stupid as dugurats?"

What had Tony said that sounded like? A moron? "I have a great deal of respect for all of you who have survived living here. I'm sincerely interested in knowing how all this works."

Still no answer. "Can't you, for one minute, accept that I really don't know what's going on? If I did, would I be fighting croggles and staying captive if I was with those scouts?"

Ten more steps then Callan said, "SEOH built the framework of the village where it is. We've been too busy surviving to spend time and resources on creating a new habitat, though we may have to as more and more children are sent here. Besides. . ." He swept a look from side to side. "This area has its own threats, different than the jungle and the denser forest, but just as lethal."

I had so many questions to ask, it was hard to figure out where to begin. But I didn't want to lose the chance to learn more with him willing to share.

"Tell me what qualifies as a tek-nah-tee?" When he made a grumbling sound at that, I added, "Please. If you'll answer my questions, I'll answer yours."

Either my offer, or my tone, must have gotten through to him. Tension loosened in his shoulders.

"Tek-nah-tee seek to control, and destroy, the world through technology."

"That leaves me out then." I pushed a mottled green leaf the size of my head out of the way of my face and admitted, "I don't care one way or the other about technology. How else are you different from them?"

Fine lines formed in his face when he frowned. "Tek-nah-tee have no gifts and don't believe in ours."

"Gifts? Such as?"

"Healing with hands or divination...via scrying, to name a couple of simple ones. I'll not share all our abilities."

I didn't blame him. Never give an enemy that kind of information and I was still marked as enemy. Gabby had just such an ability, or a gift.

But I wouldn't expose her.

Callan called that a simple ability...and healing with hands? Hadn't we just done that? But what about the internal power I'd used to kill the vine and the croggles?

Would he consider *that* a gift?

"You asked me to explain healing so how did you kill that croggle?" Callan asked again, as though *he'd* lifted my thoughts.

"I was just thinking about that. Can you hear my thoughts?"

"No. We have no bond."

I didn't know what he meant, but let it go to answer his question. "You felt energy when you helped me heal, right?"

He nodded, albeit reluctantly.

I explained the only way I could. "I start feeling this thing inside me, an energy, something stronger than just being a human. That's as good as I can describe it. Anyhow, that energy starts building and releases when I need it...like when I had to kill the flower vine and the croggles."

He didn't need to know that I'd tried and failed to call up the energy a couple of times today. That'd make me, and Gabby and Tony, too vulnerable. Better to let him think I had a weapon I could use against him and Mathias should my group need one. Though I'd given my word I wouldn't use it against Callan, neither could I let them kill my friends. If it came to that, I'd have to figure out something.

Muscles in his jaw pulsed as he thought deeply. "How long have you had this power?"

"I don't know." Seeing his quick temper flare, I held up my hands. "Before you get angry, give me a minute to explain."

He sent a curt glance my way that warned he was losing patience. "I'm listening."

"I woke up this morning in the middle of a desert with no memory of who I am or where I came from."

That surprised him. "What desert? And how can you not know?"

"I might have hit my head. I don't know, but when I came to, a beast was chasing me and I ended up getting caught by people I didn't know, then taken to a school I'd never seen."

"You recognized nothing?"

Hearing interest in his question, I rushed on. "No, well, that's not true. I did recognize the land and the mountains, but had never heard of the place where the school was located called Albuquerque."

"I don't know Albuquerque."

"What about the Sandia Mountains?"

"No."

"Then you probably won't know The Byzantine Institute of Excellence that we came from."

"No. Is this the school where your *friend* Tony said the computer sent you here?"

I was encouraged to see him considering everything we'd told him even if he had slurred the word friend to remind me of my association with his perceived enemy. "Yes, but it didn't really send us here so much as we got sucked into it and landed in what you call a transender."

"Are you sure someone was not playing a prank on you? Could this computer be an advanced Cyberprocessor?"

Colors flashed behind my eyes and alarms went off in my head. I'd heard that term. "I don't think we were tricked since there were only three of us in an enclosed room when it happened. And the computer we got sucked into was one that had been discarded. All of them in the room looked as if they were useless or old."

Stopping in mid-stride, he reached for my arm. "There were *more* computers?"

"Sure. Remember Tony said all those names like Mac, Dell, whatever?"

His mouth tightened at the mention of Tony's name.

I made a mental note not to bring up Tony again until after I convinced Callan that *none* of us were tek-nah-tees. I pushed the conversation back to what had spurred his interest.

"There were a bunch of computers in one room plus I saw some newer-looking ones in several classrooms." I didn't pay attention to his hand, hoping he'd leave his fingers where they held my arm. I liked the warm feeling of his skin touching mine and picked up a low vibration, as if the energy lying dormant inside me recognized him.

"I don't understand," he said. "Is this a tek-nah-tee school? Or a museum?"

"I have no idea. Don't even know how to spell tek-nah-tee."

He rattled it off without thinking, his eyes staring into the distance. "You would know if this school was TecKnati owned. They mark all their possessions with the ANASKO triangle emblem."

"What's that look like?"

"Three circles and an A." He released me and started walking again, lost in thought. "This makes no sense, but if you truly came here on your own..."

With Callan sounding open minded about what I'd told him, I decided to jump on this opportunity to make him an offer. "If you'll let the three of us–me, Tony and Gabby–leave, we'll take you and the others back with us. We'll show you the school and the computers. We'll get you out of here. Then we'll figure out how to get you back to your world."

He turned to me, hope and excitement flickering in his eyes for a moment, until they dimmed and he shook his head. "You arrived in a different transender than I did. We have to travel back through the same one we came here in. The scouts made it clear that to return any other way would result in death."

"Why would you believe them? How can using a different one matter?"

He smiled as if I'd asked a foolish question. "As MystiKs, we may not have entire cities devoted to science and space exploration, but neither are we ignorant of the laws of transitional travel. If we don't return to our world through the same path, our molecules would rearrange. We might either die slowly or explode upon arriving."

Not good.

Transitional travel sounded strange, but not wholly unfamiliar. I'd leave all the technical and scientific discussion for Tony. Right now, I wanted to keep Callan talking and find mutual ground for us to work out an agreement. I had to offer him something worth our freedom. "*If* we can get back the way we came, then I give you my word I'll find a way to help you escape this place."

"You make it sound possible."

I heard hope in his voice along with disappointment. I understood. I longed to find out who I was and where I belonged, but a sick worry crawled around inside me, warning that I would never get those answers if I didn't return to the Institute.

He asked, "How can you help us go home without SEOH's permission?"

"I don't know what this SEOH is."

"He's the leader of the TecKnati. Each City has its own SEOH, but one is superior to all others. He created the Sphere. He sent us here. He's the one responsible for the deaths of our children."

"Sounds inhuman."

"He *is* human. And he *will* die." The brutal chill in Callan's words told me he would fight for the honor of killing this

SEOH himself. He seemed to shake the emotion off and asked, "Something doesn't make sense. Explain about this school in Albuquerque. Tell me more about where you come from, something that might allow V'ru to fill in what you do not know."

"Who's V'ru?"

"He's an elite member of the records house, revered for his abilities. He has access to all of known history. If there is information on your world and this school, he may have it. But he will need the date the school was opened or something more than just a name."

Why hadn't Callan taken this V'ru to check the transender area? Maybe V'ru wasn't cut out for fighting croggles.

Callan wanted information on the school. I dug up what I remembered from my conversation with Hannah on the way to Suarez's class. That and the green book I'd read in a matter of seconds. "I only know what I've learned since waking up today, but Albuquerque is in New Mexico and that's part of America."

His face went still as stone. "America?"

"I might have that wrong. Someone mentioned New Mexico was a state...that's it. One of a united states."

"United States," he whispered. "I have heard of a United States...in my world..."

I wanted to shout. This had potential. "Really? Where do you live?"

He snapped out of whatever had distracted him. "I live in ATL/5, one of the ten cities."

I read somewhere in Hannah's book that there were fifty united states. Wouldn't that mean there were at least that many cities? "What ten cities? Aren't there more?"

"No." He shook his head, his tone solemn. "Life outside the renaissance cities is too dangerous." His words drifted off with his straying gaze that focused on nothing. He murmured to himself, "How can...ancient...I don't understand."

"What? Ask me, Callan. I want to work together. I'll tell you anything I can."

"Give me more information."

"Like what?"

"About the school. How old it is, anything. As I said, the more information I have to give V'ru the better he will be able to answer my questions."

If this V'ru was all that good, he should be able to confirm whatever I told Callan. "I read a book that said the Institute has been there for four years, so that would mean they opened it..." I paused, calculating the current year based on the date Suarez had written on his board in class. "They opened it in 2009."

Callan stopped dead in his path then stepped away as if too close to a poisonous snake. "The *year* 2009?"

"Yes." Had I said something wrong? "I saw 2013 written by an instructor as part of today's date on his board, so I'm pretty sure 2009 is correct." Had I screwed up simple math? "I'm telling you the truth but you can ask Gabby if you don't believe me." I tried to reassure him. "Regardless of the date, believe me when I say I *will* help you leave here."

"You can't." Horror spread across his face.

"Why not? What's wrong?"

"Because, if what you say is true...that's not my world."

"I don't understand. You said you know of America."

Disbelief rocked his expression. "I do, but I don't exist there."

How could that be? "Now I don't understand."

"I live in the year 2179. The United States did exist in 2009, long before the K'ryan Syndrome. Even if I could travel in your transender, I wouldn't survive in a world where I haven't yet been born."

I thought I couldn't be shocked any more today. My heart pounded faster as what he said settled into my mind. He came from the future? If so, that meant...

The significance of his words hit me like a fist to the middle, raising an even greater concern. If his words were true, Gabby, Tony and I were from the past...and would die if we tried to return to our world in the wrong transender pod and arrived in the wrong year.

Even if I convinced Callan that we weren't TecKnati, how could we be sure which pod we traveled here in?

How were we going to get back to our world?

CHAPTER 23

2179 ACE, in ORD/City One

There must be a faster way to exterminate MystiK brats.

SEOH ANASKO stepped away from his floor-to-ceiling window view of Lake Michigan, a swatch of blue a hundred and seventy floors below his penthouse office in ANASKO Central Tower. His image reflected back from the glass–his face cosmetically altered to allow little room for emotions to show, his hair surgically implanted and a bull of a body even if he wasn't tall–all tools to rule the furkken unwashed masses.

He turned to face Vice Rustaad, his second in command and most trusted confidant...who was pissing him off right now.

Rustaad watched him through the icy gaze of a forty-six-year-old man with the soul of an AI. He wore his short, sealskin-brown hair slicked back in a take-no-prisoners look. A mimic of SEOH's own head of thick, dark hair. A former competitive swimmer, Rustaad's discipline was evident in the way he maintained muscle definition at his age, and a competitive edge second only to SEOH's. "I understand your frustration, SEOH, but the fact remains that we have a potential problem."

SEOH had chosen Rustaad years ago because nothing stood in Rustaad's way once he was committed to a goal...such as winning a gold medal in the International Alliance Games that had replaced the Olympics after the K'ryan Syndrome. SEOH would love to know if Rustaad really had anything to do with the "accidental" death of his closest friend–another gifted swimmer–as the rumors suggested. According to the media,

Rustaad's childhood friend had posed the only threat to Rustaad's winning his last two titanium medals in swimming.

My kind of man.

Undeterred by SEOH's foul mood, Rustaad went on to say, "With the threat against TecKnati children–"

"I still don't totally accept that our children died from some *power* woven into the treaty. " SEOH could only admit that brutal truth within the soundproof walls of his private sanctum, and even here he resented the need to speak of the unspeakable.

"But the evidence shows–"

SEOH held up his hand, cutting off Rustaad. "That our three TecKnati children died as a result of vengeance and a traitor inside our group. Has to be someone who alerted the MystiKs of our complicity in the deaths of *their* three children, then assassinated ours."

SEOH's opinion hadn't changed in the past thirteen months that Rustaad had wisely not brought up the topic again, until now. Damn him for his persistence. SEOH understood collateral damage in any war–and make no mistake about it, he was at war with MystiKs–but he hated losing those three TecKnati teens who'd shown such brilliant potential.

No loss being greater than the death of his oldest son, one of his three most prized possessions. SEOH still couldn't believe his perfectly healthy seventeen-year-old boy had clutched his throat, gasping for air as he'd played his holo games. The security vids in SEOH's home had recorded the entire event.

Screw the furkken treaty.

If not for Furk, the decrepit TecKnati who'd been the tiebreaker on the board of twelve before he'd finally died, there wouldn't have been a treaty. Furk had wanted to leave a legacy, and he had, in a way. His name had morphed into a curse used by TecKnati and MystiKs. Fitting.

Rustaad still had the stubborn jut to his chin he'd walked in with this morning and continued. "My investigation has been thorough and the results speak for themselves, SEOH. There's no way the MystiKs could have known fast enough about the deaths of their children–that I personally eliminated–for them to retaliate so quickly. Each of our three teens collapsed in identical manners. Asphyxiated. No weapons involved, as stated in the penalty clause the MystiKs added to the treaty."

"Words on a vid screen."

"Words written by the hand of a Hy'bridt, initially on lambskin that was blessed by the rulers of all seven Houses and ratified by you," Rustaad amended, bowing his head to remove some of the sting of his words. He added, "Your media campaign was exceptionally successful, but some MystiKs continue to circulate word that they warned us this was how the Damian Prophecy would come to pass. They claim the prophecy begins with the deaths of three children on each side of a battle line."

Prophecy garbage.

But after losing his oldest son, SEOH had taken measures to protect his youngest, the fourteen-year-old future TecKnati prodigy who would follow in SEOH's footsteps. Until the BIRG Con meeting with the MystiKs, Bernardo would be kept under heavy guard with a medical team on hand. His son might be unhappy, but no one, not even a prophecy, was touching one of his only two remaining male children.

As for his middle son, well, the less thought about him, the better.

Rustaad pressed on. "Much as I hate to give them credit, the MystiKs *can* stand in the way of our future." He clasped his hands behind his back, tone even and dry as old bones, an influence of being raised in a TecKnati boarding school with AI instructors. "Twenty years ago, I wouldn't have thought the MystiKs could become this dangerous, but I have disturbing reports that confirm what we only suspected months ago."

"Go on."

"The young MystiK G'ortians, some of whom are in line to be the next leaders, intend to unite the Houses and, when they do, the MystiK power is purported to become ten times stronger when joined together against one target."

"Damned new generation." Accepting that supernatural abilities could interfere with science went against everything SEOH believed, everything he'd been taught.

He grunted, glancing again out the window at the crisp sky, one that was pollution free, thanks to ANASKO. How could intelligent humans believe in the 'abilities' of these MystiK wackos?

Easily. Most of mankind were lemmings, willing to follow anyone even if they were being led off a cliff. "Have people forgotten that *technology* rebuilt civilization from the K'ryan devastation and has handed them a world they enjoy today where the climate no longer destroys the earth? Where hunger is a choice?"

Before Rustaad could respond, SEOH corrected himself.

"No, *not* technology. *TecKnatis.*" He thumped his chest with his thumb. "*We* created this ideal environment that the MystiKs benefit from as well. *We* have placed the protection of the laser curtains around the Ten Cities. *We* prevent the rabid humans from entering our cities. The MystiKs should be on their knees thanking us for dealing with the feral C'raydonians."

But SEOH would never admit *some* things that had happened to the C'raydonians, not even to Rustaad. No shared secret was safe and this could not be found out.

"Quite true," Rustaad agreed, his nod from across the room reflected in the window facing SEOH. "And all of this progress has come about due to your recruiting the most brilliant TecKnatis to work here at ANASKO, because ... you set the bar for thinking beyond the box."

SEOH looked over his shoulder, eyeing Rustaad who didn't have the genetic makeup to suck up. Still, a wary man was a wise one. SEOH understood the point Rustaad made, that ANASKO had attained this pinnacle of success because SEOH not only pushed the greatest minds to reach new heights, but also because he considered the impossible to be possible.

That, in fact, had been a direct quote from the media about his HERMES space program after ANASKO transported plants and animal life from Jupiter's second Galilean moon back to earth. SEOH missed the days of unrestricted development. But the weak stomachs of today's world had outlawed so much, even importing or building sentient predator guardians that could morph from shape to shape as needed. Manufacturing one now would land him in prison, a cage the most hardened criminals feared. Gone were the glory days where he could take whatever action needed to protect what remained of the world.

Guard and preserve the TecKnatis.

He turned all the way around, ready to solve the problem digging under Rustaad's skin and move forward. "If the G'ortians are the issue then we simply capture the rest of them. That will clear the way for the return to unfettered domination of technology in this world." *My domination.*

"I agree, but we're running short on time with the MystiK's BIRG Con coming up. If plan B has a hitch—"

"It *won't.*" SEOH let Rustaad see the truth in his eyes. "Neither of us can afford to allow Plan B to fail under *any* circumstances. Even if I would consider signing the Amity Treaty again at this BIRG Con, the minute the reclusive MystiK leaders walk into the same room with each other they'll realize they're all missing children of their ruling families. That would be enough for them to join forces and turn their powers on us ... *if* they really can do what your reports claim."

Holding his thoughts silent for a long moment, though a deep furrow formed between his eyebrows, Rustaad calmly said, "You've never allowed arrogance to influence strategic planning. Why now?"

"A warning, Rustaad–take care how you choose your words."

"I'm the last person who wants to be on the receiving end of your wrath, but you brought me on twenty-four years ago with the specific orders to watch your back. I intend to fulfill my duty even at the risk to my person." Not missing a beat, he continued. "Our analysts have not come up with a viable scientific explanation for the interference with our last two HERMES shuttle launches. Have they?"

SEOH ground his back teeth, sure that there *was* a scientific answer, but since none had been discovered he had to admit, "No, they haven't."

"Then you must consider my intel that the leader of the Governing House did in fact combine powers within his house to interfere with those two launches to show us he was serious about stopping our space program and he isn't even G'ortian. Can you only imagine what might be possible if the G'ortians succeed in uniting the Houses?"

If not for losing his son, SEOH would be glad he'd had the next in line for the Warrior House eliminated. "I'm not convinced they're capable of the damage incurred in those two aborted launches. Not without help. Logic says we have a traitor, which is why I retaliated." He paused, giving that statement weight. "Someone inside our program who sabotaged the HERMES system only to give substance to the MystiK claims of power."

Rustaad pressed his opinion in a stronger voice. "We erred once in underestimating the MystiK abilities and lost three geniuses–future TecKnati leaders–as a result."

Rage bunched in SEOH's chest and rolled down to his fingers that fisted, searching for a target to crush. "Do you think *I* need to constantly be reminded of their deaths?"

"Of course not, and I don't like bringing up the subject. But–"

"That's why we're capturing their prodigies instead of killing them, so what's your point?"

The dark silk suit covering Rustaad's chest rose and fell with a soft sigh, the most reaction anyone would see from the man. The gunmetal greenish-gray uniform appeared at first glance to be the same all TecKnatis wore, but was very, very different. The color a shade darker, the texture richer, the construction handmade. Plus Rustaad wore the ANASKO tri-circle insignia, awarded to only the most deserving, the most loyal of TecKnatis.

Rustaad cleared his throat and continued. "My point is this. In spite of our captives being no older than seventeen, and many much younger, they're proving exceptional at surviving in the deadliest part of the Sphere."

That did give SEOH pause, but as long as the brats were isolated from this world and their families they were not a problem. He couldn't expend energy on something that didn't deserve his time. Especially not right this minute. He had an impending meeting with his damn board of twelve. They were waiting to be updated on the Sphere.

Eleven now, he corrected himself. "I know you're not here just to debate the power of the MystiKs again, Rustaad. What is it you want?"

"I want you to put aside your prejudice against the supernatural and open your mind to the possibility that if we underestimate MystiKs we risk making a major mistake, one that may end with them ruling this world if they unite."

Rustaad had a way of presenting the inconceivable in a deadly tone that warranted credibility. SEOH tossed back, "I think spending ten million credits out of my own pocket to build a laser grid says I'm giving serious consideration to their power potential."

"I'm not discounting what you've invested in this project, but your primary reason for building that grid originally was to allow you control over all Ten Cities. Control over TecKnati and MystiKs that depended upon TecKnati resources. Finding out the laser grid harmed MystiK powers was a bonus."

"Point taken." In the interest of getting this behind them, SEOH finally let go of his irritation long enough to give Rustaad's point the respect that his second in command was asking for and deserved. In a more thoughtful tone, SEOH said, "I don't see how MystiKs can join together if they're as untrusting of each other as we've been informed. Their lack of unity is one of our best weapons against them. Seems like that alone should be enough to undermine the prophecy you keep nattering about."

"We have to expect the unexpected. *You* taught me that."

"I've allowed you resources to analyze that furkken prophecy, and for what? You said we only needed to grab those two G'ortians..."

"Callan and V'ru."

"Right. Now you say we need more. We can't succeed by chasing invisible threats."

"I understand, but the prophecy is written as a puzzle we're using Cyberprossessing and scientific expertise to unravel. Based on what I learned this morning, I now believe we should locate and confine the five remaining G'ortians we know of."

SEOH missed the days when technology ruled and the MystiKs were nothing more than a group of harmless spiritualists. How had things gotten so out of control? But Rustaad *was* a brilliant strategist whom SEOH trusted, an allowance he rarely granted anyone. "Why?"

"Because at first we believed the prophecy meant the final step would require the G'ortians to join as one. But as we're unraveling the meaning, we now believe that one specific G'ortian will unite all, and we have no way of knowing which one."

SEOH raised a hand in deference. "Then do it. Grab them."

"We will, but we can't move too quickly. G'ortians disappearing draws more attention than losing the other MystiK adolescents. And still, capturing those other five may not be enough."

SEOH breathed through clenched teeth for a moment, determined not to lose his patience. "Now what do you want?"

"To prevent the MystiKs any chance of outplaying us. I'm concerned about the unknown element in all of this that could jeopardize everything we've worked toward. To win this war for domination, I believe we must strike from *all* sides at once."

Now Rustaad was talking SEOH's language. "I'm listening."

"First we capture the other five G'ortians, all of whom are future MystiK rulers, and take them out of play, which will prevent their prophecy from coming to fruition."

"You're sure."

"As sure as I can be. We interpret the prophecy to mean that a specific G'ortian will guide the future of the world."

I hate that mumbo jumbo crap. But SEOH believed in TecKnati analysts, the ones he'd hand selected from the best to work on his secret project. "Go on."

Rustaad lifted his hand, two fingers unfolded as he counted. "Next, we need a successful activation *on time* of the laser grid to neutralize *all* MystiK power before the leaders meet. But to insure our final step in this plan, we must have number three–to locate the sentient computer before the MystiKs do and perfect time travel in both directions, not just into the past."

"I do want that computer for many reasons, starting with keeping those crazy MystiKs from destroying it. But even if we don't get our hands on it before the BIRG Con, we have confirmation that our people in the past are on track with DNA testing and inoculations. As long as we can travel back in time, we're still good."

Rustaad stared unfocused for a moment then said, "True. But gaining that computer would be a game changer, even more so than the grid system."

SEOH sighed, wishing he could just blast the MystiKs to hell and back with a T-970 missile. "Speaking of the laser grid, is everything still on schedule?"

"Yes, but I'd prefer another test before the BIRG Con–"

"No. We can't risk the MystiKs figuring out what we're doing. If we didn't have that idiot Troade in our pocket, the head of his House would have found out about the test we ran in City Three that caused their MystiKs to get sick." SEOH would never allow someone with so little loyalty and backbone to remain in his camp, but MystiKs obviously didn't demand the level of loyalty that TecKnati expected. Creature comforts were Troade's addiction and SEOH made sure the weasel MystiK got everything he wanted.

For now.

Rustaad shifted his pose, slightly, not enough to indicate any change in his non-existent emotion. "We've taken some large risks over the years, but this one is huge. With such a tiny window of time to activate the grid before the MystiK leaders meet the first day of the BIRG Con, we should have a contingency plan."

"No. You've convinced me to treat their powers like any other dangerous weapon. That damn grid has to work, and *when* I want it to work, so we can shut down these invisible powers for-*ever*. Our engineers have confirmed the grid will function exactly as intended. All you have to do is make sure the final grid connections between cities are completed during the twenty-four hours the leaders are between cities traveling, when they are unable to communicate with anyone from a distance. If that doesn't happen, there's no contingency plan that will save us from the fallout."

Rustaad's chest hardly moved with his shallow breaths as if he wasn't alive. "You're right."

"Of course, I am. And I'll remove *any* obstacle, human or otherwise, that gets in my way."

Inclining his head in agreement, Rustaad spoke with the quiet strength of an eagle in flight. Silent, but deadly. "We *will* be prepared for anything and everything."

Scratching his neck, SEOH slowed his pacing, a new idea forming. He'd never been half in on anything and certainly not now. "We need to combat the prophecy crap they're spewing with a counter-campaign that sways public opinion, even for those of the MystiKs like Troade who enjoy life through technological advantages. That way, when we take control through the grid and/or the computer, the majority will not buck us. Lemmings do not fight."

"What are you thinking?"

"We launch a massive campaign to remind the world that it's TecKnati scientific and technological advances that brought us back to a civilized existence after the K'ryan Syndrome. Get a marketing team working on feel-good initiatives. I want to see a presentation by tomorrow."

A musical hum turned SEOH's attention to a holographic image of his AI female assistant. He said, "Yes, Leesa?"

Her soft voice floated into the room. "The ANASKO Board is assembled for your meeting."

"Thank you." When the image disappeared, SEOH pinched the bridge of his nose. "I wish I knew who was stirring up the board this time." SEOH would eliminate that headache just as he had Komaen and Furk. A fitting end for Komaen, a man whose name translated as "being sent to eternal sleep."

"They are old, SEOH. With Komaen himself gone, the rest are more cranky than actually problematic as long as–"

"I keep them content about the Sphere?" SEOH finished.

"Exactly."

"Let's go." SEOH led the way to his private interoffice shuttle that whisked him and Rustaad away at a speed that would blur the eyes, but which the human body hardly felt. Another technological breakthrough thanks to ANASKO's efforts.

ANASKO headquarters had been built as an octopus-like structure, with arms spreading from the main building that supported entire divisions and landing pads, the interoffice transport shuttle capable of moving in any direction.

They stepped out of the shuttle into a circular conference room protected by hyper-glass that only a quad-laser could penetrate. Turbo-projectiles were mounted within the infrastructure of the compound that could be launched within two seconds if the ANASKO defense system picked up an approaching threat that could not be otherwise contained.

A paranoid man worried about threats.

A powerful man prepared for an attack.

Once inside the spacious room, Rustaad marched to a titanium antigravity podium positioned the side of the massive circular table where he would perform vid relays as SEOH directed him.

SEOH sauntered to his spot at the table where he stood between AB One, or ANASKO Board member One, and AB Twelve. The seat for AB Seven remained empty, waiting for the board to replace Komaen. The board would make a decision soon, once the four most qualified candidates completed the complex steps of high-level clearance. It had already been over a year and a half since Komaen met his demise, but one could not rush some procedures, especially those written by his own father.

Names were not used in meetings to limit any social intrusion on business. SEOH had no choice but to use Komaen's *now* after SEOH had awarded a special tribute to show his deepest respect for the man he'd quietly eliminated. "Good morning, ANASKO Board. I have the quarterly progress report on the newly christened Komaen Sphere that you requested."

He nodded at Rustaad who moved his fingers silently at the podium control panel. Individual holo-vid screens appeared immediately in front of each seated board member.

SEOH continued. "This is a short vid showing the adaptability of the MystiK children in the current trial Sphere." He waited as several scenes scrolled by with images of happy children living in stylized cabins built from natural sphere materials. Next to the lush setting landscaped with exotic plants and welcoming grass, some of the children splashed in a man-made lake while others played games. All were dressed in simple, but colorful, tunics also made of natural materials that looked as though they were found within the Sphere.

Well, materials found within *one* part of the Sphere.

AB Five lifted his wrinkled gaze to SEOH. "I see only one who could be close to maturity age. Your original report indicated a number of sixteen and seventeen-year-old MystiKs captured."

SEOH had no intention of telling this bunch just how many kids, or which ones, he'd captured. The board of twelve only needed enough information to keep them content that the children were safe and happy.

All eyes lifted to SEOH when he opened his arms, palm out, the expression of an indulgent father on his face. "As many of you pointed out when we first discussed this, the MystiK teens are no different from our own and had to be given the same consideration as our children in this situation. Because certain children are not in view does not mean they're not within the Sphere. When have we ever been able to control youth when they were out of our sight?"

Most of the men chuckled agreeably with knowing looks, having dealt with errant teens in their own lives, even if the experience was decades ago and more memory than reality.

SEOH gave them a smile in commiseration. "We do have Mathias of the Governing House and Callan of the Warrior House. In fact, we even have V'ru of the Records House."

That snagged their attention. Approval murmured through the room.

Capturing V'ru had been an accident, but a providential one since the boy rarely left his family home. V'ru had been near Callan, an unexpected double trophy that SEOH had no problem taking credit for capturing.

AB Five thumped the table, shoving his frown at SEOH. "But where *are* Callan, Zilya, V'ru and Mathias? Are they adjusting well or not?"

Once the room quieted again, SEOH explained in a patient voice he had to dig deep for. "All the children are doing fine, better than fine. Our scouts informed each of the captives that they would only be in the Sphere while the MystiKs and TecKnatis work out our differences for the joint benefits of our children. Mathias and Callan are future leaders of their respective Houses, headstrong teens. I doubt any of you will be surprised to learn that those two took a few of the more adventurous children with them and went exploring. I find that to be a positive sign."

"How so?" AB One asked from his left.

"The Sphere was originally created to test the adaptability of plants and animals," SEOH said, just getting warmed up for his speech. Discovering life on a planet previously thought of as only a subsidiary moon had been significant and eye-opening. And the timing could not have been better as he'd already envisioned a way to use the fact that life could exist elsewhere as a strong reason to eliminate the MystiK vermin once and for all, without damage to TecKnatis.

MystiKs should jump at the chance to rule their own planet once he took away their power in this world.

He could feel the anticipation in the room and launched into his presentation. "When we faced the possibility that the next transfer of MystiK power to the new rulers coming of age might interfere with our HERMES Intraspace plans. . ." He paused for effect, adding, "The greatest program in the history of mankind," then continued.

"The Komaen Sphere offered a second value for our investment by becoming a holding facility for these teens while we negotiate with the MystiKs. Their families must meet us halfway and agree that the only way we will continue to survive and thrive as a civilization is through a joint effort."

Wrinkled necks wobbled with heads nodding. Thumps from fisted hands on the table drummed three times around the room, the premier sign of agreement.

He had them. "The exciting thing about how these children are adapting so quickly and clearly enjoying the Sphere is that first of all they're secure and content. Number two is that this is a longer-term peaceful option for the MystiKs who do not want to...work with us."

AB Five had taken Komaen's place as SEOH's most annoying board member. He sat back, fingers tapping silently on the table. "Are you suggesting that all of the MystiKs would consider *living* in the Sphere? It's only slightly larger than the ten cities."

So AB Five believed.

"Putting them in the Sphere would be better than what happened to the C'raydonians when they refused to cooperate and threatened the TecKnatis," AB Four muttered.

SEOH withheld a smile at the single board member he could always count on. One of the TecKnati children who'd died of asphyxiation on the heels of the first MystiK child Rustaad eliminated had been AB Four's only son. That board member would enjoy seeing where Callan and Mathias were really living in the Sphere.

But no one other than SEOH and Rustaad could be privy to *all* the activities that went on in the Komaen Sphere.

Rumbling conversation swept around the table until SEOH answered AB Five. "The entire MystiK population would clearly not fit in the Sphere. But if we can't come to an agreement with them before the MystiKs hand over power to their next generation of leaders, who are consistently showing more abilities and less willingness to work with TecKnatis, we have to accept the possibility of significant technological and scientific destruction at their hands."

The room erupted with a clash of opinions, arguing with each other whether this level of power was even possible and, if so, would the MystiKs risk destroying their own world?

The majority feared MystiKs. Which worked in SEOH's favor.

SEOH might not believe the MystiK power to be indefensible, but many of these old bastards had lived during the first effects of the fallout from the K'ryan Syndrome and still shuddered over several unexplained phenomenon that had occurred since then.

Catching Rustaad's eye, SEOH nodded, ready to add fuel to SEOH's self-made fire.

Screams spewed from the vids, drawing silence in the room when every set of eyes watched in horror as the last space launch ended in disaster with flaming metal debris slicing through people racing from the observation stands. TecKnati friends and family were lost that day.

The downside of living to an old age, as these board members had, was that every one of them had been affected by disasters such as this one.

And every board member believed the MystiKs had been behind the destruction. SEOH had made sure they believed.

"Gentlemen," he said softly this time, addressing them as human beings instead of numbers. "We owe it to the future of this world to stop the insanity. What I'm suggesting is that if the MystiKs refuse to join us in developing and protecting this fragile world we call home, that we protect our future by gifting them with a planet to make their own. We start by taking their next most powerful generation of leaders and sending them to the planetary outpost first."

That is, if we don't manage to eradicate the entire bunch by sending the K-virus back into the past once the inoculations for the chosen few to survive are completed at the Institutes.

CHAPTER 24

Where was Rayen? Had they killed her and Gabby by now?

Tony paced along the groove he'd worn in the hard-packed, green dirt floor of the crappy isolation hut. The hum of energy circulating through the walls taunted him.

No way out of here. Not alive.

When the sound stopped all at once, the change was chilling. He moved to the center where he could turn in any direction, prepared for the worst.

An opening appeared, then a young girl stood there holding a gourd-like flask and a bowl. When she stepped inside, Tony looked past her shoulder until she said, "There are guards outside."

"Figures." He swung his gaze back to her. She might be a little younger than him, but she didn't look like she'd survive more than a day on the streets of Camden where he'd grown up in Jersey. Slender, fine-boned, her hair in strawberry colored cornrows, her tunic some shade of red. She didn't look too threatening, but you never knew. Sure, he could probably overpower her and figure a way to use her to get past the guards, but that wouldn't help Gabby or Rayen and right now he was tired of being alone. "What's your name?"

"Neelah." Her voice fluttered when she spoke and gave him the impression she might talk. Which surprised him. It was kind of nice not to be treated like an evil incarnate the way Sparkle Face treated him. Neelah extended the flask and bowl. "Here's some water and fruit."

"Thanks." No chance to make a run for it, so Tony accepted the food, trying not to act too grateful, even if he was. He took a deep swig of...water? The stuff smelled like perfume and had an oily aftertaste.

Feeling her eyes on him, he managed to look as though he liked the water. "My friends okay?"

Her face brightened with interest that found its way into her pleasant tone. "One is still with the healer and the hunting party hasn't returned."

She didn't seem to be in a hurry to leave, so he decided to make a stab at getting information. Plus he liked the sound of her voice. "How old are you?"

"Sixteen. How old are you?"

"Seventeen." He squatted down to put the bowl on the floor then took another long drink from the flask. Once he got past the weird taste, the water refreshed his raw throat. "What's with all this House talk? You from the same place as what's her name? Zilya?"

She glanced over her shoulder and when she looked at him again her eyes had lost the happy creases. She moved forward, squatting down to his level. "No. She's of the Governing House, as is Mathias."

Neelah said that with a load of disdain.

Discontent among the natives? That could be useful.

Wouldn't Rayen get her panties in a twist if Tony figured out how to get the three of them out of here first?

He hadn't found a reason to smile since walking into Suarez's classroom this morning and getting tied to Rayen, but he beamed one now. All girls liked to be appreciated. He'd learned that about the same time he learned to walk. "What's so special about Zilya? I mean, can't be looks 'cause you're gorgeous."

That hit the mark with Neelah. Her face visibly relaxed and a shy smile touched her lips. "All who come from the Governing House believe they are above the rest of us, even Etoi."

"You talkin' about Zilya's prune-faced girlfriend?" He lifted a handful of fruit, tasted a piece after deciding that if they wanted to kill him they wouldn't waste food by lacing it with poison.

Not when they could use spears to turn him into a human pincushion.

Neelah nodded, her lips now curling in a sneer. "Etoi is a Rubio level servant. The very highest of rank for her position, but she is still just a servant. Nothing more."

"What's the deal between your group and the tek-nah-tees?"

"You're our enemy."

"Not me, babe. I'm not one of them. Don't even know what that is or what you guys are." Tony had an idea. "Can you write those names on something?"

She cocked her head at his request then swirled her finger above the ground and the letters carved into the surface even though she never touched the dirt.

"Awesome! How'd you do that?"

Neelah grinned, dark brown eyes shining at the compliment in his tone. "I have *other* gifts."

Tony had never been slow to understand when a girl was coming on to him. "I have no doubt, babe." He straightened his shoulders even as his mind raced with conflicting thoughts. He wanted to encourage a possible ally, but she could just be jerking his chain so he kept her talking. "How'd you end up here?"

"I was in the wrong place at the wrong time, like Etoi, except that she's glad to be here with Zilya. Etoi believes she will be treated as more once we return, if we ever see home again, but she's wrong."

"I still don't understand." He shook his head. "Who were the TecKnati trying to catch if you were grabbed by accident?"

"It appears that the TecKnati have devised this plan to prevent Zilya and the other future rulers from attending the BIRG Con or taking over their respective Houses afterwards."

"Taking over? Like becoming crowned or something?"

She shrugged. "I don't know this crowning, but once a MystiK is presented at the BIRG Con, they're acknowledged as leaders in training. They begin their official duties as they will assume the role of House leaders within ten years, or upon the sudden death of the existing leaders."

"So these TecKnati people grabbed you instead of the MystiKs they wanted. Yeah?"

She gave a sad nod.

"That sucks."

Her smile peeked out again. "You speak in the strangest way. I must go. But I'll return if I can."

"So you don't think I'm a TecKnati?"

"Oh, I'm hoping you *are* one."

That made no sense. Did she want a TecKnati ally? "Don't take this wrong, babe, because I'd love to have you come back to visit, but if ya think I'm your enemy, why you wanna be friends with me?"

She stood to leave. "I'd befriend the devil himself to get out of this place." She paused then, her face determined. "And I'm not the only one."

In the next instant she was gone and the walls buzzed again, but Tony felt better after the water and fruit. And Neelah's information. He shifted the fruit bowl and flask near a wall so he could pace. The longer he walked in circles and criss-cross patterns the more frustrated he got at being stuck in this place when Mathias had no reason to lock him up.

Or kill him.

He slammed his fist into his palm over and over, ready for a target. How could everything he'd worked for at the Byzantine Institute disintegrate in the blink of an eye *because* of a computer?

Until now, he'd believed his skill with computers would rule the day. That his natural abilities with technology would afford him control over his future and, most important, the chance to find his little bro.

He'd never get Vinny back if Tony had to depend on other people. Gram had done all she could when Tony and Vinny got dropped in her lap as small boys. She'd held off child services as long as possible, but the day had come that the social worker put Gram in the position of losing one or both, forced to admit she couldn't afford to care for two children.

At eight years old, Tony had begged the don't-give-a-damn social worker to take him and leave his little brother who'd only been four at the time.

That's when he was given his first lesson in logic.

Younger children were easier to place, sort of like mutts were cuter as puppies.

Tony squeezed his eyes shut, fighting off the misery of thinking about Vinny. Gram was too old to fight the authorities. She barely managed to keep her and Tony alive, even with him working every minute he wasn't in school.

The day she told him only wealthy and powerful people got to choose their futures, Tony chose his and studied nonstop.

He'd jumped at the opportunity to be tested as a candidate for the Institute three months ago. Money and age didn't matter to the Browns. If he made the grades, he got a full ride to a prestigious university. But the Top Ten Project meant going to MIT a year early if he won the competition.

No. Not if, but when.

That was a year closer to finding Vinny.

First he had to get out of this freakin' prison hut...and this nightmare.

If Neelah came back, he'd find out just how willing she was to go against Zilya and maybe Mathias. He should've asked her to go find out what was happening at the healing hut.

Gabby could be dead from her reaction to the vine if that goofball healer in the skirt didn't kill her. And Rayen had beaten one croggle, but that Callan couldn't be trusted. He might spear Rayen and serve her up to the croggle.

Even if Mathias has any doubts about Rayen and Gabby, he's still convinced that I'm the devil's spawn.

He hoped Gabby and Rayen were having better luck.

If they survived.

He swiped a layer of sweat off his forehead with the back of his hand.

Friction sparked in the air, alerting him to potential company again. Good. *Just give me someone who isn't a kid, or a girl.* Someone he could pound out his frustration on if they refused to let him out.

Stepping to the middle again, he faced the blurry change in the wall where everyone had entered so far. Fists raised, he shifted his body into a fighting stance.

When the opening finally appeared, a tall guy stood there in a metallic jumpsuit Tony couldn't decide was green or gray.

Dark, short-cropped hair and a sick-looking tattoo on his exposed neck. Dude made a good candidate for the Scorpion gang from Tony's old hood. The guy was shoved inside so hard he fell flat on his face at Tony's feet.

Looking over at the opening, Tony found Etoi standing half inside the hut with her spear propped on the ground.

She sneered at the guy on the floor. "You two should get along fine, TeK scum." When her gaze jumped up to Tony, she took in his raised fists and rolled her eyes then disappeared as the opening vanished.

The guy on the ground let out a painful groan. The tat snakin' around his neck was a cobra, which writhed as he moved. Tony was so gonna have to get one of them. Floor guy bent his elbows and pushed, tryin' to get up.

Ah, crap. Tony dropped his fists and hooked one of the guy's arms, giving him a tug.

Once Cobra guy was on his feet, he dusted his hands then wiped green off his face and stretched his jaw back and forth. "Not broken."

"Who are you?" Tony asked.

"A scout of course. Phen. You're?"

"Tony." *That's all this guy needs to know.* "You're a TecKnati?" Tony asked just to be clear.

"Course I am." Phen eyed Tony. "Where'd you come from?"

"One of those pod things. Transender."

"What TecKnati brought you here?"

Shoving his bottom lip up, Tony shook his head. "Don't know any TecKnatis, except you. I traveled here with friends."

"Not possible."

"Why?"

"MystiKs can't travel in a transender without an escort."

Tony tossed his hands up in the air and walked away then swung around. "I'm *not* a MystiK or a TecKnati. Got a third choice?"

"C'raydonian, but you couldn't be one of those."

Based upon Phen's dark tone, Tony didn't want to be one of those either. "What's going on between you guys and the MystiKs anyhow? You have a throw down?"

Phen's forehead wrinkled and he stared harder. "Your clothes and speech...I've never seen or heard anyone like you."

Making a chuffing noise, Tony gave him a wry smile. "Not surprised. There's only one o'me."

"You say that as if it is a positive."

Tony caught the insult and considered poppin' the mouth that uttered it, but he had a chance to find out how to get out of here if this guy played 'escort' in the pods. "Where's home for you?"

"TeK City Two."

"What planet, dude?"

Phen's eyebrows lifted in amusement. "Earth. What planet are you from...*dude*?"

Earth. No way. Unless this was some military experiment gone bad. But that didn't explain gettin' pulled into a computer. Would Phen tell him anything if this was some whacked out military program? Nah.

Back to Tony's immediate problem—finding a way home. "Do those transenders return to their original destination?"

Eyeing Tony with wary observation, Phen answered with a superior attitude. "Yes. They can only return to where they were initiated, but don't get any foolish ideas about hijacking one. I told you. A MystiK can't travel in one without an escort."

The way Tony saw it, this was outstandin' news since neither he, Gabby nor Rayen were MystiKs and they hadn't needed an escort the first time here. But he'd have to figure a way out of this prison hut first. "I'll make you a deal."

Phen listened silently, his stance noncommittal.

"Let's work together to get outta here. In return, I only want to know how to call up and operate a transender."

Phen smiled at some inner thought. "I *will* escape and without your help. I'm not telling you anything about a transender."

"How can you be so sure you can—"

The power that constantly hummed through the walls went silent.

"See you on the next trip," Phen whispered and put his palms together. He shoved them between the vertical reeds that made up the walls and pushed his hands wide, creating an opening he stepped through.

Tony hesitated only a second then jammed his way out of the hut, too.

Power hummed behind him the minute he stepped clear.

His knees went weak.

That was a close call. *I coulda been a fried Italian.*

Taking in his surroundings, Tony caught sight of Phen who'd run thirty paces away and stopped, swinging his head as he looked for something. Two more steps past a wide thatch of inky black plants twice as tall as Tony that reminded him of bamboo, and Phen halted, his attention drawn to his right. A smile appeared on his profile, as if he'd hit the Jersey Lotto.

When Phen paused, a small-sized hand appeared from behind the bamboo stalks and passed Phen something he shoved in his pants pocket. Then he nodded and snuck off down a path that had been cleared through the trees dotting the village.

Tony followed, tryin' to keep his footsteps soft. He slowed next to the stand of bamboo and leaned forward to see who was there. No one.

When he caught up to Phen, the scout had reached the fog wall surrounding the village.

The guy was running straight for the deadly haze.

Tony called out, "Stop! The fog'll kill ya!"

Phen spared a quick glance over his shoulder but didn't slow down, rushing headlong into the puke-colored mist.

Tony tensed, ready for the blood-curdling scream...that never came. What happened?

Crap. He couldn't lose the TecKnati.

Besides Rayen had stepped in to keep the crazies from executing Tony and had saved the three of them from a killer plant. And Gabby had tried to help Tony when the vine first attacked him. This was Tony's chance to do something to help them get out of here.

He ran five strides and reached the fog where he realized how Phen had gotten through.

The angle of Tony's approach hadn't allowed him to see that someone–probably the person who helped Phen escape–

had cleared a narrow path through the protective wall.

And that tunnel was squeezing closed.

No time to lose.

Plunging ahead, Tony lifted his St. C medal and kissed it. "Please don't let me die now." Then added, "Not 'til I get laid...at least once."

CHAPTER 25

Gabby realized her mistake too late. She stared at the little girl Rayen had risked her life to protect from a croggle. "Can't I just, like, hand you stuff when you need it, Jaxxson?"

He paused from what appeared to be him checking the child's pulse. Her skin had turned too bright a pink to be healthy. Jaxxson said, "I need to get her blood pressure calmed down. She's having a reaction to the Sphere. You said you wanted to help."

But she hadn't thought that would entail putting her hands on the child. And Gabby had also thought she'd have a chance to search for a way out of the village if she tagged along with Jaxxson.

Not going to happen from inside this dome thing surrounding all three of them.

Jaxxson had walked her through a canopied area where two girls who looked about twelve were making aqua-blue orbs appear and disappear for a group of very young children who ooohhed and awwwed. They were inside a woven pavilion type of enclosure. Sort of like a tent only in ratty shape and held together with vines and patched with leaves, but since the leaves were all different colors it had a kaleidoscope look to it. Different but cool.

Jaxxson had walked over to a luminous white bubble that hovered on one side of the kiddie area. The bubble looked about the size of a small bedroom. He'd placed his hands on the outside of the dome and murmured words until the opal glow shimmered in front of him and a section opened up that allowed him to enter without bending over.

He had told Gabby to follow him.

She hadn't seen much choice.

The wall returned to its original form as soon as she'd stepped inside and thankfully found the floor to be flat. She'd tentatively pressed a finger against the dome wall. Her finger sank into the strange surface then stopped as if hitting a solid material.

That had curtailed any hope of her wandering around and snooping for exit points in the village.

"Gabby?" Jaxxson drew her attention back to the child who was lying on a pillowy cloud-type of bed that hovered about three feet off the floor.

She backed up a step. "You know why I don't want to put my hands on her."

The little girl raised a timid, silver-eyed gaze to Gabby. Her tiny bottom lip quivered.

Turning her guilt-ridden anxiety on Jaxxson, Gabby snapped, "Just great. Look what you made me do."

"Nobody's making you do anything. Refusing to offer comfort is your choice."

Now she sounded like an ogre. She inhaled a breath and flexed her fingers, determined to keep the unspoken truce intact between her and Jaxxson, who stared up at her from where he knelt beside the girl. One of his hands had moved from the child's wrist to above her elbow.

Gabby stepped back to the bed and squatted down beside Jaxxson. She'd never been able to walk away from a kid in need, not after spending her life being ignored by everyone around her.

"If you can tell me how to shield thoughts from my mind...I'll try," she implored Jaxxson with a soft voice to keep from upsetting the little girl.

Maybe a child's thoughts wouldn't be as abrasive as an adult's. Thoughts that could be so negative or hateful they had sent Gabby to her knees in the past, leaving her emotionally shredded.

Jaxxson answered her in an equally calming voice without looking at her. "Your body is still healing from the vine infection, but the weave I placed on your wrist will also prevent anyone's thoughts you don't want to hear from impacting you. Unless the other person is so powerful a telepath that they could force their thoughts on you. I doubt Be'tallia is such a threat."

Gabby exhaled a breath, still trying to accept everything in this place. The twinkle in his eyes made it easy for her to joke. "Oh. So I'm wearing the equivalent of a Batman wristwatch for telepaths, huh?"

He chuckled and said, "I have no idea what you're talking about."

"Never mind. But why didn't you tell me about this wristband sooner?" Gabby crabbed at him.

"Because you must learn to trust touch, even when you lack external protection. Place your hand on Be'tallia's forehead to soothe her." He returned to treating the child, moving his palms to cover the girl's abdomen while smiling at her.

Gabby lifted her hand and slowly extended it, fingers trembling.

Be'tallia's gaze jumped from Jaxxson to Gabby, watching with huge silver-gray eyes, several shades darker than the party dress she wore.

Breathing hard, Gabby finally lowered her hand to the child's forehead and braced herself.

No thoughts came crashing into her mind.

Jaxxson hadn't lied. Call her paranoid, but she'd been tricked in the past and hadn't liked it one bit.

But here she was, touching another person who actually smiled at her.

Gabby started laughing, not a loud sound but a private little *hot-dang* one.

Jaxxson gave her a way-to-go glance then returned to whatever he was doing to heal the little girl.

Giddy with having accomplished something she'd been denied for so many years, Gabby used her other hand to hold the child's miniature fingers. "You have pretty hands and long fingers. Bet you could play a piano."

Be'tallia's gaze moved from Gabby to Jaxxson who seemed intent on something then chuckled. His beautiful brown eyes twinkled at the child who nodded, lips curling into a half-smile.

Gabby felt like an outsider. Again. But were those two really communicating telepathically? "Did you just talk to her mind-to-mind?"

"Yes. Why?" He seemed perplexed by her tone.

Refusing to sound like the terminally uninformed, she just said, "Isn't that rude to do with me sitting here?"

"No. It's no different than if you were to ask for a word in private with me."

How could she argue with that? "Wouldn't it be nicer for the three of us to talk?"

Jaxxson kept working some sort of magic with his long-fingered hands, moving them up to the child's neck as he spoke. "Be'tallia isn't ready to talk. Her throat's still raw from screaming when they kidnapped her. Speak to her with your mind if you want to communicate with her. It will help her relax around you."

Oh. Dang. Gabby flushed with embarrassment over not realizing the little girl might be in worse shape than just having a skin reaction. Poor thing had been ripped from everything she knew.

But talk to her mind to mind? Be serious. "I don't know...I, uh, that wouldn't be a good idea."

"Why not?"

Her temper lived just below the surface on most days and the only thing stopping Gabby from yelling at Jaxxson right now was that she didn't want to upset Be'tallia. But her words came through clenched teeth. "Because I don't know how to communicate that way and I'm not messing around with anyone else's mind."

"You can't harm Be'tallia's mind. She's the second born of the ruling family over the House of Developers. She's been trained since birth, how to both use *and* protect her mind. You could choose no better person with whom to test your skills the first time."

Could she do that? Gabby swallowed hard at the idea of actually trying to use her mental ability instead of avoiding it. Then she remembered the weave on her wrist. "What about the bracelet you put on me?"

"It'll only reinforce what you want. You did *not* want to

hear Be'tallia's thoughts so the bracelet helped you avoid that. If you *choose* to communicate then the bracelet will also help."

Could she control mental contact and actually speak to Be'tallia with her mind?

Was she really going to give this a try? Maybe. "You said it was wrong to enter another person's mind so how do I talk to her without forcing myself into her mind?"

Jaxxson nodded, as if she'd earned points with him. "Give me a moment to explain to her."

While he was silent, Gabby watched the interplay between him and the child. Be'tallia concentrated as she listened to something he told her telepathically then her eyes widened as if surprised. She finally nodded with a serious expression Gabby wouldn't have expected on the face of a five-year old.

Jaxxson explained, "I had to tell her that you'd never been trained to speak with your mind."

"That jolted her?"

"Yes, but not in a bad way. It's as much a part of our culture as learning how to levitate."

Of course he'd say that. Why had I been expecting him to say that telepathy was as much of his culture as something like learning to ride a bicycle? Did they even have bicycles? "Are you sure I can't hurt Be'tallia?"

"Yes."

"Okay, then tell me how to do this."

"I'll first have her reach out to you so that you can feel her tap on your mind. When you do, allow yourself to relax and stop worrying about hearing someone else's thoughts. You'll hear her."

Gabby took a deep breath and relaxed her hands then nodded at Be'tallia. In the next moment she felt a light bump, bump, bump in her mind, just as if Be'tallia had used one of her tiny fingers to tap against Gabby's forehead. Heart thumping wildly, Gabby slowly released her fear and opened her mind. She heard, *Hello. Who are you?*

Goosebumps raced up Gabby's arm at the sensation of hearing Be'tallia's sweet voice really inside her mind. Tears pooled in her eyes. She'd never experienced anything so wonderful.

Gabby replied, *Hello to you, too. I'm Gabby. Thanks for letting me try this with you.*

Your parents have gifts?

No.

Be'tallia's smooth forehead creased. *You talk to friends? Yes?*

The child really couldn't fathom that Gabby wasn't communicating with others this way already. She shook her head. *Nope. Never met anyone who could do this until now.*

Be'tallia screwed up her face in that funny frown that kids had when they thought an adult was trying to joke with them.

Gabby couldn't stop grinning. She'd never been so happy as in this moment. *Do you talk to your friends this way?*

Yes. Be'tallia looked away, sad. *But not here. I call out, but no one answers. I miss them...and my mother.*

Gabby felt moisture pool in her eyes. Be'tallia sounded so lost.

Having spent the majority of her life feeling lost herself, Gabby wished she could fix this for the little girl.

And Gabby yearned for the world Be'tallia lived in...until she realized this child hadn't lived in a perfect world. Certainly not a safe world.

Be'tallia's gray gaze lifted to peer at the top of Gabby's head. *So many hair spools.*

Out of knee jerk reaction, Gabby lifted her hands to her hair where she'd fixed her ponytails as well as she could and retied the ribbons. She grinned. *I know it looks pretty funky, huh?*

Funky?

Strange, Gabby explained.

Not strange. Beautiful. Be'tallia's awe brushed across Gabby's mind like a gentle breeze. The child had a cherub's face and innocent mind filled with tranquility.

Gabby wiped a watery eye and said, *Thank you. I've never been called beautiful.*

Jaxxson looked over at her for a brief moment, a small frown creasing his brow, but he said nothing.

Be'tallia's eyes crinkled with humor. *Do they not see you?*

From the mouths of babes, as the old saying went. *People are different where I come from. None are special like you.*

Be'tallia's mouth spread wide in happiness.

Gabby had no way to thank this wonderful child who'd allowed a perfect stranger to speak to her telepathically. If she could do this with a child maybe she really could train herself to the point of touching others.

And have a normal life.

Wait a minute. Gabby wasn't touching Be'tallia.

Sometime while she'd been fixated on talking with Be'tallia, Gabby had moved her hands to her lap where she now yanked them up in front of her face. Then she looked at Be'tallia and sent her a thought. *I'm not touching you.*

The little girl shook her head.

How can we still be talking without touching?

Babies touch. Big girls don't have to, Be'tallia explained, her telepathic voice sounding wry.

Unbelievable.

Then Be'tallia added, *You made my head better.*

Did this child mean what Gabby thought she meant? Turning to Jaxxson, she said out loud, "Be'tallia said I helped her head to feel better."

"Uh huh."

"I'm not a healer."

"You sure?"

How could she answer that? "I don't...can't...never have..."

Jackson patted Be'tallia's cheek, making her giggle. He told her, "Your skin is no longer red. You'll be fine and you *will* be safe with us." Then he sat back on his knees and crossed his arms, facing Gabby. "You work very hard at proving you can't do something. Perhaps you should try figuring out what you *can* do."

She didn't react to his not-so-gentle verbal smack. Even though she'd heard that often from instructors, psychologists *and* her father...*you don't try hard enough.*

Jaxxson hadn't meant that as a criticism so much as an observation. But he was certifiable if he thought she could heal anybody. She could accept the telepathy part only because she'd struggled her whole life with hearing other people's thoughts. And even now she had a hard time believing she'd just spoken to someone mind-to-mind.

But a healer?

If she'd been a healer she could have saved her mother from being a destructive alcoholic. Or healed her own wrists. "I think Be'tallia was confused because *you* were working on her the whole time we were talking."

"Perhaps." He shrugged. "Now for the next stage of healing."

"Why? Isn't she better?"

"She'll be fine. In fact, her throat is healed."

Gabby glanced over at Be'tallia who had the sly I'm-hiding-a-secret-from-you look. "So now you can talk?"

"Yes." Be'tallia's grin exposed a gap in her teeth.

Nice to see that children in other worlds still grew up with some of the same issues like losing their front teeth.

Returning to Jaxxson, Gabby opened her hands. "I'm confused. What's this next step?"

Holding her gaze with his steady, dark-eyed one, she felt a stronger thump on her mind this time and realized Jaxxson wanted to speak to her silently.

She panicked for a moment as he waited patiently then slowly opened her mind. Trusting a child was very different than trusting someone who said he was her enemy. When she didn't hear anything, she asked him, *Can you hear me?*

Yes. When we bring Be'tallia out of this protective dome, she will lose the soothing effect I infused in the bed beneath her. She'll begin to remember that she's been torn from her family. I've found one thing that seems to help ease the children through this difficult time.

You mean separation anxiety? Gabby asked.

We have other terms, but yes, that's correct.

What do you do?

I'll show you.

After telling Be'tallia that she was going to leave the dome and that she might feel different but to remember that she was safe, Jaxxson lifted her into his arms and stood. When Gabby popped up next to him, Jaxxson wrapped his fingers around her wrist before she could stop him.

He murmured a brief string of strange words.

In the next moment, all three of them stood outside the

dome in the canopied area with the other children.

She withdrew her wrist from Jaxxson. "Why'd you do it differently this time?"

"Before, you'd have become upset if I'd touched you. You now know you're not controlled by your gift, but that you're in charge. You knew I wouldn't force my mind on you and that you were safe with my touch. Another step in developing your gift."

He was right about one thing.

She'd never trusted contact with another person since losing her mother, but she did believe that Jaxxson wouldn't harm her.

She wasn't sure she liked that knowledge, after all Tony was still stuck back in the prisoner hut. So until all of them were free, none of them were free. She might trust Jaxxson now, but could she trust him if that Zilya chick and Mathias wanted her dead?

Jaxxson carried Be'tallia to where a group of children huddled together on the ground giggling over something. When he asked them to make a space, the children parted, revealing a pile of odd little puffy animals that squirmed and crawled all over each other.

The critters reminded Gabby of furry four-legged troll dolls with large blue-green eyes, fat lips and a pug nose. Their ears sat up like a horse's and short, thick, multi-colored hair sprouted out the tops of their heads. They had plush cinnamon-colored coats except for the same poofs of rainbow hair sticking out around their paws and at the ends of their long rat-like tails that dragged behind them.

"What are those?" Gabby asked, grinning at the funny creatures.

"Pupples." Jaxxson sat Be'tallia down on a woven mat covering the ground and petted one of the little animals. "They're the dugurat offspring."

"They look too young to be weaned from their mothers."

"They are. We rescue as many as we can and bring them in for the children. The dugurats breed constantly, but are easy prey. They'll defend their young, even attacking viciously to protect their pupples when threatened, but are otherwise docile.

They have a low percentage of survival, because a dugurat brain never grows much beyond the size it is at birth."

"Never heard of a dugurat before." *Well, except for Etoi using that term to basically call Rayen an idiot.*

"I hadn't either prior to coming here, but we have V'ru of the Records House with us. He knows just about everything there is to know about all things."

"V'ru? That's a strange name."

"He was named after an ancestor and is a rare MystiK who was gifted with the knowledge of all his ancestors upon his birth."

"Shut the front door."

"What?" Jaxxson stopped moving his hands. "What door?"

She lifted a hand, waving her fingers. "Sorry. It's an expression from my time we say when we hear something phenomenal. If this V'ru came to life with all that knowledge, did he still have to study?"

"Oh, yes. His has been a life of continuous study, but that's expected of a gifted one such as he, to whom current leaders turn for valued information."

Poor guy. She thought her life sucked, but she definitely wouldn't want his job. Gabby took in Be'tallia who'd sat quietly, now looking like a ragged princess doll that had been dragged through the dirt. Her face was starting to show the stress of her thoughts. A tear slipped from her eye.

Gabby squatted beside her. "Be'tallia?"

The child turned to her and whispered, "Yes."

"These pupples are all alone, away from home. They need someone to hold them so they know they're loved."

Be'tallia glanced at the pupples, still not reaching for one.

Gabby looked up at Jaxxson who was watching Gabby with the strangest expression on his face. She started to ask what bothered him, but Be'tallia was her first concern. "You may need to take her back to the dome."

He shook his head. "She must be given a chance to adjust. Keeping her in the dome will only delay what she must come to understand. I see you're not pleased, but my powers can only heal the body, not the mind or the emotions."

She supposed he was right. Gabby's father had always

provided the best in medical care for her mother, but no one had been able to heal her mother's damaged psyche when rumors of her father's affairs with younger women had surfaced.

Jaxxson reached over the children and lifted two pupples that made weird little grunts and growls, sounding like pig-puppy chatter. He placed one in Be'tallia's lap where the pupple started licking the little girl's fingers then pawing the front of her dress.

Gabby wanted to encourage Be'tallia, but she knew what it felt like to have everyone trying to make you "be better right now." When the little girl picked up the pupple and held it against her cheek, Gabby stood and turned a thrilled smile on Jaxxson.

He then handed her the other pupple.

She'd been itching to hold one and didn't hesitate to take the ball of fluff, running a finger over its salmon pink, aqua and butter yellow tufts of hair sprouting everywhere. Bringing the bundle of nipping, licking, squirming energy to her face, she laughed when it yipped at her.

She sensed a deep curiosity coming from Jaxxson.

Letting her gaze wander over to him, she found his eyes concentrating intently. As if he knew that she'd never held a pet because of her fear of touch. True, but another reason had been the constant moving from one city or country to another.

Pets were like children. Both deserved a stable home.

After a long moment, he said, "We can only heal others if we understand how to first heal ourselves."

She started to explain, once more, that she wasn't a healer, but just then Zilya came rushing up with a little boy in her arms. A toddler. She thrust the child at Jaxxson. "He's stable for now, but he started reacting right away."

For the first time, Jaxxson appeared worried. "How bad?"

"I had to resuscitate him twice on the way here."

"Where's Callan? I may need his help."

"He should arrive soon, but I don't know how drained he'll be from healing another."

Gabby tried not to feel hurt over having just been bumped as Jaxxson's assistant, but she dismissed the petty reaction with a child's welfare on the line. "Callan's a healer, too?"

Jaxxson swung his attention to Gabby just long enough to answer her. "Many of us can heal minor wounds and cuts, but he is a G'ortian, whose powers are still developing and can manifest in many different ways. He has proven to be skilled in healing mortal wounds even though he's not from the Healing House."

Zilya told Jaxxson, "We captured a TecKnati scout Etoi is delivering to the Isolation Unit. Do what you can for the child. Callan may or may not have the strength to help you after tending to serious wounds."

Gabby did the math and came up with who'd been injured. Sudden fear made her voice sharp. "Rayen! What happened to her?"

Zilya kept her voice even and calm. "She was struck by a croggle, but she'll survive."

That flew all over Gabby. "Why'd you let that happen?"

Glowering at her, Zilya explained, "She wouldn't have been harmed if she'd not chosen to protect a TecKnati. You should be thankful Callan deigned to repair her after she saved our enemy."

Oh, boy. That wasn't going to win Rayen any points. Or any of them for that matter.

The toddler started jerking spasmodically. Jaxxson snapped into all business mode. "He's stressing. We have to go."

Gabby was right behind Jaxxson when he reached the dome, but she still held the pupple in her hand. She deposited the small critter into a dress pocket and announced, "I'll help."

His answer was to grab her arm, getting them inside the hut with lightning speed.

She'd just dropped down on one side of the cloud bed and had placed one hand on the new child's head when she heard the little boy's internal screams of fear and pain.

He was in a comatose state. His mind locked tightly with hers. She had to break away, but she couldn't. Put up a wall. Not happening. What about her Batman vine watch? Why wasn't that working?

She snatched her hands away and covered her ears, but the screaming wouldn't stop. She fought against the chaos. Losing.

Jaxxson was saying something, shouting at her. But the words weren't clear.

Her brain felt like it was exploding.

He swung away from the child and grabbed both of her arms, his voice shouting in her head. *Stop it! You're killing him!*

CHAPTER 26

I scratched at the wound that continued to heal on my stomach, still not clear on how I'd survived a mortal wound from the croggle.

"Leave the scab alone," Callan admonished.

How had he known what I was doing when he walked ahead of me, navigating our way through the woods toward the village? "Itches."

"Of course. The skin is repairing."

I kept pace close behind. Following him had been no hardship since I had an unobstructed view of all that toned body. "I still don't understand how you healed me."

He tossed me another of his speculative glances, as if he just couldn't make up his mind if I was telling the truth about landing here by accident in the pod without a TeK scout. "I did not heal you alone."

"Don't look at me as if I'm hiding something from you. I told you I don't know how this power inside me works. I'm pretty sure I couldn't have fixed my insides without your hands involved."

Pondering silently, he led us through the last fringe of woods before we reached the green fog wall coming into view. "Have to talk to V'ru. This is confusing."

V'ru, whose mind worked better than a Cyberprocessor. Was he Artificial Intelligence? Some kind of computer? That reminded me... "What's the big deal about computers?"

He slowed until I reached his side and turned to me. "There's a myth about the very first computer from the sixteenth century. A technological creation with supernatural power that MystiKs and TecKnatis are searching for."

"Why? I thought MystiKs didn't like technology."

"We don't," Callan admitted. "We just want to keep it out of SEOH's hands, because he'll use it to destroy all the MystiKs."

A computer could do that? Maybe it was an AI unit. "Is he planning to use it here?"

"If this computer actually exists and he gets his hands on it, I doubt it will matter where we are when he hits the destruct button. Let's keep moving." Callan led the way to the green fog, then he opened the tunnel through it.

I stayed tight on his tracks, not touching the fog.

The minute Callan stepped inside the compound and closed the fog tunnel, he stopped suddenly, staring straight ahead, eyes unfocused. One blink and he dashed forward.

I caught up to him, striding step for step. "What's wrong?"

"The new boy we saved is reacting violently." He gave me a sharp look. "Your friend is killing him."

"Who?"

"The Hy'bridt."

"*Who?*" I was panting.

"The one with two eye colors."

"Gabby?" Not possible. "Hurt a child? You've got to be kidding."

Racing past a murky puddle of gray sludge and through hanging moss he slapped away from our faces, he said, "Do you hear humor in my words?"

Annoyed-distrustful-stone-face Callan was back.

When we entered deeper into the village, into a tented area I hadn't seen before, Callan continued all the way to a pearl-white dome.

Zilya stood in front of the dome, pounding on the curved wall that surprised me by not budging. "Let me inside. I'll stop her."

I guessed Zilya meant Gabby. But how would she stop her?

Callan raced up to the dome. "Why can't you enter?"

Zilya stopped pounding. "I don't know. Jaxxson called out that the child was dying and he had to stop Gabby from...something. That's all I got. I can't pass through the protective wall."

I placed my hand on the smooth, but shifting, surface that never appeared quite solid. The outer shell really didn't give when I pushed on it. "What is this thing?"

Frantic to get inside, Zilya gave me a straight answer for once. "A personal space some of us can create. This one's for isolating new arrivals." She grabbed a fist of my shirt. "Stop that girl."

I yanked out of her grasp. "Gabby wouldn't hurt a child. But I can't do anything unless you get me inside."

Without another word, Callan grabbed my wrist then put his hand on the wall. Nothing happened. He slapped the wall and growled through clenched teeth. "What's she doing to bar us from entering?"

I didn't know what made me do it, but I put my hand over the one Callan still pressed on the dome.

He looked over at me with suspicion.

I told him, "Try again. Both hands."

When he slapped his other palm on the wall, I covered both of his hands with mine and closed my eyes, searching inside myself for the swirling heat. My muscles tensed with the effort.

I didn't feel anything like the power that surged when I'd fought the croggles and the flower, but my chest heated with warmth similar to when we'd healed my wound.

A second later, Callan said in a hushed voice flooded with surprise, "You did it. We're in."

I opened my eyes to find we were inside a giant white bubble…and I still held his hands.

I dropped them, suddenly embarrassed to be caught holding Callan's hands. With a quick look around, I found the little boy stretched out on a puffy bed of air. His lips and fingers were a chilling color of blue.

Jaxxson had one hand on the child's head and the other around Gabby's throat. Her eyes were rolled back in her head.

I lunged at the healer, ripping his hand away from Gabby. She fell back and slumped on the floor. When I swung around to deal with Jaxxson, Callan shouted at me, "Don't touch him!"

Jaxxson turned on both of us and ground out his words through clenched teeth. "Silence everyone! This child's barely alive."

I shook with the anger of finding Gabby being attacked. If not for holding a child's life in his hands, this healer would be laid out flat. I'd been led to believe this guy would take care of Gabby. Dropping down on one knee, I checked her pulse and, lucky for the healer, I found one. I looked over my shoulder and demanded, "Why were you trying to kill her?"

Callan broke in. "I told you–"

I snarled, "*No!*" and speared the healer with the bulk of my fury.

Jaxxson's hand never left the child's head. "Gabby helped me heal the little girl from this morning."

"Really?" Callan asked, sounding just as confused as I felt. "Then why were you choking her?"

He can ask questions, but I can't? I don't think so.

"I'll explain later, Callan, but Gabby is truly a Hy'bridt. She has to be. Anyhow, she helped with that one, which was good, because I was drained from healing Gabby of the vine reaction."

It took me a minute to realize that the healer was using his voice to soothe tempers in the room. Even mine was dropping a notch, but I still noted that there was a limit to what this group could do with their powers at any one time. That might work in our favor when I found a chance to escape with Tony and Gabby. And we would, as soon as I convinced Callan and Mathias to release Tony.

Turning halfway around, I took in the return of Gabby's healthy color and that her arms were no longer swollen or streaked with infection. The healer *had* done some good. She stirred, lifting her hands to her neck.

Not understanding any of what was happening, I turned back to Jaxxson, "Why'd you heal her then try to kill her?"

Gabby coughed and sputtered, struggling to sit up at that point. "He wasn't choking me. He had his finger on my carotid artery to slow the blood flow, which saved me from imploding mentally."

I didn't have a clue what she was talking about, but she seemed fine now. I reached out a hand to help her up then pulled it back before I made contact.

She smiled. "It's okay. Jaxxson has been teaching me how

to deal with casual contact. He believes I can help heal others, but when I touched this little boy he was screaming so loud inside his head and in such pain that I lost control and couldn't disconnect from him."

Jaxxson finished explaining, his voice still calm and soothing sounding, not looking at anyone except the little boy he hovered over. "By staying attached mentally to the child when she went into distress, Gabby was actually harming him...and herself."

Gabby gulped. "I'm so sorry, Jaxxson."

"No, that was my mistake. I didn't consider that a child in this much anguish would overwhelm you, but once I intervened, you were actually healing him with me as a conduit between you."

Callan glared at me, still angry from our shouting match. I put my hands on my hips and gave him back a glare of equal fury for his part in the confusion. He narrowed his eyes then turned to Jaxxson. "How is the boy now?"

"Still not stable. Gabby doesn't have training. I need your help."

"I'll try, but I may not be able to do much for another hour or two." Callan's gaze strayed to me for a moment, letting me know he'd depleted his healing energy on *my* wounds.

Gabby butted in. "I'm not sure I can really help you, but now that I know to be careful I'm willing to try again."

Jaxxson nodded at a spot on the far side of the boy and waited for Gabby to get settled before he sank down next to her. "You and I will work together."

I wasn't so sure I liked how easily those two seemed to mesh. Just what all had happened while I'd been out fighting croggles? Gone was the girl who normally panicked at the idea of being touched.

Callan dropped to his knees on this side of the child, eyes on Jaxxson who lifted Gabby's hands and slowly placed one on the child's arm and her other palm on the boy's pale forehead.

Gabby flinched at first then nodded a few seconds later, acknowledging that she could handle whatever she was feeling through the touch.

Callan moved to place his hands on the child when I

interjected, "Thought you couldn't help for another hour?"

"I can't heal but I can assess how he is and maybe help that way."

I held my tongue, surprised I worried about Callan as I watched him place both of his hands on the little boy's chest. He let out a guttural groan of misery.

Kneeling beside him, I asked, "What's wrong?"

"This child has a damaged heart. We've lost others who had pre-existing physical problems, then reacted to the Sphere once they got here. None of those had as severe damage as this one." He closed his eyes, gritting his teeth for several moments then looked over at Jaxxson and shook his head. "His life force is down to a whisper. I tried to reach the heart, but his pain blocks access from me."

Gabby raised a desperate gaze to me.

I was not a healer, but Callan had proven his skill by healing me...after I put my hands over his. What kind of power did I possess? What was the chance I could help him now?

Or, what was the chance I might do this child harm with uncontrolled power?

Callan let out a slow breath that carried heavy disappointment, ending my debate.

I covered his hands again, murmuring. "Don't give up yet."

Heat swelled where our skin connected.

He looked at me sharply, but didn't move his hands.

Jaxxson spoke in an excited whisper. "I felt a pulse in the boy's life force, but it's not strong. Everyone keep doing what you're doing."

I closed my eyes and hoped I was doing the right thing when I searched for the power coiled inside me, waiting to be released. What if I released too much?

This time, I used what I'd learned when Callan healed me. Fearful of endangering the child further, I drew slowly. Energy snaked through my arms and out my hands. When the blur in my mind cleared, I realized I was seeing through Callan's eyes. I watched, amazed as he began working frantically to repair the child's heart. With him taking care of the little boy, curiosity pushed me to ease back from watching the organ repair and open myself more to him.

I saw a warm glow deep inside him that drew me closer.

Noises faded away until all I could hear was Callan's rhythmic inhale and exhale. A peaceful place I hadn't known existed. Was this what home felt like? Safe. Welcoming. Intimate. I wanted to stay.

Warmth radiated inside him as long as he centered his energy on the boy. Gone was the fierce warrior ready to battle and the hard exterior he'd shown me all day. Here was a heart that beat strong and cared for others.

The minute he released that focus, I brushed up against grief...heartache...despair that he kept hidden and buried deep.

"Rayen?"

Hearing my name from a distance yanked me back toward consciousness. I struggled, not wanting to leave this place I'd found, but the voice insisted. I opened my eyes to find Callan, Gabby and Jaxxson staring at me.

Their faces were a mixed bag of relief.

That's when I glanced down to find the little boy no longer blue around his lips and fingers. He was sleeping soundly and his skin flush with natural color. "Is he better?"

Jaxxson stood, helping Gabby to her feet. "He's healed. Callan repaired his heart and we infused so much healing energy into him that I believe he's over his initial negative reaction to the Sphere."

But instead of a smile Gabby shot Callan a look that threatened harm.

Callan's lifted eyebrow smirked at Gabby for daring to think she could.

I had no idea what was going on between those two, but Jaxxson must have. He nodded at me. "And we have you to thank for lending Callan the power he needed. I was quite impressed by what I felt circulate in the child's body."

All eyes went to Callan to see what he'd say about my help.

Would he send me back to isolation in spite of what had happened here?

When Callan turned to me, he avoided my gaze and admitted, "We owe you a great debt for saving this child. We probably would have lost him without your aid." He bowed his head an inch. "Thank you."

That must have been what Gabby had wanted, because now her face had a cat-sly, cocked eyebrow and smile.

"You're welcome," I told Callan, aware how he could hardly accuse me of being an enemy if I'd saved this child. Twice. But would this momentary camaraderie bode well for getting Callan to lighten up on Tony?

Jaxxson stepped toward the wall we'd entered through. "The child's safe here. We'll let him rest."

Once we were outside in the tented area again, Jaxxson walked over to a concerned Zilya and Mathias, quickly explaining what had happened.

I caught Callan before he could put me and Gabby back in the Isolation Unit. "We've proven we're not here to harm you and that we'll help you. Tony's not a danger to your village. I promise if you release him he'll not hurt anyone."

Callan's hard expression had returned. He clearly didn't want to agree, but this time he at least seemed to struggle with the decision. "I'll admit that you and Gabby have proven yourselves to not be a threat." I noticed he didn't say we were safe from retribution, but he was still talking. "But we knew with Gabby's eye colors that she had to be MystiK."

I turned to Gabby. "Really? I'm thinking that's good?"

She shrugged in a self-conscious way.

If that made Callan happy with Gabby, I wouldn't argue. One down, two to go. "And me?"

"I have no idea."

Not what I was hoping for on several levels. "At least you're honest."

Callan added, "But V'ru will know."

Mathias joined our group, asking what Callan was talking about. Callan explained what had transpired and Mathias agreed that V'ru would be the final word.

The infamous, all-knowing, all-seeing elite V'ru. I disliked him without even meeting the guy just because of the reverence in Callan's voice when he talked about V'ru. Where was this infallible center of knowledge? Probably being worshiped somewhere. "What about Tony?"

Callan held up a hand, stalling me. "First, I want to interrogate the scout we captured. If he doesn't give me reason to believe your friend is TecKnati then–" He looked at Mathias who said, "I'll consider releasing him."

I'd like to take Callan's willingness to talk with Tony as a positive indication, but Mathias had stopped before sharing his entire thought. I asked, "What if you still believe Tony is TecKnati?"

Mathias didn't hesitate when he said, "Then he and the scout will face punishment for the premature deaths of MystiK children who have perished here."

I knew the answer and still pushed for clarification. "What's the punishment?"

"We'll give them the same chance they gave these children. The guilty TecKnatis will be placed in the middle of a transender docking location where they can pit their skills against a croggle. I understand from Zilya that I have you to thank for giving us the gray box we can now use to call up a croggle without endangering our own."

Tony would never survive against a croggle. Neither would that scout. I had to find a way to sway Mathias and Callan from doing this even if they did find Tony guilty according to the rules of their world.

I didn't know the rules of anyone's world, mine included, but I did know I couldn't stand by and watch anyone sacrificed to a man-killing croggle. But then again, I had not been forced to witness the brutal killing of innocent children either.

Before I had a chance to convince Mathias that killing TecKnati wouldn't solve their problems, Etoi and several of the half-sized warriors came pounding into the village proper, the cleared area where the four of us stood.

"They escaped," Etoi cried out.

Callan stepped to the center of the group. "The prisoners?"

"Yes."

I couldn't believe Tony would leave me and Gabby to find a way home on his own. Or had something else happened to him? I wouldn't put it past Etoi to vent her hatred of TecKnatis on a hapless prisoner and dispose of Tony's body. Or had the scout taken Tony hostage? That had to be what happened, but what was the chance of convincing Callan or Mathias of that possibility?

Zero.

Mathias pushed forward, demanding. "How did the TecKnati get out of the Isolation Unit without being burned to death by the energy enclosing the hut?"

"I don't know." Etoi's dark eyes swung to me, accusing. "The scout was searched before being put inside the unit. He had nothing on him. We didn't search these *others* for weapons or hidden technology."

Callan raised his hand. "Neither of these two–" He nodded at me and Gabby. "Could've done it. They've been with me or Jaxxson the whole time." He turned to Mathias and lowered his voice, though I could still hear due to standing so close. "There's only one way to leave the Isolation Unit and that's by the hand of a MystiK in this village."

I caught the meaning beneath Callan's words. He thought one of their own had released the prisoners. A traitor.

Someone working with the TecKnati?

Mathias merely nodded, his mouth pressed in a firm line. He ordered Zilya, "Organize a hunt. Find them."

Zilya started issuing orders to Etoi and her small band of warriors. Within minutes, another thirty children around ten to fifteen in age flooded into the area, all carrying weapons capable of deadly harm. Some looked fragile and all were dressed in ragtag outfits, but their expressions were determined. A sort of shoot-first-and-ask-questions-later bunch, which wasn't looking good for Tony.

I stepped up. "I'll go."

At the same time, Callan and Mathias said, "No."

Then Callan added, "I can't allow you to help your friend." His next thought trailed off in his eyes.

One look at him told me what he was thinking. If I interfered, he'd have no choice but to use deadly force against me. My dying wouldn't help Tony, or Gabby either, but that didn't mean I liked the implied threat in Callan's gaze.

Gabby moved close to me and whispered, "You think Tony abandoned us?"

"No."

"Strangely, I don't either." She glanced around before adding, "But I don't trust that Etoi not to hurt him if she can catch him alone."

I nodded, but I couldn't stop Mathias and what had grown to be a formidable hunting party of armed warriors.

When Mathias made a motion with his hand for his hunters to head out, Callan stopped him. "I'll go with them, Mathias. Take Rayen to see V'ru."

"No." Mathias spoke just as softly, but I heard him. "I can use the exercise and you take her to V'ru. While you're at it, do me a favor and check on the preparations for the BIRG Day celebration. I know it sounds trivial at this moment, but we promised that to the children and those putting it together don't want me to see what they are creating."

Mathias rubbed his head, giving me the impression he found something tedious about this celebration.

Callan offered, "Sure you don't want to delay it until tomorrow?"

"No. This is the first tradition we've upheld here. I'm not much for parties, but I'll do it for the children. This Tony will be easy to track. Tell them to have the party ready to go as soon as I return."

Callan gave him a long, concerned look.

The grim set of Mathias's jaw softened. "Remember, our first responsibility after keeping these children safe is to give them hope. No matter what it takes to do that. No matter if celebrating is the last thing we feel like doing, always think of them first." He offered a tight, half-smile. "The scout may know this land, but the other captive doesn't. If I find Tony first, I'll return with him, or his body, in time for the celebration. Find out who *she* is before I return. I *must* know."

Then he pivoted away and took off running.

I had to be the *she* Mathias ordered Callan to find out about. But it was the dire warning in Mathias's voice that worried me. Something had changed in the way Mathias viewed me and I had no reason to believe it was a positive change.

Callan snapped around, pointing at Gabby. "You, stay with Jaxxson. A warning. When I'm in the village, he can reach me telepathically if he needs me."

So that's what had been happening when Callan exchanged looks with Mathias and that's how Callan had heard about the little boy being in distress. I asked Gabby, "You sure you're okay with Jaxxson?"

"Yes."

I believed her. She didn't have that empty, don't-step-too-close look in her face she'd worn when I first met her. Something profound had happened while Gabby had worked with the children and the healer.

Or because of something Jaxxson had done to her.

"You." Callan speared his finger at me.

How did I end up as 'you' again? "Forget my name?"

He ignored my sarcasm. "The girl is Hy'bridt and the escaped prisoner you call a friend is TecKnati. That leaves the mystery of who you are. I'm tired of guessing. You will answer V'ru's questions. He can discover who or what you are. Follow me."

My heart hammered my chest with two fists. He hadn't even suggested that I might be MystiK. Not that I wanted to be, but right now that was the only winning side in the war these kids waged with the TecKnatis.

On the other hand, wasn't that what I wanted? To find out who I really was? Could this V'ru know my history, know who I was? And where I came from?

If these children were from the future, maybe V'ru had information on the past.

On the surface, that sounded somewhat encouraging, until I considered the alternative.

What if this elite MystiK V'ru decided I had some type of connection to the TecKnati? Callan spoke of him in reverence and Mathias would make his final decision based upon what V'ru alone revealed.

What would Callan vote to do with me if V'ru declared me the enemy?

CHAPTER 27

What had happened to the jungle?

Tony kept taking in this forest, trying to figure out where that TeK scout was going. This place was just as funky looking, but not as dense as the jungle Tony had traveled through right after being dumped out of the pod. He doubted the thickly wooded, tree-looking growths that towered overhead, or the more open terrain at the base of the trees offered any more safety.

'Specially for a Camden-raised dude.

Eyeing the red moon through the canopy of branches, he used that marker to keep track of his direction since leaving the village. That moon kept sliding down.

What happened in this place when the moon set?

He swatted low-hanging branches that smelled like petro-chemicals out of the way and kept that scout, Phen, in sight. The Tek guy wound through knee-high, berry-covered bushes and trees with twisted limbs. If you could call these things he ran past trees.

Trees were supposed to have brown or gray bark, not chartreuse stripes and tubular leaves. Not puffy and corkscrew shaped things in shades of black, pink and purple.

Tony stumbled over jagged breaks in the ground that could be roots and pushed through a clump of spiky bushes that looked like the barbed wire on top of prison fences. Sweat stung his eyes, streamed down his neck and soaked his shirt.

Where was this scout goin'? Why hadn't he headed the other way through the jungle? Didn't he want to snag a pod, or transender as Mathias had called it, and fly home? The guy moved through this big-ass forest as though he had a specific direction in mind, but kept lookin' around as if he watched for someone. Or wanted to avoid someone. Who?

Don't let there be any other crazies out here running loose.

What if this guy stayed somewhere in this place, like in a guard shack, and was heading there instead of back to a transender pod?

Don't think that way.

This whole place was jacked-up crazy enough.

Tony had never touched anything that could screw with his brain, but just this once, he almost wished he was trippin' on acid. That'd mean there was an end to this nightmare. But no, he was lucid and breathin' hard from more exercise than a Jersey boy needed to work on computers. The muggy air he slogged through reminded him of a heat wave in Camden last summer.

Xena is cut out for this native crap. Not me.

But Tony wouldn't admit that to anyone.

Once he found a way home, he'd prove who'd had the skills for gettin' away from here.

The scout slowed down just before the woods thinned ahead.

Tony hurried, closing the distance to fifteen feet and tucking in behind a sprawling tree. He scanned the wide-open space beyond the tree line.

No towering pod, transender or other transport unit out there. Crapola. This might've been a big mistake.

Phen stood in knee-high, weedy grass, clearly looking for something, then must have found it. He ran two steps and shoved his hand into a...pink flower!

Tony had no time to yell a warning.

But even though the flower looked just like the one that had attacked him earlier, it made no threatening move toward Phen.

In fact, in the next five seconds, a holographic screen appeared chest high in the air near the scout who stood up, withdrawing his hand from the flower.

The screen lit up and a hot feminine voice announced, "*One hour, twenty-eight minutes left to request transender return from Sphere.*"

Tony's heart rate soared. There was a time limit for calling up a transender. He had to find Gabby and Rayen fast.

Lifting his hand, Phen placed his right palm against the translucent screen. A red line streaked around the outline of his hand then started blinking until it turned bright green. The minute that happened, the scout yanked his hand back and the woman said, "*Request acknowledged.*"

Then the screen vanished without a sound.

When Phen hurried toward the open space, Tony took off right behind him. Cobra dude was going nowhere until he told Tony how to get out of this hellhole.

A high-pitched whining started.

He knew that sound and increased his speed.

Bursting from the trees, he noticed a gigantic burned croggle–had Rayen fought *that*?–lying dead fifty yards away. Tony closed to within three steps behind Phen who'd been jogging along. Phen must have heard Tony's footsteps. He cast a ragged glance over his shoulder. "What the–"

Phen kicked up his speed.

You don't grow up on the streets of south Jersey and not be fast in a sprint.

Tony raced ahead, cringing as the whining grew louder.

On the far side of the clearing, dirt and other particles spun an orange-red tornado in one spot. The whirling image of a huge bullet-shaped metallic object started taking shape.

The spinning stopped at once. There stood the pod again.

Busting a gut, Tony growled and powered forward with everything he had. He went airborne, body tackling Phen, taking them both down hard and rolling.

Just like back home when an a-hole kid had pushed over Tony's little brother and tried to run.

Sucking gulps of thick air, Tony jumped on Phen's back while he was still face down. He shoved his knee hard and wrenched one of the guy's arms behind his back. That move exposed the rest of the guy's cobra tattoo that wrapped around a triangular shape like an A with three circles worked into the design. It had a small barcode beneath it.

"Let me go!" Phen yelled, pounding the dirt.

"Not gonna happen until you tell me what I want to know.

Asked you nice back in that hut. Not askin' this time."

"I've only got minutes to embark since the transender is here. Or it returns without me."

Good to know. But even better was the panic in Phen's voice.

Tony growled, "Then time's of the essence, right, buddy? Stop wasting seconds. What happens if you don't get inside in time?"

Phen slapped his free hand on the ground again. "*You* can't make it work."

"Pay attention, dweeb. I'm not a MystiK and I can sit here for hours. Won't take the others long to figure out we've both escaped. They'll be here soon."   And Tony had to have information before that happened.

"Okay. I'll tell. I'll tell."

Tony loosened his grip, but only a bit.

Phen continued, "Doesn't matter anyhow since you can't travel without an authorized scout. Once a transender is called up, you have to get inside in three minutes or it'll leave without you."

Tony leaned down close. "Letting you go depends on how well you convince me that you're tellin' the truth. I'll know the second you start lyin'. One lie and you're stayin' here with me. Understand?"

"Yes. Just hurry. What do you want?"

Nothing like fear to loosen a tongue. Another Jersey lesson learned early and well. Tony started firing questions. "Saw you call it up with your hand on a screen. I'm guessin' it works for more than one hand print."

Phen expelled a pained noise as if he'd made a grave error by allowing Tony to see him activate the holographic panel, but he kept answering as fast as he could spit the words out. "My palm print calls up the transender that brought me here. No one can call that one but me during a moon cycle."

"What?"

"Transenders can only travel to and from this Sphere while the red moon is in view overhead. Once the moon sets, the lunar surface energy diminishes to the point that it's too dangerous to risk coming or going." Phen continued without needing a nudge. "Human molecules have to be suspended while the unit transcends from one dimension to another. We still have a few flaws that haven't been worked out yet."

Oh, man, why can't I have an hour with this guy? Tony asked, "What happens if you miss *this* transender?"

"You can't do that to me," Phen pleaded in a voice pitched high with hysteria. "Transenders are reprogrammed daily. I can't call up another one once I've activated this one. And if the MystiKs find me again they'll torture then kill me."

"Then talk faster. What happens if a MystiK takes a transender without an escort?" If Tony had something to offer Mathias that his group could use to escape here he might be willing to let him, Rayen and Gabby leave.

"Not possible," Phen whined, stomping on Tony's hope. "The palm screen is programmed not to work for a MystiK. Even if they could call a transender, they'd die of asphyxiation once the transender returned if they didn't have the daily exit code entered as a secondary security."

That's no use. If he, Gabby and Rayen found a way to the transender that brought them, would a return trip suffocate all of them? But he doubted this guy'd know that answer.

Phen drew a quick breath. "I've got to go in the next thirty seconds. Have to take this one. Let me go...or be responsible for my death."

Decision made. Tony had no reason to cause Phen's death and he wouldn't trust Zilya not to kill this guy.

Getting up, he helped Phen off the ground for the second time today and told him. "You better hope I find a way home. If not, I'm goin' to be your worst enemy if you come back and hurt any of those kids."

Of all the things Tony expected Phen to say, "Thanks," had not been on the list.

A whirring noise started again.

Phen rushed to the transender and put his hands on the side. He swung his head around and yelled, "Same person has to palm the outside of the transender to open it."

Freebie intel. Sweet.

Two of the tall panels covering the exterior slid apart.

Phen dove inside as the panels snapped shut and the pod

started spinning...then poof, it vanished.

Dusting off as much of the red clay as possible, Tony strode back to the trees to find that flower. When he did, he couldn't convince himself to stick his hand down into those pink petals. But the longer he studied the plant, the more he became convinced it was one heck of a reproduction.

Nothing moved. No breathing in and out like the killer flower had done. But now that he thought about it, there had been *other* big-ass pink flowers around. While hiking through the jungle, Rayen had told him about watching for the flower breathing.

This one acted dead as a corpse.

Good camouflage for a TecKnati transender call panel.

As much as hesitating put him at risk of being discovered, Tony couldn't go back without knowing for sure that he could find this panel again. When he convinced himself to walk all the way up to the plant, and after he'd left his phone several yards away, he thought he'd beaten his nerves. But his fingers shook like old Mr. Belokov waiting for Sol's bar to open. When Tony stuck his arm toward the pink petals they might as well have been shark jaws.

Sweat broke out on his forehead. He leaned over, looking inside the opening that was wide enough for two arms. But he couldn't see all the way to the bottom of the dark hole.

Just do it.

But Phen and these crazy MystiKs were from another world even if Phen had called it Earth.

Time was of the essence.

Ah, hell. Tony took one for the team and jabbed his hand down into the hole. His fingers reached tentatively further...more...until he touched a round knob. Okay, good sign. Breathing hard, he pushed the knob.

Nothing happened.

Curling his fingers around it, he tried twisting one way then the other.

That's when the knob turned and he heard a loud *click*.

A holographic screen came alive just out from his left shoulder and that killer female voice announced, "*One hour, twenty minutes left to request transender return from Sphere.*"

So this place was a Sphere? More to figure out later. His ticket home was callin'.

Looking around to assure no one was sneaking up on him, Tony lifted his hand to the screen. The same red line traced around his palm, blinking, then stayed solid red.

The female voice came on again. *"Request denied."*

Compatibility bitch!

Tony knew, now, that this was not the same location where he, Rayen and Gabby had exited the transender. Would this work for *Rayen* if Tony could find a similar holographic screen near where the three of them had arrived in this place? Rayen's hand had started the computer freaking out back at the lab. So maybe that's what was needed here.

He wouldn't find out if he didn't get back to the village and figure out a way to break out the other two in the next eighty minutes. Based on what Phen had said, if they didn't find their original pod they might not be able to return at all. And they couldn't get the transender activated unless they found the right panel.

Damn.

Blowing out a breath and cracking his knuckles, Tony looked skyward until he had a bead on the moon position that he'd noted on the way here. Using that, he started double-timing it back to the village.

Now all he had to do was find his way without getting lost. Not get killed or eaten by vines. Not become dinner for some weird-ass animal. Not get stopped or caught by some of the village gang.

If he managed all that, and survived, he still had to pass through the skin-peeling fog around the village.

And he'd thought growin' up in Jersey was rough.

Tony found a stick that had a velvet-like bark and started thrashing his way back. He kept checking the moon through the speckled leaves and could swear that orb had picked up speed on its downward slide to the horizon.

Unless the moon was moving around, it should stay on his left all the way back. Simple astronomy.

Between keeping up with the moon's movement and trying to find his way back, he started sensing he was lost. His cell phone was stuck on the time displayed when he'd entered this place. Who knew technology could backfire? His best guess was that he'd been walkin' for about fifteen, maybe twenty minutes. That meant he had somewhere around an hour to find Rayen and Gabby, figure a way out of the village and call up the transender.

And what if I can't find a freakin' fake pink flower at our transender site?

Or if Rayen's palm wouldn't activate the holographic screen?

Or if Rayen hadn't returned to the village and still wandered around this godforsaken jungle with that crazy warrior and his friends?

If any of the boys from back home were in his shoes and had his computer skills, they'd just skip the village, find their way back to the right transender location and take their chances with the holographic panel to access the pod.

But Tony didn't throw *his* friends under the bus. No way.

Rayen might be clueless about technology, but she was turning out to be tough and decent.

And Gabby had paid for helping him fight the flower vine by getting an infection he hoped hadn't killed her.

Tony couldn't name one person who'd do what either of those two had for him.

Bottom line, he was going nowhere without Xena and Psycho Babe.

A wisp of movement caught his eye.

He shifted right and hunkered down behind a bush with feathery leaves that smelled like Mrs. Wolsinski's cabbage soup she cooked every Thursday. Easing up to watch, he listened for the crackle of feet snappin' twigs and branches.

Of course, these people were like Rayen who could move through a jungle or forest like a shadow.

There it was.

One of the pint-size warriors about twelve years old popped into view at a distance. One of those kids with the freaky purple eyes marched calmly through the woods, not sneaking as though they were trying to catch someone.

Tony could hide from them and try to make his way back,

but even if he did find the village he still faced havin' to get through the fog wall.

And he was runnin' out of time.

So he stood up and moved into a clear area, waving his hands. "Hey, guys. Over here. Glad to see ya."

Etoi popped into view between him and the kids. She took one look at him and came flying at him, drawing back her arm to throw her spear.

"Whoa! Hold it!" Tony dove to his side. He heard the whistle of the weapon as it just missed his head. He dove sideways, crashing into a sticky bush, kicking his legs to get free.

He heard the sound of someone running all out. Were all the girls in this place insane? He pushed to his feet, pulse ripping with adrenaline. Had to get away from Godzilla's bride.

Wheeling around quickly, he spied her.

She yanked her spear from the ground and hoisted it, spinning to face him from no more than ten feet away. Close enough for her to make him into a shish kebab.

Tony raised his hands above his head. "Wait a minute, babe. I was comin' in. Givin' myself up."

Out of nowhere, Mathias stepped in front of him.

Tony had never been so glad to see someone. Not that he wanted the crazy witch to skewer anyone else, but he doubted she'd make the mistake of attacking her boss.

Mathias yelled, "Put down your spear."

Etoi lowered her weapon, but pointed a finger at Tony. "He released the prisoner. The scout will report to SEOH."

"We'll deal with that *if* it happens. We don't know that the scout isn't still wandering around in the Sphere."

Tony mumbled, "Glad *someone* in charge isn't hormonal."

Muscles bunched from exertion, Mathias turned on Tony, snarling, "Shut up. You've caused us enough trouble." With a flick of his hand, Mathias called up his boys. "Restrain him."

"Hey, I was wavin' my hands, coming to you," Tony complained. "That's a sign of surrender." Granted he'd had no white flag, but still. "Where I come from we talk after someone gives up."

Sometimes. Other times they beat the crap out of you for

being stupid enough to get caught, but he figured these guys wouldn't know Jersey rules.

He *hoped* they didn't know them. "I've been tryin' to find my way back. You found me headin' *toward* the village, not away. Doesn't that count for somethin'?"

Mathias vibrated with anger. "You've released the TecKnati scout we captured. Nothing will save you from judgment now."

"No, no. You got that all wrong." Tony backed up, but two boys moved forward, spears jabbing at his neck. A third one stepped in front of him, wrapping Tony's hands and arms to his body then winding those crazy red vines around his legs. He protested the whole time, "Listen to me. I didn't break us out. The other guy did."

Someone slapped a wide, flat leaf over his mouth then wound a vine around that twice. No matter how hard he tried, all the sound he could make was a muted mumble. Then they tied him to a long pole that two of the taller kids hoisted over their shoulders and carried him back toward the village like a pig on the way to being roasted.

Now he couldn't even yell the information to Rayen and Gabby so they could get to a transender on their own.

Mathias might not let them go either if he thought they had any part in Tony escaping.

We're so screwed.

CHAPTER 28

Why is Rayen looking at me as if I've wronged her?

Callan kept his chin up, refusing to allow Rayen's brooding silence to bother him. She kept pace with his fast stride toward the Governing chamber. Anger burrowed deep in her gaze during the brief moments she flicked a look his way.

He had not put her in this position.

She was a prisoner. Even if V'ru cleared her from being TecKnati, Rayen was still in league with his enemy otherwise why had she helped the scout earlier and called Tony a friend?

Callan refused to believe he'd seen hurt in her face when he'd ordered her to meet with V'ru. *Never allow an enemy to get close.* Something he should have been thinking about when he'd almost kissed her in the woods.

Did she wield some power over him?

No. Even he could not accuse her of that. He'd know if anyone used power against him. The only times he'd witnessed her tapping an energy force had been to kill croggles, twice, and to help save that little boy.

She confused him.

Maybe that was her game, to confuse him and Mathias while her friend, Tony, the without-question TecKnati, had aided the scout in fleeing.

But that left Rayen and Gabby to fend for themselves, which would fit the selfish mentality of a TecKnati like Tony. So why would Rayen do anything to help him? Or continue to defend him?

Was she thinking the same thing right now? That her so-called friend had abandoned her and the Hy'bridt?

Betrayal cut. Callan knew that first hand.

Why should I care? He had a duty to his people and these three strangers were creating problems he didn't have time to deal with today, not with the stupid celebration for Mathias's turning eighteen before the moon set in less than an hour. He was no longer in a hurry to enforce a judgment against Rayen's friend.

A TecKnati, he reminded himself.

But Rayen would not look at him the way she had in the forest if he sent Tony to his death. *Why did that matter?*

Callan lifted his hand to his neck and rubbed the tight muscles, cursing himself for whatever had gotten under his skin. He never vacillated on decisions and couldn't now.

Rayen broke into his jumbled thoughts when she leaned close to say, "Callan?"

Her rich voice rushed over his skin with the edgy feel of a vibration. A confused part of his brain was cheered over her finally speaking to him and in a non-angry tone. But he must remember he still dealt with an enemy.

He intended to answer with a sharp, "Yes," but the single word came out gentle.

"Will they bring Tony back alive?"

Of course. She only wanted to know about the TecKnati. "Maybe."

"What kind of answer is that?" she demanded, her brisk tone irritating him.

Maybe a little irritation was just what he needed to shut down any stupid reactions he had when she got near him. "That's the best answer I can give. If he doesn't harm one of our own, then Mathias will very likely bring him back alive. If not, Mathias knows his first duty is to protect MystiKs, especially the next generation."

"Tony won't harm a child."

Callan stopped and faced her, his voice whipcord hard. "You told me you have no knowledge of anything before today when you opened your eyes in a strange desert, but you speak of this Tony as if you've known him your whole life. How can you make *any* claim as to his character or be so sure he's not TecKnati? Especially after he left you and Gabby to face the result of his escape."

"I may not have known him long, but I know Tony would never harm a child and I *don't* believe he'd leave us by choice. The scout might have taken him as a hostage."

He didn't want to admire Rayen's sense of loyalty to someone she claimed she hardly knew. In her position, he'd be furious with Tony. No TecKnati deserved this type of unquestioned support or the earlier sacrifice Rayen had made to step in, taking Tony's place as the fourth person to check the transender lines.

And how had Tony thanked her?

By disappearing without a word.

How could someone as selfless as Rayen appeared befriend a soulless TecKnati?

And why was Callan so furious on her behalf?

Because her commitment to Tony and constant arguing on his behalf chipped away at Callan's conviction that Tony was TecKnati.

Made him doubt himself.

That was the quickest way to wake the bear inside him and bring out the raging warrior, because warriors could not afford to doubt their decisions.

Standing firm on his opinion, he crossed his arms and gave his answer in a voice meant to quell an enemy. "Believe what you will. But the question is, what will *you* do when your friend is brought back by Mathias, proving Tony did not return on his own?"

Pain eased into Rayen's gaze over the long moment she spent thinking before quietly admitting, "I don't know."

Callan should enjoy his moment of triumph, but the disappointment riding alongside Rayen's doubt made him feel like he'd been cruel to a pupple.

Why did she cause him to question everything he did, every word he spoke...and stir up the urge to protect her from being harmed?

With her standing so close, he battled to keep his hands to himself.

Rayen might handle herself as a warrior, but she was feminine in a strong way he found attractive. And sexy. He couldn't keep his eyes off the exposed skin below what was left of her shirt. That sliver of cloth barely covered shapely breasts.

His thoughts skidded to a halt. *Wrong direction. Think enemy.*

Rayen's gaze had wandered past Callan.

He turned to find out what held her interest.

Three girls ranging from thirteen to fifteen created decorations for Mathias's celebration. They were watching him and Rayen with guarded glances. He knew nothing about decorating for a party and felt sure Mathias had raced off to hunt Tony just to dump a "leader" duty on Callan. He told Rayen, "Stay here. I'll be right back."

Striding over to the girls without a look back at Rayen, Callan searched for the right thing to say. "Are you almost done?"

All three girls turned looks of panic on him. Guess that was not the right leader thing to say.

Rayen appeared at his side, ignoring his glare at blatantly disregarding his order for her to stay put. She smiled at the girls. "Those are beautiful."

As if someone had released the air in a taut balloon, the girls all let out a breath at the same time and became active again.

Phoebe, the one in charge, lifted a pango orb made of the brightly-colored feathers from little pik-pik birds and answered, "Oh, thank you." She peeked up at Callan. "We have only to hang these along the vines and cover the floor with tullee petals."

When his gaze landed on the pile of hōzuki lantern flowers with their orange coloring and transparent skins, he followed Rayen's example and smiled. "Those are pretty."

All three girls turned adoring eyes up at him as if some mythical god had spoken to them.

Rayen angled her head at him in a way that made him want to say, "What?" The universal word every male spouted when faced with silent female accusation.

Rayen asked the girls, "What do you call those?"

Swapping shy looks between them, Pheobe once again played spokesperson. "Our version of a Physalis alkekengi wreath, which is meant for many years of happiness and health. The *real* ones are made of blown glass...at home."

No one could have missed the misery in Pheobe's mention of home.

Once again, Callan had no idea what to say that would lessen the hurt in Pheobe's voice. Mathias could always find the right words at a time like this, but he was not here. *And he shouldn't have stuck me with this.*

Wait until the next training. Mathias would pay for putting Callan in this position.

Rayen scrunched her eyebrows together in thought, glanced from Callan's face to the girls, trying to figure out something. When she spoke to the three girls, her voice carried a sincerity that reached out and touched anyone close. "But these decorations are more delicate than anyone could craft from glass. When you go home, you may become famous for creating these and be sought after to teach others this art."

"Art? You really think so?" Phoebe asked, glancing up through silver bangs at Rayen.

"Of course. Change is good." Callan caught on quickly and added, "Every generation should leave its own mark."

All three girls' faces lit with enthusiasm, then Rayen said, "Artists capture moments in history for others to enjoy over a lifetime."

The girls started chattering amongst themselves about different ways to customize the Physalis alkekengi. Phoebe paused and looked up with brighter eyes at Rayen first then Callan. "Thank you."

The other two chimed in their appreciation right behind her then went back to discussing their new possibilities. Callan experienced something he hadn't felt in a long while. Making someone happy warmed his heart. A moment ago those three had only been doing their duty, but now they had a calling as artists, even though none of them came from the Creativity House.

What would Rayen do next?

He had to get to the bottom of just who she was before this got any more complicated. He stepped away, ordering her, "Follow me and do not stray."

"I wasn't the one who took this detour," she reminded him.

He clamped his jaws shut, unwilling to say another word that would give her an opening to cloud his judgment further.

A wise plan that would have worked if Rayen had complied by not asking, "What're you celebrating?"

Ignoring her might send the message that she made him uncomfortable. A warrior never appeared weak or unsure. "Mathias will reach the age of maturity prior to moonset. In my world, reaching one's eighteenth BIRG Day marks the end of childhood."

"What is a BIRG Day?"

"It's the annual celebration of one's birth. We have a BIRG Day each year and a BIRG Con once every five years where those who have reached eighteen since the last BIRG Con are honored before representatives from all the Houses."

"So the BIRG Con is a big deal?"

He shrugged. "One may have a BIRG Day every year, but a BIRG Con only once in a lifetime."

"Must be hard for you and Mathias to keep everyone's spirits up with no idea when you're going home."

Her unexpected compassion chipped at his hard shell and struck close to his heart. She saw past the decorations and celebrating to the plight of the MystiKs in the Sphere. She'd understood more than he'd given her credit for. She'd understood the need to care about tomorrow as much as today.

Mathias would tell Callan to welcome any opportunity to improve the morale of the village, even if the encouragement came from a stranger.

He had taught Callan that part of his duty while in the Sphere was to smile in the face of disaster and on his worst days. Just like a warrior, leaders did not show weakness.

For that reason, Callan would smile during the celebration of Mathias's BIRG Day in spite of it being a huge nuisance and waste of time. In truth, Callan didn't really mind because Mathias deserved a special celebration after having spent the last year in here instead of a final adolescent year of carefree time most in his position enjoyed.

This would not be the extravagant production Mathias would receive at home, or at this year's BIRG Con, the symbolic–and often too realistic–end of childhood. As a Gild Level, Mathias would be first in line to the next Governing House leader. Mathias deserved to lead the Governing House and Callan would do everything in his power to make sure his friend got that chance.

Mathias was built of integrity, but he also understood when he had to be sly, like turning TecKnati lies into a morale booster by leaving tonight. Knowing Mathias, he would not lounge around and use the time to rest. He'd show up tomorrow evening with something for dinner. And truth be told, he would probably enjoy a night alone without sixty kids looking to him for guidance.

But Callan couldn't watch his friend's back if Mathias was outside the village and Callan was stuck inside here babysitting. TeK Scouts had told all the MystiKs they would only be here until they were eighteen. Only someone who drank shroom juice would believe that, but Mathias had been adamant about using that story to keep hope alive in the hearts of the children. Callan and Mathias had created a plan to make it appear as though Mathias did leave this evening.

A plan that Etoi or Zilya could not know about since Etoi had no leash on her tongue and Callan didn't trust Zilya.

A night of solitude might be the best gift of all for Mathias.

Callan entered the common area where a thirteen-year-old boy supervised the food being prepared for the feast. He used the word "feast" loosely. They'd been anticipating preparing fresh roasted croggle meat for this evening's celebration, but now they were reduced to tullee pods and dried banban seeds.

Rayen's gaze swept over everyone, her face closed off as she kept her thoughts to herself while matching Callan step for step.

Crossing the open area to reach the Governing chamber, Callan returned polite smiles to all the excited faces turning toward him...all but one.

Neelah rarely had a smile for anyone these days, every glare blaming the Warrior House and Governing House for pulling her away from her betrothed. Callan might feel some sympathy for the girl if she'd direct her anger at the TecKnati, not other MystiKs who suffered alongside her. Neelah was not the first, nor probably the last to leave a betrothed behind.

Entering the Governing Chamber, Callan crossed the room to one of the carved chairs and sat down, weary from using so much energy to heal.

He waited to see if Rayen would take the other one, but she'd paused just inside the door, thumbs hooked in the top of her blue pants.

Did she have to draw his attention to her narrow waist like that? "Have a seat."

"I'll stand."

So be it. Best way to put himself back on firm footing with her was by not treating her as a guest. That might also help toss a wet rag on this strange awareness of her that kept his thoughts in turmoil.

Rayen took one look around and moved further inside the doorway then crossed her arms. "Where's V'ru and what makes him so special?"

Callan wanted to slap himself. He'd forgotten to tell V'ru to meet him. Holding up his hand in a sign for Rayen to wait, he sent a brief telepathic call to V'ru, asking him to join Callan to interrogate a prisoner.

Finally, he answered, "He's a G'ortian, a rare descendant of the Records House. He's on the way."

"Did you just call him telepathically?"

"Yes."

Even motionless, Rayen emitted a silent power. "What's a G'ortian?"

"Someone of unusual gifts and powers that develop very young." That's how he saw V'ru, but not himself. When he looked in the mirror he saw a waste of power that should have gone to someone else, someone like his twin brother who would have used it to lead. G'ortian abilities were too unknown, too unpredictable to be used by a warrior.

Rayen asked, "Are you going to give Tony a real chance to tell his side of what happened today?"

That again? "What is it you think he can explain about escaping that's not obvious? At least, to everyone else but you."

"I told you. Maybe he had no choice and was taken as a

hostage." Her words were given in an even tone, but there was nothing easygoing about the snap of her dark eyes.

"If your friend was taken hostage then the decision will be simple."

Rayen's body relaxed, the combative edge leaving her gaze and tone. "Good. I was worried you'd just find him guilty no matter what."

He hated to destroy Rayen's moment of relief, but she had misunderstood him. "If your friend *was* taken hostage, Mathias won't have to make any decision, because the TecKnati do not take hostages. If the scout does not recognize your friend, he will assume Tony is a TecKnati traitor who has gained unauthorized access to the Sphere and kill him."

Rayen looked away, her face schooled to reveal nothing when she turned to him again. "Having Tony end up dead would suit you just fine, wouldn't it?"

She made him sound heartless. He hadn't ordered her friend's death. Yet. What would she do in his place? "I only told you the truth."

"Then here's the truth, too. I hope Tony did manage to escape on his own, because I don't want him to die. He's not a traitor or anything else, and hasn't harmed any of you."

"He *is* a—"

"TecKnati. I get it. You *hate* TecKnati and you *think* Tony is one therefore you're justified in hating him."

When she put it that way, the correlation sounded completely irrational, but he'd already figured out that she had a way with words. A skill he had never developed.

With no better argument, he waved a hand at her. "I don't play word games."

She moved so quickly he couldn't get up before she towered over him, an avenging angel with her hands gripping each corner of the chair back at his shoulders, locking him into place. Yes, he could shove her across the room. She'd sworn to not use her powers against him, but he was bigger, and physically, he was stronger, and he had kinetic powers she didn't know about yet, though that gift was still evolving. The bottom line was that he didn't want to harm her.

On the other hand, maybe she'd like a little sparring match.

Talking to her might be easier if he let her work off some of that bottled-up fury.

She leaned her head down. "Word games? I'm *not* playing games with someone's life. You can't just declare someone an enemy without reason. As a leader, you're expected to be fair and consider all possibilities."

What had been *fair* about killing MystiK children?

"Mathias is the leader. I'm his sword arm." He angled his head back, trying not to be distracted by the sizzle of her emotions roiling through the air. "Regardless, do *not* think to tell me my duty. Every person here is my responsibility. And every one here *has* been harmed by TecKnatis. Do not dare to tell me how to handle the travesties committed by our enemy. Crimes they must be punished for."

"I'd understand your punishing a crime committed here, but you blame Tony for crimes he hasn't committed. That's wrong!"

He lifted a hand to cup her face and stopped himself, folding all his fingers until only his index finger stood. "Here's what's wrong–TecKnati using their advanced technology to commit heinous crimes with no chance of being caught."

"So anyone you merely *suspect* of being TecKnati is held accountable?" Rayen's low voice bubbled with fierce determination. "How's that right? Or fair?"

"You want to talk fair? They murdered Jornn, my twin brother and sent his body home for my mother to see his bowels hanging out and a triangle hole where his heart had once been." Callan grabbed the sides of his chair in death grips and pushed up into her face. "They tortured him, brutalizing every inch of his body except his face. TecKnati wanted that to be my mother's last vision of her oldest son."

Rayen stared open mouth then dropped her head, her shoulders easing, her voice lowered. "I'm sorry. I didn't mean . . ."

He hadn't meant to talk about Jornn. He'd kept that pain locked behind a strong wall, hidden from the world. Grief welled up in his throat until he couldn't breathe.

His amazing, gifted brother, the one expected to take over the Warrior House. The one who possessed all the attributes of a leader his people would follow.

Not me. But Callan would do whatever it took to protect these children and find a way home. Too many had died. No more.

"Callan."

When he shook off the suffocating grief, he found Rayen squatting in front of him.

For the past year, he'd worked himself twice as hard as any other warrior he trained for the simple reason that it kept him from thinking. And feeling.

This strange girl had done this to him. Made him feel.

He lifted a calloused thumb to stroke the soft skin on her cheek.

The sound of her voice soothed the beast that wanted out to rampage and kill his enemies. She whispered, "I understand your pain. I'd probably feel the same way if I lost a brother or sister that way." She lifted her hand and touched his arm. "I'm not judging you. I only wanted you to think twice before condemning an innocent person."

Callan lifted his other hand to her face, holding it there in indecision. He wanted to touch his lips to hers, to feel the warmth radiating from her.

"Are you at a disadvantage, Callan?" a young voice called from the doorway.

Rayen stood quickly and backed away.

Callan took a breath, shaking off the strange feeling that had come over him and called out, "No, I'm ready to meet." He stood, angling his head toward the door and said, "This is V'ru of the Records House. He'll tell me who you are."

CHAPTER 29

Staring at wonder boy V'ru, I wanted to ask Callan if he was the one playing games now. Was he serious about taking advice from some boy whose head didn't reach my shoulder and who wasn't even in his teens yet?

V'ru was gangly stick arms and legs, huge brown eyes and a toothy smile that fell away the minute he stared up at me. He wore a cloth wound around him that brought the word "toga" to mind, but he was so skinny the loose clothing looked as though someone had wrapped a toothpick with a napkin. His thick black hair fell mop-like into his face as one small hand kept shoving it out of his eyes.

This was the all-knowing wise one?

"V'ru, this person is known as Rayen," Callan said, by way of finishing introductions.

"How old is he?" I muttered, seeing my fate in the hands of a kid who would topple over if I blew on him. Not just my fate, but Tony's, too, if Mathias showed up with the Jersey Jerk captured.

"*He* is eleven years of age and prefers to be spoken to directly rather than treated as though he does not hear you," V'ru said, as though admonishing a small child.

I lifted my hands and struggled to keep a straight face. "No insult meant."

V'ru merely dipped his head slightly, accepting the apology, which caused his hair to slip into his eyes again, then stepped forward to ask Callan, "How may I assist you?"

"We found Rayen and two other unknowns at a new transender location today. We have determined the other female in the trio to be Hy'bridt."

That garnered a slight slant of V'ru's eyebrows in surprise before Callan continued. "We *suspect* the male with them to be TecKnati." Callan glanced at me as if to say, *see, I can be fair, too.*

Even though I now better understood his rabid hatred of his enemies, I still couldn't allow anyone to take the life of someone who had not personally caused harm, or judge him based on what others had done. I was betting my life that Tony was not TecKnati. Sure, the Jersey Jerk could be a pain, but that didn't warrant a death sentence.

I considered it a move in the right direction that Callan had used the word "suspect," but that may only have been to prevent me from protesting further.

V'ru held himself very straight, his fragile hands now clasped behind his back. He spoke as if he stood before elders six times his age. "And what do you know of this one?"

This one? I lifted a hand. "Stop right there. I'm not *this one.* If you don't want me to refer to you as if you aren't here then call me by my name. Rayen."

V'ru's eyes rounded even more at the order. "I see what you have had to suffer, Callan."

What did that mean?

Callan gave V'ru a friendly look unlike anything I'd seen cross his face since meeting me. He clearly had a fondness for this kid. "It's not so bad, V'ru, but I need your answers to help Mathias make a decision on what to do with the three of them."

How could anyone make life and death decisions based on a conversation with an eleven-year-old boy?

V'ru made a quarter turn with his body as if he were on a spindle and asked me, "State your family history."

Spearing Callan with an impatient glance, I summarized what I knew quickly. "I don't know my family history. I woke up this morning in the middle of the desert near the Sandia Mountains with a beast chasing me and with no idea who I am or where I'm from. Some people picked me up in a transport unit with wheels and took me to a school."

"Wheels?"

I nodded, noting that I wasn't the only one who thought that odd.

"Intriguing. How do you know your name is Rayen if you do not know who you are?"

This kid *would* ask that. "I...uhm, let's just say I do have some innate knowledge, like the fact that I'm seventeen." No point in mentioning the ghost or that I'm allergic to peanuts.

Time stretched from one long second to the next as V'ru appeared to study on something before asking another question. "Why did you come here?"

"To this Sphere?"

"Yes." The word might have been short, but V'ru loaded it with serious *of-course* attitude.

"I didn't have a choice. I was in an equipment room at the school with Tony and Gabby, looking for a computer when I turned one on and got sucked into it."

"Computer?" V'ru looked from me to Callan. "That is...not possible."

Callan interjected, "I thought the same thing, but I believe she *is* telling the truth." He paused, then added, "About the computer."

Meaning I might be lying about everything else? I let that go and spoke to V'ru again. "Anyhow, Tony and Gabby grabbed my arm to keep me from disappearing, but they got pulled in, too. Next thing we know we're in the thing you call a transender, then spit out here where we end up fighting for our lives *and* saving little kids."

I sent that last comment in Callan's direction to remind him that two children were alive right now because of what I had done as well as the efforts of Gabby and Tony.

His eyes wouldn't meet mine, but I could tell I'd hit the mark by the way his fingers curled into fists and uncurled.

V'ru cocked his head at me. "What year were you born?"

"I don't know, but I'm guessing if I'm seventeen that I was born about 1996."

That answer turned V'ru into a statue, staring at me as if I weren't human. When the kid did speak it was with a hushed awe. "No one has ever perfected forward travel through time. Not even the TecKnati."

Callan nodded, "Exactly, so how can this be?"

"Either she lies–"

I snapped, "It's not a lie."

"–or the TecKnati have developed technology I cannot access." V'ru sounded as though that was beyond improbable. He looked right at me when he said, "Give me your blood."

"What?"

"I said–"

I waved him off with my hand. "I know what you said, but I've given up enough blood today."

"Why do you fear me?" V'ru appeared completely baffled.

Fear a skinny eleven-year-old? Insulting. "I'm not afraid of you."

"Then hold out your hand."

Callan explained, "V'ru needs a sample of your blood to process."

I could accept that, though I didn't like getting jabbed with another needle. The Institute had already taken blood samples and fingerprints. With V'ru stuck in this Sphere, I doubted the kid would get results back faster than the school.

Still, to show good faith, I extended my hand with the palm up. V'ru nodded at Callan who produced a short blade from where it had hung from a loop on the belt slung around his waist. I breathed a sigh of relief that he hadn't cut my throat when I'd stood over him earlier. Now he just pricked my finger then backed away as I offered the bubble of blood to V'ru.

What exactly would this kid do with the blood?

Reaching out with two narrow fingers, V'ru carefully lifted a smudge of blood between his thumb and forefinger. He swirled the drop for a minute between his fingers then took a deep breath and closed his eyes.

I watched Callan for his reaction, but he seemed content to wait on whatever V'ru was doing.

When V'ru opened his eyes again, he reached into a pocket on his toga outfit and produced a small cloth to wipe his fingers clean. With his arms shoulder-width apart, he lifted his hands, palms facing out.

A bright, translucent image in the shape of a rectangle came to life, similar to the computer screens that I'd seen in Mr.

Suarez's classroom. But this one had no structure holding the image floating in the air.

I pointed. "That's–"

Callan answered, "–a holographic monitor. Shhh. We have to be quiet while V'ru uses his gift to analyze."

V'ru moved his hands back and forth in front of the monitor, tapping in places and pausing images that streamed past faster than I could process. When the kid slowed down, the screen image coalesced into one of a stark, light-filled landscape and a cliff-dwelling abode that brought up the word "home" in my mind. More memories surfacing?

Could this kid actually tell me who I was? My heart started beating faster. I sucked in a sharp breath, excited. *Home!*

V'ru pushed the screen to his left as if it slid on a track and I felt as though something vital to me disappeared.

I spoke first, aware of half-formed thoughts pushing at me. "I've seen a projection like that before. That's driven by a Cyberprocessor, isn't it?"

"Some are," V'ru allowed, considering me with a curious expression. "MystiKs do not utilize Cyberprocessors, but you are not MystiK."

I'd survived deadly beasts, a trip through a computer and spear tips to face this judgment-by-child without trial? *I don't think so.* "I'm getting tired of saying this, but I am *not* TecKnati."

"I believe you."

Callan said, "What?" as I said, "Really?"

Addressing Callan first, V'ru explained, "I must have more time for a complete analysis, but this one–Rayen–has no residue of the K-enzyme, the metallic ink in her system. This ink is what all TecKnatis use to mark their human population."

I gave Callan a victorious smirk. "See?"

"However," V'ru continued. "As I said, I need more time to study on this. Your physiology is not of the ancient times that you claim."

Callan returned the smirk, but added a dose of suspicion. "So you *did* lie about coming from the year 2013."

"No, I didn't, but if your boy recorder here is so smart what year am I from?"

Callan and I turned to V'ru who said, "If you know what a Cyberprocessor is then you cannot be from the year 2013 as it was not created until the year 2129, month July, the day 17, time–"

I cut in, "Okay, I get your point and I don't know how I know about Cyberprocessors, only that I do. Just like I know I traveled here from 2013."

No judgment showed in V'ru's expression, in fact nothing crossed that blank little face. He said, "What else can you tell me about when you woke up in the desert?"

"Nothing except that I did recognize the mountains I saw in the desert, but then they took me to the city called Albuquerque."

With a touch of his finger, V'ru slid the floating monitor back in front of his face again, tapping several times before the image returned to the scene with the strange house. "As one of the ten MystiK cities, Albuquerque did exist–"

Callan's eyes rounded. "Really? I've never heard of that."

V'ru paused with a look of strained patience on his face. "That is because you are not a historian. Albuquerque is the city you know as ABQ/City Seven."

"Oh."

"As I was saying, Albuquerque existed in a territory once known as the state of New Mexico during the year 2013, established in 1706 by–"

"That's all we need on Albuquerque, V'ru," Callan said with heavy politeness to smooth over his interruption.

Good thing to know I wasn't the only one anxiously waiting for some concrete information.

"I don't know about it being MystiK or not," I said, wondering if that would work in our favor or against us. "But since Gabby and Tony *are* familiar with that area, yet aren't familiar with MystiKs, I'm not sure we're talking about the same place."

V'ru opened his thin lips to speak, but Etoi raced into the room, announcing, "We caught the TecKnati."

I turned to face her. "Tony?"

Etoi ignored me, only speaking to Callan. "The one who released the scout. Mathias sends for you."

"I'll speak to Mathias about the recaptured prisoner, but we are almost at the time for celebrating his BIRG Day. Go oversee the final preparations."

"I should help with guarding the TecKnati." Etoi was clearly annoyed at Callan sending her to do a mundane job of preparing a celebration, even one for Mathias. Or maybe especially because it was for him.

V'ru seemed perplexed. "Should we not postpone the BIRG Day so there is no rush, Callan?"

"No. It's important to hold true to our customs, even here. Mathias and I both believe we must not become lax with rituals that are significant to our Houses."

"Do you believe what the scouts told us about leaving here at eighteen?" V'ru asked with the first emotion I'd heard in his voice. The boy yearned for home as did all the other children. On top of that, he clearly feared being left.

This new information confused me. "So you get to *leave* at eighteen?"

Callan only said, "That's what the TecKnati scouts told us when we were dropped here."

I'd think that good news, if not for the way his gaze had shifted away when he'd explained that. I didn't know that he lied, exactly, but he hid something.

But why would the TecKnati release one of their MystiK captives? Surely they realized Mathias would go straight to his people and bring the wrath of the MystiKs down on the TecKnatis.

Anyone would declare war to regain their stolen children.

If I'd thought it was hard to understand the world I'd fallen into earlier in the day, that was nothing compared to this world in this Sphere.

Callan's smile expanded, but with a forced effort. "Of course, I believe we'll leave here at eighteen. My guess is that the TecKnati will use each leader they return as a pawn in negotiating with our Houses. This is clearly about the HERMES space launches that our leaders interrupted. The sooner our Houses know where we are, the quicker they will find a way to return us home."

"That will be soon?" V'ru asked, sounding more like a boy of his age and less like a stuffy know-it-all.

"Yes." Callan nodded with conviction. "Once our Houses and the TecKnati come to an agreement this will all be over. I want you to continue analyzing the information on Rayen while I speak with Mathias." Callan turned to Etoi. "Go now and check on the preparations."

I watched those two march out with their orders, fairly sure that I was the only one who realized Callan had not told V'ru and Etoi the whole truth. I didn't know how I knew, but I did.

Why?

I had to reevaluate Callan and didn't like what I suspected.

Anyone who'd mislead these kids and raised their hopes only to have those hopes crushed when Mathias didn't leave was capable of ordering the death of a stranger just because he had a scorpion tattoo and an attitude.

Callan couldn't see beyond his grief over his brother to pass up a chance for vengeance.

When Callan bent his head, ordering me to follow, then stepped out of the chamber, I rushed to catch up.

If he was willing to kill Tony, he'd better be prepared to kill me as well.

And that meant I had to be prepared to do whatever it took to stop him.

CHAPTER 30

Hanging vertically from the pole that was more rigid than it first looked, Tony struggled against the vines, but nothing gave. He sucked air through the slim opening allowed by the leaf covering his mouth. Smelled like one of those cinnamon candies cheap restaurants had on their counters.

He wasn't sucking any mints ever again.

When the kiddie army stopped, someone cut the vines wrapping him and he hit the ground as hard as bag of cement. That hurt.

Mathias stepped into view, found a handhold between the red vines still wrapping Tony like a neon-red mummy and hoisted him to his feet.

For a second, he thought he was in a different village. This place looked like Party Central with hanging strings of multi-colored flowers, twined vines and a whole bunch of globe plants that reminded Tony of Mr. Tan's Japanese lantern flowers.

Did this bunch celebrate executions?

Gabby walked into view. She shadowed the healer, Jaxxson, who was no longer looking at her as if she topped his list of inconvenient chores. What had happened for him to be giving her the eye, the guy look that said he was interested and waiting to pick the best time to make his move?

Gabby would shut him down in a heartbeat. If Rayen didn't get to him first.

But at least Gabby looked healthy again. When her gaze danced over the crowd and landed on Tony, she broke into a run.

Never thought he'd be so happy to see Psycho Babe.

Mathias put his arm up to stop her from getting close.

Instead, she leaned her head past Mathias. "You okay, Tony?"

Do I look okay, babe? He shook his head, trying to talk, but the only sounds that came out were garbled noises.

"Uncover his mouth," Gabby demanded of Mathias.

You tell him Gab!

"No."

Well, at least she tried.

When Gabby's attention shifted past Mathias, Tony followed her line of sight and, halle-freakin-lujah, Rayen stepped out of that feather structure with Callan, Etoi and some skinny punk kid. Rayen would find a way to get this leaf off Tony's mouth so he could tell Rayen and Gabby he'd found their way home.

But that red moon had dropped pretty low by the time this bunch of munchkins had carried Tony through the fog wall around the village. By his estimate, they had something like forty-five minutes left to call up the transender.

Maybe less. *Cuttin' it short here, people.*

Etoi peeled off from Callan, heading over to where Zilya spoke to Neelah and some other girls who were busy hanging a bunch of feather balls from vines looped between tree limbs overhanging the area. Like the old ladies in Camden draped green, red and white bunting to celebrate St. Anthony's day. 'Cept these colors were weirder–purple, oranges and some crazy green blue. Etoi did spare the time to send Tony one more death glare on her way.

"Where did you find him?" Callan asked Mathias when he reached Tony.

Mathias pointed toward the forest area. "On that side of the village. We flushed him from where he hid. Alone. There's no sign of the TecKnati, but I doubt the scout's still here."

Callan nodded. "Take this one to the Isolation Unit."

Tony started shaking his head and grunting noises in Rayen's direction.

Rayen stepped forward. "I want to talk to him."

Callan turned on her. "He has proven himself TecKnati."

"Just give me a moment. Please."

He worked his jaw back and forth then rolled his eyes and said, "And you'll believe what he says?"

Rayen's gaze shifted to Callan. She stared hard into the badass dude's eyes before saying, "Sometimes you just have to look a man in the eye and take his measure to decide if he's telling the truth."

Was that some kind of jungle alpha talk?

Callan didn't speak for or against Tony, but he shifted his gaze to Mathias who granted Callan's silent request by giving a jerky nod of his head. "Do it quickly."

Rayen turned to Tony. "Were you leaving me and Gabby?"

Tony shook his head, hoping Rayen would believe him, but why should she, just based on Mathias bringing Tony back strung up as if he'd abandoned his friends?

Rayen studied on it a moment then asked Callan, "Will you loan me your blade?"

No, Rayen. *I swear I wasn't leaving!* But Tony had no way to shout beyond making panicky sounds.

Accepting the knife, Rayen reached for Tony's hand that was pegged against his thigh by the vines. But instead of a slice, Tony felt a prick at the end of his finger. What the heck?

Rayen lifted the blade point with a drop of blood perched on it. She turned to the little guy who had followed Callan here, but Rayen spoke to Callan. "If you're so certain Tony is TecKnati, then ask V'ru to test this blood for the K-whatever ink."

What? Tony watched as Callan gave V'ru a hand sign to call him forward. The kid touched the blood and rolled it between his fingers.

Just great. Now my life depends on some kid in middle school playing chemist with my blood?

After cleaning his fingers, this V'ru character lifted his palms and a holographic screen appeared, Tony forgot about blood, MystiKs and TecKnatis. How had junior pulled up that wicked screen from nothing but thin air? *So* frickin' awesome.

Lowering his hands after a moment, the kid announced, "There are no trace elements of the K-enzyme metallic ink in his blood."

What did that mean? Was it good news? Or bad?

Rayen lifted her fist and gave it short pump. "All right." She swung around to Callan. "There's your proof."

So good. Unless . . .

"However," the pipsqueak kid added. "I must complete a full analysis for a final determination."

"Now wait a minute," Rayen groused. "You have your proof."

Callan shook his head. "That's one marker, a simple one. We'll give V'ru time to be thorough." That forced smile popped up on his face again. "Send the prisoner to the unit. It's time to start the celebration."

Rayen took one look at Tony and suggested to Callan, "Why do that when he escaped from there once? Wouldn't you prefer to keep him within sight until you make a final decision? Besides, don't you want everyone here for your party?"

Mathias considered this. "The prisoner can't break the bindings." When he seemed ready to agree to anything to get this celebration moving, Mathias snapped fingers at two of his hunters and pointed. "Seat him there."

Gabby followed Tony and sat down next to him. She leaned close, whispering, "Rayen and I believe you. We'll figure a way to get you out of here."

He owed Psycho Babe a hug ... and to stop calling her Psycho Babe. He nodded and made a grumbling noise.

Gabby whispered, "I don't know what you're saying, but I have a way to find out...if you're game?"

He nodded. At this point, he'd play Ouija Board with his nose if she could figure out what he needed to tell her and Rayen.

"It means having to speak to you mind-to-mind," she explained.

Just when he was ready to kick her nickname to the curb, she says something like that. He rolled his eyes, glad he couldn't speak right now because he was sure she wouldn't want to hear what he thought of her crazy solution.

Mathias stepped up and told Gabby, "Move away from the prisoner.

Instead of blindly jumping, she held up her hands. "I don't have a knife."

"Now."

She stood, but growled her discontent, making sure anyone close by knew she thought Mathias was a tyrant.

Now Tony wished she could've at least tried the Vulcan mind meld or whatever she was talkin' about.

The celebration turned out to be what looked like a birthday party. Tony couldn't believe while the time for callin' up a transender ticked off the red moon clock, this bunch was servin' some kind of fruit cocktail like it was a birthday cake and each one comin' by to hug Mathias and saying goodbye.

Was this a farewell party?

Where'd they think Mathias was going?

Some kids beat gourds and blew through reeds, while others twirled and danced with orange and yellow vine streamers. The littlest ones clapped their hands and threw flower petals into the air like confetti, then they'd stare at them for a second and the petals would remain suspended. Several others were concentrating, and around them spun vine streamers and whole flowers as if they were mind activated. Everything seemed frenzied though, as if they were forcing happiness.

Finally the main whoop de doo ended, with Zilya saying a few words, holding a politician's smile in place. Her eyes held a boat load of denial, not believing something about this party.

Mathias took time with each of the kids, praising them for the decorations and laughing at their antics.

When Gabby had left Tony's side, she'd passed by the healer who frowned when she bypassed a seat next to him.

She'd planted herself shoulder-to-shoulder with Rayen.

She and Rayen had both kept visual tabs on Tony throughout the party.

Like I can go anywhere being wrapped up this way?

Rayen whispered something to Gabby who nodded, then winked at Tony as if she sent a message.

If I get out of this, I'm going to teach Xena and Psycho Babe some useful hand signals.

Mathias finally stood and everyone applauded. He lifted his hands for silence. "Thank you for a BIRG Day celebration that exceeded my greatest expectation."

You got some low expectations there, buddy.

Mathias continued, "I must go now, but if I'm given a choice know that I will return. However, until that happens you must stay united and follow Callan's leadership."

Zilya spoke up at that. "I am the next highest in rank from the Governing House."

"That is true," Mathias agreed. "But I am designating Callan who is better prepared to lead our group in this Sphere. As you well know, I hold the power to make that decision at any time our people are under threat such as we are here."

"As you wish." Zilya shrugged as if she couldn't be bothered. The minute Mathias turned from her, Zilya whispered something to Etoi who chuckled, as if they both thought this whole production was funny. Maybe they didn't expect Mathias to leave at all. That would be a mean trick to play on these little kids. Tony wished he could hear what Zilya and Etoi were whispering, but Mathias kept talking.

"Protect and watch over each other. Never give up hope of leaving. We will win this war. Our families *will* find us. This I believe with all my being."

Mathias gave a pointed look at Callan who came to his feet and offered, "I will join you on the walk."

What walk? And would that be the time to make a run for the transender? But how could they when he couldn't even talk to Gabby or Rayen?

Giving Callan a quick head dip, Mathias added, "I ask Rayen to join us as well."

Nooooooo. This was a bad time for Rayen to leave. *We probably got less than twenty minutes now.*

Mathias's statement also startled Zilya and Etoi whose confused gazes darted from Mathias to Callan to Rayen. Zilya jumped to her feet, mouth open to protest.

With a lift of his hand, Mathias cut her off. "This is my choice."

Rayen didn't stand, but she did say, "I want to know that Tony and Gabby will be safe while I'm gone if I agree to go."

You tell 'em, Rayen. But don't go.

Callan addressed Zilya and Etoi. "As long as those two don't attempt to escape, they're not to be harmed. To do so will result in painful punishment."

Etoi blanched at whatever Callan alluded to, which gave Tony a moment of relief about being left tied up.

With that settled, Rayen spoke quietly to Gabby then stood and followed Callan and Mathias from the common area.

Gabby got up and crossed to Tony. She squatted down and reached up to pull the gag off his mouth.

When she did, Etoi shouted, "Do *not* touch him!"

Gabby didn't even look back when she answered, "Chill. I'm only letting him breathe."

Go Gabby!

Etoi grabbed her spear and rushed over to point it at Gabby's back.

Tony shook his head. Much as he wanted to tell Gabby what he'd found out, he didn't want her hurt.

Gabby shoved up to her feet and pivoted to face the spear, looking down as she scoffed. She slapped aside the tip. "Everyone has the right to be stupid, but you're abusing the privilege. Taking his gag off doesn't constitute trying to escape. But if you want to stab me then argue that point with Callan. I'm game as long as I get to watch *you* being punished."

Careful, Psycho Babe, but man that is so hot. Tony let out a muffled chuckle when Etoi backed down.

Sulking, Zilya stood off to the side, not offering an opinion.

Jaxxson strolled up. "There are better uses for your energy, Etoi. Such as helping the others clean up, and making sure the smallest ones retreat to their chambers before moonset." When she turned away sharply from him, he added, in a lower, tighter voice, "Please follow Mathias's example by giving the children encouragement. Do not spew venom when they face enough hardship."

Etoi stomped off without agreeing or spouting another snotty comment.

Jaxxson's serious gaze bounced from Tony to Gabby. "Do you give your word you'll not attempt to escape or help him escape, Gabby?"

"Yes."

"Then you may remove his mouth covering." The healer moved on to each group of children, touching their heads lightly and issuing compliments on the decorations and food.

When Gabby sat back down, Tony noticed her hands had been clenched, ready to fight.

He had a whole new respect for Psycho Babe.

She slipped her fingers inside the leaf across his mouth and started tugging it down, whispering to Tony as she did. "If Rayen can't talk sense into Callan then maybe Jaxxson can. I've gotten to know him today."

Tony sucked in a deep breath of air and sighed. "Finally. We don't have much time."

"What're you talking about?"

"I followed the scout back to his transender location."

"You *did* break him out of the prison hut?"

Tony didn't know whether to be impressed that she thought he was capable of that, or insulted at her you-did-try-to-leave-us tone. "No, someone here shut down the power. When the scout jumped out, I did, too. Barely made it before the power zapped back up. Has to be someone in this village who helped him, but that's their problem."

"We have to tell Jaxxson."

"We can tell him on the way *out*, but right now we need to grab Rayen, because I've found our ticket home."

Gabby's lips parted. "What are you talking about?"

"I saw how the scout called up the pod. Then I tackled him and made him tell me everything about how to get into one. I think we have to call up our original transender to go home, but we have to do it before that red moon sets." He nodded to the darkening horizon. "I'm guessin' we don't have more than twenty minutes, tops."

"But...I don't want to go home. I'm staying here."

CHAPTER 31

Worry tightened the muscles in my shoulders. Where were Mathias and Callan going? Did this walk mean Mathias really intended to abandon his own people? How could he leave Callan alone to deal with that hateful witch Zilya and her annoying shadow Etoi plus a village full of small children?

Something didn't fit here.

Callan followed Mathias with his head held high, but anxiety radiated off of Callan's every move and tensed neck muscles.

I fought the urge to put my arm around him, doubting he'd welcome my comfort right now. He still hadn't decided if I was his enemy or not.

I couldn't let this go any longer. "Are you really going to do this, Mathias?"

Callan answered instead. "This is not your concern."

"Then why am I going with you?"

Before Callan could say another word, Mathias cleared his throat as if he had something blocking his words. "Let me explain, Callan." Then he addressed Rayen. "The TecKnati scouts told us we would not stay here past turning eighteen, but Callan and I have figured out that this is only to demoralize our group when it doesn't happen. So we're pretending I am leaving, then I am to come back tomorrow, explaining that the TeKs gave me the choice to be locked up back home or to stay here."

Now I understood. What a nice thing to do for everyone considering how dangerous it was out in these woods. "Exactly how long are you going to be gone?"

Callan had given Mathias a questioning look, then must have decided there was no point in keeping the rest secret. "Just twenty-four hours. Mathias will enjoy a much-deserved break."

I asked, "But why did you bring me instead of one of your people, Mathias?"

"Callan has shared with me about how you battled two croggles and how you fought for, and then helped to heal, the little boy."

That didn't really explain why I was walking with them, but I let it go since it sounded as though Mathias had a more favorable opinion of me now.

Mathias had entered the forest and stopped in a small clearing, evening twilight feathering through branches and leaves, slanting cold fingers of darkness and quieting all bird sounds. He turned to Callan with a look in his eyes that gave me chills.

When Mathias spoke, his voice sounded raw. "It's time for you to know everything."

So this is where all my bad feelings were coming from.

Callan's face fell at hearing that *he* didn't know everything. "What do you mean?"

Callan hadn't shown even the slightest indication of fear while facing the croggle, but some worry shadowed his eyes now, and darkened his skin that started changing rapidly, a physical action that I'd decided was tied to emotions. What would cause such a severe emotional reaction in Callan?

Mathias looked resigned as he glanced over his shoulder where I saw a glimpse of the red moon low in the purple sky, but no green stripes.

Were the TecKnati really coming for him? Had one arrived during the ceremony and everyone missed the signs but Mathias?

But Callan missed nothing, and should have seen, too.

Mathias scrubbed his hands over his face then told Callan, "We don't have much time."

"What have you kept from me?" Bitter disappointment seeped into Callan's voice.

I wished for some way to figure out exactly what had Mathias acting so spooky.

Mathias drew a deep breath that shuddered through him, then he told Callan, "I had you bring Rayen for a reason. V'ru told me what he'd learned so far."

Callan's stony silence weighed heavier than the humidity clinging to my arms.

I couldn't stand the tension between these two. "Do you believe what I've told you, Mathias?"

"Yes."

Chill bumps raced up my arm at finally hearing the right answer. "So you'll tell Callan to release us?"

"He can release you, but only if you promise to help them find a way out of the Sphere."

That got a reaction out of Callan. "What can she do?"

I had no idea, but I told Mathias, "You have my word."

For the first time since meeting Callan, I heard true worry enter his voice when he asked Mathias, "You're still only going away for a day, right?"

Mathias took another look up at the sky. "No, I'm disappearing. For good. There'll be no coming back."

"What?" Callan's golden-brown hair turned bright blond and the splattered aqua shapes on his skin darkened into dark blue storm clouds. "You've been holding out on me?"

Mathias kept speaking quietly, every word forced from deep inside. "Yes, I haven't been completely honest, but you'll soon understand why I had to do this. And just as I have lied to you, you will lie to the others as well when the time comes."

"No, I will *not*." Callan quivered with anger. "*You* said we are to be leaders. Leaders do *not* lie to their people."

Mathias grimaced as if Callan had cut him with his blade. "Listen. I could not tell you what would happen before now or you would have focused on the wrong things. Your duty is to keep their spirits up and convince those children they are going home. If not, they *will not* survive. I was here for eight months longer than you. I watched our children lose their will to live without hope and they died."

I heard things in Mathias's voice that weren't coming out in his words. He still hid something from Callan.

Crossing his arms, Callan snarled, "I have *believed* you, trusted you. And now...*now* you tell me you won't come back? Tell me the truth, all of it."

"I always did tell you to be prepared for anything, including my not being around to help."

Walking several steps away, Callan muttered, "But I thought you meant if a croggle killed you. I would never have let that happen."

"I–" Mathias choked on the word and his shoulders jerked straight as if he stood at attention, muscles clenching. Sweat broke out on his skin.

Callan spun around and stared at him, lips moving but no words coming out.

I lifted a hand toward Mathias and he shot me a warning look. "I did not bring you to interfere."

"Why did you bring me?"

"To understand why you must *not* break your word."

Callan took a step toward Mathias who shouted, "Don't touch me!"

"Why?" Callan shouted back and took another step toward him, a cautious one. "What's happening? Talk to me."

Mathias gritted out his next words. "I am not the first to turn eighteen in the Sphere. Anatoli arrived with me."

"I know that name. He's of the Cultivation House."

"Yes," Mathias continued. "And he reached his BIRG Day a month before you arrived."

Callan's eyes opened wide. "Where is he? He should have told the House leaders about us or stayed here to help us."

"He's not to be blamed for anything and you will not tell the children where I've gone when you return to the village."

"Anatoli left and..." The struggle to understand what was going on carved anxiety in Callan's face. "Did SEOH send Anatoli to a prison a telepath can't reach into? Being G'ortian, maybe I can help. Tell them to take me."

"No, SEOH hasn't figured out how to do that, but he has proven to be far more sly than any of us anticipated." Mathias's body jerked with a spasm. Sweat now dripped from his forehead and arms, as if his body wrestled with something. He groaned.

Callan rushed forward, but at that moment, Mathias flew up ten feet off the ground with his arms stretched above his head like a puppet whose master had yanked the strings. He hung there in midair.

Callan roared, "*Mathias!*"

I reached for the heat within me to do battle and called out, "What holds you? How can I kill it?"

Sweat poured down Mathias's face when he lowered his chin, speaking through gritted teeth. "I'm sorry I lied, Callan. You've been a brother to me, but now you'll know why I could not tell you. I did what you must do. Lie to protect the others."

A howling noise started deep in the forest and gained volume. Like a killer wind bent on destruction. But what was it?

Callan shouted, "What are we fighting?"

Mathias looked right and left, terror riding his gaze. His body shook. He yelled back, "Give Rayen her freedom. Trust her to use it wisely."

Streaming bands of black energy shot through the opening, whipping past me. Heat built inside my chest, rolling through my body. I lifted my arms into the energy shooting around us on the ground. Sparks crackled with contact between my power and the attacking energy. Something clasped my wrist and yanked me up a foot off the ground.

Mathias screamed.

Steel bands of strength latched onto my waist, pulling my body backwards. The force holding my arm drew me up, threatening to rip my body in half.

Mathias shouted, "Noooo, Rayen. Your word."

My heart thundered in my chest. I fought tears over the pain tearing through me.

Callan yanked on my body, shouting, "*Let go!*"

I couldn't.

But whatever had my wrist released me and whispered in my mind, *Next time.*

I fell backwards, landing against something hard and warm. Callan.

The energy still swarmed, alive with distorted faces and glowing yellow eyes, but didn't touch me or Callan. A dozen or more black spirits howled through the clearing.

Wind blasted branches and scoured leaves across my face and body, held wrapped in Callan's arms. His shouts were nothing more than hoarse noises filled with raw pain. I looked up as the horde of black ghostly bands whipped around Mathias one at a time, round and round until the only part left in view was his agony-filled gaze, staring at nothing.

All at once, the howling ended.

And Mathias was gone.

An unearthly silence reigned.

I couldn't stop shaking. So that's what the TecKnati meant by the MystiKs leaving here at eighteen?

Somehow, Callan managed to get to his feet with me still clutched against him. He turned me to face him and I wanted to cry over the misery in his eyes.

Instead, I wrapped my arms around him and held on. He pulled me tight into his embrace, his breaths coming in ragged shudders. I wanted to comfort him, but his strength comforted me. My mind raced to understand what had happened. These deadly spirits had to be something created by the TecKnati for them to attack at moonset on the day a captive reached eighteen. That made MystiKs fair game when they were no longer technically children.

Demonically brilliant.

Mathias had spent all these months knowing he faced this end to his life.

Only a truly cruel person could come up with that kind of torture.

Mathias was right. Those children in the village couldn't know what had happened to him, or that the same fate waited for anyone else they depended on. Or for them.

I pressed my lips against Callan's chest, tasting the salt of his skin. He tucked my head against his shoulder, unwilling to give me up and I didn't try to push away.

Mathias's message was clearer now. He hoped that I wouldn't abandon Callan once I knew that there was no way for Mathias to return.

He was right.

Callan finally drew a breath that had a sound of finality to it. He eased his hold on me.

I placed a hand on his chest and took a step back. "I, uh," I mumbled, at a loss for what to say. Saying I'm sorry he'd lost his friend didn't begin to cover Callan's loss.

He touched my chin with his fingers, lifting my face to meet the eyes of a warrior, but he had to swallow before he could speak. His voice came out hoarse, but strong. "Mathias is right. You can't tell anyone about this."

Nodding, I added, "My word."

I still had to get Gabby and Tony back to the safety of Albuquerque. An hour ago, I would've had no problem abandoning this place. Lifting my fingers to brush his cheek, I made him an offer. "I'll stay to help you protect these kids and search for a way out of here, but I want you to free Tony and Gabby to leave if we can find a way to get them home."

He didn't answer at first. Lines formed at the bridge of his nose in a sign that he struggled with a decision. "You would stay?"

Looking deep into that haunted brown-eyed gaze, I realized I'd do far more than that for him. "Yes."

"And you're certain that Tony is not TecKnati?"

"Yes. He's from 2013, not your world."

He took my measure with his next look. "Then I'll free him. He and Gabby will be allowed to return to their home."

CHAPTER 32

I hoped Gabby and Tony would understand about my staying, but Callan and his band of youngsters needed someone with my strange superpower to fight monsters. Someone more than Etoi, Zilya and matchstick V'ru.

The upside of staying would be spending time with V'ru who might shed some light on where I'd come from if my blood wasn't as old as Tony and Gabby's. Maybe, if I survived all this, I'd get a chance to search out my family, wherever they might be.

When I returned to the village and entered the common area, I was a step behind Callan who'd shed any grief during the walk, at least grief that someone could see in his face. I knew his insides were shredded from watching what had happened to Mathias.

A commotion was erupting.

Callan stopped short in front of me and called out in a voice that belonged to a leader, "What's happening?"

As usual, Etoi jumped in first. "V'ru has completed his analysis of the TecKnati's blood."

Just the way she put that raised the hairs on my neck. I saw Gabby standing next to Tony, who was still wrapped in vines, but now had his mouth uncovered and a scowl on his face.

I stepped forward, speaking directly to V'ru, "What'd you find out?"

Lifting his narrow chin, V'ru pointed a finger at Tony. "That one has a genetic marker of the TecKnati–"

"An enemy!" Etoi shouted. "The lack of K-enzyme ink means nothing!"

Tony spoke up, "We got bigger problems, Rayen. Need to move this along so you and I can talk."

I lifted a hand to let Tony know I understood and to wait a second then I turned to Callan. "Can you shut up Etoi for a moment so we can get to the bottom of this?"

Callan shoved a dark look at Etoi that would have shut up a croggle. "Not another word unless I ask you a direct question."

For once, Etoi clammed up and nodded respectfully.

I asked V'ru, "What does this genetic marker mean?"

"That he is of the TecKnati lineage."

"I still don't understand. Tony's not from your world."

"I did not make that claim."

At the eternal end of my rope, I asked bluntly, "Callan needs to know if Tony *is* or is *not* a TecKnati from your world."

V'ru turned to Callan. "No, this one's blood is older, from the year 2013, born in 1995, the month of–"

"Got it." I stopped V'ru from rambling on then added, "Thank you," before reminding Callan, "You agreed to free Tony."

"I did." He called out, "Jaxxson, release him."

With Gabby and Jaxxson's help, Tony was shaking off vines and stretching stiff limbs before hurrying over to me. He said, "I know how to call up the transender, but we've got maybe ten minutes to get back to where we first arrived."

What? Now?

Gabby strode right behind him, a determined look in her eye. "I'm not going."

"You want to stay?" I asked, taken aback by her words.

"Yes. This is the first place I've ever felt...normal."

Tony released a tired exhale. "What about your family, Gabby?"

"I doubt my dad'll even notice I'm missing."

"That can't be true, Gabby." Tony looked to me, but I wasn't the one to convince her to go.

"If you're sure," I said to her. "I plan to stay, too."

Tony raised his hands. "Whoa. Listen up, you two. We *all* have to go, because we need Rayen's handprint to call up the transender and to make it function. And two may not be able to return without the third one. We're all in this together. And if we don't get into the right transender before that moon sets...there may not be any other way home."

My chest hurt from the sudden pounding of my heart. I'd promised Callan I'd stay. Given my word. But I couldn't condemn Tony to being trapped in this dangerous place.

Taking in Gabby's mutinous face and Tony's worried one, I ran my hands through my hair, needing a way out of this.

Jaxxson stepped forward and spoke to Gabby. "You can't go with us to our world once we find a way out of here. I'd rather you go home, because I would not leave you here."

From the softening of Gabby's face, I figured she caught Jaxxson's meaning, too. The healer was saying if he got the chance to return to his home, he wouldn't leave if it meant Gabby would remain alone in the Sphere.

That was, if Jaxxson didn't turn eighteen here first and leave a different way, as Mathias had.

What about Gabby? Would the same thing happen to her if she turned eighteen? Granted, she was only sixteen, but I couldn't let her stay and not know what risk she faced, but neither could I share what had happened to Mathias. And Tony would definitely turn eighteen if we got trapped here for any length of time.

Which left me with having to leave the Sphere to get her *and* Tony out of here.

Something silent passed between Gabby and Jaxxson that brought a watery smile to her face. She turned to me. "I'll return with you."

Tony muttered, "Halle-freakin-lujah."

That left the final decision to me, who Tony believed was the only one who could call up his ride home. But I'd promised Callan...

V'ru spoke up. "I have the results of Rayen's analysis as well."

All commotion ceased.

I asked, "What'd you find out?"

"First, tell me what beast chased you in the desert?"

"I don't know, some strange thing that could change shape."

Callan's eyes widened at that then he sent a stern look to V'ru, one that questioned where the young boy was going with his question.

V'ru nodded, as if puzzle pieces slipped into place. "That confirms what I have determined. You are of C'raydonian descent–"

Every child in the common area gasped.

I had no idea who or what a C'raydonian was, but it sure didn't sound good.

"That is all they have time for," Callan snapped, grasping my hand, a serious edge to his words. "You must go. Now!"

"Wait. I need to hear more from V'ru and I said I'd stay. I don't want to leave you and the children here alone."

"I'll tell you what you need to know on the way, but...you'll never be able to live with yourself if you fail to take your friends home."

I didn't think that was the real reason Callan had decided I had to leave right this minute.

He squeezed my arm, letting me know he was sincere and not just trying to get rid of me. "Go home with them. That may be the only place to find a way to free us."

There was something he wasn't saying. But what? And what was a C'raydonian? I thought there were only MystiKs and TecKnatis.

Callan started barking orders at the children. "You three finish getting the young ones to their chambers. Etoi, pull together ten hunters who can travel to the transender location where we originally found these three. Get moving."

I grabbed Callan by the arm. "I can't do this."

He stepped close to me. "Yes, you can, just as I can, and *will*, take care of this village...until you return."

The faith he showed in me was humbling. I put my palm on his cheek. He was right. I had to take Tony and Gabby home, but could I really find a way back here? I had to. For him. For all of them. And what if V'ru could tell me more about myself? "I *will* return as soon as I can. Just as soon as I get those two back to the school."

"I know. But we need to move out. The moon is close to setting."

When I turned to leave, I noticed one person who wasn't joining us. Zilya had watched the entire exchange through eyes flashing dangerous thoughts. I didn't have time to waste wondering what was going on between her and Callan.

After giving me a wide berth as if I were a threat, Etoi whipped together a band of young hunters, all the while her expression saying she didn't like doing it. Callan led the march through the fog wall, out to the jungle side of the village. Once the kids entered the dense foliage made darker by the setting moon, every fourth child lifted his or her hands in the air and light glowed from their palms. At that point, they raced forward, beating a path to the transender and making it impossible to talk.

I took the last position, watching over all of them and trying to convince myself I wasn't doing the wrong thing and that Callan was right.

Tony and Gabby had ended up in this dangerous place because of me. I owed them and could pay them back by taking them home.

When our group reached the edge of the jungle next to the transender landing spot, I searched beyond the thick leaves for croggles. Callan stepped up to me, barely winded from the run. He said, "Hurry. Giant croggles only come after a transender lands, but the baby croggles are more active and appear unexpectedly sometimes. If you go quickly, you should be safe."

"What did V'ru–" I started to ask when Gabby yelled, "*No, Tony!*"

I saw Gabby rushing toward Tony who had knelt next to a pink bloom identical to the attack flower and stuck his arm into the center of it.

Was the guy suicidal?

Running over to him, I got there first and grabbed Tony's free arm.

"Let go, Rayen. I got this. It's not a real flower."

When a holographic panel like the one V'ru had used appeared next to Tony, he stood up, pulling his arm free, grinning his who's-the-man-now grin he'd had when I first saw him enter Mr. Suarez's classroom.

A female voice from the panel announced, *"Four minutes left to request transender return from Sphere."*

Tony told me in a rush, "Put your palm here." He pointed to the panel. "And hold it there until you get a red outline."

I hadn't gotten the information I wanted from Callan, but with minutes counting down, I did as Tony instructed. A red line traced my palm then started blinking, and finally the outline glowed green. The voice said, *Request acknowledged.*

"That's it!" Tony shouted. "You *did it*, babe."

A whirring sound began out in the open space.

I turned, searching for Callan who was right behind me. I grasped his shoulders. "What was V'ru saying about C'raydonians?"

Tony stuck his face next to Callan's. "We gotta go. That thing takes off in three minutes whether we're in it or not."

"Move." My one word shoved Tony out of the way. I pleaded with Callan, "I have to know."

He lifted his hands, cupping my shoulders, disappointment rippling through his voice. "C'raydonians lived in our world at one time."

Lived? "And?"

"They were...after the K-virus...they..."

"Say it!"

"They were rabid. Dangerous to the rest of the survivors." He sounded guilty having to admit that. "C'raydonians were hunted to extinction by sentient beasts fifty years ago because everyone feared them breaking through the laser curtains protecting our cities. The last ones disappeared forty-five years before I was born."

"What?" I felt lightheaded. "That means—"

"That you shouldn't be alive."

"Why...how could I end up in 2013?"

Tony yelled, *"Come. On. Rayen!"*

The whining noise screeched louder. Wind swept from the open space and into the jungle around us, rattling through the dense foliage, whipping the blood-red earth into a frenzied, dense funnel cloud.

Callan shouted down the wind. "The C'raydonians had time travel to the past. You may have been thrown into a portal in an attempt to spare your life and have been bouncing your way back in time. The beast that chased you is a sentient machine built to track and kill C'raydonians. It may have followed you into the same time travel portal."

I shook with the news. My people were dead. My family. I should be dead.

We were hunted...as dangerous beasts.

Callan sucked in a quick breath and rushed on. "V'ru spoke to me in my mind before I left. He said many young people were lost in the C'raydonian Siege. He warned that the TecKnati would be thrilled to discover a living C'raydonian to imprison and run tests on..." His fingers tightened on my shoulders, demanding I heed his words. "Staying here puts you, and us, at risk. You *must* go."

I didn't believe he really thought I was a risk to him if I remained. Not the way he added "and us" almost as an after thought. "I don't understand."

"I'm telling you to stay in the past. Where you're safe, Rayen. If the TecKnati find you here, they'll take you to SEOH and he'll kill you." He whispered, "Don't come back for any reason. I don't want you to die."

Tony grabbed my arm, pulling me around. "Now means *now!* The pod's spinnin' into view."

Out in the field beyond the jungle, a whirling circular mass of gray metal emerged.

I let Tony pull me away to where Gabby stood looking as if she was going to bolt in some direction, but I wasn't sure whether she'd head for the transender or back to the village.

When Tony released me and pulled Gabby's arm, she followed him. I fell into step behind them, ducking my head so I wouldn't be swallowed by the winds.

My insides were ripping apart.

I didn't care if I was C'raydonian. I couldn't be rabid. Just couldn't.

At the edge of the field, I stopped and turned. Callan stood two steps behind me, as if determined to protect me to the last second.

I closed the distance between us and reached for him.

He yanked me into his arms, covering my mouth with his, letting me know in the most honest way he could that he didn't want me to go. His lips embraced mine with fierce determination, just as he did everything else. His arms banded my back and hugged me close. All the turmoil and chaos disappeared.

Nothing existed except this moment.

A life I had more questions about than answers.

But nothing could make me question what I felt for Callan. I might not fully understand it, but I knew no one would ever mean as much to me.

Warmth burst inside me, but not like it had before. This time the heat that rushed through my body with the power of a tidal surge, threatening to consume everything in its path.

Just as his lips were consuming me with every touch.

Tony yelled, "*Raaayen!*"

I broke away, regretting the separation as if I'd lost an arm or leg. "I *will* return. Don't even waste your breath arguing. I'm coming back. That's a promise."

I kissed him quickly once more and swung around, running across the field where Tony stood with his mouth gaped open and Gabby grinning. When I got to the transender, I looked at Tony. "What now, Jersey?"

"Oh, uh, put your hands up on the pod."

I did, joining my hands with his and Gabby's and two panels slid open. Tony scrambled in, pulling Gabby in right behind him.

Turning for a last look, I saw a sad smile on Callan's face. He didn't think he'd see me again. I just knew it. Leaving him was killing me, but I would come back. I waved and dove inside as the panels started sliding shut. Then something I needed to know slammed into my brain.

I shouted at Callan, "When are you eighteen?"

For a second I thought he hadn't heard me.

He hesitated then called out, "Not soon."

The last words I heard as the panels snapped closed.

My next breath came out harsh and shaky. I couldn't breathe

when I realized Callan had already started fulfilling the role Mathias had just vacated.

He'd just lied to me.

CHAPTER 33

SEOH looked up from his rare wood desk–real mahogany wood –where he'd been scanning the latest hologram report on production in City Three as Rustaad entered his office. "Your message said there'd been developments in the Sphere."

"Odd ones."

Pushing back in his chair, SEOH rested his elbows on the chair arms. "Vid report or a Scout report?"

"Scout. We lost one today. A croggle attack."

"How could that happen when they have full control over summoning the beasts?"

"Phen T-112 said his Scout partner accidentally hit the button while they were in the middle of transender landing space Zulu."

"Accidentally? No TecKnati can be that stupid."

"T-112 explained it as the other Scout 'fooling around' with the MystiK child they were delivering."

Idiot. "In that case, the croggle did us a favor by eliminating a waste product." He turned back to his hologram.

Rustaad gave a mild smile of agreement. "I've called for an immediate review of all Scouts being sent into the Sphere to determine future suitability."

"How did Phen T-112 stop a croggle with the stun unit?"

"He didn't. A foursome of the older MystiKs attacked the croggle and took T-112 captive."

SEOH slammed his fist down on the chair arm. "Did they get any information out of him?"

"No. Fortunately, this worked in our favor. The MystiK we planted in the Sphere freed T-112 and sent information with him."

Easing back against the plush leather only the elite TecKnati enjoyed, SEOH chuckled. "They're too stupid to realize we'd put one loyal to us among them."

"Perhaps, but that's not the odd part of the report. He claims there are interlopers in the Sphere."

Too impossible to consider. "Were there any unauthorized transender trips to Komaen?"

"Not from here. Our security system released no alert of a transender traveling from here to the Sphere or back without authorized hand recognition. But when I looked closely, our system picked up a transender landing in the Sphere that did not originate here."

"What? Did someone hijack one of ours?"

"I don't know. Every person is scanned for identification when they leave home base and when they exit a transender upon return to home base. I ran a thorough check on the systems. Nothing shows up."

SEOH pounded his desk. "If it's a closed world–and it damn well better still be–where did interlopers come from...and are they MystiK?"

"Two questions I can't answer as yet, but I will very soon. The Scout said one of the strangers that fought the croggle killed it on her own, with nothing more than stabbing a stick into the beast. Next thing the beast exploded into flames. That's far more powerful than anyone we anticipated having in the Sphere."

"Her?"

"Yes, her."

SEOH mulled over everything Rustaad had shared and decided he'd been too lenient with this program. "These brats are more versatile and adaptable than we anticipated. It's time we changed the plan."

"To what?"

"They've had it too easy playing in their village that *we* set up for them with no real trials. I have something in mind that'll test the best from their Warrior House." He paused, then added, "Mathias should be out of the equation by now, right?"

"Yes."

"Then what I have in mind will be quite entertaining and even more of a challenge. Call a meeting of the Sphere engineers for tonight. I want changes made. Now."

"Is it worth another meeting with the board to approve the expense?"

SEOH hadn't reached this point to lose. He could not allow anyone to come and go into that Sphere who could put everything at risk. "I'd pay out of my pocket to see the face of the one called Callan confront what I have in mind. His Warrior House is a bigger worry than those blasted Governing MystiKs. They're enough of a pain in my side, but Callan has some paying up to do."

Rustaad moved to leave.

SEOH's voice stopped him. "Plus I want those Sphere interlopers caught and brought to me. I can't imagine a MystiK figuring out how to get inside the Sphere, but let me find out the intruders are TecKnati...and blood will run."

"Very well. I'll arrange the meeting in the battle room." Rustaad indicated the soundproof room where SEOH brought his most loyal and brightest minds to discuss things the board would never know about.

When Rustaad turned to leave again, SEOH added, "Wait. _I_ have good news."

"Oh?" Rustaad paused, completely still. At times it appeared the man didn't breathe.

"Another sign that the Byzantine Institute in the past is on track."

"Do we know if they found the Genera-Y computer?"

"Unfortunately not yet. If only we could communicate directly with them." SEOH shook his head at the frustration of having operatives who were assigned a mission but could not make contact with anyone in the future. "But no matter, we did receive verification that the genetic monitoring program is performing just the way we intended. They've clearly begun to identify MystiK ancestors and have the female Bio-Genetics Research Center up and running at the Institute."

He smiled at Rustaad's raised brows, adding, "It's true. I received a report today that several entire families of MystiKs in three cities disappeared. These must be descendants of females going through the Bio-Genetic program in the past."

"No TecKnati children missing?"

"Not a one."

Rustaad actually grinned. "My admiration SEOH, the egg removal program works."

"Absolutely. I wish there was a way to communicate with the agents we sent back to the year 2009 to let them know the eggs they've removed from MystiK ancestors have wiped out entire lines."

"The agents we sent are exceptional scientists and well-trained TecKnati who'll continue to perform their jobs regardless, even if they never learn of the results. This is outstanding. And neutralizing MystiKs this way defies their power, because the treaty's specific words were 'no TecKnati shall kill a MystiK born since A.C.E. 2127.' Fools weren't bright enough to consider that the treaty did not prevent sending someone into the past to prevent a MystiK birth." His grin deepened.

Caught up in Rustaad's unusual show of emotion, SEOH even chuckled, more than pleased with the results of his plan. "Our agents in the Byzantine Institute have clearly reproduced ANASKO technology for engineering the removal of eggs from a female without leaving a mark on her body."

"MystiK female ancestors will not suspect they've been sterilized. Excellent."

CHAPTER 34

When the panels on the transender pod slammed shut trapping us inside, I froze, digesting Callan's last words.

C'raydonians were hunted as a rabid race.

All my people were dead.

And Callan would turn eighteen soon.

It was Gabby who shook me loose from my stalled state when she asked Tony, "What now?"

"Don't know. This was all I found out."

A low hum started again, picking up volume until the sound screeched.

Gabby dug her fingers into my arm and yelled at Tony, "Grab Rayen's other arm."

"Why?" Tony acted appalled that she thought he should cling to a girl.

"Don't go back to being a jerk just when you've shown signs of evolving into an intelligent life form," Gabby shot at him, raising her voice over the increasing whine. "You're the one who wanted to do this. You're the one who said it took all three of us, so either grab her arm or say goodbye."

I didn't know whether Gabby was right or not, but just as my body felt pulled in multiple directions and everything began to blur, Tony's hand latched onto my other arm.

I clenched from head to toe against the sensation of being warped while suspended in a spinning free fall. My body turned into a human bungee cord, stretched thin and sucked forward.

With my hands slapped against my body, I shot through a rotating tunnel of blurry muted colors...toward a flat surface.

The equipment room floor.

Tucking at the last minute before I hit, I slammed the concrete floor and rolled.

Gabby slapped down next. "Ouch."

I pushed her out of the way just before...

Thump!

"Ah, man, that sucks." Laid out flat on the floor, Tony dropped his arms and groaned.

Gabby muttered, "Are we really back?"

Forcing myself to sit up, I gripped my dizzy head. "Think so."

"Think I'm gonna be sick," Tony grumbled.

"Do it and *you* clean up." Gabby pushed herself up, holding her head, too.

A ding sounded three times out in the hallway.

Doors opened, voices filled the silence and the sound of hundreds of footsteps slapped through the halls.

Tony shot upright, fingers clutching his forehead. "What time is it?"

We all turned to the black-and-white school clock hanging on the wall.

"5:00!" I shoved to my feet. "I'm late for a meeting in Maxwell's office."

Tony struggled to his feet and offered a hand to Gabby, giving her a tug up. "Don't panic. Maxwell knows it takes five minutes to get from most classes to his office. I hope Suarez didn't send anyone here to check on us. We were supposed to report in to him by now."

Would my fingerprints reveal anything?

Was I really a C'raydonian? That would be putting a lot of trust in an eleven-year-old boy living in a strange Sphere. I had to know what they found out in *this* world from my prints. As bad as I wanted to tear out of here and go see Maxwell, I also needed to keep Mr. Suarez happy for any chance of staying in this school.

Leaving would mean losing my one shot at getting back to Callan. Every minute of waiting to return was already driving me crazy. "What're we going to do about the computer?"

Tony and Gabby both looked over where three circles spiraled on the computer screen I'd touched earlier.

Gabby spoke first, echoing my thoughts. "We can't lose it."

"No," Tony agreed, picking up the laptop and folding the case shut like a book then shoving it under his arm and wrapping up the power cord. "No one's touchin' this but us." Then he turned to me with a cocky grin. "You go see Maxwell. I'll explain to Suarez that we got so involved working on this that we lost track of time."

I hesitated, not ready to leave these two with so many questions still raging in my mind about what had happened in the Sphere.

Gabby brushed the wrecked mass of ponytails back from her face. "I was dodging the front office when I came here to hide. Better swing by and see if I'm in any deeper hot water than what I usually trudge through." She smiled up at me then Tony. "Can't be any worse than facing croggles, huh?"

Tony snorted. "Guess not, sweet cakes."

I even smiled, but the mention of croggles brought another beast to mind.

I held up my hand to stop both of them from leaving the room. It was time to come clean. "I need to tell you this, even though you've probably gotten pieces of it in the last few hours. I came to in the desert this morning with some big hairy beast chasing me that morphed into a more streamlined shape when I climbed into the rocks. I saw it again, outside this room, right before we got sucked into the computer. This time it was a black bird."

"Like a crow? Or a vulture?" Gabby asked.

"Maybe a raven, but who knows with my memory holes. All I know is that it was here for me, and I'm concerned about who else it'd hurt trying to get to me."

Gabby and Tony shot quick glances at each other then back at me.

Maybe I should've kept that to myself since V'ru's information *had* confirmed my first suspicion that the beast was after me. But I didn't want to hide this from them after all they'd been through.

Gabby spoke first. "Do you think it'll attack just anyone here?"

"I don't know. The minute I was around other people, it stopped chasing me. And, I'll explain later, but V'ru said they were created to track people like me...C'raydonians."

"When'd he tell you that?"

"V'ru spoke to Callan in his mind and he told me as we were running for the pod."

Tony chuckled. "Didn't look like no *talkin'* goin' on to me during that lip lock." He shrugged, and added, "Don't give me that look, Xena. I'm not insulting him." He scratched his head. "Morphing animal-to-bird things, huh? Just try not to burn down the school if you have to kill the thing."

For lack of a better description when I'd first entered the Sphere and spoke to the MystiKs, I had called these two friends.

Now, I found that word lacking when I considered the value I placed on both of them. But I couldn't waste another minute. "Where can we meet up again?"

"If you're going to Maxwell's, we can wait for you in the hall outside the front office," Gabby suggested.

"Good by me," Tony agreed.

Sticking my head into the hallway first, I sniffed for the stench of the predator and smelled a faint residue. But nothing strong enough to indicate the thing was nearby. At least, for now, I wouldn't be as concerned over this beast.

Could I draw on my power to destroy it if the thing attacked me? If I could even use the power outside the Sphere?

I could only imagine how a display of power like that would go over in this world or with the Browns. That'd probably get me in worse trouble than kicked out.

I had to stay here, no matter what.

Signaling to Gabby and Tony that all was clear, I took off for Maxwell's office, rushing through clumps of students gathered around lockers. When I reached the office, I looked down at my clothes that were torn and dirty. And my shirt was half as long as it had been this morning.

I ran nervous hands over my hair, pushing it back from my face that I hoped was not filthy.

After a knock on the wood door, I was called inside where I found Dr. Maxwell sitting at his desk. Mr. Brown stood off to one side again and Mrs. Brown was perched on one of the two chairs facing the desk.

"You're late," Mr. Brown announced. "What happened to your clothes? Did you try to leave the Institute?"

"Uh, no." I looked down again as if I'd forgotten the shape I was in and the instrument attached to my leg. Guess one of my questions had been answered. Traveling to the Sphere hadn't activated it. I actually smiled as I answered, "Mr. Suarez assigned me to work with another student on the Top Ten Project together. We had to dig through a bunch of old, dusty computers and stuff. Some of them snagged on my clothes."

"Something snagged and ripped off the bottom half of your T-shirt?"

"I should have been paying better attention. I will from now on." In other words, I wanted to stay. "Sorry. We got...sucked in so deep with the computers we lost track of time."

Mrs. Brown brightened. "Getting involved in a project and working as a team is encouraging."

Dr. Maxwell pointed at the empty chair. "Have a seat, Rayen."

Sitting down, I took in Mr. Brown who stood with feet shoulder-width apart and arms crossed, creasing his crisp gray suit at the elbows. Questions hovered in the man's intense eyes, shadowed beneath his furrowed brow, but he seemed in no hurry to ask them. Had Nick told him about my head injury?

If he had, they would be shipping me off already, right?

Lifting a paper, Dr. Maxwell said, "We have the report from running your fingerprints. You don't show up in any criminal databases."

Leaning forward, hands gripping the arms of my chair, I asked, "What does that mean? I don't...exist?"

As that question fell from my lips, I realized I'd been hoping that V'ru had been wrong. That I did belong in this time frame. That I did have people. . .family looking for me.

Dr. Maxwell answered, "Oh, yes, everyone exists, even if they are only a cog in a wheel. But without knowing where you came from or who your family is, we can't generate documentation, which means we'll have to hand you over to social services. We can't take the liability of keeping you here."

My mouth went dry. I couldn't get separated from Tony and Gabby. Or that computer. I needed to get back to help Callan. "Social Services? Are they here in the school?"

"No, their office is downtown, about thirty miles away."

Thirty miles might as well be another world away. I was emphatic when I told Dr. Maxwell, "No. I want to stay."

"You don't have a choice." Dr. Maxwell leaned back, looking extremely content with this news. Maybe even pleased.

Sweat formed on my palms. I couldn't go somewhere else where no one knew me, and somewhere far away from the computer Tony carried with him. I turned to Mrs. Brown who had championed me earlier and seemed no happier than me about this. "I really want to stay."

She asked, "Have you remembered anything about your home, Rayen?"

"I know the Sandia Mountains. That's my home." The words were out of my mouth before I realized the truth behind them. Those mountains did feel like home.

But at what point in time?

"Really?" Her face lit up. She turned to Mr. Brown. "I've got an idea. Rayen might not be in law enforcement data files for fingerprints, but she's clearly Native American at least on one side of her family. She might be in the BIA records."

I asked, "What's BIA?"

"Bureau of Indian Affairs." Mrs. Brown's enthusiasm picked up momentum. "She *could* be listed in local tribal records. If so, Takoda would be able to tell us."

Who was Takoda? And could he really help?

I watched the interplay between the Browns, pinning my hope on Mrs. Brown. The husband and wife exchanged some silent looks until Mr. Brown's face shifted from rock hard determination to something less resistant.

That gave me hope that Nick hadn't said anything. Yet. I asked Mrs. Brown, "Does that mean I can stay?"

The uncertainty of this moment sent terror through me, which seemed ridiculous after facing deadly creatures and carnivorous plants in a strange Sphere.

But I had nothing if I got kicked out of this Institute. I'd lose the only friends I had plus any chance of returning to the Sphere–and Callan.

Mr. Brown unfolded his arms and shoved his hands in his pockets. "You can stay while Takoda researches the Tribal Records–"

What had Tony said today? *Halle-freakin-lujah!*

"–but it's a long shot so don't hold your breath."

I *had* been holding my breath and let it out now that I had a reprieve, even if only a temporary one. "When will you have this information?"

Mrs. Brown said, "Probably within a day or so."

Not much of a reprieve.

Dr. Maxwell had been scribbling notes the whole time and stopped writing. His jaw rigid, he forced his flattened lips to lift with a polite smile that failed to hide his lack of support for this plan. "You can sleep in dorm eight. Mrs. Brown provided a duffle of clothes and personal items for you on the chance that you could stay." He sent a scathing look up and down me. "Try to do a better job taking care of those items than the ones you're currently wearing."

"I will." I stood, turning to add, "Thank you, Mrs. Brown." I gave a nod to Mr. Brown who made no move to acknowledge it.

Outside the administrative offices, I searched until I found Tony, who was reading a paper posted on a glass window to the offices.

"Where's Gabby?" I asked, walking up to him.

"Down the hall." Tony pointed to his right without taking his eyes off the paper. He mumbled, "She had to go somewhere."

I searched the hall. There went Gabby, the prancing rainbow with bouncing ponytails, alongside Hannah who had guided me through the building this morning. Had it only been hours since I woke up in the desert?

I gave another look down the hall, concerned about Gabby leaving us. Hannah had no reason to harm Gabby. Right? But after having fought our way through one battle after another today, I had the urge to grab Tony and follow her to make sure she was safe.

"Oh, man!" Tony slapped the wall beside the window. "I can't believe he's doin' that to me."

"What?"

"Suarez said he posted a roster for the Top Ten Project and that he made a few adjustments." Tony wheeled around, snapping his knuckles. "He's teamed me up with Nicholas Brown."

Had Suarez also put me with someone else or assumed I was leaving? I searched the list and found my name matched up with Hannah. Annoying, but not so bad.

But Tony still stomped around.

I didn't understand the problem. "I thought you wanted someone good at computers." Lowering my voice, I said, "Maybe someone who can work *on* them...and not inside one."

"Very funny, Xena," Tony said, not smiling. "You don't understand. There can only be *one* Top Ten winner sent to MIT, the second member of the team can have another school, but both can't go to MIT."

"And that means what?"

"Nicholas is no slack, but he knows I'm better with computers, which is why he probably pulled rank and got himself teamed up with me. We have to choose a team leader. There's no way Nicholas will agree to me runnin' our project, which means when we win that he'll get first choice and walk away with MIT a year early. I'm so screwed."

I had yet to figure out what this MIT thing was, but clearly Tony wanted it badly. "Is this another one of those bus situations?"

"This is a fleet of buses."

"Can we fix it?"

Tony's voice bottomed out. "I don't know."

I spoke even softer, glancing over my shoulder to make sure no one else was near before saying, "We traveled through a computer to another world, fought giant monsters and attack flowers then found our way back. Nicholas can't be as difficult to deal with."

Not as difficult as me trying to figure out how to stay after tomorrow if this Takoda person didn't supply documentation that couldn't possibly exist if I was C'raydonian...and from the future. But Tony didn't need any more bad news at the moment.

"I suppose," Tony grumbled. "Let's get something to eat. I'm starved."

"What about Gabby? Where'd she go anyhow?"

Tony waved that off with his hand. "Hannah said Gabby had been scheduled for testing at the Bio-Genetic Research Center at the hospital."

A frisson of worry fingered across my neck at the word hospital. Nicholas had warned me about staying away from there, but then he'd been toying with me earlier. Still the worry remained. "Will Gabby be safe?"

"Of course. It's a women's center for cryin' out loud. What could happen to her there?"

I looked down the hallway as students streamed past us and scratched my head. "I don't know. What could happen to three students in a school equipment room...with a computer?"

My eyes tracked over to a boy who seemed familiar from the back. I would have dismissed it if not for catching a glimpse of a snake image on his neck.

Had that been a cobra tattoo? Like the one on the TecKnati scout, Phen?

The boy disappeared into the sea of students.

I shook my head at my runaway imagination and followed Tony. No way could Phen be here.

The End

NOTE FROM AUTHOR

Thank you for reading *Time Trap*, the first book in the new Red Moon Trilogy. There will be two more books out in 2014. The next one is *Time Return* that will be out February 2014 and the last one is *Time Lock*, coming Summer 2014. Visit http://www.MicahCaida.com to keep up on news and for chances to win signed copies plus other prizes.

If you have a moment, we would really appreciate it if you would post a review online at the bookstore and/or Goodreads (Micah Caida on Goodreads) and visit Micah Caida on Facebook.

Thank you,
Micah Caida

TIME RETURN,
THE RED MOON TRILOGY BOOK 2

Rayen promised to return, Gabby must return, and Tony can't return.

Three teenage friends are connected by a shared secret that forces a decision with consequences no one saw coming. When Rayen arrives on the Red Moon sphere again, she finds shocking changes. Her arrival causes more upheaval and danger for the MystiK children, creating a heart wrenching challenge for Callan who must choose between duty and holding onto the one girl he can't have. But walking away is harder than he expects when a new MystiK male in the sphere is poised to take Callan's place. Under threat of attack from an unexpected enemy, Rayen and Callan must put their personal feelings aside to unite a village in chaos.
Choices backfire, trust is forfeit and alliances shift as elements of the Damian Prophecy begin to fall into place and the time of reckoning is closer than anyone expected.

Read *TIME RETURN* February 17, 2014

ACKNOWLEDGEMENTS

Micah Caida is a blend of two voices, two minds and two personalities – both with supportive families and friends. We thank all of you. Additionally, we appreciate our early readers who gave us feedback that was invaluable. Thanks to Alex Bernier, Duncan Calem, Angela Catucci, Alexandra Fedor, Lynn Fedor, Emily Gifford, Sophie Pajewski, Emily Skeel and Adam. A special thank you to LH for one piece of advice that made a huge difference – you know who you are and why we're thanking you. It takes a team of professionals to produce a quality book. Our deep appreciation to Cassondra Murray who spends days checking for last copy edits and continuity issues, which is no small task with the world building in this book. Thanks also to Judy Carney for the first copy edits, Kim Killion for the gorgeous cover and Jennifer Jakes for formatting. Extraordinary artist Andrew LoVuolo created the Micah Caida website that is out of this world and web architect Scott Martin (JorleyMedia.com) worked his magic building a high-performance engine that makes it all run.

We love to hear from fans – micah@micahcaida.com
Website – http://www.MicahCaida.com/
Facebook – Micah Caida
Twitter – Micah Caida
Goodreads – Micah Caida

AUTHOR BIO

USA Today bestseller Micah Caida is the melding of two voices, two personalities and two minds of best selling authors, which often turns up the strangest ideas. Micah enjoys exploring how different characters react and deal with similar situations. Life is often filled with the unexpected – both good and bad. While creating the Red Moon series, Micah hit upon a very unusual "what if" that exploded into an epic story filled with teenagers who face impossible odds, but are the only ones who can save the world from itself.

For more on Micah visit MicahCaida.com